DRAGONBORN

Donna Sundblad

Each Voice Publishing

Published by Each Voice Publishing

ISBN: 978-1-7328744-6-6

Cover Design: J. R. Thomas-Charlton

Editor: Ian Rumple

With Gratitude

While writing may be a solitary occupation in some ways, in other ways, it takes a community of support to see a book come to publication. For this book, I first want to mention my husband, Rick. Thank you for listening to me talk about characters and scenarios like they are real people. For leaving me alone to write and putting up with a schedule that has me up writing at all hours if the muse dictates it is time. Your quiet support means a lot to me as we walk through this life together, still firmly clutching a few dreams of youth.

I also want to thank my friend, Becca Krummert, for all the hours we spent together and her valuable feedback during the initial writing of Dragonborn. And to my beta readers, Heather, Gail, and Rene, for taking the time to read the first completed draft and for much-appreciated input and encouragement.

Thank you to my editor, Ian Rumple, for helping me hone the Dragonborn world by challenging me to clarify how things work in this magical land.

Special thanks to Julia Rose Charlton, my cover artist, for using her artistic ability to capture Jurom and Aurora for the cover. In this regard, I must also mention Michelle Cox for helping me find the right cover concept.

And I must mention One Voice Publishing for pulling all the pieces together. Thanks for sharing your remarkable skill.

Lastly, I thank all my readers. Especially the sideline cheerleaders, who are always asking when the next book is coming out. You don't know how much it helps prod me along!

Dragonborn

PART I

CHAPTER ONE

Nerius Azwix darted through the streets, searching for a place to hide. To catch his breath. He cut down a narrow alley, dodging a cart filled with grain, and spooked the horse harnessed to it. The animal reared, wide eyes staring in fright, front legs pedaling the air. The cart teetered, shifting the mountain of golden grain in its bed. The crash behind him sent the grain cascading into a roadblock, slowing the pursuit of the king's men.

He ducked beneath the awning over the back entrance to the Rusty Peg Pub and yanked the door handle–locked! His grimy hand clasped the amulet hanging at his sweaty neck as he placed the other hand on the door. "Recludam." Scraping of the bolt on the other side flooded him with relief. For once, the hit-or-miss magic of the amulet worked. The hinges creaked as he pushed into the murky backroom. He shut the door and slipped into the shadows behind the ale barrels stacked to the right side of the room. The sound of boots pounding the cobblestones passed by in the street. The tension in his shoulders eased. He'd lost them. He let out a sigh of relief, but it caught in his throat at the clack of booted footfalls on the boardwalk. The person stopped outside the door. It creaked open, leaking sunlight across the dirty floorboards. Nerius held his breath; his lungs burned from the long run. *Why didn't I lock the door!* He peeked between the casks as he ignored the sweat dripping into his beard. Booted feet stepped to the center of the room. The jangle of chainmail left no doubt it was one of the soldiers. *Why does there always have to be a hero?*

Nerius cursed his lack of magical skills one more time. All of this trouble for a small bag of pilfered coin? The pompous nob he took it from would never miss it. An invisibility spell would be quite helpful to get me out of this trouble! He grabbed the tarnished amulet in his fist and whispered, "invisibilia."

The hum of an unsheathed sword raised the hair on the back of his neck. The man at the center of the room clutched a sword at the ready. Nerius held his hand in front of his face and stared at his dirty fingernails. The spell hadn't worked. He ripped the useless amulet from his neck and threw it over the barrels. It clattered to the floor on the opposite side of the room. He peered between the ale drums and waited. The soldier stepped into view as he investigated the noise. Nerius shoved his full weight against the stacked casks. They toppled and crashed, knocking the soldier to the floor. Nerius grabbed the sword from the man's hand and sliced his throat before he regained his wits.

With the bloodied blade dripping in his hand, he swung the door to the street open and hurried to hide behind the supplies piled on the other side of the room. The barkeep rushed into the small storeroom from the barroom and froze when he saw the dead soldier. Nerius knew the man. Everyone called him Skunk because of his body odor. He often bought stolen goods from Nerius, but could he be trusted not to turn him in? *No*. Not only was a reward offered on the wanted posters plastered around the village, but now, with this dead soldier, the price on his head just went up. Officials didn't know his name, so they dubbed him the Red Knave because of his red hair, and Nerius embraced the name. Azwix was the surname given to every abandoned child, and he hated the reminder that he wasn’t wanted, even at birth.

The barkeep stood at the threshold of the open door scratching his lice-riddled head through his knit cap. He peered left and right down the street. Nerius held his breath. What he didn't need was for him to call the soldiers back here.

As he crouched in hiding behind a pile of crates, his legs started to shake. He bumped the stack piled to his right, and the topmost box teetered and crashed to the floor. Pocket watches and gold jewelry littered the floor. *Skunk’s booty*. He resisted the urge to grab a handful and pocket it as his stomach flip-flopped. The metallic smell of the soldier’s blood wafted in the small room and sickened him. His heart raced with panic. It had been that way since the older boy he called his brother tricked him into drinking the blood of his first kill to enhance his magic. *That was 20 years ago*, he reminded himself. *Pull yourself together*. It had made him sick and didn't do anything to help his powers. Bile rose in this throat. He swallowed hard as he eyed Skunk standing with his back to him. If he had the power, he'd change him into a skunk and get out there. But his magic rarely worked. It left him no choice. He raised the sword and tiptoed from his hiding place. The toe of his boot landed on a loose floorboard. The creak alerted Skunk. He spun around to face him.

"You!"

Nerius shrugged and smiled, showing off teeth green and black at the gum line. "Me." He placed the tip of the sword against Skunk's chest. "Close the door."

Skunk shut the door and swallowed hard. "Don't kill me, Red!" He raised his arms, filling the room with his stench. "I—I have something I can give you if you spare my life… something said to make you powerful… said to come from the corridors of the Labyrinth."

That drew Nerius' attention. He drew a small circle in the air between them with the bloodied tip of the sword. "And what is this… something?"

"It's a book. A–a book of powerful magic."

Nerius poked the blade tip through Skunk's tunic. His heart raced at the thought of spilling the big man's blood. Of falling to his knees, sick and puking his guts out, unable to get away if he had to. But the possibility of powerful magic lured him to risk it. "If this is a book of such powerful magic, why is it you are the one standing at the tip of the sword begging for his life?"

Skunk licked his lips nervously, casting a glance at the pile of stolen booty stored to his left. "I planned on using it to take my… uh… belongings through the Labyrinth. It's supposed to let you control the corridors." He forced a chuckle. "How about we do that together?"

"You're saying with the magic of this book, you can control the Labyrinth?"

Skunk bobbed his head up and down. "Mind you, I haven't tried it yet. Just found it buried in the desert while I, uh, was getting rid of a body. I haven't used it cause it was wrapped in a skin with a warning.

I–I can show you." He shrugged and offered a weak smile. "It's right over there." He ticked his head toward the pile of ill-gotten gains stacked against the wall behind Nerius.

"Thanks, I'll check it out." Nerius ran him through. Skunk's brown eyes grew wide with surprise and transformed into sightless, glassy orbs. His bulk dropped to the dusty floorboards with a thud. His right hand landed in the soldier's pooled blood. Nerius dragged the smelly man's feet away from the door and opened it a crack to peek into the street. He cursed under his breath when he spotted soldiers running back in his direction.

He piled Skunk's body on top of the dead soldier. His boot slipped in the blood, and he landed on his rump. From the corner of his eye, he spotted his amulet, scurried toward it like a crab on all fours. He scooped it up into his bloody palm and tried the invisibility spell one more time, changing the incantation slightly. "Envisibilia." Still didn't work.

He rushed to his feet and rummaged through Skunk's booty, looking for the book of magic. Right now, it was his best chance to get out of this mess. Hopefully, it would prove more successful than the no-good amulet he'd bought from that persuasive woman who called herself a sorceress. As he rummaged through the crates, he stuffed his pockets with gold chains and coins. He lifted the lid to a small chest and paused. *Something wrapped in animal skin.* It was heavier and bigger than he expected. He drew back the skin, revealing gold and black filigree. He struggled to read the title. "Obligandi Ignis?" If he was right, that meant *binding fire*. That made no sense. *But even if this book doesn't help my magic, it will fetch a good price.* He brushed the delicate tracery with his fingertips. It shimmered and slithered as if alive. He yanked his hand away. The sound of boots on the street didn't allow time to figure it out. The title of the book had changed… *breathing something*. He'd learn all that later. The barred door rattled. He threw open the cover. Under a faded imprint of a hand on the first page were the words, "Place your hand on the page."

He slapped his hand on the image, "Come on, come on… I need the power, not games."

A flash of buttery light coursed through his hand and up his arm, highlighting his veins like fiery threads. He struggled to pull his hand away but couldn't. A string of light burst from his chest and snaked about the room as if searching. It turned and struck his breastbone like a startled snake. Nerius gasped as the light drew back into his chest. Fire from within heated his face, his head filled with the knowledge of powerful skills yet to be mastered, of experiences he never had. Within seconds, the cord of fire connecting him to the book dimmed and vanished.

Nerius gasped for air, but a surreal calm washed over him. Somehow it would be alright. Mentally, he no longer feared the pounding against the door. Newfound power filled his every fiber–including the power to become invisible. But there was no need for that now. He lifted his hand from the page and swept it to the left. The bolt moved to the side, sending a knot of soldiers falling into the room in a tangle of arms, legs, and drawn swords.

He tried to laugh, but realized he still wasn't breathing. He dropped to his knees. The book fell from his hands as he grasped his throat and pounded his chest, trying to release the hold on his lungs. From the floor, the palm on the page glowed with golden light. Radiant beams shot from the book and hit his chest and forehead and forced air into his lungs. He watched the soldiers scramble to their feet in confusion, as if he were looking through someone else's eyes. With his new breath came new clarity. He knew what to do.

He snatched up the animal skin and wrapped it around the book with a quick spell to make it invisible. For a moment, he hesitated, marveling that his magic worked, and yet he knew it would. It wasn't his magic. It was the book, and he knew it. He stashed the invisible book into the small chest to protect the pages and slipped it into his satchel. Another spell hid that from sight, too. Then, with a wave of his hand, he made himself invisible.... *Didn't work! The spell I need most!* He cursed under his breath as the soldiers grabbed his arms, pushed him to his knees, and tied his hands behind his back. The smell of his victim's blood overpowered him, but this time with an excitement... a hunger.

As they marched Nerius to the dungeon, he wondered why the invisibility spell didn't work, but he didn't worry about it. His newfound knowledge and the book gave him more than hope–it gave him power. *I just need to master it*. Fellow thieves called to him from cells as the guards forced him to the more secured center of the prison–and the dungeon. They stopped in a room furnished with a long, roughly hewn table, a few straight-back wooden chairs, and a stone fireplace that took up an entire wall.

The stocky guard behind him poked him between the shoulder blades as he barked an order to the youngest-looking guard of the three in the room. "Ervig, get the key. You unlock; I'll run this ruffian through if he even hints at making a wrong move."

Ervig grabbed the ring of keys and unlocked the heavy door. A stench wafted into the room as the door opened. He cast a nervous glance into the dim passageway, a shadowy stairwell that curved to the left. "Gunteric, why can't you and Claus take him down there?" the fresh-faced Ervig asked. "You know I hate the dark."

"Well, get moving, and you won't be down there long."

Ervig reluctantly grabbed a torch, lit it in the fireplace, and headed into the stairwell. Gunteric gave Nerius a light jab. The prisoner cursed under his breath as he followed the golden circle of light cast around the guard in front of him. His newfound invisible treasure thumped against his hip, with each step empowering him even as he descended into the cramped, damp stairwell carved into the stone foundation beneath the jail.

Behind him, Gunteric prodded again with his sword until they stopped outside a thick metal door where musty air mingled with a rotten smell. It was no secret–no one ever left the dungeons. Regular prisoners held in the cells upstairs were let out to beg for their food during the day and were returned to their cells in the evening. Word had it that those held in the dungeon were lucky to be fed once a week.

Ervig placed his torch in a sconce next to the heavy metal door and fumbled for the right key as he stood between Nerius and the dungeon. His hand shook as he fit it into the lock. The stubborn bolt clicked open, and Gunteric nudged Nerius forward with the point of his sword. "Welcome to your new home with the other filthy rats."

Nerius inched forward, unable to see beyond the limited circle of light cast by the torch. The burly Gunteric shoved him forward. Nerius gagged. *The smell!*

"Close him in," Gunteric barked.

The younger guard obeyed as Nerius stumbled into the blackness. The door closed behind him with a clank of finality, leaving him in total darkness.

"Lucem hyacintho globus," he said in a quiet voice. The spell sounded more like a question as he waited to see if it worked. The bluish glow of a lucium sphere appeared in his palm and grew into a ball of light. His heart raced as the cerulean light fell across skeletons of forgotten prisoners in various forms of decomposition. Water trickled down the wall into a small slime-covered pool.

He found a flat ledge to sit on, set the sphere next to his leg, and pulled the invisible chest from his satchel, hidden by the invisibility spell. *The soldiers may forget me here, but by the time they open that door next, I don't plan to be here. But how long will that take?* Before he could do anything, he had to study. He opened the chest and waved his hand over the invisible contents. The dragonskin protecting the book shimmered into existence. *Dragonskin? How did I know that?*

He laid the book on his lap and gently peeled the dragonskin away. One of the minuscule thorns covering the skin pricked his finger as he stashed the skin into his satchel. "Ow!" As he read, he sucked the blood from the small puncture on his filthy finger, but before he realized it, he vigorously licked the dried blood from his fingers as he studied. Power filled every fiber of his body as he read about how drinking the blood of his victims sealed his covenant with the book. In the back of his mind, a faint memory of drinking blood from a bowl tickled his thoughts, but it wasn't his memory. For now, he pushed the thought away and concentrated on the book. He held all the power he'd ever wanted and more in his hands. He turned page after page, devouring the knowledge. It would take time, but he held the power to take worlds. To accomplish that, he would need a dragon. *But first, I have to find a way out of this place.*

CHAPTER TWO

Nerius sat with his back propped against the damp, cold stone deep in the kingdom dungeon. The isolation, endless echo of dripping water, and rancid smells would normally have driven him mad. But he wasn't alone. The *Book of Darkmore* sat open on his lap while the lucium sphere hovered over his shoulder, casting enough light to read the faded writing. He devoured the knowledge–the power. Power to transform his fear into a hunger to know more, do more, and get more.

He practiced as he read. His first major feat cleared the air of the foul smells. No more stink of putrid rotting flesh, rat feces, or pooling slime-covered water smelling of rotten eggs. A rat skittered along the wall and stopped to sniff the air. Nerius grabbed the lucium sphere and shined it around his cell. The bluish hue fell across the half-decayed body in the shadowy corner to his right. Rusty streaks painted wet tracks into the scummy water where a mischief of rats feasted on green gunge growing on and around the pool.

For the first time, he wondered how the rats entered this windowless oubliette. Perhaps if he changed into a rat, he'd be able to escape. He turned his attention back to the book. It offered information on how he could transform others into animals, but not himself. At least not yet. He wasn't finding the help he needed and fear started to gnaw in his stomach that he might die here after all.

Keys jangled in the lock. A guard opened the door enough to throw a loaf of bread into the dank cell. That unnatural clarity returned to Nerius as if seeing the world through another's eyes. He reached out with a claw hand, straightened his fingers toward the arm, slipping back through the opened door, and cast the spell. "Recensere rat." As he said the words, his fingers curved like talons.

The man on the other side of the door fell to the floor. In a flash of light, he transformed into a rat, his voice nothing more than a high squeal followed by squeaks and hissing. Red magic particles flowed from Nerius's uplifted hand, raising the frightened animal into the air, and drew it into the dank dungeon. "Come join me, rat. Come feel what it’s like to know you will live out your life here." He threw his head back, laughed manically, and dropped the guard rat next to the bread he'd thrown into the cell.

The rat glanced at the book and the prisoner with wide eyes.

"Don't worry," Nerius said as he wrapped the book in the thick thorny skin and placed it into the chest before packing it into his invisible satchel. "You can fight the other rats for this bread, and then… well, I will leave that to your imagination."

Nerius walked to the door, the guard rat scurried at his heels. He kicked the rat back into the inky darkness, yanked the keys from the door, and tossed them onto the floor. "I'll even leave you the keys, which is more than you did for me. Oh, but wait. You have no hands." His eerie laugh echoed as the door creaked and clicked shut with finality.

The high-pitched squeal of a frightened rat followed Nerius up the stairs but faded as he neared the top. The torch he carried flickered on the stone walls as the stairs curved to the right. He slowed when he heard voices, not because he feared them, but more to give himself time to think of a way to pay them back. "What's taking Ervig so long?" he heard one of the two remaining guards say.

"He probably pissed himself down there in the dark." The two guards shared a hearty laugh.

Nerius snickered. *They have no idea.* He stepped into the square guardroom, where one guard sat with his legs propped on the tabletop next to an empty plate. He picked his teeth with the nail of his little finger. The other man sat with his back to Nerius, focusing on slicing a thick slab of cheese.

The guard with his feet on the table spotted Nerius. In his haste to stand, he fell backward on his chair, hitting his head. The second guard rushed to his feet and spun around to face the escaped prisoner. It was the guard who had thrown him into the dungeon.

Nerius’ lips stretched into a toothy grin, showing off his rotting teeth as he reached toward the guard with a claw-hand. "Effingo me!"

Muddy red particles fell from over the guard's head. He stared with frantic wide-eyes while trying to brush it from his hair. The guard shrunk by about six inches and lost most of his bulk until he looked just like Nerius.

Nerius waved his hand in front of himself. "Effingo mihi." Again, crimson particles rained from thin air, this time over his own head. The guard rubbed his eyes in disbelief as he stared at himself. He balked at the smell of his hands, pulled them away, and stared at the dirt… at hands, not his. “What the what?”

The second guard stood, massaging the growing lump on the back of his head. When his eyes fell on his companion, looking like Nerius, he rushed the man. The two of them scuffled; the Nerius lookalike screamed, "Claus, what are you doing?"

Claus punched him in the face, bloodying his nose. He forced the Nerius lookalike to his feet, drew his dagger, and pointed it at him. "Back down those stairs, scum. I don't know what you did to Ervig to get up here, but I promise it won't happen again."

"It's me! Gunteric!" the Nerius doppelganger cried as Claus grabbed a fistful of his shirt.

"Yeah, right. And I'm Xazdos, the god of Music." He forced the Nerius lookalike toward the door with the dagger at his back and walked by the real Nerius, looking like Gunteric. Claus grabbed a second torch to light the way, wondering what fate had befallen poor Ervig. Before he disappeared around the bend in the stairwell, the Gunteric look-alike stretched out his hand, "Effingo mihi." A second transformation changed him again. He straightened his cape across his shoulders, walked down the corridor past the cells filled with prisoners, and stepped into the sunshine looking just like Claus, still carrying the invisible satchel at his side.

As he walked through the marketplace, no one took notice of him as he pilfered coins, jewelry, and other treasures to add to the stash he planned to bring with him into the Labyrinth.

CHAPTER THREE

Flickering torchlight filtered into the dungeon as the door opened with a screech. Claus shoved the prisoner inside. He stumbled and fell. Ervig scurried toward the light, his nose twitching. *I have to get to that door. Somehow let Claus know it's me*. Whiskers sprouting from his eyebrows, cheeks, and even very short whiskers around his mouth sent messages to his brain. Something wasn't right. In confusion, he skidded to a stop. The prisoner leaned on one arm. "Claus, please, it's me! Gunteric! He's bewitched us."

"Nice try." The torchlight glinted against the keys on the floor. Claus stepped into the dungeon, snatched up the keys, walked out, and pulled the door shut with a loud clank. The lock clicked.

Darkness fell over the dungeon like a shroud. "Ervig? Ervig, are you in here?"

Fear flooded Ervig. *It is Gunteric!*

Gunteric wept in the dark like a woman, and if Ervig could, he'd do the same. *I have to do something! I have to get out of here and find a way to cancel this spell and catch that villainous wizard.* He scurried to the door, hoping to squeeze beneath it, but the armored door fit tighter than new boots a size too small. Behind him, he heard Gunteric groping toward the door, still blubbering. "It's me, Claus. I swear it's me, Gunteric." He reached toward the door. "You've got to let me out of here."

Ervig scurried to the side to avoid a possible kick from Gunteric. *Trapped like a rat*. He paused. *The rats! How do they get in here?*

As much as he detested it, he followed the rat scent marked by their urine. It led to a well-used crevice. He squeezed into it, wondering if it would become his tomb. He pushed the thought aside. If he did nothing, he'd die in the dungeon.

His whiskers and sense of smell led him through the dark. As he moved forward and up, Ervig contemplated his plight. *Even if I get out of here, what can I do? I can't speak–even if I could, who would listen to a rat?*

A distant memory tickled his mind. As a boy, he sat watching dragons circle over the mountains to the north. His grandmother who raised him often watched them too. "Dragons communicate with animals, but only very special people, Ervig."

"I wish I was special… like that."

His grandmother smiled down at him and nodded. "I think you are, but that would be up to the dragons." He grew up believing such tittle-tattle until the other children started to belittle him as a dull-headed nitwit for believing it. But fable or not, right now, it's all he had. *Dragons have powerful magic. Maybe they can help... maybe even change me back. If they don't eat me first.*

Finally, daylight brightened the gap ahead. The sight renewed his energy, even though his rat belly said it was time to find food. Ervig dropped into the dust at the back of the jail. The world seemed so much bigger, and the mountains where the dragons lived so very far away. Distant voices floated from the marketplace, giving Ervig another idea.

He hugged the foundation of buildings to avoid foot traffic in the marketplace, a place he knew well. It was his job to monitor for theft and the selling of contraband. So much human chatter overwhelmed him. Instead of looking for the mountain man, he listened for the distinctive, deep-throated bray of the man's pastel-eared burro. It sounded more like a growl and worked wonders for deterring thieves who might otherwise run off with the animal and his load. Sure enough, the animal's rumbling bray cut through the marketplace din. Ervig darted between feet, under carts, and over to the burro. The mountain man stood with his hand resting on panniers draped over the side of a wagon. Ervig mustered his courage and scurried up the rim of the wagon wheel, climbed into the bed of the wagon, and rushed to the panniers. He slipped under the flap and stole inside.

The rich scent of leather smelled like heaven compared to the stuff he'd been dodging on the ground. Now he waited. The empty bags would have to be placed on the burro and carried up into the mountains for his plan to work. Sure enough, the mountain man flipped the panniers over his shoulder, walked over to the burro, and untied his beast. He stopped and talked to the merchant in code. Ervig knew they were setting up some kind of deal, but right now, he cared little about such trivial things. All he could think about was getting to the mountains–to the dragons.

Ervig found a couple of Firnettle berries at the bottom of the sack. Thankful for the meal, he ate, and the burro's steady gait gently swayed him to sleep. Troubled dreams haunted him until he awoke hours later, disoriented. *What? Where am I?* He tried to call out, and his reality hit him. *It wasn't a dream. I'm a damn rat! Please help... somebody help!*

His world shook as the mountain man yanked the panniers from the burro's back and hung them on a rusty nail in the side of a dilapidated wooden structure. Ervig peeked out into a small fenced corral. The mountain man walked away toward a ramshackle cabin. *This is my chance.*

Ervig squirmed free of the panniers and dropped to the ground slightly, spooking the burro as he ran off into the thick undergrowth. He had no idea where he was going, except up. No one knew exactly where dragons lived, but at times he still saw them circle over these mountains. As he climbed, he mentally called out.

"Dragons! Dragons! I need help! Please, please help!" He thought of nothing but the dragons while keeping his eyes open for predators like snakes and hawks as he skittered ever upward. The suns hung low in the sky when he broke through the foliage and onto a wide stone ledge. He paused, wondering about being so exposed. But once the suns set and darkness fell.... *"Dragons! Dragons! I need help! Please, please help me!"*

A dark shadow loomed above him. *"Who calls for help?"* a deep voice boomed in his head.

Ervig stepped out further into the open, his heart pounding. *"I-I do. My name is Ervig. I am a man–not a rat–one of the prison guards in Resallat's capital, Prudek. A prisoner–a murderer and wizard changed me into a rat and escaped. He even made one of the other guards look like himself. I didn't know where else to go for help. I hoped maybe... maybe you could use your magic to turn me back. To help capture this man."*

A large prickly-looking dragon covered in sharp scaly spines the color of wine dropped in front of him with a thud. A gust of air flipped Ervig end over end back into the brush. He peeked out and blinked, amazed at the animal's size.

"Ye be brave, Little One." The dragon lowered his face until Ervig stared straight-on at the sharp blade-like horn on his violet snout.

"C-c-can you help?"

"Dragons be not able to lift the spell of another, but there be a way to change ye back. The magic of the Labyrinth. But it requires sacrifice. First, pray tell of this man of dark magic."

Ervig told the Dragon all that had happened. To his surprise, the dragon seemed most interested in the book the thief had in his possession.

"This book... be it wrapped in skin?"

"Yes, thick prickly...." He stared into the dragon's amber eyes with a new realization. *"It was dragonskin!"*

"This be serious, Little One. I know this book and the spirit of the book. Mine kind thought it to be hidden where it could not be found. Come, we must gather the Thornose to fight this evil and reward thee when the job be finished."

CHAPTER FOUR

Dark clouds roiled overhead as Nerius headed into the karst foothills outside the capital, cloaked in the magical guise of the prison guard, Claus. *As good as this disguise is, I need to find a place to hide. Somebody is bound to start putting things together between that guard in the dungeon and the one I locked in a cell looking like me.* He paused to dab sweat from his brow as he scanned the landscape. *Someplace dry and out of sight where I can study the Book of Darkmore. I wonder why it's called that, and how do I know these things?* He spotted what looked like an opening, a possible cave, and headed that way.

He'd picked his way by instinct until this point, based on his skill and the knowledge the book had planted in his head. *I know it offers so much more.* When he reached the opening, he found it to be a good size cave. "Good shelter." He used his magic to start a fire without any wood. He puffed out his chest, happy to have magic that worked. As the flames chased away the chill, he recalled starting another fire. A fire that burned most of a village. He said nothing, but knew it was someone else's memory. "I'll figure this out," he said as he emptied pilfered coins and other valuables from his pockets and satchel.

He sat on the ground cross-legged with his back against the cool stone wall and opened the book on his lap. "Maybe I can conjure up some food." The cover slithered at his touch when he opened the pages to the place he'd left off in the dungeon. Just touching the book filled him with intense excitement and euphoria. He not only liked the feeling; he craved it.

Thoughts of hunger and food vanished as he read about forcing a portal open into the Labyrinth of Times. *This is what I need.* According to the book, such a portal would give him access to other times. He re-read it. *Other times? And somehow, when I create such an unsanctioned portal, will it cause another opening? In the heavens... a slit or tear in time? I wonder what that means.* He marked the spot with his index finger as he let his mind wander. "I've never been a clever sort, but it sounds like these tears would allow me to travel into the past or future without the dragons knowing I'd done it. The possibilities are endless. Maybe I can figure out how to become a bird of some sort and fly into another time." He continued to read, and his heart fell. *Only a dragon can see these tears....* "Well, that's a pile of pebbles. Why bother to tell me about it if I can't see it?"

His read on, and his heart beat faster. It talked about the possibility of riding a dragon through these tears in the fabric of time, moving from one time to another undetected by the dragons who guarded access to the Labyrinth. *If I build a web of these tears, I could plunder one world after another and become the wealthiest... no... I could become king across all time.* "A dragon. I need a dragon." The thought was complex and unlike any he'd ever thought, as if it had been whispered in his ear.

His attention fell to the small pile of valuables he'd collected as he walked through the capital. "I need to do better than this if I'm going to be king!" His thoughts drifted back to the Rusty Peg Pub and Skunk's loot stashed in the backroom. A smile crept across his face as he gave birth to a plan. "First, let's see if we can pry open this Labyrinth." He studied the page in the book and after a few mistakes, held out two claw hands and said, "*Aperiam temporibus Labyrinthum.*" Dark red particles flowed from his fingertips and drifted to the back of the cave, building into a blood-red cloud of particles. The ground shook. Red light sliced through the magic particles from a crack materializing in the rock. It sizzled like meat on a spit and grew larger as it mingled with the swirling particles. Nerius walked over to it and stuck his arm through the opening. His heart slammed against his ribcage at the thought of such power. He withdrew his arm, shook off the numbing sensation, and headed back to the pub to collect Skunk's loot.

Looking like a guard had its advantages. It gave him a sense of authority that fit him well. People no longer saw a man with no birthname. No one questioned him. In fact, most people steered clear of him. All went smoothly until he commandeered a wagon and horse.

The owner of the horse and wagon cursed at him loudly, kicked dust at him, and challenged his authority. “Ya think ya can just come take my horse and wagon cause ya wear that uniform? Ya’re nothin’ but a sludge farmer dressed up like a chimeric.”

White-hot anger flared in Nerius's gut. He stepped close enough to feel the man's foul breath brush his face. The beat of his heart pulsed in his ears as he stared into the man's eyes–eyes filled with fiery rage. Nerius grabbed a fistful of the man's tunic as his left hand slithered to the short military dagger at his side. Quick as a snake strike, he shoved the blade into the man's gut beneath his ribs. "Don't argue with the government," he said as he twisted the blade, "… or a chimeric with a dagger."

Warm blood gushed across his hand as the fire in the man's eyes dimmed until his sightless eyes stared at nothing. Nerius breathed deeply of the metallic scent, longing to lick the blood from his fingers–to cut out the man's heart and feast on it. He shook himself. *What is wrong with me?* The rational part of him sheathed the dagger and dragged the body behind a pile of manure and straw. Even that odor didn't drown out the scent of fresh blood. A craving for blood overtook him as he hurried to the wagon, climbed aboard, and snapped the reins trying to outrun the unnatural urge.

As he headed toward the Rusty Peg, he instinctively licked and sucked the blood from his fingers. In his mind, he saw his hand dipping a quill in blood. He blinked away the vision. *Have to stay focused.* In the future, he'd study the book for a spell to give him more time. *Time to cut out their hearts to satisfy my thirst.* The thought thrilled him, almost as much as the thought of the gold and other treasures he was about to confiscate. But in the back of his mind, it scared him.

He cut down the alley to the back door of the pub. So much had changed in a day. Yesterday soldiers chased him as a common thief down this same alley. Today, he stopped outside the pub disguised by magic as one of those soldiers. No longer just a thief but now an emerging wizard with more power at his fingertips than he thought imaginable. Soon to be a rich man. A future king. But for now, just a prison guard.

When he walked into the dimly lit backroom, his eyes fell to the dark stain on the floor–the place where he'd spilled the blood of two men. That same delight rushed through him, filling him with a shining euphoria that boosted his self-confidence and energy.

Sounds of passersby in the alley snapped him out of it. He walked through the piles of loot left to him by Skunk. *Much too much work.* Thoughts of failure started to crush him until he remembered the book. He yanked the chest from the satchel and pulled out the book. Before he opened it all the way, the rope of buttery light snaked through the air and hit him in the forehead. It gave him the spell he needed. "Transi hinc illuc." Instantly the loot disappeared. The energy flow stopped, leaving Nerius slightly disoriented. A loud crash outside the door startled him. He ran to the door and blinked in disbelief at the horse running down the alley pulling the front wheels of the wagon like a riderless chariot. His wealth lay scattered amid the ruins of the stolen wagon.

“What the jig!” He cursed under his breath but quickly spoke the spell again and transferred the swag back to the backroom. "I need a bigger wagon." He stuffed the book back into the invisible satchel at his side. "But first, I need a drink."

He stormed into the bar. The new barkeep raised his brows in surprise to see someone coming through the back. "Who are you? How'd you get in here?"

Nerius straightened his cape and realized blood covered the front of the uniform he wore for the first time. "Give me an ale. That's what I'm here for." He stepped up to the bar.

The barkeep filled a mug until foam ran down the side and set it in front of him with a trembling hand. "Any word on who killed that soldier or Skunk?"

"Looking into it." He downed his drink and thought of having another, but he needed to get on with his business of moving that plunder from the backroom before someone else realized it was more than stock supplies. As his temper cooled, he came up with an idea.

He checked Claus’ purse, pulled out a silver river coin, and tossed it to the barkeep. "Keep the rest. I'll let you know what I find out." He walked out, sure the man would never mention a guard coming from the backroom wearing a blood-soaked uniform. Not with the potential of more silver to line his pocket.

He marched out the front door into the bright sunshine and shielded his eyes against the light. He squinted at a couple of uniforms walking toward the pub at the far end of the street. One wore the same face he currently brandished. *He's free!* He rushed toward the alley, wondering why the spell had worn off? *Does that mean....* He couldn't think about it. He spun around and cut through the tavern to the back entrance and bolted the door to the street. *Chances are, those guards are heading here*. His hands fumbled with the book. "I need a way to move this stuff, now, and me with it!"

The golden rope of light tickled his forehead and once again deposited the spell. "Transi hinc illuc." Nothing happened. "Transi hinc illuc," he repeated. The clack of boots on the boardwalk sent him into a panic. He hid amid the booty while flipping through the pages with trembling fingers.

The handle of the door rattled. Hopefully, they'd go around to the front. *By then, I should be out of here.*

"I'll wait here," a voice on the other side of the door said. One set of booted feet walked away. Nerius flipped pages frantically, looking for the spell. Finally, he spotted the words… the words the book had given him. His eyes scanned the page. The words were right, but he had to visualize what he was moving and where he was moving it to. From inside the pub, he heard the barkeep say, "Back so soon?"

He pictured the piles of loot in his mind. "Transi hinc illuc." As he said the words, he visualized the cave. The booty dissolved into thin air, and in a blink, he was hiding in plain sight. He rushed behind the barrels of ale and mead on the other side of the room as the door from the tavern opened into the storage room. *Now, what do I do?*

"Get away from me, you crazy old man." There was no doubt it was the guard's voice. Nerius felt trapped. *Can I transport myself with the same spell?* To be safe, he held the image of the moneychangers of Cathedral Square in his mind. "Transi hinc illuc."

Instantly he stood outside the offices of the wealthiest men in the world. He walked around to the back of the building to the stables and hitched a horse to the sturdiest wagon available. He'd make a quick withdrawal and be on his way.

CHAPTER FIVE

Ervig hid behind the large, blade-like horn on the violet snout of the dragon, Vellath, son of Therus. This spot, free from the sharp spines covering the dragon's armor-like scales, offered protection from the wind and even the rain as he stared at the world below. Everything looked so small except for the two dragons flying on each side of him.

"We be watching for a tear," Vellath said to his companions. "It be as we feared. The Book of Darkmore be found."

Ervig dared to ask. "Tear? Tear in what? And this book? Is this the book I saw?"

The dragon on which he rode narrowed his amber eyes until they looked cross and angry. "If ye want to know what the Thornose know, ye must swear an oath never to tell another, for we be gifted to see the future… and we be tasked as guardians of the Labyrinth of Times."

"I swear," Ervig said quickly. "Help me to understand what we are fighting. I want to help."

"Ye must place thy hand upon mine nib horn and swear the oath. If ye break thine oath, be aware that ye shall revert to life as a rat… never again to attain thine true form."

The thought sent a shudder through Ervig's tiny, furry body. "I am a man of my word." As he said it, he hoped with all his heart that he would be a man again.

The other two dragons didn't fully agree with Vellath's decision to share this special dragon knowledge, but Ervig could see Vellath had the authority to make the judgment call. He ordered the other two to go off in search of "the rogue portal." As they veered in opposite directions, Ervig learned Vellath's nib horn was the blunt nub in front of the sharp blade-like spike on his snout. Ervig feared the air current would whisk him to his death as he stretched flat to reach the nib horn. Beyond the smooth spot, tiny thorn-like barbs gave him a foothold as he reached with his right paw toward the nib. When his paw touched the velvet-covered bump, he sensed a oneness with the dragon. The connection startled him.

"This be an oath of allegiance to the order of the dragons–a secret covenant. Ye shall agree not to speak of it with any other human. And ye shall promise to use thy abilities and judgment to serve alongside the dragons of the land."

Ervig didn't hesitate. He had nothing to lose and everything to gain. "I so swear."

"In ages past, a dark evil entered the land. That evil was banished to the Pyre by the Thornose. But one of the fire spirits hid and was overlooked. It lived within one man… a man with sinister aspirations." Visions of a man with a dark, muddy-red aura edged with black played in Ervig's mind. "He captured mine mother, mate of mine father Therus, after wounding her. He tortured her and skinned the flesh from her flank as he bound her with his magic. He told her he would take her apart bit by bit and eat her… to absorb her power. While he didn't eat her flesh, he did drink of her blood!"

The sight sickened Ervig and frightened him to think that such a twisted mind existed in the human race.

"When he fell asleep, his hold upon her dimmed. She escaped but left behind a pool of her lifeblood. This dark mage used her blood mingled with his own as ink to write the book ye saw."

Within his mind, Ervig watched the book come into being–the book used to make him a rat–the book that allowed his prisoner to escape–the book that left Gunteric looking like the prisoner, Nerius Azwix.

"Within the pages of the book, he wrote each spell with this enchanted blood giving it a power unknown to dragonkind. A life of its own. Finally, he placed the pages within a cover crafted from the skin of people he tortured mingled with dragonskin… mine mother's skin… skin he stripped from her as he tormented her. He made them one using dark magic. The book drew life from the blood. It absorbed the man's cruelty… his greed… his blood lust and combined it with the power of dragon magic and that of the fire spirit. It burns with a binding fire that links the man and book. The man who wrote the book became one with it. After a time, the book overpowered the man. It absorbed the life of the host. Without a host, it lies dormant until it be awakened by a new host."

Fear filled Ervig as he thought of his prisoner. "Nerius Azwix." He murdered two men in cold blood. Was that before or after he took possession of this… this book of evil magic? He changed me into a rat and left me to rot. Who knows what became of Gunteric! Or even Claus! Or what he's done since he escaped!

"The malevolent spirit grew powerful and deceptive," Vellath's bass voice drew him back to the visions unfolding within his mind. "This spirit of binding fire that promises a human host power and wealth feeds the evil within a man. It absorbs the wickedness within each host, breeding a growing evil that passes from one human host to the next. Each host be more malicious and vile than the one before it. To defeat this spirit, the host must be separated from the Book of Darkmore, for from it, the host draws power each day. If he cannot, the book then draws life from the host, until they be no more.

"But that be not the end. The fire spirit lives on within the pages, and the book be protected–cannot be destroyed. It must be hidden where it be not found. Mine mother gifted our race with a skin–her skin–able to shroud the power of the book written in her blood."

Ervig felt sadness as he witnessed images in his mind of the swath of lavender skin wrapping the book. He wasn't sure if it was his sorrow or that of the dragon, but he recognized the skin and the book. "I know who the new host is. It's a man, Nerius Azwix, known as the Red Knave. He is a murderer and thief. He has that book. What can we do to separate him from it? He carries it in an invisible satchel at his side."

"Here be the way," Vellath said, "and also the way ye shall return to man form. With this covenant oath, the spell I place on thee be protected even within the Labyrinth. When ye complete thine task, it shall be removed… unless ye choose to treasure it and walk the land as one Dragonborn." The details of the plan filled Ervig with hope. Not just hope that he would become human again, but that he would catch the Red Knave and separate him from the power of the Book of Darkmore. But it also crowded his thoughts with fear of the unknown.

Vellath swung his head right and left. Ervig almost lost his footing. "What! What?" He didn't see anything.

"A tear in time," the dragon said. The seriousness of his tone filled Ervig with dread.

The other two dragons swooped in to join Vellath and Ervig. "A tear," the first said. “The prophecy be coming to pass. Now there be three.”

The other two dragons developed a plan based on Ervig's helpful knowledge of the man who held the Book of Darkmore. Ahead of them, the dragons' fears were confirmed as a gash of purple light sizzled in the sky. "It be a tear in time," Vellath announced again.

"We be too late?" his companion on the right said.

"If we don't find the rogue portal, he shall escape with the book," the dragon on the left warned. “We be possibly too late already."

In the distance, Ervig stared out at a jagged purple slit burning in the clear sky. By the dragon's reaction, this tear was very bad, but only they could see it. “I see it! But what does it mean?”

The dragon on the right drew nearer. “The human sees it? Only dragons be able to see them, and not all dragons. How be this possible?”

“He be Dragonborn,” Vellath said as Ervig stretched forward again with his paw on the nib. "Help me understand these tears."

Again, visions flashed through his mind. He witnessed the man he saw torture the dragon with the Book of Darkmore opened in his hands. Buttery golden light poured from the page. The man shielded his eyes for a moment and then lay his hand upon the page like one swearing an oath. Threadlike fire climbed his arm, and a rope of fire burst from his chest. It lingered, and then the fire slipped back into the book. The man set the book down for a moment and then raised his hands with fingers bent like an eagle’s talons. His lips moved, but Ervig could not hear the words. A small swirl of red energy shone in the dark and spun as it expanded. The ground beneath the man’s feet shook.

“This be when the first breach tore through time. Mine mother said it sounded like a roar of an angry dragon. It shook the ground. When it first happened, we knew not what it was.”

Ervig, watched as the man in the vision picked up the book and jumped through the portal. He appeared to be weak as he stood in a small cave clutching the book to his chest.

“Humans within the Labyrinth be drained of their powers,” Vellath said. “But outside the Labyrinth, the book replenishes the man. What ye be witnessing here before us be the result of an unsanctioned portal created in this way with dark, unholy magic.

“The Thornose dragons be gifted with visions of the future and be guardians of the Labyrinth. We sanction travel from one time to another, but these tears be a threat from unlawful and unsupervised travel between times.”

The immensity of this knowledge hit Ervig. If a criminal like the Red Knave had access to travel from one time to another… The thought sent a shudder through him. "What does this portal we are looking for look like?" Ervig asked.

Vellath said, "A true portal cast light of blue. What we be seeking now be a rogue portal of red energy. It may be not easy to see. It could be hidden within a forest, under a rock cropping, inside a cave…."

Ervig understood, but he was good at finding criminals. "If I know the Red Knave, he won't be leaving this time empty-handed. That greed will slow him down. He'll probably need to make more than one trip to carry his stolen items into the Labyrinth.”

“The prophecy foretells of four new tears. So this be the first of four.”

“Last I saw him, in Prudek. He wore a guard uniform. I’m pretty sure it was him, even though he wore the look of a guard I work with. Even his face. But, if he is still dressed that way, his red cape should be easy to spot."

The pupils in Vellath's amber eyes narrowed to slits. "There be something red down there on that wagon."

With Ervig's rat vision, he saw no detail other than the snowcapped mountain peaks to his right. The foothills beneath him looked more like a quilt sewn by his grandmother.

They dropped quickly. Ervig's claws and furry belly held tight against the prickly violet hide as the airstream tried to tug him free from the dragon's snout. "There, look, a red radiance." His heart beat faster. "Coming from that cave."

The dragons veered and landed hard. Ervig flipped from Vellath's snout and rolled toward the cave. "Hurry," Vellath said. "Follow him. Remember what I told thee! The book protects him, and he protects the book. If ye take his life, the book be ready to take thine and give it to him. Ye must catch him soon after ye step into the next time… while his powers be drained. Separate him from the book."

* * * *

A shadow fell over Nerius as he unloaded the wagon, still wearing his Claus disguise. He shielded his eyes and looked up into the sky. Three dragons swooped toward him. Dragons! He eyed the strongbox full of gold in the back of the wagon. It was too heavy to move quickly, even with his current muscular arms. For a moment, he toyed with the idea of trying to ward off the dragons with magic. I could bind a dragon, a single dragon, but I don't know of a spell that could work against three dragons. His hand fell to the invisible pouch and book of magic at his side. As long as I have this, I'll have all the treasure I can want. Without hesitation, he spun on his heel and dashed into the cave.

Behind him, the dragons landed hard. Their talons sliced furrows in the rocky soil. As the rock shattered into splinters behind him, Nerius dove for the swirling red light of the portal he had forced open. The darkness of the Labyrinth welcomed him. He'd already piled most of his booty just inside the opening with the aid of his magic.

Rogue portals were one way. Once closed, there was no going back. He laughed. "No one can follow me once I shut this door." He thrilled at his power to control. I can open a portal anywhere. The trumpeting of one of the dragons on the other side of the portal startled him. He expected fire to follow him through the opening as he raised his claw hand and ordered the portal to close. Black particles drifted into the swirling energy changing it to dark violet. Slowly it retracted, turned black, and blinked out of existence. He breathed a sigh of relief. But what he didn't know is that before it closed, a tiny body slipped through, dropped to the floor, and scampered into the shadows.

CHAPTER SIX

Ervig's heart raced as he scurried through the contracting portal. His miniature body dropped with an almost imperceptible thud to the cold stone floor on the other side. He moved his tail, thankful it didn't get clipped and wondering what that might mean to his human body if such a thing might happen. With practiced military discipline, he shoved all such nonsensical thoughts from his mind. He had to move fast. Vellath had warned the spell Nerius placed on him would wear off quickly as the Labyrinth purged all magic, enchantments, and spells–other than dragon magic. And while the book tapped into dragon magic, it was not pure. The prisoner's powers would drain to nothing if he stayed within the Labyrinth for long enough.

Oscillating shadows created by the dimming portal light worked to camouflage his small furry body as he scampered out of sight. The portal blinked closed and darkness wrapped around him. For the moment, he thanked the stars for his rat vision and the information his whiskers provided as he sensed his way through the pitch black. As a rat, he did not fear the dark. His whiskers and sense of smell helped him to find his way quickly to a shallow alcove.

He lay there panting as pain wracked his body; his limbs stretched, his torso felt like it was exploding as it expanded, but his head hurt most as he transformed back into a man. He clenched his jaw to stifle even the slightest moan. The process left him breathless and his uniform soaked with sweat. *My uniform!* For a moment, he lay there thankful he wasn't naked as the coolness of the stone floor refreshed his body. He placed his hand on his face, thankful to have a hand, a human nose, and two legs! But in the dark, he couldn't see a thing. He strained to listen, unsure how to proceed.

The blue glow of a lucium sphere cut through the darkness and filled the area with subdued light. Ervig peeked from his hiding place. Nerius held the sphere in his palm. He no longer looked like the clean-cut, muscular Claus. For a brief moment, his thoughts shifted to his friends, wondering if Gunteric was still locked in the dungeon or if he and Claus had regained their true forms. He pushed them from his mind. He didn't have time to think about what might be happening in his time. A wave of sadness rushed over him. According to what the Thornose dragon told him, he'd never see his home in his time again.

In the pale blue light, dark energy flashed around Nerius as he organized and stacked his loot. It wasn't light but the absence of light. At the center, closest to his body, he saw a hint of muddy pink. Somehow he knew this meant Nerius was immature and dishonest. He didn't need special sight to know that, but the dark energy that surrounded the prisoner sent shivers up Ervig's spine. He forced himself to shrug it off. *Stay focused.* It was up to him to make this man pay. *But how? If I kill him, the book will take my life and give it to him.* His lack of experience in such things made him nervous, but he had the element of surprise on his side, and the wisdom and knowledge passed on to him by Vellath. *Somehow, I have to separate him from the book.*

He placed his hand on the wall beside him as he watched the prisoner. Its coarse grain felt cool to the touch. Dark bands of various widths ran through the rock. It didn't feel like anything magical. As the dragon had predicted, the Labyrinth not only erased the magic that turned him into a rat and which had changed Nerius into Claus, it also dispelled the invisibility enchantment on the heavy satchel hanging at the Red Knave's side. *Wonder how long it will take for his powers to weaken.* All Ervig knew for sure was the longer Nerius stayed in the Labyrinth, and the more he used his powers while in the Labyrinth, the sooner he'd become powerless. Ervig hoped he'd stay busy cataloging the booty he'd stashed on this side of the portal, but to his disappointment, the prisoner used his magic to bundle the hoard of ill-gotten gains and then shrank them into a manageable pack that he slipped onto his back. For now, his powers seemed to be fully intact.

A sense of fear kept Ervig in his hiding place, watching from the shadows. Nerius picked up the lucium sphere and hurried forward with the heavy satchel at his side and the pack on his back. In his haste, he stumbled and landed hard on his stomach. The lucium sphere fell from his hand, rolled down a slight dip in the floor, and stopped outside a tunnel opening. Overhead, a colony of bats took flight. Nerius covered his head and cowered as the cloud of winged mammals rushed over him and swooped upward.

Ervig leaned back into the alcove. Amid the sounds of wings fluttering, his ears picked up tiny voices. *Bats! I'm understanding bats!* They were not happy to have their hibernation interrupted. But all the ruckus gave Ervig a new idea as he struggled to keep up with his new skills and instincts–to learn quickly enough not to lose his prey. His nerves had him on edge as he tried to call upon his newly acquired dragon magic. *Here goes.* "Mutata in vespertilio," he whispered.

The quick spell encircled him with a spiral of energy. At first, his skin tingled. Then pain tore throughout his body as he endured the agony of transformation into a whiskered bat–the only kind of bat he knew well enough to visualize. The kind of bat that hung in the stables back home. He'd always thought of bats as rats with wings, but now he knew that was not the case. This form flooded his mind with new information. It left him reeling. He tried to focus. To get his bearings. Again, he had whiskers and fur, but this time he also had wings. He flapped his wings and flitted upward where he clung to the wall. Flying took more out of him than he expected. He emitted a call and listened to the echo. In his mind, it created a map. *This is perfect!* He knew every nearby nook, stalagmite, and tunnel opening, and to his surprise, in the light of the lucium sphere, he could still *see* Nerius as humans see. But, he didn't have to see him. His silent calls tracked the prisoner as a moving living object that made his way to an opening ahead on the right.

Ervig swooped to keep up. He'd learned from Vellath that the corridors of the Labyrinth shifted. His purpose was to follow the Red Knave and capture him when he made his way into the next time while he was drained of his powers and to confiscate the book. The prisoner headed into the tunnel, and Ervig followed him, emitting another burst of high-pitched sound beyond the Red Knave's hearing.

Information bombarded him as Ervig captured details of a maze of interconnecting circles. Within these moving circles were corridors and rooms. Smaller circles broke apart with pieces that rotated, creating dead ends. He could see the Labyrinth stretch time, clip it and reattach it to a new timeline. Others connected to complete a different circle. Some were circles within circles. Ervig updated his mental map as he interpreted each echo.

The human walked ahead of him, carrying the lucium sphere. Ervig was happy to see it because even that low-level of magic would help drain the prisoner of his powers, and keeping the stolen cache on his back bundled with magic would drain him even faster. *Flying is my energy drain*, Ervig thought. Ervig wished for the mobility of his rat body and, for a brief moment, wondered if he could create a rat that could fly. For now, he stuck with what he knew and flitted forward following his prisoner.

Nerius stepped into a wide-opened circular area with cascading levels linked with stairwells and tunnels. Ervig's sonar showed some openings led to dead-end rooms, but it seemed the Red Knave could see this, too. He climbed a stone staircase up to the second level. Ervig flew up to the second level and clung to the wall. From here, he watched as the floor shifted. The bottom half of the staircase folded flat, and the floor rotated and disappeared! He stared into a circular room beneath them with more rooms and stairs. The walls began to shift. Ervig folded his wings and swooped in to stay close to his prisoner. He latched onto the backpack strapped to the Nerius's back.

Nerius cursed under his breath and stopped to rest. His labored breathing was a good sign. Even in the cool underground environment, Ervig smelled the prisoner's sweat. Nerius let out a long breath and said, "Satis est." His backpack fell from his back, and Ervig quickly flittered toward the ceiling before it hit the ground. He worried that Nerius had spotted him, but if he had, it didn't seem to matter. Nerius picked up his pack, carried it into one of the side rooms, and dumped his plunder into a pile. He raised his claw hand above it. "Ad magnitudinem." Red particles rained over the treasure as it changed back to full size, cramming the small room." Nerius stepped back outside the door and raised his hand one more time. "Colonade in perpetuum." The outside appearance of the room transformed into a colonnade with three columns. "That should make it easy to find."

Ervig wondered if it could be permanent if magic other than dragon magic was erased in the Labyrinth. *But magic erased is generated outside the Labyrinth. I wonder....* No time to dwell on questions; he'd save those for the next time he talked with a dragon. Instead, he focused his attention on Nerius. If he continued this way, he'd die powerless before he ever opened another rogue portal. Ervig's hopes lifted. That would certainly make his life easier. *I can leave the prisoner and the book hidden here in the Labyrinth!*

He no sooner thought it than Nerius lifted his arms, fingers of both hands bent in a claw pointed toward the wall calling for a portal. A weak stream of red particles drifted toward the wall. A crimson light sparked into existence like a lit fuse and exploded into a swirling pool of scarlet energy. Nerius stumbled toward it, so weak the satchel dropped to the crook of his arm. The weight of the book within it yanked him off balance. He fell sideways through the portal. Ervig thrust into the air, cutting a path straight through the portal into natural sunlight. The brightness blinded him. He dropped into the shade beneath broad-leaf shrubs on a karst hillside to let his eyes adjust.

Nerius stumbled and collapsed in a cloud of dust as the portal blinked out of existence. The satchel fell from his arm skidded a few feet down a slight slope until it stopped on a patch of sparse grass. Ervig's mind screamed for help. Here in the middle of nowhere, what could he do? *"Someone, please, help me before his magic comes back!"*

"Get ye the book," a voice called to his mind.

Ervig quickly transformed into his man form. This time he expected the pain, and it didn't seem so bad because his mind focused on his duty. All that mattered was getting his hands on the satchel. He stood, and for a moment dizziness spun the new world around him as he hurried toward his prisoner in a drunken zig-zag pattern. He willed his arm toward the satchel. The leather strap brushed his palm, and he instinctively clamped it in his fist. He stood staring at his pale prisoner as he caught his breath. "Nerius Azwix, you are under arrest for murder, thieving, and defrauding." It felt strange to speak audibly–almost distracting. His mind raced to imagine what the charges would be for turning him into a rat or for stealing Claus' identity.

Nerius looked up at him with wide eyes and a pale pallor. "You! How–." He scrambled weakly on hands and knees, staring at the satchel.

"Stop!" Ervig shouted, but the criminal ignored him as he grabbed hold of the satchel. The two of them struggled in a tug of war for possession. The Red Knave rushed him and hit him hard as he pulled the strap of the satchel free. "You'll never be able to stop me now." He hugged the satchel to his chest; his eyes fluttered as if he'd just received a large dose of laudanum. A huge shadow eclipsed the sunlight and surrounded them in the twilight. In one swift blur, talons of a giant claw caught the strap and ripped it from Nerius' grasp.

"No! No!"

Ervig grabbed the prisoner by the arm and pulled him to his feet. "It seems I have stopped you." He glanced at the dragon overhead in a hazy sky, wondering where he was to take the prisoner. *"Should I put him back in the Labyrinth?"*

"No!" A rush of wind peppered Ervig's face with grit as the dragon swooped and caught the Red Knave by the back of his tunic. As the prisoner lifted into the air Ervig's training kicked in. He tackled Nerius' legs and grabbed hold. *"What are you doing?"* Ervig shouted to the dragon's mind.

The dragon's leathery wings beat the air without an answer. They quickly gained altitude. Ervig stared at the diminishing mountains as his grip slid to the man's ankles. Ahead of them, he spotted a small village in the distance. *"Is that where we are going?"* The Red Knave kicked his legs. Ervig panicked as his grasp slipped. He dangled high above the rolling foothills clutching the ankle of the prisoner's boot. To his dismay, the prisoner's boot started to slip from his foot. *No! No! No!* The boot pulled free, and Ervig dropped into a freefall with the boot in his hands. His chainmail pulled him quickly toward his death with Nerius' laughter fading overhead. *"Help!"*

The dragon's deep voice filled his head. *"Ye be Dragonborn. Help thyself!"*

Ervig's thoughts raced as fast as his heart. *The dragon is right. I need to stop thinking like a limited human.* His fears dissipated; he knew the right thing to do. "*Mutata in Falcon.*" Feathers sprouted in a flash of energy and pain and pointed powerful wings lifted him high, snatching him from certain death. As a fast-flying peregrine falcon, his eyesight zeroed in on the dragon as it released his prey and let him fall into a cistern. Nerius dropped out of sight, pulling the satchel with him.

Ervig reached the spot and circled above the opening. Nerius hunkered at the bottom of the dry cistern clutching the satchel with the dragon resting on his haunches at the rim. Anger burned within Ervig's gut. *"I thought you wanted to stop the Red Knave! You didn't stop him at all. You gave him back the book! His power!"*

"Hurry, Little One," the dragon said. *"Time be short."*

Ervig landed beside the dragon. *"Hurry! Hurry and what? Who are you? What are you talking about?"*

"I be Tezoth. I saw the rogue portal open. I carried the one you call the Red Knave here to give him time to regain a little of his power. Ye must follow him one more time into the Labyrinth."

Dread filled him. *"The Labyrinth... again? Why?"* This dragon didn't understand–he hated the dark and tried to keep up without being spotted amid the shifting corridors. And even more, he hated the dark aura surrounding the prisoner. It had almost erased the prisoner's original aura, and it filled Ervig with a healthy fear of the man's power.

"I perceive ye to be Dragonborn. Ye must practice thy foresight," the dragon said. *"The ancient prophecy foretells that he must be entombed in the temple of the human prophets. Humans here in this time have no temple. No foresight. Ye be chosen to move through time. To stop the man and the magic of the book... for a time."*

Below them, the Red Knave gained enough power to generate a rogue portal. Above them, the rumble of a tear in time tore across the sky. *"Quickly, Little One. Ye must move quickly. Ye be the one that knows what must be and how to accomplish it."*

Ervig wanted to scream with frustration. As a military man, he liked to have a plan. To have time to think and strategize–and orders to be carried out. One didn't go into battle blind! The dragon seemed so sure. He was not. But as the portal grew in the wall of the cistern, he changed into a jumping spider and dropped onto the prisoner's shoulder before slipping into the cold darkness on the other side of the portal's red energy.

Four pairs of large eyes offered excellent eyesight and eliminated his fear of the dark. Two large eyes in the middle and two smaller ones looked forward, while the second row of two tiny eyes let him see behind, and two other large eyes looked upward. In all, this jumping spider form gave him 360-degree eyesight.

CHAPTER SEVEN

Gamalar and his mate Hennah circled the mountains in the north after an early morning hunt. She carried a large-horned binturong in her talons while a malachite-eyed dhole hung limp in Gamalar's grasp. The transparent nictating membrane that worked as their third eyelid provided them with perfect vision in the low light. Peach pastel layers of haze crept across the eastern sky as the second sun peeked above the horizon.

Gamalar paid little attention to the suns. Instead, he focused on the purple energy that sizzled from five openings torn into the fabric of time by humans—humans who used dark magic to create unsanctioned portals that forced access to and from the Labyrinth of Times. As a youngling, these tears in time wrought fear within him. Now they just made him uneasy. Nervous. *They leave us to be so vulnerable.*

He swooped and glided alongside Hennah. *She's been so quiet.* He wondered if she was thinking about that threat as well. "What be troubling ye, Hennah?"

Hennah didn't answer. Her blue-green scales shone dark like coal in the shadows of the low morning light, with her blue underside brighter than usual as the first rays of the sun lit them from below.

Gamalar vibrated the tip of his left wing as he did when courting her, but she didn't even notice.

"Hennah!"

She snapped out of it. "I be sorry, Gamalar. What say ye?"

"What be wrong, Hennah? Ye seem lost within thyself?"

She veered closer. "I cannot say. I feel something be wrong. But I know not what it be. I see it not. Not here and not in a vision."

Her premonition heightened Gamalar's senses. "I think it best we return to the roost. Now."

"Aye."

As they turned with the suns at their back, a rumbling crescendo roared across the heavens and climaxed with a boom. A shock wave buffeted their large bodies and shook them to the bone. The malachite-eyed dhole slipped from Gamalar's left talon and dangled from his right. Hennah stared at him with wide amber eyes. "What be happening?"

Purple energy unzipped the heavens right in front of her sluicing them with a tingling sensation. Gamalar butted Hennah with the full weight of his body and knocked her away from the opening. She tumbled end over end a couple of times with the weight of the Binturong pulling her into a spin and dragging her downward. Gamalar watched in horror until she righted herself with the binturong still in her grasp. Once he saw she was safe, he positioned himself in front of the new tear. Hennah joined him, and the two of them treaded air and stared at the energy spilling into their time.

Hennah let out a puff of smoke as she exhaled. "It be a hundred ages since a new tear!"

Gamalar's mind raced as he tried to make sense of what was happening. "We must hurry back to the roost."

"Aye!" Hennah followed her mate straight to the roost nestled within the tallest mountain. Many of the Thornose gathered in confusion. "It appeared just after dawn," one dragon said in disbelief. His mate roared. "Why see ye it, and I see it not?"

While all heard the tear, it didn't take long to realize how few saw it. Gamalar had been aware that many did not see these breaches in time, but at this moment, it caused panic. Dragons who had ignored the prophecies now misquoted and misinterpreted some of the ancient foresights. Talk of escaping through the Labyrinth spread. Gamalar roared, and many quieted. "Thornose be not able to traverse the corridors of the Labyrinth uninvited. Know ye not the basics of the Labyrinth?"

His announcement stirred a buzz of excitement. They'd been warned for centuries about the possibility of more rents in time. But the passage of decades had given many of the Thornose clan a false sense of peace and confidence that the book and its evil had finally been confined. The elder dragon stepped up to the highpoint and overlooked the chaos. "Dragonkind! We be warned again and again that this be expected. For those who held on to false hope, this new tear shatters that misplaced hope. It be proof that the evil spirit of the book lives on."

Tozoth, a reddish-violet dragon much the same color as Gamalar but smaller than most Thornose males, landed beside the elder. All present knew him to be gifted with prophetic visions. Until now, many had ignored him or even slandered him, but now all gave him their full attention.

"Be warned. A second new tear be coming. The human scoundrel be escaping the Labyrinth he unlawfully entered! After that, another tear be coming. This vision be sent through mine twin, Tezoth, from another time. He be a witness to the human who now possesses the Book of Darkmore. On his heels be another human… one Dragonborn."

Dragonborn! A human! Gamalar snorted at the concept, and he wasn't alone. The topic of Dragonborn humans had been disputed for centuries. Some speculated it was the answer to overcoming the power of the book. Gamalar refused to believe such a thing. *Impossible!*

Tozoth stretched his wings to draw attention back to his message. "For ye doubters, let me say that this human be Dragonborn through Vellath, son of Therus. And it be him who sent this… this Dragonborn into the Labyrinth in pursuit of the book and the one who carries it! This man be the first of the Dragonborn."

Gamalar's mind spun. *First! Does that mean there will be a second... third? How many? Has Hennah such visions?* Vellath, son of Therus, brought credibility to the idea of a human Dragonborn. *Dragonborn be sanctioned!* Everything within him fought against this concept… this joining with humans in a covenant of trust, but he had to let go of his old thoughts and beliefs.

Tozoth lowered his wings. "Tezoth, mine twin, be witness… that this Dragonborn not only communicated with Vellath but changed into a bat, spoke with a second dragon, transformed into a bird and even a spider as he gave chase to the book and this human who is called the Red Knave."

How can I argue with these proofs? Gamalar wondered. *But still, I must be vigilant. Look what humans already be responsible for. It be this Red Knave human who opened another rogue portal and another tear in time. This human be so careless. So dangerous, with four breaches leaving our world in peril of invasion from other times and more promised to come.* As these new facts overcame his former inclinations, he could no longer dispute that humans… Dragonborn humans would join them in this fight. *I must be sure.*

The elder dragon gathered scouts to scour the land for the rogue portal and the one who bore the spirit of the book. Before he left, Gamalar joined Tozoth on the highpoint. "Prove to me that what ye say be true."

Tozoth did not argue. Instead, he leaned his head forward, and the two dragons touched nibhorns. The vision came to life in Gamalar's mind. What he saw left no doubt. "It be just as ye said, Tozoth. I be sorry I doubted ye. I must join the scouts to seek out the portal."

He quickly flew down to Hennah and told her he would meet her back at the nest. "I be joining in search of the portal. If I return not for the late feeding, meet me at the nest."

Before she replied, he took to the sky with the other scouts, but the rouge portal was not found in their time. During the search, two more tears ripped the heavens just as Tozoth had predicted. But from the vision, Gamalar knew that wasn't the last of the tears. He felt trapped as he joined Hennah at the roost to eat. All the herd talked about the new tears and what Tezoth had predicted.

Hennah stood beside Gamalar as he stared up at the sky. "This dark destiny be no longer a topic of natter or conjecture. It be time to act," he said.

"Aye, mine mate."

Gamalar walked away from the beast he'd been eating, and Hennah followed him as they lumbered to their burrow within the warren. "Act how?" Hennah asked.

Gamalar stretched out within the shallow depression of their nest and lay his head upon his front legs. "At first, I suspected Tezoth fabricated his vision; that he be covering for his brother's inability to capture this — this Knave human. But I challenged him privately, and Tezoth shared his twin's vision nib horn to nib horn with me. I now be a witness to the human with the red hair trapped in a dry cistern with the book. He broke into the Labyrinth through a rogue portal and escaped with the Dragonborn human giving chase. Tezoth's witness be seen through the eyes of Vellath, son of Therus, who be at the cistern. He witnessed the Dragonborn change from a falcon to a spider. I know no dragon who be able to do such things. And so this Dragonborn followed the red-haired human and the book to another time. He hesitated not to give chase. He be there to trap the human with the book in a secret room within the temple of the prophets… human prophets."

Gamalar struggled with it. *Human Dragonborn, human prophets, human temples!* Gamalar found it all quite bothersome. *"Why do we need human help? After all, it be a human that gave birth to this trouble in the first place."*

Hennah curled up beside her mate and lay quietly for a few moments. "In time past, a human who found their way into the Labyrinth of Times stirred little concern among us because the shifting corridors promised certain death to those not chosen to enter, for it stripped away all powers except those of the dragons."

"I know; I know. Ye be ready to tell me how the Knave's predecessors be no ordinary humans. How the Wizard Darkmore created the powerful Book of Darkmore with dark magic drawn from dragon's blood mingled with the power of the Tryx fire spirit." He did not lift his head but turned his eyes to look at her. "I know this. But I still say remove the human, and the problem be gone."

Hennah let out a sigh. "Ye know that in the beginning, the dragons understood not that the strong magic of the book survives the Labyrinth. We know not everything, Gamalar. I have the gift of foresight, yet I see not the entire future. When Therus' mother, Tharza, left the Labyrinth of Times as her *Donum*, she told him of a future bleak and riddled with foes and friends most unexpected. She and her mate, Bardes, talked at length about what they knew, but even they knew only in part. But one thing they be certain of—if nothing be done, the world they lived in and love be certain to end. Thornose know not everything, but Tharza knew to leave us the Labyrinth and her mate Bardes knew to give us the energy to power it. Ye could say if they never left their Donums we be not in this trouble. But we know not what they saw. Some things be not for all to see or know. We be able to act upon what we know, not what we know not."

Thought of the book sent a chill through him that reached the flesh beneath his violet scales. *That book be written in dragon's blood... the blood of Therus' mate, Zaylan.* Gamalar lifted his head. "Ye be right. When Zaylan recovered from her wounds, she spoke of the time she cast the Tryx fire spirits into the Pyre. I know little of the Tryx, and yet she warned that the spirit of the book be Tryx and that the human with the book be one with the Tryx."

"Aye," Hennah stared into Gamalar's eyes. "We know not all things, but with the warning, she offered the secret to the spirit's defeat. 'Cast the spirit of the man into the book and dispose of it.'"

"That sounds easy enough, but when she tried to trap the wizard and the book in the Labyrinth, he broke free by creating a rogue portal. And that be where our problems started. He moved through the Labyrinth to a new time, leaving three rents in the heavens in his wake. And Zaylan died shortly after."

Hennah let out a long sigh. "Aye. Some say it be the result of a remnant curse from the man who tortured her."

Gamalar saw the worry in his mate's eyes and regretted his words. "Most say she passed from a broken spirit."

He decided to change the subject to something less foreboding. "Do ye ever wonder about her Donum? The spheres?"

"Aye, but I also wonder about Therus' Donum. A tree? And it be not a pretty tree."

"We shall perhaps learn more about that tomorrow."

"What? What be ye saying?"

"All those able to see the tears in time be called to come to the Sacred Garden tomorrow."

"Ye mean… we be called to travel through the Labyrinth?"

"Aye."

The two dragons slept little as their minds raced with the possibilities.

CHAPTER EIGHT

The naked Therus tree loomed at the center of the lush Sacred Garden. Its sun-bleached branches cast a shadow under the twin suns like a tangled sundial. *Hennah be right. It be out of place here amid the verdant greens, bright yellowbark willows, and the rainbow of colorful blossoms. Why does the Therus tree bear no leaves, no blooms, no bark? It offers little shade. But somehow, it leads dragons through the corridors of the Labyrinth?*

Dragons of the Thornose clan clustered around the ancient tree in silent reverence. It represented the presence of the ancient and honored, Therus, son of Bardes, keeper of the Labyrinth of Times. The tree marked his resting place in the Sacred Garden, but it was more than a marker. The tree was his *Donum*—the gift of himself left behind to help the Thornose clan in their role as guardians of the Labyrinth. Today's gathering cluster of Thornose dragons could see the tears in time. According to the elder dragon, this tangible indicator made it clear that they were *called* to understand the tree's secrets, but it did not guarantee they would be chosen to know its power and its tie to the Labyrinth of Times.

Gamalar glanced at Hennah. Her large amber eyes pinned, excitement constricting her pupils into narrow slits. As a pair, they could be chosen to carry a branch from the Therus tree through the Labyrinth. *But where?* Gamalar wondered. *Where be we going? What be it like?* All he knew was that in whatever time they moved to, if chosen in that new time, they would serve as overseers and guardians of the Labyrinth. Beyond these responsibilities, the two of them were also expected to start a new Thornose herd. *Which means what? There be no Thornose dragons where we be going? Or that we be the smallest of herds among others?*

Gamalar anticipated the adventure with mixed emotions–excitement tempered with caution. He thought of other dragons sent out over the decades. Therus' son Vellath was among them. *That was what... a hundred ages ago?*

Gamalar pondered his conversation with Hennah and how they didn't know everything. *Everyone thought that the Book of Darkmore be secreted away for good because, after the original three tears, new breaches in the fabric of time stopped.* But centuries later, two more slits slashed through time, leaving two more unholy, dangerous tears. *The leaking purple energy from the new tears signaled the book be again in the hands of a human imbued with dark powers.*

We dragons often speak of things to come, but we still be lulled into complacency. Even me. He scanned the gathering, wondering if others felt the same. *We no longer heeded the prophetic warning but talked of them as something that never be in our lifetime.*

Because the humans in this time had no temple of the prophets, one thing was certain. Some of us be sent out. He looked at Hennah. Their eyes met. *Be we among those to be sent outside this time?* Gamalar understood time connected the past, present, and future. *Be we the ones entering the time when the temple of the prophets exists?* His regret for leaving the familiar overtook his thoughts. He glanced around at the other dragons. *Do any of them have misgivings about leaving? Fear of what might happen once they enter the Labyrinth? What if we do find the Red Knave? Dragons travel in pairs. Will only two dragons be able to overcome the evil?*

He glanced at Hennah. The blue-green scaley spines along her back ridge shimmered with iridescent colors in the sunlight. *What if something happens to her? Will it leave me without a mate, in a world without dragons?* He feared the unknown and the known–the evil. The longer the spirit occupied its human host, the more powerful it grew. Each time the fire spirit moved to a new host, it brought with it knowledge of the previous host. *It grows worse and worse.* Beyond stopping the Red Knave, the goal was to confiscate the Book of Darkmore so the spirit of the book could not claim another host.

He scolded himself inwardly and repented of his misgivings by focusing on the Therus tree. None of the dragons gathered for this ritual knew where they were going if chosen or what they'd find. They all placed their faith in the Therus tree to show them what was next.

In faith, Gamalar knew Therus would show him and Hennah the way through the Labyrinth if they were chosen and that together they would step into a new time to face an unknown world.

As much as he had reservations about what could go wrong, the possibility of a new start in a place where humans hadn't polluted the air, filled him with a hint of optimism. He tried to contain his expectations to avoid disappointment. For all he knew, he might go forward to a time when the humans already filled the air with the hazy residue they suffered from in this time from the burning of sea coal. As he struggled to manage his hopes and fears, he yearned for a future with clean air, free from the evil threat of the Book of Darkmore and its fire spirit for his offspring.

From the front of the gathering, the elder dragon's voice drew his attention. "Do ye have questions?"

Gamalar had hundreds of questions but asked only one. "How long before we depart?"

"*If* ye be called *and* chosen to enter the Labyrinth of Times," the elder dragon corrected. "The secret of traversing the Labyrinth be given to each one here this day, but the time of the choosing be not known–even to me. Only those truly chosen shall traverse the Labyrinth with unclouded guidance. Any who enter without being chosen shall be trapped in a shifting maze without end. Those standing here this day be called but not yet chosen."

The tip of Gamalar's tail tingled. That often happened when his nerves were on edge, but as a young dragon, not much older than a hatchling, he learned the prickling sensation to be a sign–to move forward. He couldn't argue with it, but he wondered at the meaning of being called but not chosen. He had no time to ponder such a riddle because the elder dragon invited each of the dragons to step forward to burn the Therus tree. One by one, smoldering branches plopped to the ground and were plucked up by the dragons.

Gamalar aimed using the razor-sharp thorn on his purplish-blue snout to line up his target as he stepped forward with Hennah at his side. He focused on one of the top branches. Fire churned in his gullet, burst into his throat, and blazed from his powerful jaws. Hennah targeted the same branch from his left. Even as smoke built up in his nasal passages and tickled his snout, Gamalar wondered if the placement of the branches had anything to do with what time they'd enter or if they would be chosen. For a brief moment, he felt linked to the Therus tree. He saw a face, a thin human male with hazel eyes flecked with green. He wore a pointed hat and, in his hand, he held a staff made of wood from the Therus tree set with a magenta rosa gem. The connection broke as the branch fell free. Gamalar's heart raced. *What be the meaning of the vision? Who be that human?*

He picked up the branch while Hennah gathered a Zaylan sphere by spreading the wing membrane between her tail and hind legs with the long spur on her ankle bone. This membrane worked as a pouch to carry things in flight. The sphere slipped inside, the membrane slid closed, and held the sphere snuggly in place.

Following the ceremony, Gamalar and Hennah ambled to the outer perimeter of the Sacred Garden with their Therus branch clasped in Gamalar's wing claw. They reached the ridge overlooking the human dwellings in the large valley veiled in hazy smog. Ten purple slashes now sizzled and spit sparks in the sky, struggling to cut through the miasma. It was the four new tears that scared him because no one had ever found a way to stitch these rents in time. And while moving through the Labyrinth was monitored by the Thornose, the tears left gaps that could be traversed unhindered and unnoticed through time. *If I hadn't butted Hennah away from that tear, she might be lost in another time.*

He found consolation in the fact that only the called could see this purple energy leaking into their world. *Hopefully, humans were not able to see them. Especially humans, the likes of this Red Knave.* The sight only reminded Gamalar and Hennah of the urgency of their mission. For most of their lives, there'd been only the three tears. Every dragon learned the history behind them. How the human who wrote the Book of Darkmore had tortured Therus's mate Zaylan. How he mingled his human blood with hers and penned the book of dark magic. Dread hung over him that the power of her dragon blood survived within the pages of the book even within the Labyrinth and empowered the man to create a rogue portal and escape. That portal tore the first slit in the fabric of time. Then the Wizard Darkmore

gathered his belongings and stepped back into the Labyrinth and ripped another opening in time and then a third when he left the Labyrinth and escaped to a new time.

When no new tears appeared for hundreds of years, the dragons thought the human had died. That the threat no longer existed. *Until two new tears appeared*, Gamalar thought as he stared out into the haze. Those with prophetic visions announced the spirit of the book had a new host. A human female, Lilith Shade. *Humans' names be so strange.* And so the two Tears of Shade were added to the first three Tears of Darkmore like strange constellations of purple energy burning in the sky. When news arrived that the woman had been separated from the book and buried where no one would find her or the book, the dragons held a feast. *We lived in peace. I thought our younglings be able to grow up here without the threat.* Gamalar swung his head to see his mate looking out at the same view. He turned back to the tears. *Until now.* The roar of four new tears ripping through time so close together had created a sense of urgency he'd never witnessed among the Thornose. *Ten openings now burn in the heavens! How quickly they be changing the course of mine life. Because we be able to see the tears, we be among the called.* He glanced at Hennah and down at the branch clasped in his wing claw. *I wonder if we be among the chosen.*

Gamalar rested on his haunches as he considered humans. They didn't care that the air grew thick and hard to breathe or that they were the cause. As much as the Thornose clan tried to protect the human race from selfish or harmful thoughts, somehow this foul air still happened. *Could Darkmore have wielded such influence–to blind the humans in this way?* He thought about the face he'd seen when connected to the Therus tree. A human face. *Be that the face of Darkmore... or perhaps the Red Knave, or someone else? Why else did Therus show me this human?* He'd seen the Red Knave in the vision Tezoth had shared but not clearly. All he knew for certain of that man was his red hair. The human in his vision wore a pointed hat and what hair he saw was not red. He'd never forget the human's piercing hazel eyes.

"Be ye worried about whether or not the air be clean where we be going?" Hennah asked.

For a few moments, they sat in silence. After thinking about how to answer, Gamalar finally said, *"I believe it shall look much like the Sacred Garden of Therus. Mine concern be more for the dangers of the tears in time."* He turned away from the vast valley and the smog that hung like a disease over it and circled to face the garden. Tall green grass, lush trees and shrubs, flowering plants, and the yellowbark willows all grew in healthy soil with clean air. He wanted to see and remember it before he left, just in case he should never see such beauty again.

Hennah nuzzled the prickly spines on the side of his face and rubbed her bladed crown under the needles of his beard and looked up at him. *"In mine vision at the tree, I saw a tear in time and flying through it be a dragon... not a Thornose, but a larger dragon with a smooth face and on her back be a human."*

His gaze locked with hers. *"So where we be going, there be tears in time and dragons... dragons who carry humans like beasts of burden. Dragons not of the Thornose...."* He thought of the human face he'd seen. *Could this be the human Hennah saw?*

"Breathe, Gamalar. It be a vision yet future. And I can tell you this—the air be clean." She chuckled. The light clicking eased the tension tightening the muscles across his withers.

He was about to ask her to describe the human when suddenly the branch clenched in his wing claw emitted a soft yellow glow and spoke to them mind to mind in the ancient language. *"Ineo."*

The two dragons stared at each other for a brief moment. Gamalar's heartbeat rushed in his ears. The tip of his tail tingled. He nodded once. *"It be time. We be chosen."* They took to the air with the glowing branch. Their keen eyes watched for the portal. The branch grew brighter like a beacon marking the portal's location beneath the smoggy foulness. As they dropped through the smoky film, the muted blue glow of an active portal welcomed them from the maw of a cave.

CHAPTER NINE

Gamalar looked back one last time at his world obscured by human foulness. He thought he'd have an opportunity to bid his friends farewell. Instead, he and Hennah stepped into the cave and through the portal. As the energy swirled around him, he felt light pressure as if squeezing through an elastic casing. On the other side, the pressure vanished and light from the Therus branch cut a swath through the blackness highlighting a small circular room. They blinked to stretch the transparent nictating membrane over their eyes. In an instant, they could see in the dark. The grinding of stone on stone filled the stale air. The dragons stood still as the walls shifted. *Or be it the floor?* Gamalar wondered as fine-grit rained from above as they stood at a dead-end. The wall moved and opened to a new corridor. The golden circle of light from the Therus branch brightened, and they started forward into the fresh passage.

"I feel… like I be rotating sideways and up and down at the same time," Hennah said as she stopped in her tracks.

"Aye." Gamalar paused beside her. "Our sight be showing more than we need to see. Keep thy eyes on the light. It helps." He lumbered forward, and she followed. Gamalar kept his eyes trained on what the light showed him and fought thoughts of how easily one could become lost in the Labyrinth. Doors lined each side of the new corridor. "These doors be too small for dragons to fit through," Hennah said.

"That be easy then, for if we cannot fit, it be for certain not the way."

At times shifting walls and floors moved beneath their feet and forced them to new levels. They lost a sense of the passage of time, but as his throat grew parched, Gamalar questioned, How long be we within the Labyrinth? He plodded forward with Hennah at his side. Perhaps we be doomed to wander the Labyrinth until we die of thirst. Just as he thought he could bear it no longer, the walls shifted. He put aside thoughts of thirstiness. “Hennah, stay ye near.” Together, they stepped through a new archway and stood upon an outcropping that overlooked an underground lake in a mammoth cavern. The moist air soothed their dry eyes. “Be we lookers only at the water below or drinkers as well?” Hennah asked.

Gamalar snickered and took to the air. “I be a drinker.” She chased after him and landed beside him on the shore. They drank deeply, and the cool water satisfied his thirst and energized him. They took time to spread their wings and stretch but then pressed on. Beyond the lake, a naturally formed stone bridge stretched across a deep canyon. They stood gazing at the canyon. “It be best we stop and rest,” Hennah said.

“Aye.” Gamalar took to the air above the canyon to exercise his wings with the Therus branch clamped in his jaws. “Before we rest, come fly,” he said. “We Thornose be built to fly not crawl about within the earth like worms.”

Hennah joined him. “It be freeing to take to the air.”

As Gamalar circled in a loop, he spotted a hint of blue glowing from the other side of the canyon. “Hennah, see ye that?”

"Be it a portal?" Hennah asked.

With the branch clenched in his jaws, the two dragons gracefully lifted higher into the stale air. The Therus branch cast soft petals of light across the lake. Its brightness grew more intense as they headed toward the blue light.

"This be it!" Hennah looped up and over as she circled back to glide to a gentle landing beside her mate. They settled in front of the portal, stopped to look at each other, and then stepped through the swirling blue energy together. This time the portal prickled the skin beneath their scales. “Mine skin be cold and numb,” Hennah said as she tried to shake off the odd sensation.

“Mine too,” Gamlar said as they walked into a cave lit by bright sunshine leaking through a fissure about two dragon lengths away. The nictating membrane over their eyes helped control their sensitivity to light as their eyes adjusted. They stopped at the threshold and peeked at the world beyond. Blue skies and a stunning mountain vista welcomed them to their new home. Gamalar breathed deeply.

The pure air was unlike anything he'd witnessed in his life. Cleaner and fresher than even the Sacred Garden. The light of the branch died. He dropped it to the ground with a thud, and it rolled from shadow to the light of the two suns.

Hennah lumbered into the light. Her blue-green scales radiated with iridescent color, and the blue on her chest and stomach looked as if it were more vibrant than ever. "Here be a good spot to plant." She scraped the talons of her wing-claw across a spot, etching an "x" into the hardpan. Gamalar picked up the branch in his jaws and joined her. Together, they clawed the top layer of hard-packed, stony soil; their talons created deep furrows until they reached rich dark soil.

Hennah stretched her neck and gently plucked the branch from Gamalar's mouth, placing the burnt edge into the hole. Then, she spread the membrane between her tail and hind legs using one of the longspurs extending from her ankle bone. The Zaylan sphere rolled out onto the ground. With her snout, she rolled the Donum sphere into the hole. Together, Gamalar and Hennah scooped dirt into place around it. When they finished, they stepped back and studied the branch sticking out of the ground like a large dead stick.

Time ticked, and the two dragons looked at each other with unanswered questions. If they failed in this first task.... Just as Hennah turned to walk away, the ground beneath their feet vibrated. The branch grew taller. Loose dirt and small pebbles bounced around its thickening trunk. Crackling sounds and rumblings from the quaking mountains filled the air as the branch transformed, bigger and thicker until a Therus tree stood before them in just minutes.

"The Therus tree has taken root, Hennah. This be our new home," Gamalar said. "Do ye desire to spy out this new land and find food?"

A soft clicking emanated from his mate. "I be tired, Gamalar. All that walking be wearisome. I say we rest before we fly above these mountains and search out this new land. Though I be hungry, it be sleep, I need to be fresh, vigilant, and strong. For we know not what be ahead."

"Ye be wise, Hennah. We rest a short time but then must find food." He lumbered to the spot just outside the portal cave and scraped the hardpan into pebbles creating a shallow bowl. Hennah joined him, and the two curled up in the softened depression together.

"I wonder what be these pink stones."

The transparent stones sparkled in the sunlight within the loosened dirt Gamalar had scraped away to make the beginnings of their nest. “They be crystals,” Gamalar said as Hennah’s eyes grew heavy. Thoughts of the shimmering stones faded as she drifted to sleep.

Gamalar awoke with a start. The tip of his tail tingled. He pushed to his feet, lifting his bulk to his full height, which woke Hennah. A shadow fell across the tree.

"What sort of dragons be ye?" a voice asked as a cloud of dust stirred around them. Hennah rolled to her feet as a large green dragon with smooth scales and a white patch of skin on the front of her neck landed near the mouth of the cave. A row of curved barbs lined the boney ridge on the back of her long neck. At the base of her neck, between her well-muscled shoulders, she bore a longer, slightly curved horn that glinted in the suns’ light.

Hennah blinked and stepped closer. "We be of the Thornose clan? And ye?"

"I hail from the Goldenhorn clan."

The two females circled one another. Gamalar worried for his mate's safety. The Goldenhorn be so much bigger than mine, Hennah. His muscles tensed, ready to spring into action if necessary.

"It be a Goldenhorn I saw in mine vision, Gamalar." Hennah cast a glance in his direction and then trained her vision on the larger green dragon.

The Goldenhorn dragon paused and eyed the smaller Hennah. "Pray tell, where do ye hail from?"

Hennah looked up into the larger dragon's strange eyes set like jewels within boney eye ridges. The dragon’s eyes caught Gamalar’s attention as well. What purpose do such round multi-faceted eyes serve?

"Gamalar?" Hennah called him back to the question. "Will ye answer her question, or shall I?"

He said, "We be travelers through the Labyrinth of Times. The Labyrinth chooses this place in time to be our new home."

"And that?" The Goldenhorn ticked her large snout toward the Therus tree. "What manner of tree be that?"

Gamalar hesitated. It was important to protect the Therus tree. Hennah walked in a wider circle and sidled up beside him. "This be a Therus tree," she said.

Light shimmered in the Goldenhorn's round eyes. "A Therus tree? Such a tree be spoken of in our prophecies. Be it from the garden? The Sacred Garden?"

Gamalar stared at the smooth scaled green dragon in wonder. "Ye know of the Sacred Garden?"

"'The prophecy says, 'The day the Therus Tree from the Sacred Garden reveals itself, shall mark an eon of fortune and an age of growth… a uniting of four unlikely allies.'"

This prophecy intrigued Gamalar. "Mine name be Gamalar, and this be mine mate Hennah. As she said, we be of the Thornose Clan. What be these allies ye speak of?"

"Mine name be Naroath of the Goldenhorn Clan. Welcome to Vodatha–thy new home. The understanding of the prophecy be hidden from us. However, the existence of the Therus Tree marks it true."

CHAPTER TEN

Ervig marveled at his newfound courage. *That dragon somehow changed me when I took that oath!* He no longer feared the dark as he did in the dungeon. He didn't even notice it. Though it helped that in his spider form, his unique vision worked even in the dark. Somehow, he knew how to extend his legs muscles to flex them using hydrostatic pressure as he crept to the edge of the shoulder bag carrying the Book of Darkmore. He was even able to regulate his heart rate to control that hydrostatic pressure. *Being Dragonborn has increased my knowledge and experience beyond anything I thought possible.*

Ervig had always been a quick study, but so much had happened so fast. A couple of days ago, I awoke in my bunk and reported for duty among the guard. Since then, I was turned into a rat, escaped the dungeon, talked with dragons, and flew on the snout of a dragon! And I took that dragon oath–learned so many things before I entered the Labyrinth with the hope of removing the spell. It's all so outlandish! I wonder what Grandmother would have thought. She always said I was special.

As he moved through the Labyrinth on the backpack, becoming Dragonborn stood out above all he'd experienced. When that power touched his mind, it was like it coursed through his veins. The knowledge and the understanding that came with it! It changed me. But what's next?

As he clung to the backpack on his prisoner's back, he had to admit it wasn't without its challenges. In the world beyond the next portal, I must somehow get Nerius to a temple and then separate him from the power of the book. And there is the never going home.... Not that I had anyone there since Grandmother's death. He shook off the melancholy threatening to distract him. He had his duty. For now, the longer he and the Red Knave stayed within the Labyrinth, the better.

He settled in for the ride waiting for Nerius to step through the next gateway, or die depleted of the power he needed to open that portal.

The Knave slowed. The soles of his boots shuffled along the smooth floor until he reached a dead-end. “Well, I’ll be a snitching sneazel!” He stumbled but caught himself. “I need to get out of here.” The Red Knave created another lucium sphere to light his way. That’s good. Use your magic. Ervig didn’t know how much of Nerius’ power had come back, so the longer he stayed within the Labyrinth using his magic, the better the chance he would deplete his powers. Hopefully, he hasn’t learned that was the reason for the weakening of his power.

* * * *

Night fell across the temple complex at Nalhdyn Hold. An irrational restlessness troubled Prophet Calder Glimmergaunt. He tried meditating but couldn’t shake it, so he got up from his bed, slipped on his casual prophet’s robe, and walked to the oval scrying pool in the temple courtyard. His shadow stretched out beside him under the almost full moon as his bare feet padded the cool mosaic pavement of red feldspar, marble, mother-of-pearl, and precious stones. The fountain of the twin prophetesses at the center of the pool sent minute, silvery ripples dancing across the mirror-like surface of the water. He rested his hip on the rim of the pool and stared at his dimly lit troubled reflection. He ran his fingers through the water in search of answers. Within seconds, a vision reflected from the water's surface. A man in uniform at the gate. A copper-color dragon hovered overhead and dropped a second man to the ground. The same dragon he’d seen in many visions but still didn’t understand why. The man in uniform forced the other man from the ground and held him at knifepoint.

The lips of the man in uniform moved. Calder wished his visions included sound. He watched his hand reach out and accept a bag from the soldier. As the scene unfolded, he wondered at the man’s unfamiliar uniform. The uniformed man with the knife forced the man dropped by the dragon toward the temple complex and through the large archway. A sinking feeling washed over the prophet as he watched himself take them into the library to the last row of shelves.

"No!" The word tore from his throat in a harsh whisper. He covered his mouth and scanned the darkened windows to see if he had spoken too loudly. All stayed dark.

He glanced back at the vision unfolding in the pool. Terror grabbed him until he found it hard to breathe. We are going to that room.... His heart beat faster as he saw his hand reach for the sconce and pull it like a lever. The secret door opened. Darkness piqued his sense of the dangerous relics locked away for their dark menacing magic. The prophets' aversion to magic ran deep. The Labyrinth's magic had taken many lives, and those who toyed with magic always ended up using it for evil. The vision faded, filling Calder with cold dread. He stared at the moonlight dancing across the pool as he wrapped his arms around himself. He breathed deep and strove to dispel the fear clinging to him. What dark magic could lead me to reveal that room to a stranger… two strangers? What was in the bag? He glanced at the sky expecting to see the dragon, but instead, only light wispy clouds scuttled across the face of the moon. What does it mean? he wondered. More importantly, when will it happen?

* * * *

Journeying as a jumping spider on the satchel gave Ervig plenty of time to think and strategize. He toyed with the idea of becoming a giant spider and using his webbing to secure his prisoner, but he didn't know if that was possible. He could transform into other things he'd seen and knew existed, but he didn't know of any giant spiders. When Nerius stopped to eat, Ervig longed to fill his stomach with even a crumb, but for now, he stayed hidden to prevent the Red Knave from figuring out the connection of how he was able to follow his prisoner into other times.

To his dismay, Nerius lay down on his side, placed the shoulder bag under his head as a pillow, and closed his eyes. Situated under the man's stringy hair, Ervig found himself at the nape of the prisoner's neck, wishing he'd taken the form of some deadly spider. Nerius' snores tore through the silence. Ervig wondered if spiders slept. Not something he'd ever considered.

Ervig clung to Nerius' tunic collar as the man stirred. He sat up, stretched, scratched, and let out a few mild curses about his aching back. "By my bones, I need to get out of this bloody Labyrinth. It's enough to make a man daft." He lifted his hand, his fingers forming the claw. Red particles drifted in a stream toward the wall joining into a swarming small energy spiral, but the portal didn't grow. It was big enough for a man to climb through, but it would be a tight fit. "Son of troll," Nerius cursed under his breath as he shuffled over to the opening.

He's weak. His magic is gone! Ervig considered jumping through the portal first to start calling for help from the dragons, but his guard training didn't allow it. He had to stay with his prisoner because if the portal closed before Nerius climbed through, it would separate them. Dead or alive, I need to take him to the temple.

Nerius' boots shuffled across the uneven floor toward the weak portal. Ervig held tight to his shoulder. When they reached the portal, Nerius stuck his head and shoulders into the swirling energy. On the other side, Ervig jumped from his shoulder into the sandy soil. Pain racked his body as he visualized himself as a man. Within minutes, he stood in his uniform and yanked Nerius through the portal. He dropped him to the ground and tied his hands behind his back.

"Bullspit! How! How did you get here? Son of a troll."

Ervig ignored the string of profanity and called out mentally for help from the dragons. Silence. Will the dragon hear me?

His mind raced. Everything happened so fast. I didn't even have to think about changing from spider to man. It was as natural as scratching an itch. But now, standing there as a man brought with it doubts. I had called the dragons as a rat and as a bat. Now that I'm human…. Panic tightened his throat and made it hard to breathe as he stared down at his prisoner, who lay like a corpse in the dirt. What do I do now? I'm so… tired.

A female voice filled his mind. "Well done, young one. Welcome to thy new home. Mine name be Migjok of the Thornose clan."

Home! As he scanned the sky, relief flooded him, and he spotted the speck that quickly took form and loomed larger and larger. A coppery-colored Thornose dragon dropped from the sky. The ground beneath Ervig's feet shook, and his knees went weak. The dragon rushed toward him. Ervig cringed, unsure of what to do. The dragon reached out with her wing claw, grabbed the satchel strap, and dragged the bound prisoner toward her. "You must separate the man from the power of the book. He be using his magic to steal thy strength and mine for his own."

Nerius screamed as Ervig stepped toward him with his blade drawn. The prisoner clenched his eyes shut as Ervig slipped the edge of his dagger beneath the strap with a trembling hand and sliced it free. He yanked it from the prisoner's grasp and stepped back a couple of steps with the satchel clutched to his chest. Sweat soaked his tunic beneath his jerkin as he dropped to his knees. How could he steal my strength so quickly!

Nerius groaned. "No! You can't! You don't know what it will do to me."

"Take the satchel to the temple."

Ervig sucked in a deep breath and nodded as he let it out. "Where is it?"

"It be south of the mountains in the west, along the Inkish River."

"The west?" Ervig glanced at the twin suns as they dropped toward the purple silhouette of mountains at the horizon. He let out a long sigh. "I'm tired. I haven't slept or eaten in a day. It will take me weeks. And this cabbage head just made it worse." He sat back on his heels, overwhelmed. Behind him, waves lapped the shoreline of a lake. He longed to rest. Maybe even sleep for a couple of hours.

The dragon left the prisoner lying on the ground and ambled over to where Ervig knelt.

"Ye be thinking like a man. But ye be Dragonborn."

Ervig looked up at the dragon. "What is that supposed to mean? You don't know what I've lived through. I'm hungry and tired."

"It means ye took an oath of allegiance to the order of the dragons–made a secret covenant. Ye agreed not to speak of it with other humans. And ye promised to use thy abilities and judgment to serve alongside the dragons of the land."

Ervig nodded. “Yeah, I did, but I don’t see how I–”

A large shadow fell across them with the rush of wings propelling sand into the air. Ervig shielded his eyes as grit from the shore peppered his face. He opened his eyes to see another dragon different from the Thornose. The dragon’s smooth orange-colored scales shimmered with yellow highlights. It had two front legs instead of wing claws and a line of curved barbs along the boney ridge on its long neck, leading to a longer golden spike high between its shoulders.

“Greetings, Migjok,” the new dragon said. “This be the Dragonborn?”

Ervig ignored the fact that the dragon talked about him like a piece of furniture.

Migjok pushed Nerius to the side with his tail. “This be our prisoner. The one who bears the foretold evil. He swung his large head around to look closely at Ervig as if examining a bug. This be Ervig… I think he shall be dubbed, Ervig Rainyriver, for he doth moan and whimper like a dreary day.”

Ervig propped his knuckles on his hip. “Just let me eat, and I’ll do whatever it is I must do.”

“I be jesting, Little One. Eat! Regain thy strength.”

Ervig frustration mounted. “Fine. Eat what? Air?”

“There be fruit on the trees over yonder. Or ye can eat the seeds of those lacy white flowers over there. Do ye need to be fed like a pet?”

“Pet? No. It’s just that…. Well, humans need sleep and food, and I haven’t had either since I started this… this chase.”

A clicking noise emanated from the dragon.

“Are you… laughing at me?”

“Yes, ye shall be Ervig Rainyriver.” Migjok swung his head toward trees not far from where they stood. “That fruit be what ye need. Then ye shall mount upon Nimbus. She shall carry thee to the west.”

Ervig found his legs. “Nimbus? That’s you?” he pointed to the bigger orange dragon with yellow highlights and a large white patch on her throat.

“This human has no humor,” Migjok said.

“If you were starving and tired, you wouldn’t think it funny either.”

“Who are you talking to?” Nerius glanced around as he slowly backed away from the dragons. “We need to get out of here!”

“I be Nimbus.” The big dragon turned. Her tail swept the sand into a dune before she walked over to the trees and snapped off a branch in her powerful jaw. She carried it to Ervig and let it drop. Clusters of red fist-size fruit filled the branch. “Thank you.” Ervig plucked one and tasted it. “Delicious.” The slightly sweet but tart fruit almost instantly energized him. “This is exactly what I needed. What is it?” He wiped red juice from his beard.

The same light-clicking noise emanated from deep within the dragons’ throats. Ervig shook his head. “You are laughing at me.” He laughed and nodded as he looked from one dragon to the other and gorged himself.

“It be dragonfruit,” Nimbus said. “Do ye have the strength to ride?”

Ervig stood. Surprised that his vigor had returned so quickly. “Yes, I think I can ride.”

Nerius squirmed, trying not to get too far from the satchel. “Who are you talking–” He screamed as Migjok wings beat the air and hovered above him. The dragon grabbed him with the talons of his hind legs and hovered higher. “To the temple. Be swift, Nimbus, for this evil must be contained speedily.”

“We shall be in Nalhdyn Hold before ye,” the larger dragon challenged.

“Let the one whose feet touch the mountains be the first to brag,” Migjok called as he carried the screaming Nerius higher into the air.

Nimbus bent her foreleg and leaned forward. “Come, young one. Climb to mine back and take hold of mine goldenhorn.” Ervig clasped the heavy satchel, climbed the dragon's leg, and settled on a flat smooth spot of leathery skin. "I could just turn into a falcon or something."

"You be welcomed."

Ervig let the jibe go and tied the cut satchel strap together, hung it over the goldenhorn, and held fast with both hands. Nimbus raised her wings, and with one sharp downward movement, they lifted into the air. At first, Ervig marveled at the changing landscape, but quickly his weary body dropped to Nimbus' flat, leathery skin around the goldenhorn, and he fell asleep. When he opened his eyes, the suns had set, and he couldn't see where they were in the pale moonlight. A short time later, the eastern horizon began to brighten, and when Nimbus landed in the Nalhdyn mountains, Migjok and the prisoner lazily circled in the sky above the temple complex.

CHAPTER ELEVEN

Ervig stretched his free arm over his head to work out the kink in his back before climbing to the ground. Sleeping slumped on Nimbus' back was much more refreshing than he expected. He grabbed the strap of the satchel from the goldenhorn and clambered to the ground. Chilly wind leeched the warmth from his body as he stood beside the dragon. He wrapped his cape around himself best he could while keeping the book away from his body. Nimbus stared up at Migjok and the prisoner in the sky. Ervig followed her gaze. *I wonder if I will see these dragons once this is over and the Red Knave is locked away, or am I to be on my own? Alone.* His grandmother's words spoken on her deathbed echoed in his mind. *"Ervig, you are a strong man with a good heart. You will find your way."*

He pushed aside his concerns and pondered the task ahead. He needed to get rid of the book. *"Which way do I go?"*

"Follow, ye, the river. It be the way to the temple." Nimbus glanced back into the cloudless early morning sky where Migjok circled with the prisoner in his clutches.

Ervig nodded and pulled his cloak tighter around himself to stay warm as he started down the road that followed the Inkish River. *It looks low.* His boots kicked up a cloud of dust carried away by the stiff breeze. *As beautiful as this world is, it needs rain*. He paused to stare up at Migjok and his prisoner silhouetted against the light of the early morning suns. *He's flying lower. I must be getting close*. As he followed a bend in the road, he spotted a walled complex in the distance. *There it is. It's bigger than I expected.*

The dragon and prisoner circled lower as he approached the perimeter wall coated with a pinkish lime plaster. Beyond it stood the complex where the Nalhdyn Temple of the Prophets stood. He glanced over his shoulder. He could no longer see Nimbus beyond the curve in the road.

I don't want to even get near this book again. The way Nerius could steal my strength and energy like that. Even the dragon's strength! This book is the reason I'm here. Because of this book, my life will never be ordinary again. Resentment simmered in his gut.

Overhead, Migjok glided in lazy circles. Nerius drooped like a damp rag from the dragon's talons but still cried out occasionally for help. They were far enough up that his cries sounded more like a pesky mosquito than a man in distress. As Ervig neared the gate, Migjok circled in a downward spiral with the prisoner hanging limp. When they landed, Nerius lifted his head and stared at Ervig with a pale face. Dark circles rimmed his red eyes. He raised his hand like a beggar looking for coin. "Please, I need the book. I have to touch it. Just for a minute.... Please!" His arm dropped to his side.

With a downward swoop of his wings, Migjok lifted into the air and hovered low to the ground. *"Bring ye the book to the prophet."*

Ervig was used to doing his duty. *It's no different than locking the Red Knave in the dungeon. Except when this is all over, there's no going back to the barracks. Once I finish this task, what is my duty? Where will I live?*

Beyond the pinkish perimeter wall of Nalhdyn Hold, the first rays of the suns highlighted tiled rooftops. In the background, nestled amid a sea of mountains, sat the massive multi-story temple. Ervig walked up to the gate with an uneasy feeling. He lifted the brass knocker glinting in the suns' light. The clang of brass echoed as he waited for someone to answer. *What kind of place is this that doesn't have a guard at the gate?* No sooner did he think it and the gate opened with a whisper. A robed man with a violet aura tinged with yellow, who looked as if his skin never saw the suns, stared at him wide-eyed. The violet energy showed him to be a spiritual man, but what concerned Ervig was the yellow. *Indecisive people can be a danger to those who depend on them.*

"I must speak with you," Ervig said as he shoved the bag with the book in it toward the pale-faced man. "I've been sent to you with this book of dark magic, magic that can end the world as we know it." The man's hand shook as he accepted the satchel. He held it out away from his body like something to be tossed into a cesspit.

Ervig turned at the sound of Nerius' whimpers. The prisoner hit the ground in a puff of dust carried off by the wind. Ervig rushed to his side and forced him to his feet, bound his hands behind him, and held his dagger at his ribs. "Hurry," Ervig called out to the robed man at the gate. "Don't let him get too close to the book, or it will grant him power we can't control. I'll follow you at a distance."

The robed man stood motionless; his brow wrinkled in an I-don't-know-what-to-do look. "Listen," Ervig said. "His magic changed me into a rat! Do you want that?"

The prophet shook his head. "No. No, certainly not. Come," The prophet said in a quavering voice. "Follow me." He opened the door wide to let Ervig and Nerius through the gate. As the prophet closed the gate and fumbled with the lock with nervous fingers, Ervig moved to the side to keep Nerius away from the power of the book. With the gate secured, he turned and said, "Come with me."

Ervig followed the robed man through the complex thankful it was still so early. When they finally stepped beneath the central archway of the temple's first floor, Ervig felt like his task was almost finished. They veered right and stepped into a vast library. Ervig followed at a distance as they walked by long tables with chairs and shelves filled with scrolls. The robed man glanced over his shoulder at him with worry as they entered the next section. High desks against the far wall filled the perimeter of the room. *What kind of temple is this?* He wanted to ask but didn't want to risk creating suspicion. Instead, he said, "The prisoner is known as the Red Knave and is wanted in multiple…." He paused, looking for a way to explain it, and chose the word "…worlds."

* * * *

Calder Glimmergaunt forced one foot in front of the other. He continued to hold the satchel at arm's length like a poisonous snake, but it grew heavy, causing the muscle in his shoulder to burn. Other than that, he felt like he was walking in a waking dream. Behind him, the uniformed officer said, "The prisoner is known as the Red Knave and is wanted in multiple… worlds."

"Worlds?" Calder repeated. *A heretic! There is only one world!* His mind raced to make sense of it. The vision was true, but the man's words were false. *Am I doing the right thing?* He'd never heard anyone say such a thing before, never read even a hint of more than one world in the scrolls. If it wasn't for his vision, he would take the man in uniform into custody for trial. He switched the satchel to his other hand and decided to test the man. "There is only one world." He glanced over his shoulder to watch the man's reaction.

The soldier's brown eyes grew wide but didn't let up his hold on the sickly-looking one the dragon had dropped at the temple doorstep. "I mean… villages. Every village and town is like another world to me. He is wanted in several villages. Please, we must enclose him in that secret room of yours. Keep going. Stay ahead of us. Don't let him near that satchel."

Prophet Glimmergaunt felt uncomfortable that the "secret" chamber was known by this outsider. *I can't reveal the location of the chamber of forbidden artifacts! This could be a trick to reveal its whereabouts. Maybe I should take him to the storeroom until I can sort this out.*

* * * *

Nerius slumped, forcing Ervig to half carry, half drag him through the library. "Please," Nerius mumbled. "Just let me near the book for a minute." Ervig did his best to ignore the man's pleas. In the next sector of the library, a handful of robed men and women were lighting lamps hanging from the ceiling. They stopped and stared, but when they saw the High Prophet carrying a satchel by its strap like a censor hanging by a chain, they looked away.

At the rear of the library, they walked into an area filled with shelves stacked with junk. When Prophet Glimmergaunt reached the last row of shelving, the yellow almost overtook his aura. *He doesn't trust me*, Ervig thought. The prophet stopped and faced Ervig and lifted his hand. "Stop right there. I need some answers. How do you know about the room? And… and do you plan to just leave this man locked inside?"

Ervig nodded. "We have no choice. He is a wizard of the dark order. A murderer and thief. The spirit of the Book of Darkmore has touched him… it lives through him. It's in that satchel you're carrying—the book, I mean. The only way to separate him…."

* * * *

A sinking feeling washed over Calder Glimmergaunt as his emotions warred. *Nothing good ever comes of magic. If I had my way, it would be banned throughout the land. But sentencing a man to death by locking him away and forgetting about him…* It troubled him. As he stood at the last row of shelves in the northwest corner of the temple trying to decide what to do, life started to return to the prisoner's eyes. A sinister evil stretched his face into a wry grin. His shoulders straightened, and he stood up, bearing his weight. A cold wave of fear froze the prophet in place.

The guard glanced around. "What are you waiting for! Open the door to the room!" he shouted. His voice echoed throughout the hall. The prisoner jerked free and jumped into the air. In one easy movement, he slipped his legs through his arms with his hands still bound. Now they were in front of him.

Calder spun and dashed between the shelves filled with broken pieces of relics. He skidded to a stop at the dead end and yanked a sconce draped in webbing. A secret panel slid open. Fear paralyzed him as the guard and prisoner struggled. "Get the book in there," the guard yelled.

Calder stared at the satchel still held out at his side and back at the guard. The Red Knave twisted free of the man's grasp and wrapped the dangling edge of the rope binding his hands around his neck. Calder trembled as he backed into the dark room and shoved the satchel onto a shelf littered with other relics. He swiped his hands across the front of his robe as if wiping any residue of magic from his palms. The sound of scuffling on the other side of the door scared him. *What will I do if the wizard overpowers the guard?* For a brief moment, he thought of all the power for evil locked away in the room where he stood. *Maybe I could ward off the dark magic.* He shoved the thought aside. *I'd rather die than put my trust in magic.*

He inched toward the door and peeked out at the two men. The guard slammed the Red Knave against the wall, and the two of them stumbled backward through the door into the darkness of the secret room. Calder scrambled back to get out of the way and reached into the folds of his robes for the two starstones. He rubbed them together vigorously until they filled the room with a warm buttery glow.

The two men crashed against the far wall rattling a chain connecting leg and handcuffs to the wall. They slid to the floor. The guard pulled his head free from the rope and grabbed the Red Knave's bound hands, shoved them against the wall, and locked one of the leg cuffs around his wrist. The prisoner bucked. "No! No! You can't do this."

Ervig stood on shaky legs, gasping for breath. He glanced at the prophet still holding the starstones in his trembling hand. "We need to get out of here."

"Just… just leave him here to-to die?"

"The moment he joined with the book, he signed his death warrant. There's nothing we can do about it. And if we don't get out of here. One of us could become the next host." Ervig cupped the prophet's elbow in his hand and steered him through the door and back into the musty storage area of the library. The prisoner screamed and bucked; the chains rattled as the door closed. The two men walked through the halls together, but Calder saw no one. Heard nothing. He couldn't just murder the man. He walked the guard to the gate. The two talked briefly. Calder could see the man was as troubled as he was. He tried to talk about the dragons, to ask how they were involved, but the guard just shook his head and said, "They are trying to help us."

Calder watched the guard walk down the road away from the temple until he was out of sight. He turned on his heels and hurried back to the library, his robes billowing behind him. *I can't just let that man die. Somehow, I have to help him.* He rushed through the library to the northwest corner of the storage room and opened the secret door. He froze at the threshold. A rope of golden light emanated from the satchel and licked the man's face. He stepped into the room, wondering what he should do as the light filled the prisoner's mouth.

Light shot out the man's eyes as he let out an unearthly shriek. His entire face glowed. The skull beneath his skin shined through until it burst into flame. Calder back-peddled toward the door. The light withdrew to the satchel on the shelf leaving behind smoldering skeletal remains. The dead man's boney finger moved–pointing toward the book with his hands still bound. Calder backed out of the room, bumping into the doorjamb in his haste, and yanked the sconce. As the door slid shut, the smell of burned flesh lingered in his nostrils and on his robe.

* * * *

Nerius Azwix struggled against the chain, keeping him from the book. The rope of light warmed his face as he used his last ounce of power to lift the chest from the satchel. His power wavered, and it fell back onto the shelf. Sweat stung his eyes as he tried to muster enough magic to bring the book to him. *I need the book! I need strength.* But the energy from the book devoured his last grain of vigor.

"You are too weak," a voice sounded in his mind.

The door to the room slid open. From the corner of his eye, he saw the prophet step into the room. Nerius opened his mouth to scream out for help, but the fiery energy filled his mouth and bore into his eyes. He shrieked. And then the book made a promise. "Give yourself to me, and you shall live again."

Pressure squeezed his chest, making it hard to breathe. *I don't want to die!*

The rope of fire stroked his face. *"Give yourself to me, and you shall live again."*

"Yes! I give myself to you. I want to live!" A calm washed over him, and his spirit withdrew to the book. For a moment, he looked down at his old body, nothing but smoldering bones. He lifted the boney finger to point it toward the book and mingled his essence with two others within its pages, waiting for another to come and free them.

Ervig sat staring into the campfire as he chewed a long blade of grass. Guilt held him in a tight grip. *Nerius Azwix was a scoundrel but leaving him to die....* The large Goldenhorn, Nimbus, eyed him. It made him uncomfortable. *"What?"*

"What be next for thee?"

Ervig tossed the blade into the fire and watched it vanish in a thread of light. *"That's a good question. I don't know what I should do? Why do you ask?"*

"The future."

"The future? What about it?"

"Thy choice can change the future. Could even save the Red Knave from the fate we delivered him to this day, for ye be destined to save the land."

Ervig's curiosity piqued. *"The land? How? From what?"*

"It be easier to show ye if ye be willing."

Ervig shrugged. *"Certainly, what do I have to do?"*

"Let us fly, and I shall show thee." Ervig climbed the dragon's muscular leg and took a seat on the flat area behind the golden horn. He grabbed the spike with both hands, and with a mighty sweep of her wings, Nimbus took to the air. The cool night air made Ervig's eyes tear. *"Be ye ready?"* Nimbus asked.

Ervig swallowed hard, trying to overcome a sense of uncertainty. *What do I have to lose? "I'm ready."* The words barely left his lips, and visions burst into view within his mind's eye. The visions showed the two of them flying through a tear in time. On the other side, a pristine valley stretched beneath them. The two landed, and there Ervig built a home. Nimbus hunted for them providing meat, while Ervig cultivated the land. Then he saw another human… a female. She became his mate.

Outside the vision, Ervig found a sense of satisfaction, of belonging, even as the vision continued. Nimbus taught Ervig and the woman the ancient language. Together they chronicled prophetic visions. Magic would save humankind. Dragon magic. When the vision ended, Ervig blinked at the bright morning sky. He had no idea he'd been flying for so long.

"Be ye willing?" Nimbus asked.

Ervig had no doubt. *"For that? I am ready."*

Nimbus flew directly to a tear in time to the north. As they flew through it, the prickly sensation reminded him of passing through the Labyrinth portal, leaving his skin cold and numb. For a moment, it took his breath away. *"So where are we?"*

"We be 700 years in the past."

"What? Seven hundred years!"

* * * *

Calder Glimmergaunt looked around the table at his fellow prophets. Driven by what he witnessed, he'd led the cause to snuff out the use of magic. The first step was final. Moving forward, magic–all magic would be discouraged in general and shunned among the prophets. From here forward, prophecy would be the desirable gift among their students. At the coming of age, initiates would be forced to choose between magic or prophecy. Those who chose magic would be sent to study at Tachnir. "Going forward, it will be against the law for a single individual to have both powers." The prophets unanimously agreed, and the law passed with the hope that people would gradually move away from magic altogether.

CHAPTER TWELVE

"Seven hundred years," Ervig repeated as he rubbed the tingling sensation on his arms. For the first time, he realized he never had human skin when he had slipped through the rouge portals. *I felt numb then. I wonder if that is why.* Below him, the Inkish River snaked along the valley floor, but it didn't seem dark like ink in this time though things looked slightly blurry. He rubbed his eyes with the heels of his hands. *"I can't see very well."*

"It be a mark of traveling back in time."

"What! Will it clear up?" He peered down at the ground, still out of focus.

"Aye."

Within a short time, his vision returned to normal. Sure enough, the river no longer flowed dark, murky, and low. Instead, it ran clear like a mountain stream during the winter thaw. To the west, the Nalhdyn mountains rested like a slumbering giant. "Where are the villages? The people?"

Nimbus circled lower and followed the river. Thatch rooftops dotted the shoreline. "There be the humans."

"So, how does this work? It muddles my brain. I mean, we shouldn't be able to do this. We could change history."

"That be right, Little One."

The two of them flew along the valley toward the west. Behind them, in the distance beyond the eastern mountain range, Ervig witnessed the hugest body of water he'd ever seen. It stretched along the entire horizon for as far as he could see. Suddenly he realized he hadn't been paying attention to the history lesson delivered by his winged companion. "… Here, there be no dragons."

"What? No dragons? At all? How do you know?"

"Remember how ye called out when ye be a rat?"

“Yes.” That memory seemed a lifetime ago. The experience almost seemed normal now.

“The dragon, Vellath, heard thee. When ye called me, I heard thee. If there be dragons here, I would hear them; feel them.”

“So what do you plan to accomplish by coming here?… As the only dragon?”

“Not me.” The dragon turned her massive head and looked at him with her multifaceted eye. “It be what **we** shall do.”

“And?”

“We shall work to stop the dark magic of the book carried by the Red Knave and its hosts.”

“We can do that?”

“We can try.” The dragon circled lower over a small valley tucked within the mountain range. "Hold ye tight with thine legs,” the dragon warned as she lifted her wings and created a backdraft. As Nimbus’ feet grabbed at the rich earth, deep furrows stirred a rich earthy scent into the air. When they came to a sudden stop, Ervig lurched forward with his hands squeezing the goldenhorn and his knees hugging the dragon’s sides. He let go and climbed to the ground willing his stiff legs to obey as he stepped onto the fertile soil. His trousers stuck to his inner thighs where the skin had chaffed and bled. His knees buckled, and he dropped to the ground.

“Come,” Nimbus said.

“I-I’m having problems standing up.” He leaned one hand against the dragon’s side as he took a step. “I’m having trouble walking!”

“It be like thy vision. It will pass.”

Ervig followed him with an awkward gait. His sore legs barked at him as he willed them to march into the heavily wooded tree line. “Where are we going?”

Small saplings snapped as Nimbus forged into the trees. Dappled sunlight danced across the forest floor as the branches of the canopy overhead swayed with the wind.

“We be looking for Blunt-Leaved Yellowcress.”

Ervig just wanted to sit. His feet hurt, his legs not only stung but itched, and he longed for sleep. Nimbus stopped, and he sat on the ground cushioned by humus. The sweet fragrance of the forest helped Ervig relax.

"Here it be. See this vine?" Nimbus stood beside an old tree with a wide trunk wrapped in a vine with broad yellow speckled leaves. "This be the Blunt-Leaved Yellowcress."

"And?" Ervig's tired nerves were frazzled. He didn't want any more riddles, or prophecies, or anything that made him think.

The dragon turned and stared at him with a look that reminded him of his grandmother when she was cross. "It be thy medicine."

"Medicine?"

"For thy legs."

Ervig sat up. "My legs? What do I need to do?"

"Ye can make a tonic from the leaves and drink it, or slice into the vine and use the bitter gold fluid as a salve. There be much medicine in this forest. It be here to help thee while ye be here."

Ervig pushed to his aching feet, walked over to the big tree, and sliced off a piece of the woody climbing plant. Golden liquid oozed from the severed vine. He pulled down his trousers and applied the first drop of golden juice to his inflamed skin. What a relief! He sliced open the length of vine and smeared it across the inside of his leg. He shuffled closer to the tree with his trousers around his ankles and sliced another segment. By the time he opened it up to apply it, the redness and sores on his first leg had vanished.

He pulled his trousers up and glanced up at his dragon as he did a little jig lifting one leg and then the other. Finally, he stopped and shook his head. "Sorry that I was cranky."

She leaned in and placed her forehead against his. He stared wide-eyed. What am I to do now?

"That be encouraging." The dragon let out a light clicking noise.

He reached up and tentatively patted the side of her snout. "Why do you say that?"

"Because ye and I shall spend much time together, young one."

“Please, just call me Ervig.”

“Ervig,” she said. “There be one more thing required of thee."

CHAPTER THIRTEEN

That *one thing* would take years. Ervig was to play a role in passing on Thornose prophecies to future generations. Not speaking them but writing them in the ancient language of dragons. *"First, ye must practice thy Dragonborn powers,"* Nimbus said. *"For they be needed. And ye must build thy shelter and prepare thy nest for thine mate. Then ye be ready to learn the language, to write the symbols, and know the meaning."*

In the beginning, Ervig thought the task to be impossible. *"I'm just one man. How can I do this?"*

"I be thy help. I deliver what ye need to build thy shelter. Ye use thy power and knowledge to put it together."

Nimbus held true to her word. She gathered materials, and Ervig worked at the craft of building using both his magic and his hands. First, she brought wood while Ervig practiced clearing and leveling the site near the healing forest. Then he used his power to dig a hole for a support pier. He tried a variety of spells. They worked as well as a child digging in the sand with a spoon. *"I think it would be quicker if I just dug the whole without magic."*

Nimbus snickered. *"Did ye think that perhaps thy spell be not specific?"*

"What do you mean?"

"How many holes do ye need?"

"Eight."

"And when ye have eight, what be thy plan?"

Ervig explained how to build a foundation. *"And so I need to place eight-cut logs into these holes this way...."* He moved his hands vertically through the air. "*...for support for the cabin. It will make it strong and stable."*

"Mine suggestion be to try a spell such as, '"Omnia quidem haec planta verticaliter servare.'"

Ervig understood what the dragon was teaching him. *Complete several steps at once! "Omnia quidem haec planta verticaliter servare."* He stared in wonder as eight tree-length logs lifted into the air and pounded into the ground until only three feet stuck out. They were correctly spaced and level with each other. "This is… is…."

"It be time-saving." Nimbus looked at him and blinked.

Learning to wield more complex spells made the work go faster. Once the floor was in place, the logs Nimbus had piled high soon transformed into walls. Nimbus flew back and forth to the building site and added to the growing pile of rocks for the chimney and fireplace.

In the evening, they sat around a fire and ate whatever Nimbus had hunted for dinner. Even after he finished the cabin, Ervig ate outside with Nimbus most nights. She enjoyed his company and he hers.

As he crafted furniture, he often thought about the woman in the vision Nimbus had shared with him before they flew through the tear. *I wonder when she will come.* He longed for human companionship but kept the thought to himself. He didn't want to hurt Nimbus by insinuating she was not adequate companionship. *When Nimbus said we'd be spending much time together, I didn't realize she would be my only companion. It is my third summer in the past. At first, it was fun practicing magic with Nimbus, learning to harness my knowledge with my new enhanced abilities to build the cabin and furnish it. But if I am true, I'd say there is more of a sense of accomplishment when I use my hands to make things.*

He poured his free time into glass blowing and gathering and working with medicinal plants from the forest. While he crushed bark from the leatherleaf tree into powder, he stopped to rest his wrist and glanced over at the shelves lined with an assortment of small glass vials and urns crafted from sand Nimbus collected from the shore of the large body of water beyond the mountains. He chuckled as he remembered the first time he saw her with the bulging manticae on her neck. He'd rushed to see if she was unwell. She laughed and explained the pouch was for carrying young. "But we use it to carry many things." Then magically, she transferred the sand to a pile on the side of the cabin.

To work on his glass blowing technique, he started crafting vials first. Now the vials held various tinctures and potions and offered a clear visual that he did not possess the glassblowing craftsmanship of his father. The big project he had planned was window glass. It wouldn't be perfect, but he didn't care. The cabin was close to being done, and he cared for the garden with his magic. He could fix the window glass with magic too. It was nice to have something to occupy his days. To keep his mind and hands busy. Glass blowing proved to be an activity that provided a relaxing break from building, planting, and harvesting. To his surprise, it stirred up memories of home that he'd long forgotten. Memories from before he lost his parents.

As he added new potions to his collection, he didn't bother to use magic to fix lopsided vials but used them as a measure of his progress at improving his skill. Once the walls were up and much of the furniture crafted, he decided to tackle blowing the window glass. When it was ready, he used magic to set the glass into the window frame. His heart dropped a little when he saw it in the sunlight. It did allow light in, but he was disappointed at the bubbles, waves, and varying thicknesses, making it impossible to see outside clearly. He rested his hand against the glass and cast a spell. The opaque glass transformed until it seemed almost invisible.

While he enjoyed glassblowing, the things Nimbus taught him about the healing properties of the plants created a whole new interest for him. With the combination of his Dragonborn abilities and his natural interest in healing, he learned to enhance many healing properties to do even more.

One evening, as he finished crushing bark, he took a break and walked over to the window to see if the suns had set as he rubbed soreness in his elbow. The suns hung low over the mountains painting bright oranges and yellows pastels across the sky. *My work keeps me busy, and while Nimbus proves to be a real friend, I long for human companionship*. The longing often haunted him. Mostly at night. The first of the twin suns dipped behind the mountains as a couple of long-tailed harriers chased each other. *Maybe I can create a woman from a harrier.* He chuckled at the absurd thought.

I wonder where Nimbus is. He turned from the window and stared at the room in which he spent so much time. *How long have I been here on this side of the tear? It has to be at least two to three years now.* He'd held onto the vision of the future that brought him here. When he tried to talk to Nimbus about it, she always put him off, saying things like, "The cabin needs to be completed." *Well, the cabin is done.* He walked over and added a log to the hearth.

Nimbus had tried to encourage him with other prophetic visions, but Ervig's thoughts always returned to the male Goldenhorn carrying the female human–the woman who was to be his mate. *Will I even be alive to see it?*

A rush of wind buffeted the small structure. He listened for Nimbus' trumpet as he turned toward the door. When he swung the door open to greet the dragon, he froze with one foot on the threshold. He stared out at a maroon dragon with a gold belly. At one point, he would have thought the dragon huge, but he was smaller than Nimbus. *It's them!* Upon the male Goldenhorn's back sat the woman from the vision clutching his goldenhorn. Tears stung Ervig's eyes as he stared at the young woman with auburn hair tied back in a braid that trailed halfway down her back. *It's her. It's her! The woman from the vision. And the loveliest creature I've ever seen.* She looked at him with blue eyes wide with wonder, and he hurried over to meet the two of them as he mentally called Nimbus home.

"Welcome!" he called out in his audible voice. It felt strange and foreign in his throat. The young woman glanced down at him, her white-knuckled fingers still strangling the goldenhorn in front of her. She blinked. "Welcome?" Her eyes scanned the wilderness. She let out a deep sigh as one remembering to breathe and looked down at Ervig again. "Where are we?"

"Come down from there, and we can talk over a cup of tea. Would you like some tea?"

She laughed lightly. "I think right about now I could go for something stronger than tea, but tea will do."

He offered his hand to guide her as she clambered from the back of the violet dragon. "Thank you. It feels so good to stand on solid ground again." With her feet firmly planted, she dropped his hand and placed her knuckles on her hips as she scanned the mountains, took in the garden, the cabin.

Ervig scratched the back of his neck. "The question is, *when* are we?"

She arched one brow as she crossed her arms. "When?"

A dark shadow fell across them, and a stiff wind kicked up and transformed into a whirlwind of grit. Ervig rushed his new guest to the porch of his cabin. "That's my dragon, Nimbus."

Nimbus landed, and the two dragons circled one another and greeted each other with trumpeting sounds loud enough to shake the snow from the mountaintops.

"Come in, come in." Ervig could hardly contain his excitement as he opened the door to the cabin. The woman stepped inside and stopped.

"What's all this?" She stared at all the herbs and plant parts hanging on the walls and from the rafters to dry. For the first time, Ervig saw his existence from an outside perspective. "This," he said, "is how I pass my time most days since I finished building the cabin. There in that jar, that's wild wheat I'll be planting when the weather warms. Along with drying things for food, I gather, experiment and process...." He pointed to his collection of vials and jars.

Her eyes grew big. "Really? What have you learned?"

"Have a seat, have a seat." He moved a log over to the table and sat it on end like a stool. "Sorry, I still need to make some chairs." To his delight, she didn't balk but sat and started lifting the vials scattered across the tabletop, smelling the contents, and trying to read the labels. She squinted.

"You won't be able to read them," he warned as he grabbed the pot of water warming on the hearth.

"You're right? What language is this?"

He smiled. “It’s not the language. I’ve confused the perception of the writing. If you want to read it, you have to drink the elixir that unscrambles it.”

“Why would you do that?”

“That’s a long story, and we’ll have plenty of time to talk about all that later. For now, I’d love to hear about you. It’s been a long time since I’ve had another person to talk with.”

He handed her a cup made from half of a large nutshell. He dropped a couple of pinches of bearberry tea into each cup and added the hot water. Again, she took in her surroundings as Ervig added the steaming liquid to her cup.

He sat on a log across the table from her finding it hard to believe she was finally there. She fingered her face, “What? Do I have something on my face?”

He blinked and shook his head. “I’m sorry. No. I just haven’t seen another person in so long.” He shrugged. “I guess I can’t believe you are here.”

She stared at her tea. “Well, I guess I am.”

“How did you get here?” The words no sooner fell from his lips when he thought of the dragon’s oath. *I’m not allowed to talk about it with any other human, or I might turn back into a rat–forever.* “I mean, what’s your name? Where are you from?”

“My name is Kaibelle, daughter of Tybalt, the potter of Stanlow of the harbor. My father is—” Sadness clouded her face. “My father was a true craftsman. Best in the village.” Her eyes pooled with unshed tears.

He patted her hand. “Don’t feel you have to say more. I understand.” But he didn’t understand what he wanted to know. *From what time did she come? I’ve never heard of Stanlow.*

A smile wavered across her lips as she lifted her cup and took a sip of tea. “What of you? What is your name?”

“I’m Ervig… Ervig Greenfields. Before I came here, I worked as a guard at a prison. And then I met Nimbus.” He shrugged. “To the best of my calculation, I’ve been here for a few years. I know a little magic, and now as you can see, I'm learning about herbs and plants and the magic locked inside them."

"Greenfields. That's an unusual name."

"It is my birthname?"

"Birthname?"

"Yes, the name I was given to mark my birth story. My mother was out hunting with my father. Her birth pangs started, and they started back toward home, where my grandmother lived with them. She was to help with the birth. They didn't make it back, and I was born in a green field under a cloudless sky. I—I didn't know my parents. I have a few vague memories, but they passed in a mudslide when I was very young. But I do have my birthname and the story that goes with it." He shrugged. "My grandmother raised me."

"I like that. Where I lived, we didn't have birthnames."

"Well, you can be Kaibelle Potterschild. It's still part of your birth story."

She nodded. Her lips quivered, but she forced a smile. "Yes, I like that."

* * * *

As Ervig became acquainted with Kaibelle, Nimbus and Kaibelle's dragon, Beroan, shared their stories. Unlike humans, they took no oath of secrecy. Nimbus bragged about Ervig's abilities. *"He be able to take animal form, and his mind be keen for understanding the magic of plants. And he be able to build things like that dwelling they be sitting in."*

"Does he understand why he be here?"

"Not totally. But do we? We be here because we foresaw, but even dragonkind cannot begin to see the complete unfolding of what be the future. What we may have changed by coming back to this time."

"That be true enough," Beroan said. *"And what of us. Does this become our home?"*

A tendril of smoke curled from Nimbus' left nostril as she stared out at the mountains. *"It be our home."*

"Have ye a nest, or do ye sleep with thine pet?"

Nimbus' eyes narrowed. *"Ervig be not a pet. Yes, he be a companion."* She let loose a snort of annoyance followed by tendrils of smoke. *"And a good one. He be a good and pure heart, and he be mine friend."* She glanced through the window at the humans. *"What of thy human? Be she pet or friend?"*

"I know her not well enough to say. Her family be killed by one wielding the dark magic of the book."

"Do ye not know what her Dragonborn gifts be?"

"Our time together be short. I only know she be able to see the essence of life. Not just see it but read the colors."

"Mine human can see the essence but reads it not well. And thy human, she understands she must not tell another human she be Dragonborn?"

Beroan let out a low growl of frustration. *"The Thornose explained it to her. Beyond that, what can I know? I be still not certain about partnering with humankind. Can they be trusted? And why be we the ones to go back in time? It be not Goldenhorn blood that inks the pages of the book of dark magic. It be not a Goldenhorn dragon that be changed in the future to join the evil one who holds the book."*

Nimbus chose not to argue but changed the subject. *"Be ye ready to see thine new home?"*

Beroan stared through the window at the two humans sitting inside the cabin at the table. *"We just trust them? Leave them on their own?"*

"We be not here to make them keep their oath, Beroan. We be here to guide them. They be chosen for a reason. Ye and I shall help discover what that be."

As the two dragons flew to the small mountainous island to the north, Nimbus pondered that Beroan would be her mate. Not a comforting thought. *While he be attractive to look at, his temperament be quite callous.*

Over time her perception of him changed. As she hunted with him and worked with him to train the humans, his interest in the truth became clear. His passion to fight the evil of the book matched hers.

He knew the ancient prophecies as well as she did, and that commonality gave them something to talk about with each other. After a time, he confessed, *"I trusted not the humans, for I worried that by working with them we be possibly contributing to the problem we be trying to rectify in the future."*

Honest communication and more time spent with the humans proved them trustworthy. Beroan's heart changed toward their mission, Nimbus, and the humans. *"I be ready to start teaching them the ancient language."*

"I think they be ready, too."

Nimbus enjoyed Beroan's companionship, and one evening as they fed side-by-side, he brushed his face against hers. His scent lingered on the side of her snout and up to the bony ridge over her eye. She stopped feeding and let out a snort as she raised to her full height. Beroan stretched his neck. A rumbling vibration started low and grew louder as we wooed her. Golden highlights edging his scales shimmered against the dark maroon. Nimbus bobbed her head and took to the air. Beroan thrust into the air while still making the courting call. He circled her and then came up behind her.

Without looking back at him, she said, "*I accept thee, Beroan, son of Migjok as mine mate.*"

CHAPTER FOURTEEN

Ervig and Kaibelle found it easier to accept one another as mates than the dragons did. They were both only children who had lost their parents. And even though they didn't speak of it, the presence of dragons in their lives made it clear they were fighting for the same goal. As time passed in the valley, it was easy to forget about the fight. They learned to use their Dragonborn skills without speaking of them to make life in the valley easier. Kaibelle helped with the garden and joined him in harvesting plants from the forest. Ervig added a lean-to to the side of the cabin. It helped to keep some of the mess he made out of the house. When he surprised her with a loom, she didn't question how he had built it and when she showed him her new potter's wheel, his eyes shined with wonder, but he never asked where she found the materials she needed.

The dragons taught them more about the healing properties of herbs as well as medicinal plants and fungi, but once they started teaching the humans the ancient dragon language, that became the dragons' key focus. "Ye almost be ready to learn to write it," Beroan said with a snicker.

For food, Ervig and Kaibelle learned how to use their unspoken abilities to grow peas, lentils, barley, and oats, along with flax, which they used to make clothes, nets, and paper. While magic alleviated much of the work, they both still enjoyed working with their hands. Ervig's glass blowing technique improved, and along with his bottles and vials, he crafted drinking glasses for the two of them and even added a second window at the back of the house to allow more light for Kaibelle as she sat at the loom.

By the time they had their household fully furnished, Kaibelle had curtains hanging at the windows. "You know, Ervig, when I came here, I didn't think I could ever be happy again."

He walked over to her as she stared out the window and wrapped his arms around her. "And you are happy now?"

She turned to look at him and nodded. A smile flickered across her lips as she took his hand and rested it on her stomach. "Ervig, I know the dragons want us to start writing out the prophecies in the ancient tongue. Do you think our child will learn to speak it?"

His dark brown eyes grew wide as he stared at his hand on her belly. "You? You mean?"

Tears of happiness pooled in her eyes, and she nodded. "Yes."

The two of them worked diligently to get done what they could before the baby was born. Ervig created a quill that never had to be dipped in ink and used it to transcribe scrolls dictated by Nimbus. Kaibelle's experience as the daughter of a potter came in handy as the dragons tasked her with creating fired tiles holding the same prophecies. The earthy scent of wet clay often brought memories of home that she cherished but never voiced. As she painted the symbols on the tiles, she thought of the decorative touches her father brushed on earthenware jars used to hold apothecaries' ointments and dry drugs. *Maybe someday I'll make something like that for Ervig's collection.*

The time to give birth arrived. Kaibelle stared at the son in her arms. Fine wisps of strawberry blond hair covered his head. As he suckled, his orange-yellow aura told Kaibelle so much that she wished she could share with Ervig. *Our son is intelligent, detail-oriented, scientific, creative, and a perfectionist*. She looked at Ervig. "You still think Kylar is the right name?"

He nodded. "And I think his birthname should be valley−Kylar Valley because he is the firstborn in this valley the dragons carried us to."

She nodded. "But what do we call this valley?"

He blinked. "You mean the hidden valley? Lost valley? We don't have a real name for it."

"Lost Valley." She smiled. "Kylar Lost Valley."

"He will have fun explaining that in the future."

With the birth of Kylar Lost Valley, progress on the tiles slowed, but Kaibelle made steady progress just the same. But when their second son, Erik Morning Caller, arrived, work on the project slackened a little more. The family grew, and three more brothers joined Kylar and Erik: Rikard Greenfields, Tomas Two Blossom, and Carn Spider Brook. Each new addition required more time to provide and care for their family. The dragons' hatchings took up some of their time, as well, but neither dragon nor human lost sight of the goal. They made steady progress on the scrolls and tiles as the dragons and humans bonded on every level.

Ervig sat outside the cabin in the shaded lean-to. The higher end of the lean-to roof abutted the northern cabin wall leaving enough room for Nimbus' head to fit as she passed on the prophecies to the Dragonborn in the ancient language. The youngest of her hatchlings lay sleeping on the flat spot around her goldenhorn as Ervig's hand moved with practiced fluidity inking every symbol as if it were his native language. He and Kaibelle had become quite fluent in the ancient dragon tongue over the years, but bits and pieces of the message often left him with a sense of foreboding for his family. He jotted the last stroke of the final symbol, set down his quill, and rubbed his eyes. Kaibelle would use his parchments to create the last of the tiles. *"Sometimes, this still seems so overwhelming."*

Before Nimbus could respond, laughter broke into their serious world as two of Ervig's young sons ran toward him. His six-year-old boy, Tomas, chased his strawberry blond toddler brother, Carn. Giggles filled the air. Ervig stood and snatched the younger boy into his arms, tossed him into the air, and caught him as his older brother tackled his legs with a hug. With his arms still wrapped around his father's thighs, Tomas stared up with a gap-tooth smile. "Mum says we're going dragon-riding. Me and Carn too!"

Ervig set his youngest son down, and he took off running. He glanced at Nimbus and shrugged. "We can't leave them here."

Nimbus let out a light clicking noise. She'd grown to love the human younglings–all five of them. In them, she saw the hope of why they came back to this time, but a hint of sadness mingled with her happiness. As of this telling, she and Ervig had finally finished the writings of the prophecies, and Kaibelle would soon fire the last of the tiles. Within a short time, it would be time to let the humans go back to the humans. Their work together done. It saddened her, but she had her brood to care for and raise.

The sound of stirring dragon wings beyond the cabin drew attention to Beroan and their two older hatchlings. Jurom, the oldest, was close to his first fire breath but hadn't mastered the skill. They landed in front of the cabin, where Kaibelle carried a pallet of tiles crafted of fire clay. She set it beside the fire pit and stretched the muscles in her back. The move accentuated the growing mound under her apron. Their sixth child would join the family soon.

She slowly got down on all fours and lined the fire pit with tiles while Beroan waited. After placing the last one, she covered them with wood shavings, leaves, and dried manure. She stood and wiped her hands on her apron and nodded to Beroan. *"They are ready."* She stepped back and called to Ervig. "We're firing. Keep the children over there." The three older children watched through the open window while Ervig held Carn, sucking his thumb, with Tomas at his side.

Once Kaibelle stepped back, Beroan lifted his head and stretched his muscular neck forward. A stream of fire spewed from his mouth and spread across the pit like liquid.

"One more firing, and that's the last of them," she said as she walked over and rubbed her hand up and down the dragon's side. She looked over at the eldest hatchling as a puff of smoke escaped his nostril, followed by a sneeze. *"And Jurom, I have a task for you, if your father will allow it."*

Jurom's green scales shimmered in the sunlight. *"Tell me Mother Kai-Belle. What be it? What can I do?"*

"Come to the porch, and I'll show you."

Jurom bounded toward the door like a horse-size puppy. "Slow down, slow down." Kaibelle laughed. Beroan walked around the fire pit to join him with his middle hatchling following at his side. Kaibelle disappeared into the cabin for a moment and walked out carrying a large bundle of hemp fabric.

Jurom's boney brow ridge raised as he tried his best to hide his disappointment. He sniffed it. *"What be it?"*

"Let me show you!" She flipped the fabric in front of her and let it fill with air before blanketing the ground. *"I made them just for you."*

Jurom circled the human gift cocking his head to make sense of it. *"What be it?"* he asked again.

"Dragon panniers."

Jurom looked up to his father. *"What be panniers?"*

"It be a way to carry valuable items too many to carry with claw or talon."

Jurom's blue-green eyes changed to a violet hue. Even though he didn't say it, it was clear he was upset as Ervig, and the rest of the children joined together to investigate. Nimbus followed with their third youngling cradled on her shoulders. Kaibelle put her hand on Jurom's boney eye ridge and rubbed it. *"These are special because they're going to be used to carry the tiles to your home."*

Jurom blinked and looked at his mother. *"I thought humans know not where we live?"*

"That be the future. The future where our home be called Jurom after thee. In the future, humans shall not know where we live, until the time be right."

Beroan stepped forward. *"Ye be the carrier of the tiles, Jurom. In times to come, they be known as the Jurom tiles."*

Jurom's eyes darted from Kaibelle to his father. *"Be they heavy?"*

Kaibelle rubbed his snout playfully. *"Yes, they're heavy. That's why we need your help. We need a strong dragon for the job."*

The lilting click, click, click of the dragons melded with the children's laughter and Jurom's excitement. Kaibelle grabbed her youngest son as he darted in the direction of the fire pit. *"I thought maybe you could take some of the tiles tonight, and then we can bring the rest with us tomorrow."*

Everyone agreed that was a good idea. Ervig and his three oldest sons, Kylar, Erik, and Rikard carried piles of tiles out the door to the grassy area where Kaibelle knelt, carefully wrapping and packing them into the panniers so they wouldn't scrape against one another. She said, *"As a potter's daughter, I feel like my father is with me in all this."*

Ervig carried the loaded panniers over to Jurom. *"Let's see how they fit."* Ervig lay the panniers across the young dragon's back and fastened them securely to his short goldenhorn. The look on Jurom's face said it all. He didn't like the feel of the load on his back, but the honor of being chosen for such an important task had him beaming with pride.

* * * *

After solidifying their plans for the next day, the humans offered short goodbyes, and the dragons headed north. Jurom beat the air almost effortlessly carrying the weight of the tiles across his back. His parents talked of the humans and how they would be missed. *"What do ye mean missed?"* Jurom asked.

"Ervig, Kaibelle, and their younglings will be leaving the valley soon to live among their own kind."

"But why? Be they not happy here?"

"Yes, they be happy. They know not that their time be drawing near to move outside the valley, Jurom, so talk not of it with them. Mother Kaibelle be expecting another youngling. This be what marks our time together to be near a close."

"I do not want them to go."

"Worry not, Jurom. For now, we shall live together on the island."

That news seemed to alleviate the young dragon's concerns as the family of dragons crossed the sea. The hatchlings carried by Beroan and Nimbus slept the whole way while Jurom chattered on and on.

Nimbus glanced at her mate, *"So ye heard the youngling within Kaibelle as well?"*

"Aye, I did."

"Ye knows what this means."

"Aye. Some Dragonborn traits be passed to human offspring. Not all offspring, for I sense it not in the first five human younglings."

"The one yet to be born. Her gifts be powerful."

The two of them circled their island home as the suns set, wondering how the consequences of all this would play out in the future they came from.

PART II

CHAPTER FIFTEEN

The following dawn, Nimbus hunted food for her mate and whelps as they slumbered in the roost nestled within the dormant volcano. She pondered the future. *How be this present reality changing the future from which I be? The Thornose be not here, and so we have not a Therus tree.* Her thoughts focused on the unborn human who touched her mind. The fact that it reached out and spoke with her and Beroan, much like her own hatchlings before they entered the world, raised the possibility that the child could be the reason for them coming to this time. It could be the heart of the promise they looked forward to with hope. *But what be next?*

A vision flashed within her mind. The Therus tree, the dormant volcano, a human eye with two irises—one looking east and the other west, a human female with a dragon's head, and a tear in time. *A Thornose head. What be the meaning of a human female with a Thornose head?* She pondered the question as she carried breakfast home to her family. *How long be it before a Thornose travels the Labyrinth to this time?* Clearly, the Thornose head showed it to be a future prophecy of sorts. *And the preserving of Thornose prophecies....* When she reached the roost, Beroan stretched his wings and trumpeted his welcome for both his mate and the food she carried. Jurom copied his father's greeting at a higher pitch and ran toward the carcass his mother let drop on the cold volcanic rock. His siblings ran to catch up, but they stopped short of taking a bite. Their father would be first to eat.

Beroan feasted as Nimbus lingered with her hatchlings and waited their turn. After feeding for a few minutes, he invited his children and mate to join him. But this morning, Jurom's excitement took away his appetite. *"How soon be we able to leave?"*

Nimbus nudged him with her snout. "*Eat, Jurom. Ye be carrying the tiles on the flight back and need thy strength."*

Kaibelle stacked cooled tiles on the grass and checked them for cracks while Ervig pulled the last tiles from the fire pit to cool. It amazed her that they had not only finished this task that once seemed so overwhelming but had become a family. *A growing family.* She cradled her belly in her arms as she sat back on her heels to admire her husband's violet aura. It had drawn her to him from the beginning as a magical visionary. Same as Mother. Her thoughts carried her back to that day she became Dragonborn. How the dragon warned that her parents were being hunted. She had dropped her basket of mushrooms and ran as fast as her feet would carry her and broke into the back door of the shop only to find her father sitting at his potter's wheel. *For that brief moment, all seemed well until Mother burst into the room. 'Tybalt! I feel it. The evil is here.' I didn't understand. The way Father grabbed my arm and tugged me toward the back door saying, "We have to get her on her way." The way mother joined him, pulling me toward the door. That lavender aura edged in violet. I realized they were Dragonborn. "What do we need to do?"* Her question echoed in her mind as she remembered the sadness in his eyes. *"Kai, we must send you to safety, for the future depends on you."*

As she watched Ervig, she wished her parents could have met him. At the moment, red tinged the edges of his violet aura, highlighting his strong will and heightened survival instinct as they prepared for this trip. She pulled in a breath as her unborn child pushed against her ribs. She ran her hand across her stomach. *The future depends on me.*

She scanned the piles of tiles. *Years of work. It's why I came here. Once we install the tiles, what will be next?* She rubbed the small of her back to work out the ache from bending over. "I think I'll let you and Kylar finish bringing the rest out," she called to Ervig. "The baby is telling me it is time to rest."

Ervig cast a worried glance in her direction as murkiness tinged the red of his aura. "We can always put the trip off until after the baby is born."

"No." She shook her head. "I know we are to go."

Ervig stacked another load of tiles on the ground and nodded with resignation. "I know."

* * * *

Ervig glanced out at the mountain landscape as Kylar walked beside him with a smaller load of tiles. He loved living here but thought of his sons' futures. What good was it to have all these sons to carry on his line if there were no girls to become wives? *And what about this trip? Is it safe for the younger children?*

As he and Kylar stacked the last batches of cooled tiles ready for transport, large familiar shadows fell across them like low-lying clouds. Kylar shielded his eyes and looked up as the dragons circled overhead. The other children danced about at the sight of their friends. Ervig hurried to Kaibelle's side. "I know *we* must go, but what of the children? Are you sure they should come with us? If they should fall as we fly…."

Kaibelle placed a reassuring hand on his arm. "Stop being such a prophet of doom. The children have been looking forward to this trip, and I'm not leaving them here. Kylar can care for the boys, but he's only ten summers old. We are not leaving them."

As the dragons circled nearer to the ground, he patted her hand and nodded as the wind kicked up ash from the pit.

Jurom dropped to the ground a little too fast, lost his balance, and rolled into a lopsided somersault before coming to a stop with his empty panniers draped across his face. Kaibelle hurried over to check on the dragon and straighten his makeshift saddlebags. "Are you alright?" Suddenly the baby within her stirred.

The dragon blinked. His multifaceted eyes grew wide enough to see into the Midlands.

"Jurom?" Kaibelle waved her hand in front of his face as Nimbus hurried over to her son.

He blinked. *"What be that, Mother Kai-Belle?"*

Kaibelle looked at Nimbus. *"What is he talking about?"*

Nimbus lowered her great head and looked her son in the eye. *"Jurom, what did ye see... or hear?"*

"I heard a voice, Mother. I thought maybe I be hearing someone calling from the Midlands. But I see nothing–no one."

"What did it say? This voice?"

Jurom nervously looked about. *"My name... it said mine name. Said, 'Jurom, I will be born at Jur-Jurom.'"*

Kaibelle placed a hand on her swollen belly. *"My child? You mean my child spoke with you? How can that be?"*

Nimbus shook her great head in mild disbelief. *"I know not."* She didn't mention that she and Beroan heard the child. *"It be a mystery."* And that was the truth, for Dragonborn were sworn to keep their dragon gifts a secret. *But what of this child. It has taken no oath. What means this for the future of humans if such skills be passed on to offspring?*

The prophecy of the unborn prodded her to hurry things along. *"Let's get those tiles packed,"* Nimbus said. *"The sooner we get moving, the sooner we be home."*

* * * *

Kaibelle nodded but couldn't help but feel the dragon was hiding something. It left her a little uneasy for the first time in years. She knelt beside her husband to help pack the tiles. Her mind raced. *Should we leave the children here after all?* She watched Ervig from the corner of her eye as he steadfastly packed the tiles into the panniers. She had to say something. *But what?* "Ervig?"

"Yes?" His distracted attention focused on situating the titles so they wouldn't crack during transport.

She paused, taking a long look at the children wondering what to do. Suddenly a young voice filled her head. *"Mother, do not fret. It is meant to be."* Energy flashed through her. The breath caught in her throat as her hand flew to her stomach.

The sudden movement caught Ervig's attention. "What is it? Kai? Are you alright? Is the baby coming?"

She looked at him with wide eyes and stared past him to see Beroan focused on her. *"Did-did you hear that?"* she asked her dragon friend.

He closed his eyes and nodded once. *"We understand it not."*

"I'm fine." She looked away from Ervig. She never liked withholding the truth from her husband, but this was especially difficult. This was their child. She turned her focus to the tiles as she gathered her wits. Handling them calmed her. She knew clay. How to work it, mold it, fire it. What she didn't understand was how the child she carried could speak to her before it even took its first breath. None of her other children had done that, so why now. *What does this mean?*

Ervig gazed into her eyes with unspoken concern flowing at the edges of his aura. They'd learned to navigate this challenging thread in their relationship, but it didn't go unnoticed. He said, "Why don't you prepare the children for the ride while I finish up."

"Good thinking." She placed her hand on his shoulder and used it for leverage to help her stand. She walked away feeling like a puppet controlled by a puppeteer. But the child's voice played over in her mind telling her to *fret not*, and so she lost herself in preparing her five sons to travel. The youngest, Carn, would ride wrapped in a sling on his father's back, so she started with Tomas and Rikard. They eagerly mounted Nimbus to be tethered to her goldenhorn, where they would ride in front of their father. The youngest hatchling lay curled in front of the goldenhorn. Erik and Kylar would ride with her on Beroan tethered in the same fashion, with the middle hatching joining them.

The ride did little to calm her thoughts. Kylar and Erik sat between her legs, on each side of the goldenhorn to which they were secured. They had chattered with excitement as they took off and climbed above the valley, but now clouds stretched beneath them like a snowy landscape quickly boring their young minds. Soon the monotone view lulled them to sleep as they lay with their heads upon the sleeping hatchling. Amid the quiet with the cold wind in her face, Kaibelle tried to speak with the child within her. *Nothing.* It left her feeling guilty and full of questions. She hadn't said anything to Ervig because she wasn't sure if it had to do with her Dragonborn powers.

The dragons dropped through darkening clouds, and Kaibelle stared in awe at the sprawling, verdant island below. "It's beautiful." The words no sooner escaped her lips, and Kylar woke up. He sat up and rubbed the sleep from his eyes for a moment. When his eyes fell to the expanse of water and the vast island, his jaw dropped. He drank in the view of volcanic peaks blanketed in tropical forests. "Mother, I've never seen such a place."

"Neither have I, son." The island loomed closer. Rivers and waterfalls created a network through the trees. A rainbow hung above a large waterfall cascading into three separate falls, which filled an emerald green lagoon at the bottom. The entire island was like a lush garden untouched by human hands.

Kaibelle woke her second oldest. "Erik, wake up. Look where we are." Jurom flapped his wings with renewed excitement in the air beside them. *"This be mine home,"* he said proudly to everyone who could hear him. Kaibelle studied her two sons sitting in front of her to see if they heard the young dragon. Kylar's violet aura with pink highlights remained unchanged but as unique as ever. *My artistic magic visionary. But can he hear the dragons?* She really couldn't tell, and, for the first time, she wondered at all that was happening around her. Since coming to this time, many layers of mystery and communication went on all the time. As exciting as all this was, she longed for an ordinary life for her family. A sense of routine. A sense of complete honesty. *A simpler, quiet life... Like regular, everyday people. Regular people. I thought that's what my parents were, but they were Dragonborn.*

She let it go as they circled the sleeping volcano, and the boys squealed with glee. The clouds cut out the sunlight and blanketed the opening in shade. "Mother, look. Is this where the dragons live?"

"Yes, Kylar, it is."

"Hold ye fast, Kaibelle," Beroan warned as they started to drop. Her boys gripped the goldenhorn they were tethered to, and Kaibelle wrapped her hands over theirs to be sure they were secure. A small lake loomed into view within the grassy crater. Beroan landed gently, jostling them slightly. For a moment, she sat, thanking the stars they all landed safely. Then, she blinked in disbelief at her peaceful

surroundings. A small waterfall splashed on the opposite side of the lake across from where they landed. "Isn't this beautiful?" She leaned forward to untie her boys when the baby kicked her ribs hard enough to take her breath away. "Ohhh!"

Kylar stared at his mother wide-eyed. From a few yards away, Ervig asked, "What is it?" His voice sounded a little shrill and panicked as he worked to untether Rikard and Tomas. "Kaibelle, are you alright?"

She closed her eyes and took a deep breath. "I'm alright, but I'm going to need some help getting to the ground. I'm afraid I'm about to have a baby."

Nimbus lay partially on her side to help Ervig dismount with his children, who quickly ran toward the small lake. *"The water be deep,"* Nimbus warned.

Ervig called to the children. "Stop!" To his relief, they obeyed his command. Carn whined and squirmed to get down from the wrap on his father's back. Ervig loosened the wrap and freed Carn to run around with his two oldest brothers. He gathered the three youngest near the dragon hatchlings to play, and Nimbus created a corral with her tail to keep them safe. "Thank you," Ervig shouted over his shoulder as he hurried toward his wife. Jurom jumped his mother's tail to get into the corral, the tiles on his back weighing him down enough that he landed with his belly on the girth of her tail. He dragged himself the rest of the way over to greet Kylar and Erik.

Beroan bent his foreleg, and Ervig made quick work of the climb to his wife's side. "Help the boys down first," she said. He used the rope that had tethered the boys to the goldenhorn as a sling under their arms and lowered them to the ground, and ushered them into the area under Nimbus' oversight. Without a word, he rushed back to Kaibelle. He helped her climb to the shore. When they reached his foreleg, she paused and let out a deep breath trying to breathe through the pain of her cramping abdomen.

Once they reached the ground, Beroan stood to his full height. *"A storm be brewing. Beyond yon water-veil be an alcove. It be a comfortable nest for ye to birth."*

Ervig glanced around as he supported Kaibelle. "You tell me what you can do."

"If the water is warm, I would love to go to the alcove. But what of the children?"

Beroan walked to the water's edge and lowered his head above the water. Flames shot from his jaws and licked the surface of the lake. He turned around and stirred the waters with his massive tail and then repeated the process. *"It be warm,"* he. *"And the children be cared for."*

Ervig helped Kaibelle into the water. She closed her eyes. "This feels lovely." As he guided her, she opened her eyes and looked into Ervig's brown eyes filled with concern. "But I think it would be good to get to that alcove soon."

His eyes grew wide. "Hold on. Hold on." He paddled with one arm and pulled her along as she rested on her back, her belly cutting a wake across the surface. The dark sky overhead grew ominous. *Kylar will know to get the children under shelter.* Pain squeezed her as they reached the falls and slipped beneath the veil of water. Ervig pulled himself onto the stone ledge and stood within a large alcove poised to help her out of the water. "This is perfect. Warm… as if the floor is heated."

"Ervig, the baby is coming!" She placed her arms on the ledge but didn't attempt to get out of the water.

He jumped back into the lake. "Right now?"

She pushed. "Right… now."

The baby entered the world of the dragons. Ervig pulled the infant from the water and held it for a moment in disbelief. "A–a girl. We have a daughter." He blinked away tears. "A girl…." His lips brushed her forehead, and he handed her to Kaibelle. "Let me tell the others." He broke through the curtain of water and shouted to the dragons and boys on the shore. "It's a girl!" Ervig shouted verbally as the rain started to fall. Tears on his face were washed away by pelting rain as he watched his children jump up and down at the news. He started to laugh as Nimbus used her tail to keep the children corralled and safe as she walked toward the tunnel leading to the roost. *"We be seeing ye in the morning, Ervig."*

"It's a girl, Kaibelle," he said again as he ducked back through the waterfall to his wife.

"Sure is." A lavender and violet aura swirled around the baby, edged in red. It didn't surprise her that the child was a magical visionary with a strong will and unshakable determination… *and survival-oriented.* She wanted to tell her husband but held her tongue as she handed him the baby and climbed into the alcove. She lay on her side on the warm stone and cradled the baby against her breast. "I'm going to enjoy a little time with our daughter, Aurora… Darksky."

He climbed up next to her. "Aurora? I like it. But Darksky?" He brushed the baby's red fuzzy head in the dim light. "I mean, she could be Aurora Dragonsroost."

She smiled. "It's raining. Part of her story… her history. Just like Kylar Lost Valley, Erik Morning Caller, Rikard Greenfields, Tomas Two Blossoms, and Carn Spider Brook. Each birthname is part of their history. A story they will tell others. I'm afraid Dragonsroost could be dangerous for her in the future. So, the way I'm thinking, we flew above the rain on the way here. We enjoyed sunshine above the clouds. And our daughter was born below the dark sky. Dark sky people will understand but Dragonsroost? How would she explain that?"

For a moment, silence hung between them as they considered their fractured history. He was Ervig Greenfields, she was now Kaibelle Potterschild. Ervig didn't argue about his daughter's name for Aurora meant rainbow, and in his mind, she was a rainbow in a dark sky, and that was fine. He'd heard the child before her birth and wondered what lay ahead. He wondered at her lavender and violet aura edged in red. It was darker than Carn's aura but similar. *What does it mean? I wonder if Kaibelle can see these colors around our children as I can.* He glanced into Kaibelle's eyes and knew that the name she chose was her way to say that she knew the baby was special without breaking her dragon oath. He nodded. "Aurora Darksky." He glanced over his shoulder toward the flow of water, creating a curtain between them and the others.

"I hate to just leave you, but I do need to go make sure the children eat and then get them to sleep here in a strange place."

"Don't go just yet. Stay just until I fall asleep. I want you here… with our special little Aurora."

CHAPTER SIXTEEN

Ervig glanced at his wife with fondness as she sat on the ledge of the alcove with her feet dangling in the water nursing their daughter. *She's already grown so much, and I still haven't finished with the tedious work of preparing these walls so we can install the tiles*. At least with Kaibelle's help, she could install tiles while he worked on prepping the walls. But the baby could change all that. Not only could Aurora sit on her own now, but she had learned to crawl and get into the bowl of gypsum mortar. *Aurora can't be contained in this alcove much longer. How much longer will Kaibelle be able to help me. If I have to finish this without help, Aurora could be ten summers old before I finish.*

When Kaibelle finished feeding Aurora, she worked at his side with the baby in a sling across her torso as she focused on the precise work of installing the tiles in the correct order.

"Have you ever wondered why we're doing this?" she asked.

Ervig stopped with the empty trowel in his hand as he wiped the sweat from his forehead with his sleeve. "What do you mean?"

She carefully situated the tile in her hand on the fresh layer of mortar and pressed it into place, then studied her husband with that look of mentally measuring her words so as not to break her oath. It was a language they understood well. "We have all these writings on parchment, right?"

He nodded; brows arched in an unasked question.

"So, why do we need to place them here among the dragons? I mean, they already know all this. It makes me wonder why we're doing this."

With a great splash, Nimbus' large head broke through the waterfall. Ervig and Kaibelle jumped. "Nimbus!" As Ervig's heart slowed down to normal, a pang of guilt and shame flashed through him as if they'd been discussing some forbidden subject, but the light clicking from Nimbus made him laugh as he turned to apply the next layer of mortar to even out the wall.

"Thy question be surely valid," she said. *"This travel back, forward, and between times scrambles logic to be sure."*

Ervig and Kaibelle cast a glance at one another and nodded.

"This be not goldenhorn prophecies but given to us through the Thornose clan. It be asked of us to honor their foresight in this way."

Lines of deep thought etched Ervig's forehead. "But for what purpose? There are no Thornose dragons here. And–and you see things future…."

"That be true, but these writing be for a future time when the Thornose live in the land... and not just Thornose but other dragons. These writings be here as a guide to dragons from all times. They be given to us by Zaylan, mate to Therus. It be her blood used to write that evil book.... Think about how the writings start."

Ervig looked at Kaibelle. She read the first tiles already in place at the top of the wall. "Fire be the tool that unlocks the message?"

Nimbus chuckled again. *"If ye use fire on thy human parchment, ye will unlock nothing but ash. This message ye place here now be for the Thornose yet future. Thy daughter shall be the caretaker of the ancient Scroll of Prophecy for thy kind."*

Ervig raised his hand to stop her. "That's enough. You're right. It scrambles the logic. Perhaps someday I'll be able to see the entire picture." Inwardly, he didn't want to hear it because it filled him with fear. His eyes fell to his sleeping Aurora in the sling. When he looked up into Kaibelle's eyes, he saw the same fear.

The work progressed, and Aurora grew into an active toddler running and playing with her brothers. Kaibelle spent less and less time in the alcove to keep a watchful eye on her children. It slowed progress as Ervig had feared. With the solitary nature of the work, he missed her company–his family. It left him alone with his thoughts.

It was one thing for Kaibelle and me to agree to come through the tear in time, but now the way the dragons talk—the consequences for that decision seem to predetermine our daughter's purpose in life.

"Caretaker of the ancient Scroll of Prophecy? What does that mean?" he muttered. It made him think of the book that started this trouble in the first place. *And the same dragon–Therus' mate tied the two together in the past. Or is that the future now? Was she somehow writing herself a message?* He sat on the floor and pressed his head against his knees. Substantial doubt churned in his gut. *If I don't finish installing these tiles, will it save my daughter trouble in life? Or would it mean that somehow, I never have a daughter?* He raked his fingers through his hair and cursed himself for his doubt. *I need to get out of this room and clear my head.* For the first time in a long time, he transformed into falcon form, cut through the veil of water, and took to the sky.

His oldest four boys swam in the lake as he circled above them. Aurora rode upon Jurom's back as he flapped his wings and walked along with Carn leading him. A sinking realization washed over him. The dragons had already touched his daughter's destiny, and there was no changing that. And while it wasn't an easy life, it was a good one. If not for the dragons, he wouldn't know Kaibelle, and he wouldn't have his five children. He flew back through the cascading water of the falls into the alcove and quickly changed back into human form. He rolled his shoulders forward and then back to stretch. *That did it. I feel better. Ready to work. All of this is my part in making a better future, and I will complete the work.* He picked up the trowel and bowl of mortar. With a quick spell, the mortar became pliable again. He read the last tiles fastened to the wall and arranged the subsequent tiles on the floor in order. Before he even put the trowel to the wall, an almost imperceptible splash drew his attention to the ledge. A strawberry blonde head popped up.

"Kylar!"

"Hi, Da, Mother said you might like some company, and so I thought I'd come to see you. I saw that falcon…." He wiped the water from his eyes and glanced around the spacious alcove with a frown but shrugged off his question. It wasn't the first time he had spotted the disappearing bird. The tiles lining the walls grabbed his attention. He pointed to the dwindling pile of loose tiles. "Is that all that's left to do?"

Ervig nodded as he marveled at his eldest standing there in a puddle collecting around his feet. *He's grown so tall.*

"Maybe I could help you." Kylar gestured to the tiles stacked on the floor. "You know, I can read the ancient language."

Ervig's first thought was to send his son back to be with the rest of the family to protect him from knowing more than he should. But he changed his mind. *The dragons know he can read the language. Better to equip him with knowledge for the future than to let him face it in ignorance. With his mind, he probably knows every symbol from memory.*

It turned out that the boy made for good company. Ervig enjoyed passing on his masonry skills to his son as they installed tiles side by side. It slowed progress at first, but it didn't take long for Kylar to get the hang of it. And it didn't take long for Ervig to realize how much his son had grown. Part of him wished he could keep the boy young–to protect him from a world where the evil Book of Darkmore could change everything in an instant.

Ervig paused with a tile in one hand and his trowel at his side. "I miss time like this," he admitted.

Kylar nodded as he concentrated on the placement of one of the lower tiles. "I was going to surprise you, but I guess it won't hurt to tell you. I've been writing about everything, so you can read it when we get home." He flashed his father a smile.

"You wrote about it–like about all this?" He waved the empty trowel in a wide-sweeping gesture.

"Oh, not just this. I've been writing everything since I learned to write." He shrugged. "It makes me feel like I get to talk to someone when everyone is working so hard."

Ervig's mind raced. He'd never really looked to see what Kylar was doing. He never thought it to be more than random scribbles or drawing. *A way to keep him busy while we did what we needed to do.* Now it worried him. *Is it allowed? Can he write about life among the dragons? –Why not? After all, he hasn't taken an oath.*

"Da, are you alright?"

Ervig looked at the tile in his hand and let out a nervous laugh. "Of course, of course. I guess I sometimes forget you're old enough to read and write."

Kylar puffed out his chest as he looked up at the tiles. "'Fire be our tool. The Thornose.... I've always wondered–what is a Thornose?"

Ervig's heart pounded in his chest. "That's great, Kylar." He put the tile and trowel on the floor. "I'm a little hungry. I think I'll go check on your mother and get a piece of dragon fruit for the two of us." Without a pause, he hurried to the ledge and dove into the water.

* * * *

Kylar watched his father disappear into the water and beyond the falls. He glanced around the cavern in wonder but got back to work. He slathered a thin coat of gypsum mortar onto the wall. In the solitude of the alcove, he became more aware of the noise of the falls splashing into the lagoon behind him. The curtain of water hid him from the rest of his family. *It feels strange. Since Aurora was born, I rarely have time alone.* He savored the moment. *No little brother tugging on my arm to play. No keeping Aurora occupied and out of mischief. Just me working with my hands.* It excited him that his parents chose him to help with the tiles. As he smoothed the mortar, his chest swelled with a sense of pride. *Da trusts me enough to leave me to work alone while he checks on Mother and gets us some food.*

He pressed another tile into place. The job wasn't hard. It just took a long time, and the tiles needed to stay in the correct order. He knew the order because he helped draw the symbols on the tiles for his mother as he copied from the parchment penned by his Da. It's how he learned to read. Covering the walls with the ancient symbols gave him a sense of satisfaction–of accomplishment. Most tiles told stories. *I like the tales, but they all sound like some other world. Sometimes, much like the world Mother talks about in the yarns she tells, when she wants us to fall asleep.* He pondered the words on the tiles. *It is clear that, at some point, these symbols will come to life somehow.* He didn't understand it, but just reading about it excited him.

His thoughts drifted back to his father's reaction when he read aloud from the tiles. *The look on his face.... He didn't know I could read. I hope that won't change things. I don't want to have to play the care minder for the other children. I'd much rather help with the tiles.* He decided not to mention what he read in the future.

As he tapped the next tile into place, he stopped. The symbol for *secret* or *mystery* always caught his attention. It reminded him of a person without a head running with three drops of water around where the head should be. This time it was speaking of a secret gift. *A gift to be opened by the priestess.... A gift from the Thornose. That word Thornose.... What could it be? I think it must be a dragon of some sort. And by the look on Da's face when I read the word, he knows what they are.* He continued tapping tiles into place. The rest of the message talked about opening the gift. *To accept it, one must use the word 'apparet' but, to open it, they must use the word 'aperta.'* Kylar paused to figure out the riddle. *A gift opened with the ancient language. The receiver will know where to find it.* He frowned. "What can this mean? What kind of gift could it be? How will the person know where to find it? What will they find when they open it?"

The splash of his father shooting up through the water's surface next to the ledge startled Kylar from his reverie. Da slapped his wet hand against the warmth of the stone ledge and pulled himself into the alcove, careful not to smash the dragon fruits tucked into his waistband. He pulled one out and handed it to Kylar.

He quickly set his trowel on the floor and took the fruit. As he did, he whispered, "*apparet,*" under his breath as he imagined receiving the secret gift. He scraped the red skin off the fruit with his teeth and spat it into the water. He never ate the sour skin. As he bit into the juicy pink flesh of the fruit, he watched his father take over the placement of tiles. It wouldn't be long, now, until all the tiles were in place. *Then what will happen to us? When will the stories on the tiles take place? Will we go back to the cabin? Or will we go somewhere other people live?*

"Kylar? Kylar? Did you hear me?" Ervig asked.

Embarrassment burned across his cheeks. "Sorry, I was daydreaming."

Ervig smiled. "What I was saying is that you've made me realize we work too much. Let's finish our fruit and go have some fun for a change."

They swam with the dragons and the other children. Ervig showed them how Jurom could fetch a rock from the bottom of the lake and, they all took turns throwing it. Kylar wondered how the dragon could recognize the same rock among others littering the floor of the lake.

Later that night, as Ervig lay beside Kaibelle while she nursed Aurora, he told her what happened with Kylar in the alcove. The look on her face told him she already knew. He asked, "Is it that he is gifted? Or is it that he grew up around it all these years as we've worked on making the tiles?"

Kaibelle smiled in the firelight, but it wavered and died on her lips. "I don't know. I don't think we can know because of the oath."

He nodded, and the two of them talked about it no more.

CHAPTER SEVENTEEN

Kylar worked with his Da each day as Kaibelle cared for her children. For the most part, their conversations centered on things the rest of the family were doing, like Kaibelle teaching the children to work with clay. The boy laughed as he tapped a tile to level it and scraped the excess mortar away. He stopped and studied the tiles he'd just placed. "I wonder if a Thornose is a kind of dragon," he said thoughtfully. "This is talking about a Thornose egg."

Ervig shrugged. "Could be. Maybe it's a bird. We'll probably never know."

"There's one thing I don't understand," Kylar said as he set the next tile. "Why are we doing this? For the dragons?"

"It's an agreement we made so we could live in our house in the valley. They don't have hands, and they needed it done."

Kylar's brow creased with thought. "You agreed?"

Ervig started to sweat. "Yes." *Did I break the oath? I swore to never tell another human what the Thornose know as guardians of the Labyrinth of Times. Kylar has read the prophecies. I didn't say anything I shouldn't.... Did I? What was I thinking? I did say we agreed–with the dragons! Oh, my stars! How will I explain that! What will happen to my family if I turn into a rat!*

Kylar nodded slowly. "And so, what happens when we finish?"

Dread shot through Ervig. He stared at his hands. *No pain, no change from man to rat.* He stared at his hands with thankfulness for his fingers. *I'm still a man.* He breathed a little easier. His pulse slowed to normal. "Then it's time for us to move on."

"Really?" Kylar's eyes grew wide. "Where will we go? Back to the cabin or someplace else? Will there be other people?"

Ervig looked straight ahead at the tile in front of him. This conversation loomed close to forbidden territory. "Your mother and I haven't decided yet, but when we agree on a direction, that's the way we'll go."

"I wonder what it will be like." Kylar let it go as he slathered a thin layer of mortar onto the wall, but their short conversation resurrected questions in Ervig's mind. "*Where do we go?*"

Nimbus' light-clicking laughter filtered into his thoughts. *"Ervig fret not over thy future. Thy work here be almost complete. Tonight we discuss where ye be going after our younglings be sleeping."*

* * * *

Kaibelle worked the squishy, sticky, off-white clay with veins of red with her hands. She smiled as she glanced from one child to the next as they pinched, rolled, and flattened the clay in front of them. "If we had a wheel, we could do more."

With Nimbus' help, they harvested the clay from the bottom of the lake. As their small hands worked the clay, it turned an unusual pink hue. *As a potter's daughter, I've never seen anything like this clay.* Once dried, she couldn't break it even though it was air-dried and not fired. *I could make pots for cooking, but I don't think I'll have time. The tiles are almost in place.* This was why she had the children working with the clay. In her mind, they were fashioning a keepsake to take "home." *Carn and Tomas don't even remember the cabin in the valley.*

Tomas and Carn rolled out a small rope of clay. "We're making snakes!" Tomas said with a smile. Erik rolled out a thinner cord which became a stem for what he said was a flower. Kaibelle smoothed her lump of clay and, with the help of a touch of magic, turned it, with wet fingers forming it into a small urn with a lid. *A gift for Aurora.* She made it large enough to store herbs or ground grain. Aurora sat beside Jurom on the shore playing with pebbles. When Kaibelle was satisfied with the urn, she cast a silent spell and dried it. "Here, daughter, this is for you since you are too young to make something for yourself." She placed the unbreakable urn in the baby's chubby hands. The toddler's blue eyes sparkled with delight. She smiled and lifted it with arms wobbling to hold it to Jurom's face. The dragon touched his snout to it. Light of many colors burst around the dragon and child.

Kaibelle thrust her hand into the light and snatched the container from her daughter's fingers. Aurora wailed, but Kaibelle almost didn't notice as her pulse drummed in her ears as her heartbeat against her ribs as if she'd run the length of the Inkish River. The urn in her hands brightened from the familiar blush to a vivid white. Five red glyphs emerged on the surface. *A tree–a Therus tree. A mountain.... No, a volcano, this dormant volcano. One eye with two irises. One looking west and the other east. It looks human, except that it has two irises. And a female human? With–with a dragon head? A Thornose head!* She'd left the Thornose behind in her own time. *What can this mean? And* what is this fifth symbol? *A thick horizontal bolt of lightning? No, I think it's a tear in time.* She let out a long sigh. *Now, what does this mean?*

Suddenly Aurora's cries broke through the fog of distraction. Jurom rubbed his green snout gently against the child's head, but she didn't stop crying until Kaibelle set the small urn on the shore in front of her. Aurora looked at her mother as she drew in a shuddered breath. Water from the lake fingered the shoreline. The morning suns warmed her. A light breeze brushed her face. *It's all as if nothing has happened.* Kaibelle dried her daughter's tears with her apron. Aurora flashed a smile. Her eyes shined with happiness as if she hadn't been crying a moment ago. She closed her eyes as Jurom rubbed the smooth bony ridges of his face against hers.

"Are you happy now, daughter?" Kaibelle asked with a singsong voice.

Her daughter nodded and blinked away the last of the tears clinging to her lashes. Happiness danced in her eyes, but a wave of fear washed over Kaibelle. Aurora's aura now shined with rays the colors of the rainbow, and her eyes, once the color of the sky, were now the color of a spring meadow flecked with golden flowers. She watched her precious daughter play with the dragon as she clasped the container with two hands, like an oversized toy. Kaibelle glanced at the waterfall across the lake. She tried to mentally bid her husband to *"come,"* but it didn't work. Finally, Aurora set the urn on the ground, used her hands to help her stand, and toddled off with Jurom. Kaibelle marveled at the rainbow of energy surrounding her. *I've never witnessed such an aura.*

Kaibelle slipped the urn into the satchel draped at her side and followed the two of them as they wandered to the water's edge. Her Dragonborn ability to see auras was one of those things not to be discussed because it offered insight through Thornose magic. *But what about that rainbow energy enfolding our daughter? I can't say a thing!*

She swiped her hands across her face and let her arms drop to her side. A large shadow eclipsed the daylight. She glanced up at Beroan's underside to see the stag he'd brought to feed them. As the mammoth creature landed, she rushed over to him.

"Beroan! I'm–I'm frightened."

"What be the problem, young one?"

She could feel his concern. *"I'm frightened for the future. For my children. Is....* She swallowed hard. "*...is Aurora Dragonborn?"*

"Dragonborn be few. And of all Dragonborn ye and thy mate be the only proven pair of Dragonborn to have younglings. While all thy sons but one show signs of being dragon-touched, thy daughter be unique. A lineal born with distinct power and an innate connection to dragons."

"Is that something good?"

As she asked it, Ervig and Kylar stepped from the lake, their clothing dripping a trail of water as they walked toward Beroan and Kaibelle. Kylar sprinted ahead to help gut the deer. "I'm starving!" Kaibelle laughed. Her children anchored her to the life she once knew and longed for now. Kylar not only knew how to dress the deer, but he also processed the hides for clothing and writing material. *He's getting so mature.*

Ervig walked over, kissed her on the forehead, and stroked Beroan's flank.

"I'm done."

Kaibelle took a step back. "You've finished? All of it?"

He nodded. "All of it. With Kylar's help, it didn't take quite as long as we thought. We should be home in time for spring planting."

Kylar looked up from his task. "I can't wait to see home. I wonder if any of our chickens will still be alive after all this time–or our cattle. At least we'll have wood that is dry to build a fire. Oh, and we'll have to make a longer bench now that Carn will be sitting at the table with us. Aurora will take the baby chair."

Ervig looked into Kaibelle's eyes. She saw the same questions about Kylar's ability to remember every detail. *What would happen if we ever talked about the Dragonborn parts of our lives?* But she knew better. For a brief moment, her mind flashed back to the circumstances surrounding her transformation to Dragonborn. It sent a bitter shudder through her.

Ervig drew her to his wet chest and clung to her. "It's going to be alright." He rubbed her back, and she listened to the steady beat of his heart. And she believed. *Everything will be alright.*

The dragons cooked the stag, taking turns breathing fire to the children's delight. They never seemed to grow bored of life with the dragons. After dinner, they sat around glowing rocks heated for warmth and shared stories from the day. Kaibelle treasured the laughter and even time with the dragons. But a cloud hung over her. Nimbus touched her mind letting her know she understood. The dragon led the children and her hatchlings into the roost, where she heated the night rocks until they glowed a subdued red and settled the young ones in for the night. By the time she walked back outside, the blue glow of a lucium sphere had drifted above Kaibelle's shoulder. She held a clay jar toward Beroan and pointed to markings on it.

"What be that?"

Kaibelle extended the container toward her. *"It's an urn I made from the clay from the lake as a keepsake for Aurora from her birthplace. After I mixed the clay, the red veins blended into the white clay to make it the same rose color as always, but when Aurora held it, and Jurom touched it.... I saw energy. It looked like a rainbow shining around them, and these symbols appeared."*

Ervig looked from Kaibelle to her dragon. "What? What is that?"

Kaibelle looked at him with brows raised. "Ervig!"

His jaw set. He crossed his arms and waited as the multifaceted eye lens at the center of the dragons' eyes studied the pottery. Nimbus had told him these lenses gave them excellent up-close vision and the ability to see when traveling in the Midlands–the space between times. Kaibelle could see the lens focusing on the jar in her hands. *"It be the dragon magic,"* Nimbus said so both Kaibelle and Ervig could hear.

Kaibelle's brow knit in concentration. "So it's Jurom's magic? It looks like the red pigment I'd mixed throughout the clay–I don't know–somehow it separated from the clay leaving it white and formed into these red-colored symbols?"

"This be a foretelling. These be symbols that guide the future for thy kind. It be a message from thy daughter."

"What?" Kaibelle's knees buckled as she leaned against Ervig. "Our… our Aurora!" She buried her head against his chest. "But she is a baby!"

"What does it mean? What can you tell us?" Ervig asked as he wrapped his arms around his wife and helped her sit on the ground. "I mean, what do the symbols mean? What do we do now?"

"They each be a symbol… answers thy clan shall seek."

"Our clan?"

"Do ye know of Five Marks?"

Kaibelle wiped her eyes with the back of her hand. "You mean the old village from my time?" she asked out loud. "The original buildings are no longer standing except for what remains of an abandoned temple."

"In this time that village be not here… yet. It be thy next home."

Ervig rubbed the back of his neck and gestured for Kaibelle to stay seated. He walked over and sat beside her crossing his legs. "I think it's time for us to sit down and talk. What does all this have to do with our daughter and us? I'm not trying to divulge anything here regarding anything prohibited by the dragon oath. I'm just trying to figure out what we are doing when we leave here."

Kaibelle linked her arm through his and leaned closer. "Exactly."

Nimbus and Beroan admitted that they could hear Aurora before she was born. "I did too," Kaibelle admitted. Ervig nodded. "Me too."

"We believe she be Dragonborn within thy womb," Beroan said. *"The jar bearing the symbols be a guide for thy descendant. Place within it the deed to thine home in the valley."*

"What?" Kaibelle stood. "This might all make sense to you, but for us…. It makes me long to go back to my time, my life. When things made sense. The deed to our house? That makes no sense."

Firelight shined in Beroan's eyes as he tipped his head to study his charge. *"Thy world as ye knew it be no more, for the evil we fight destroyed it."*

She slumped back onto the rock. "Destroyed?"

"What's destroyed?" Ervig looked from Kaibelle to the dragons. For the rest of the night, they spoke in an open conversation where both humans and the dragons heard everything discussed. The conversation carried them in a whole new direction. The following day they would leave, and when they arrived at the cabin in the valley, they wouldn't be planting spring crops. *"Ye must pack thy things. We be ready to carry thee beyond the Inkish River. Thy new home be the place ye once called Five Marks. We dragons stand ready to help thee until the temple be built."*

"Build the temple!" Ervig repeated. *"That thing is huge. At least in my time, it was."*

* * * *

In the dim light of the glowing night rocks, Ervig stared into Kaibelle's eyes. Aurora slept between them without a care. When Ervig asked about Aurora's eyes, Kaibelle said, "They changed when the urn changed." She longed to tell her husband about the rainbow energy shining around their daughter, but she buried that fact with her other secrets and offered a weak smile. "I wish we were able to stay at the cabin for at least a season."

"I know. Me, too, but it's better if we leave in the spring because even though Five Marks is near the water, the winters are harsh if I remember correctly. We certainly wouldn't want to arrive in time to freeze without a place to live."

She nodded and looked up at the stars dotting the night sky outside the tunnel opening. *These stars are different than in the valley–and not the same as the stars in Stanlow*. She drifted to sleep secure in her husband's love but wondering what the future held. Her dreams carried her to the Midlands–though she'd never been there. Shifting shadows churned around her. Beroan led the way. His eyes allowed them to see the way. *"Where are we going?"* she asked.

"We be going to thy home."

She followed. "My home?" Her eyes scanned for a horizon, but a dark mist veiled the way. "How did I get here?" Her surroundings changed. Her dragon was the only constant, so she kept her eyes on him as she looked forward to stepping foot on their land in the valley.

A bright light wrapped around her, and in a flash, they stood in daylight. Her stomach lurched. For a very brief moment, she wondered if she might be expecting another baby, but all such thoughts evaporated as she stared at the apocalyptic landscape. She reached out and leaned against Beroan. "What is this place?"

"This be thy home. This be the future ye escaped–the future we be changing."

"Why are you showing me this?"

"Young one, life for ye be difficult. Thy life as Dragonborn be long. Ye shall have times of sorrow. Remember what ye see here. This be not the future of the land because thy daughter holds power for a different future than what ye witness here. Thy clan shall bring forth one to save the land through all time."

CHAPTER EIGHTEEN

The following morning, Kaibelle awoke early. She glanced outside where shadows still overtook the lake, but blue skies promised mild weather above the crater as they flew home. She stood and smoothed her tunic and slipped on her apron. Aurora snuggled against her father's chest. A smile flickered and died on Kaibelle's lips. The rainbow aura lit up around her daughter even as she slept.

Kaibelle gently stepped outside and walked to the shore. The lake's surface looked like dark glass with a crescent of blue sky reflecting in the still morning air.

"Isn't it pretty?"

The young voice behind her startled her. She spun around and almost bumped into Kylar. "Kylar! What are you doing out here?"

He straightened his satchel strap across his chest. "I know we're leaving soon. I just wanted time to enjoy the lake. I think I'm going to miss being here."

She rustled his blondish red hair. "You're right. We're leaving today."

"Today!" His brown eyes widened. "I better go pack."

"Pack?" She smiled. *He thinks he has enough possessions to have to pack.* "You'll have time. Your father and I have to check all the tiles are secure one last time before we leave." The two of them walked along the edge of the lake as they talked. He bent to pick up a yellow-tipped feather and saved it in his bag.

Laughter spilled from the tunnel leading to the dragon roost. The other boys burst into the morning sunlight and raced toward their mother and brother. Behind them, Ervig carried Aurora. The boys ran straight to the edge of the lake and waded ankle deep as they tried to scoop out small baitfish to see who could catch the most. Aurora leaned toward her mother with outstretched arms, and Ervig handed her over.

Nimbus circled overhead, carrying a branch filled with bright yellow fruit. The children instinctively ran closer to the outer rim of the volcano to give her room to land. Jurom stepped into the daylight just ahead of his father and trotted to join the children as they gathered around the limb to pluck fruit for breakfast. His two younger siblings waddled behind him, trying to keep up.

Ervig helped secure Aurora in the wrap across Kaibelle's torso. "We should go check the tiles…." He scanned the lake, the grassy area, the children, and dragons. "… and if all is as it should be, we should head toward home."

Kaibelle swallowed against the emotional tightening of her throat as she bit off a chunk of skin from the fruit in her hand. She held the juicy pulp to Aurora's lips and called to Kylar. He hurried to her side. "Your father and I are going to the alcove to check the tiles are all set and in place one last time. After that, we'll be leaving."

Kylar looked into his mother's eyes with a hint of sadness. *He looks so much like Ervig.*

Kylar nodded halfheartedly, glanced at his feet, and mumbled. "I'll be ready."

"Make sure everyone eats." She mussed his hair, and he smiled. "All will be well, son," she said as she adjusted Aurora's weight in the sling. Then she turned to her dragon with the hope that she was right. *"Beroan, can you take us to the alcove so that we don't get wet?"*

"Certainly."

Kaibelle climbed onto Beroan's back first, followed by Ervig. She scootched close to the spike, and Ervig sidled up behind her on the flat spot behind the goldenhorn. They rode in silence, watching their children on the shore as they cut across the lake. The children's voices and laughter carried over the water until the waterfall splash drowned them out. Beroan's large head cut through the water and sprayed them lightly as he passed to the other side and turned his head to keep them dry beneath his snout.

"It's cold." Kaibelle hugged Aurora close to her.

"Let me warm it for ye." Beroan opened his jaws and sent a stream of fire into the large cove. Flames hit the back wall, curled to the ceiling, and rolled down the walls like an unfurling curtain until it licked the floor and died.

A filmy haze hung lazily in the alcove where the top-most symbols sizzled to life with amber heat highlighting each glyph. As one after another lit like a fuse, the image of a wraith-like dragon appeared. *A Thornose dragon! A green Thornose!* Kaibelle cast a nervous look toward her husband, who stared straight into the vision as it started to speak in the ancient language.

"It-it's Zaylan!" His brow knitted with unasked questions. "How is this possible?"

"What?" Beroan eyed the smoky alcove. "Ye see *Zaylan? How? What be she saying?"*

"She speaks of the pool–the lake, I think. She calls it the Pool of Zaylan and says it's her gift of understanding and sight to the Thornose clan."

"Thornose," Beroan repeated. *"This be for the Thornose?"* His tone dripped with disbelief.

"But how? How do we see this–this message?" Kaibelle hugged Aurora close to her chest.

The gauzy-looking dragon head answered as if she heard the question. Behind her, amber heat continued to spread from one symbol to the next. "I be Zaylan mate of Therus. This vision be for Thornose eyes only," the dragon said. "Eyes opened by drinking the panacea with unconscious wisdom. It stills voices of this world and orders words to be heard, only when speaking with thee. It opens thine eyes to thine sixth sense. Grants vision able to penetrate time and space. This be how ye see and hear mine message, now, though mine spirit rests in Nomuria. The Goldenhorn be able to read this message, but they be gifted with far vision unable to see as ye see now."

Ervig and Kaibelle stared in wonder at the dragon image floating above the floor. The apparition said, "Their gift coupled with thine gift shall work together to save the world across time from the heartless, vicious spirit of the Book of Darkmore. A spirit created by the fire spirits of the Pyre when they mingled with the darkened heart of a human who craved the power. This human studied it, toyed with the dark arts, and tapped into its power. He learned of dragon magic–ensnared me and used mine blood to bring life to the words of the book.

"He wrote each spell and chronicled the knowledge he gained within the book giving it spirit and life through the blood. Finally, he gave it skin. His own life. The malicious Tryx spirit of the Pyre grew powerful and deceptive within him. It lives on. The Evil breeds evil. Each host be more malicious and vile than the one before it. To defeat this spirit, it must be separated from the Book of Darkmore, for from it, the host draws power each day. The book be protected and cannot be destroyed–cannot be killed–and so must be imprisoned–hidden where it cannot be found–forever.

"This prophesy thine eyes witness this day be in place to defeat this spirit in thine future. But it be not thy destiny alone. For it be a task that requires the Dragonborn to work together. The Thornose clan charged to be guardians of the Labyrinth of Times. The Goldenhorn clan charged to be sentinels of the Midlands–the space between times. The little, but not insignificant, Icewing cave dwellers from the Restless Mountains can read the thoughts of humans. And lastly, and most unlikely, be human Dragonborn."

The Zaylan image floated forward and almost seemed to take on substance. Her snout came near as if sensing Ervig, then Kaibelle, and finally Aurora. The baby reached out and touched the dragon's nibhorn. A blinding golden light exploded and flooded the cove. A bolt of energy struck Beroan's head. Zaylan's image wavered as the smoke thinned. The image dissipated. Her still audible voice started to fade. "The day the Therus Tree from the Sacred Garden reveals itself shall mark an eon of fortune and an age of growth… a uniting of four unlikely allies."

Beroan stepped back. A spray of water shot across Ervig's tunic. He and his wife sat motionless on the Goldenhorn's back, striving to make sense of it all. Aurora peeked from the sling with large green eyes. The water from the falls splashed behind them.

"I heard that. Ye be saying it be Zaylan's voice? Why I be able to hear it now?" Beroan asked mind to mind to both humans as he stared at the layers of haze, attempting to see any hint of what the humans were seeing.

"Yes, it was Therus' mate Zaylan. We didn't just hear her; we saw her," Kaibelle said.

"How be it so? The queen of the Thornose be long dead. And why I be able to hear her at the end?"

Ervig shrugged. "It's Thornose magic and… I think it was through Aurora that you were able to hear what she said. I don't know. Perhaps that last sentence was for your ears and always meant for Goldenhorn ears."

Kaibelle nodded. "I know we can't talk about it, but the fact that we could see Zaylan makes it clear that we're Dragonborn through the Thornose. I think that's why we understand…. Why we see."

"This be a message for the Thornose, then?" Beroan asked once more in disbelief.

"It is. Perhaps the Thornose will no longer come to know the prophecies, and the Goldenhorn are being used to preserve this wisdom and pass it on in the future," Kaibelle said.

Ervig dismounted to the ledge and stood wrapped in the warmth and haze. "Beroan, she made it clear the Goldenhorn are guardians of the message. And sentinels of the Midlands. For now, this is home to the Goldenhorn, and when the Therus tree comes to this time, it sounds like the Thornose and others will join you."

Kaibelle climbed from Beroan to the ledge and stepped into the alcove. "Yes, it sounds like the Thornose will eventually come to this time and somehow see the message and that it will guide them to vanquish the evil book. I don't know how…." She stared at the tiles. The symbols no longer burned but had returned to their original black. Aurora looked out from the sling with wide eyes as her parents checked the tiles and found them all secured for the future.

"And so mine kind be watchers… looking for the Therus tree."

Kaibelle nodded and wondered how all this would change the future. *Will it save the lives of my parents?* Aurora started to fuss. Kaibelle patted her back. "I guess it's time for us to go."

Ervig took one last sweeping look at the tiles and helped Kaibelle climb aboard the dragon. Kaibelle took one last look at all the hard work they'd put in as Ervig took a seat behind her. As they cut through the falls, she cradled Aurora to her chest as Beroan turned his head to protect them from the flow of water. They slipped out into the sunshine with their minds spinning with questions. On the way across the lake, Kaibelle shared the other information they had heard with Beroan. They both wondered about the meaning of the four unlikely allies. "*Thornose and Goldenhorn are two. The Dragonborn humans three, but who is this fourth? These Icewings?"*

"I know not," Beroan said.

As they saddled the dragons for the trip back to the valley, a bittersweet feeling filled Kaibelle. *I'll never see this place again.*

CHAPTER NINETEEN

The dragons took to the air. This time Kylar rode Jurom. The young dragon had doubled in size in the time they lived within the island volcano. And now that he didn't have to carry a load of tiles, Ervig deemed Kylar old enough to ride on his own. He drank in the sights. On his first trip, he'd fallen asleep, but now he was old enough to ride the dragon by himself to make room for Aurora to ride with their mother and Rikard on Beroan. He looked over to see his little sister waving goodbye to the island. "Bye-bye, Jur-Jurom."

He glanced over at Nimbus. This time Tomas flew with Da, Erik, and Carn on the larger orange dragon. Below him, a massive blue sea stretched for as far as he could see. A string of islands dotted the sea as they flew toward a distant mountain range on the mainland.

Kaibelle nursed Aurora to keep her occupied and help alleviate the pressure in her ears as Beroan climbed higher into the sky, carrying Rikard, Aurora, and herself. Thankfully, the toddler drifted to sleep, and Kaibelle used a little magic to help Rikard take a nap. With the children asleep, she sat back and took in the view. Sometimes it all still felt like a dream. She scanned the sky and observed her family spread out over the sea on dragons. *Dragons, flying over the sea, this family. All impossible things before I came here. And things continue to change so quickly. Think of how much has changed since we last made this trek.* Her thoughts wandered to the urn with the five glyphs and that day when the multi-colored aura first shined around Aurora… *Aurora Darksky. Her essence is so opposite the dark skies of the day she was born. So much has happened since then.*

When they reached the mountains, the dragons landed to let the humans walk around, relieve themselves, and eat some of the fruit they carried. By the time the first of the two suns dropped near the horizon, they were over the valley they called home.

"This is where you were born," Kaibelle said to Rikard. He didn't remember it until the cabin came into sight. Kaibelle pointed. "There's our house." Even as she said it, a sinking feeling washed over her. They might sleep here a night or two before they moved on. By the time they landed, the first sun had disappeared behind the mountains on the western rim. Kylar ran to the cabin as if he'd only been gone a day and opened the door. He stuck his head out. "We need firelight."

Ervig pointed to the stacked wood in the lean-to. "Everybody grab a log, and let's start a fire out here." It amused Kaibelle that he wanted to spend time outside with the dragons now that they were home. But it didn't surprise her. He had admitted that he'd grown so accustomed to them that he wasn't sure what life would be like when they went their separate ways. *And what of Aurora?* That was her biggest concern.

The boys set up the logs, and Jurom stepped forward. His head jutted forward and closer to the ground. The boys stepped back. Kylar glanced wide-eyed at the young dragon as glowing veins of fire showed through the skin between his green scales as his gullet expanded. "Is he going to blow fire?" Rikard asked.

"Yes!" Kylar moved to stand with his younger brother as if he were a shield. Jurom let loose with a flow of liquid fire. The dry logs burst into flame. Nimbus and Beroan congratulated their oldest hatchling on his first fire while their younger hatchlings looked on with a sense of awe at their oldest brother.

"I wanted it to be special," Jurom said as Kylar stepped over to rub the bone ridge of his brow.

The humans and dragons ate and decided to spend the night outside. Stars blinked overhead in the violet sky as the children started to fall asleep one at a time. Three of them had drifted off, but an overtired Aurora fussed in her mother's arms while Kylar sat working on something by the light of the fire. She couldn't tell what he had in his lap, so she walked over to see what he was up to and encouraged him to go to sleep so she and Ervig could have time with their dragons to plan the move.

She glanced over her son's shoulder as she bounced Aurora on her hip. He held a piece of flattened lake clay, smoothed out about the length of her forearm and twice as wide on a board. A map etched into the soft surface showed the island from the air labeled *Jur-Jurom,* along with the chain of islands leading to it. It also detailed the coastal mountains and everything else between the hidden valley and Jur-Jurom. *It's every detail!* "How did you do that?"

"I took it from the bottom of the lake and wrapped it in a hide to keep it moist."

"No, I mean that…" she pointed at the clay. "…remembering all those details so exactly."

He shrugged. "I don't know. I just see it in my head."

"Give it to me for tonight. It's time to get some sleep because tomorrow is another busy day. We have to decide what things we're taking and get them packed."

Kylar let out a deep sigh and handed the map to his mother. She balanced the board like a tray flat against her palm as Aurora reached out to touch it. "It will be dry tomorrow. You won't be able to make any changes. You know that." He glanced at her as she raised the map out of Aurora's reach.

"I'm pretty much done with it. Be careful, though. It's starting to bend a little. You need to hold it with both hands for now." He stood and took it carefully from her hands. "Mother?"

"Yes?"

"Do you ever get tired of moving?"

She laughed. "I confess, I do. But this next move will be our last for a long time." She handed Aurora to him and took the map with both hands. "Can you help get her to sleep? Your Da and I need to talk about tomorrow." He nodded and carried her over to where Jurom lay warming near the fire and sat beside him with Aurora in his arms. He leaned against the young dragon's side and cradled his sister in his arms. She squirmed for a moment but quickly snuggled against his chest as he stroked her red hair. Even though she relaxed, she fought sleep as she reached over her brother's shoulder to stroke the dragon's side. With each rub, Kaibelle watched the radiance surrounding her daughter pulse with power.

She walked around the other young dragons sleeping near the fire and maneuvered back to her husband and the two adult dragons. Ervig threw a few more logs onto the fire. Oscillating shadows danced across the dragons lying on the ground behind him. As she watched him, part of her felt relieved that they would be parting ways with the dragons once they reached Five Marks and finished building the temple. *But really, what difference will it make? Ervig and I are Dragonborn, and Aurora is… what? And what of Kylar? He shows an incredible memory for details. Is that natural or the dragon influence that Beroan called dragon-touched*?

Ervig walked over, took the map, set it on the ground, and wrapped her in his arms. "How are you?" Concern colored his voice, and she couldn't pretend it wasn't warranted.

She planted her face into his chest, trying to collect her emotions. "Don't ask because I don't know." Her muffled voice quavered. She looked up into his eyes, where firelight danced like stars. "I was sad to leave Jur-Jurom… I guess the children did name it that. It's on the map Kylar has drawn." She pointed to the clay map on the ground. For a moment, a smile played across her lips at the child-like name. But her smile faded as she glanced at the cabin. "I was happy to be back here." She gestured toward their home. "And a little afraid about Five Marks. Not to mention for our children. Kylar just drew this perfect map from memory! And be careful. It is still drying." She gestured toward the map on the ground. "And Aurora… well, I don't need to say more."

Ervig turned to Nimbus. "We'll be back in a moment." Her light clicking laughter told him she understood. Together, he and Kaibelle made sure all the children were safe, comfortable, and asleep.

Kaibelle rubbed her lower back. "I'm exhausted." Ervig nodded but said nothing. He didn't have to; she could see it. He was just as tired. They rejoined their dragon companions and talked about the move and the future. Finally, Kaibelle announced, "I can't stay awake a moment longer." Ervig agreed, and they all turned in for the night.

CHAPTER TWENTY

In the morning, the children's laughter woke Kaibelle. Rikard galloped around the embers of last night's fire on the stick horse Ervig had made for Erik when he was younger. She stuffed Kylar's map into her bag so it wouldn't get stepped on, and with everyone occupied, she decided to visit the cabin.

The hinges of the door squealed as she walked into the house. A wave of emotion overtook her as she took in the home she'd known for a little more than a decade. *This is where my sons were born, learned to walk....* She started toward the fireplace. The clatter of her footsteps echoed against the floorboards, a foreign sound after living in the dragon's roost. She stopped at the hearth, collected some of the trinkets her son Erik had carved for her before they left for Jur-Jurom, and pocketed them. She stepped over to her potter's wheel in the corner and drew her finger through the dust. It coated everything. *I want to bring this with me.* She turned and considered her loom. Ervig could build another. *What of his elixirs, tinctures, and other potions?*

Her mind fought between reminiscing and letting go. *Soon this will all be a distant memory like the Vodatha of my time... And the Vodatha of Ervig's time, if they called it Vodatha in his time.* She walked to the window expecting to see her chickens scratching, but they were gone. The roof of their coop peeked from the overgrown prairie grass. Hopefully, the dragons would collect chickens for them again. She shook off the melancholy reverie and strode over to the hearth and built a fire. *Most of my family won't remember this place, but this morning I'm going to leave them with a serving of good memories like those I treasure in my heart.*

Ervig cast a sideward glance at her as she stepped out to the well to collect water. He mouthed, "What are you doing?"

"I'm packing, of course." She walked back into the house, closed the door behind her, and laughed at the look on his face. Her laughter faded to a smile and disappeared. "I better get started."

With a touch of magic, a fire burned in the hearth that chased away the morning chill as she put on a kettle of porridge. Breakfast bubbled in the pot while she wiped away dust from the table and started collecting things she wanted to bring. Up in the loft, she gathered blankets from the beds and shook off what dust she could. As she folded them, she spotted skins rolled up like scrolls beneath Kylar's bed. As much as she'd like to bring all this, there wasn't enough room. It reminded her of the map she'd stuffed into her bag. She pulled it out and smiled at his signature at the bottom as if it were a school assignment. *Kylar Lost Valley.*

When he was born here in this cabin, I didn't know what name to give him. I still felt lost and out of my time. I was still learning to interpret the meaning of the colorful energy I saw around people and was unaccustomed to giving birthnames. Now Kylar Lost Valley is a bright young man I love with all my heart. Since then, she'd learned Kylar's bright orange-yellow aura not only marked his intelligence but showed him to be detail-oriented, creative, and a perfectionist. "Well, Kylar, you certainly are detail-oriented, and I don't need dragon powers to know it." She shook the map in her hands up and down with small movements trying to figure out what to do with it. "You were the first to be born here this valley the dragons carried us to. It's fitting you are the one who drew this map. But I think it best if it stays here with your collection of childhood scrolls." She dropped to her knees and slid the map under his bed beside his scrolls.

Hinges shrieked a warning that someone had opened the door into the main room below. Kaibelle glanced over the loft rail into the open area to see her family pour into the house. Kylar led the way. Fresh in her mind, she recalled their little-used full names as each one walked in the door. Tomas Two Blossom and Carn Spider Brook stood at the door with a lost look on their faces, as if they'd never been inside a house. To their memory, they hadn't been. *We've lived in caves and under the sky.* Rikard Greenfields ran toward them carrying a couple more stick animals to ride–stick animals Ervig had carved a lifetime ago. They decided to give Rikard Ervig's last name because he helped bring him into the world following a difficult delivery. For a moment, sounds of laughter and running feet swept away the emptiness.

She brought the blankets downstairs and placed them on the floor near the door. "We'll be bundling what we can carry in these, but first, it's time to eat. Go out to the well and wash your hands and faces." Tomas looked at her with a frown. "Wash my face?"

She walked over and crouched in front of him, eye-to-eye. "When you don't have a lake to swim in, the dirt stays on your face, hands, and everywhere else. You have to wash it off."

He raised his grubby hands and stared at them with a new understanding. He followed his brothers out to the well to wash up.

Ervig stood in the doorway with Aurora in his arms. "Nimbus is hunting with the hatchlings in the foothills to let them practice their hunting skills." He set Aurora down, and she clung to his leg, wary of being indoors.

Kaibelle crouched and tried to coax her daughter to walk to her, but she hugged Ervig's leg and wasn't letting go.

Ervig finished his report. "Beroan has flown to Five Marks to find a place for us to live until we build the temple." He walked stiff-legged over to Kaibelle with Aurora still clinging to one leg while balancing on his foot. The ride on his leg broke through the fear with giggles. "It smells delicious in here," Ervig said.

Kaibelle nodded. "Before the children get back in here, I want to say I'm fine. But I have to admit that it's hard for me to leave. We need to be careful that our attachment to this place, and the past, doesn't affect the children. Our whole purpose is to create a new future, and it starts with them. We need to give them something to look forward to."

He pried Aurora's hands from his leg and lifted her over his head, moving her from side to side as if she could fly. "Like a river that they can swim in?" he asked in a sing-song voice.

She chuckled. "Yes, like a river… so they don't have to wash up." She walked to the shelf and grabbed the stack of bowls she had made so long ago. Before motherhood. She removed the top bowl covered in dust and laid it aside. She scooped out steaming bowls of porridge for each of her children.

By the time the boys walked back into the house, bowls of hot oats had lined the edges of the heavy wooden table. Kylar showed everyone where they were to sit and how to use a spoon. Kaibelle marveled. Carn sucked his thumb, unsure about eating gruel until he watched his brothers gobble it down and ask for more. Aurora claimed her mother's lap instead of the baby chair, and together, they ate at the table as a family.

The rest of the day went by fast as they sorted through their meager belongings. They decided to leave the furniture except for her pottery wheel and most of the dishes. They would bring all the clothing since they were leaving the loom behind and, even more, because she didn't particularly fancy spinning and sewing. What one child outgrew another could wear. She glanced at Aurora, who had never worn proper clothing in her life but went about almost naked most of the time. That would have to change because Five Marks wouldn't stay secluded. Others would be drawn there. For now, she decided to dress her daughter in her brothers' hand-me-downs. Once they settled in Five Marks, she would focus on making her daughter some appropriate clothing.

The rumble of a dragon trumpeting startled her from her reverie. *It's Beroan!* A higher-pitched nasal call ended with a snort. She hurried down the stairs to the door to see Jurom land beside his father. "Their back from Five Marks? So soon?" Fear gripped her. *What could be wrong?*

They went out to greet the dragons. "How did you fly to Five Marks and back so swiftly? Is everything alright?"

"We flew not, Little One. We traveled the Midlands for it be quick–like a blink." He looked toward Jurom, who stood unusually quiet. *"By air, it be a long journey. Too long for thy younglings in one day. Mine son Jurom and I will carry thy bundles to Five Marks through the Midlands when they be ready."*

"Can we travel the Midlands? If it is so fast, we could all avoid the long trip."

"Only those Dragonborn can move from one place to another through the Midlands. Our eyes be able to see toward the future, even between times."

Even though she and Ervig were Dragonborn–and maybe Aurora, her sons were not. She nodded.

By the end of the day, lumpy blanket bundles stood heaped outside. Ervig decided to go with the dragons through the Midlands to help remove the loads on their backs at Five Marks. They secured blanket bundles first on Jurom and then on Beroan. Nimbus walked up to Ervig. As "his" dragon, she bent her head for him to rub her snout. *"Wilt thy mate be comfortable if ye be coming with us?"*

He glanced over his shoulder at Kaibelle as she secured the rope to tighten Jurom's pack. *"Will you be comfortable leaving your hatchlings here with her?"*

She chuckled lightly. *"I be comfortable."*

He struggled to lift one of the bundles onto her back, and Erik hurried over to help him. He was almost as tall as Ervig and only nine summers. The bundle rattled and shifted as he girded a rope around her midsection and secured it to her goldenhorn. *"Are you sure you can carry this and me?"*

"Ye weigh less than one hatchling. I be able to fly with two and sometimes three hatchlings too young to fly, but for this journey, ye shall not ride."

Erik climbed onto the dragon's back, stood beside his father, and double-checked his knots. "Do you want me to come along to help?"

"I appreciate it, but I think I can use you here to help look after things until I get back." Erik nodded, but his eyes fell to the dagger strapped to his father's leg. He remembered seeing it when he was younger, but now his father never wore it. His head bobbed once in agreement to stay while his eyes fought to hold back tears.

CHAPTER TWENTY-ONE

With Aurora balanced on her left hip, Kaibelle waved to Ervig as he stood beside Nimbus. A large bundle fastened with ropes tottered on her back. That dream of the shifting shadows of the Midlands haunted her and left her unsettled. Not only was Ervig wearing his dagger, he wasn't even riding Nimbus. *Beroan led me through the Midlands in my dream, but it was only a dream. I think....* Dream or not, it prepared her to understand what Ervig was about to do. *Travel between times with Nimbus, Beroan, and Jurom within a bubble of this time. That bubble is massive!* She nervously rubbed her sweaty palm against her apron. While she understood the concept in a limited way, she didn't understand it at all. *What if the bubble breaks like soap in the wind? Prolonged exposure to the Midlands proves deadly to non-Dragonborn humans. If something should happen to Ervig...."*

"Worry not, Little One," Beroan said. "The Goldenhorns' special eyesight be able to see the rings of light that mark the bridges between times. They be back safely in a short time."

Kaibelle hung her faith on that promise. She wanted to run to Ervig and hug him one more time, but she stood her ground and offered him a smile. His eyes locked with hers as a tentative smile played across his lips. He waved and placed his hand on Nimbus' side.

A swirl of golden light turned the twilight to the brightness of high noon. Individual tornadoes of light surrounded Ervig and the dragons and exploded in a brilliant flash. Kaibelle squeezed her eyes shut and turned away, but a ghost of the explosion lingered. She opened her eyes and blinked. They all had disappeared, and her children clamored to know what had happened to their Da and the dragons.

* * * *

A buttery wall of light swirled around Ervig and the dragons. He could no longer see Kai or the children, but he could feel Nimbus at his side. The light went out like a candle in the wind. His eyes struggled to adjust to the darkness as a wave of dizziness overtook him. Fog settled into his mind making him feel disconnected. A pinpoint of pain shot through the back of his head. With the fingers of his free hand, he felt his scalp at the base of his neck–checking for blood. All felt as it should. At least he thought it was as it should be. Suddenly he had trouble remembering–anything. Where am I?

"Young One, close thy eyes a moment."

The familiar female voice calmed him. He closed his eyes, trying to remember who the voice belonged to. The wave of nausea fighting to overtake him started to subside.

"Does this be better?"

He tried to nod, and his head reeled.

"Walk," the voice said. "Come. Put thy foot one in front of the other. Come."

He wanted to ask where, but his mouth seemed disconnected from his mind. His leg lifted and stepped. He opened his eyes. Mistake! Swirling disorientation flooded him. "What's happening to me?"

"We be inside a bubble which distorts thy body to travel between time. Can ye see the rings?"

Ervig didn't want to open his eyes. He squinted with one eye. "I see something… a faint circle… purple… it looks like it's smoke or fog."

"That be it," Nimbus said. "That's where ye be going. Ye must walk through the rings. I be here beside thee."

As they moved forward through the thick darkness, resistance slowed his movements. "Feel like I'm crossing a river in water up to my neck."

"It shall ease as ye cross through each ring."

He pushed forward, following Nimbus' guidance. When he reached the purple ring, Beroan walked through first, and Jurom followed with a wobbly gait. Nimbus started through the gossamer ring of light. Ervig leaned heavier with his hand against her side to keep his balance. The wave of nausea subsided slightly as he looked ahead at the charcoal gray sky… not a true sky but more like a ceiling. Beneath his feet, no texture… not grass, nor stone, nor wet or dry. "I feel like I'm in a nightmare."

"For those not Dragonborn, this be worse than a nightmare. For they have not the sight to see the bridges between time and space. Can ye see the next ring?"

Ervig swallowed against the bile rising in his throat. "Is it green? So dark it's almost invisible?"

"That be it. The third be the color of a stormy sea, and beyond it be an explosion of dark colors. Within those colors be a ring of violet. Once through it, the magic shall carry us into thy world."

"To–to Five Marks?" He remembered the name but not what it meant.

"Aye."

The effort to move and nausea stole Ervig's strength. He almost missed the dark green ring. Nimbus nudged him toward the circle of muted light. As he stepped to the other side, the air burst with subdued swirling colors. It looked much like ink mixing with water as his eyes sought the last ring. There it is! Every bit of his being wanted to run toward it, but his muscular legs would do no running in the Midlands because they were already moving faster than light, even though it didn't feel that way.

"Hold to each other Beroan ordered. So we be together when we transport."

Jurom held his father's tail in his mouth when they reached the violet circlet of shadowy light. Ervig slid his hand to Nimbus' snout and steadied his other hand on Jurom's rump. As they stepped to the other side, golden energy wrapped around them and yanked them upward. Ervig squeezed his eyes just as his stomach dropped. His feet slammed into the ground jarring every bone in his body. He stumbled forward and landed on his back, gasping the fresh sea air. A slick film of sweat coated his face, arms… even his trousers stuck to his legs.

Behind him, the sound of waves lapping the shoreline helped relax his muscles. "Get thee up," Nimbus said with urgency. Ervig scrambled to his feet, alert and reaching for his dagger. “What? What is it?”

“There be danger. The myrnexes.”

Ervig held his dagger at the ready and crouched in a forward fighting stance with his weight on the balls of his feet. With his elbows at his side, he held his hands up for protection–his dagger clutched in his left hand and checked with his right hand. He turned right and left, expecting an attack. “Myr—myrnex? What is that?” He didn’t see anything, but his military training had him looking for a way of escape.

“Just watch where ye step. They live in the ground. Humans who slip into their holes return not.”

“What?” Ervig face flushed with anger. “You’re bringing us to a place where there are these… these myr… these dangerous things that live in the ground—”

“Stop, Ervig. Ye know I be with ye. Let us move to the sea and remove these bundles.”

Ervig sheathed his dagger and again felt much like a marionette with someone pulling his strings. He loosened the loads and pointed to them one at a time, saying, “Et leva.” The cumbersome bales holding his household items lifted into the air following the trajectory of his finger to a sandy plot out of reach of the high tide line. The muscle in his arm shook involuntarily. As the bundles dropped to the sand, he collapsed beside them. “I just need to get my bearings before we go back.”

“Stay here with Jurom. We be back shortly. Jurom, stay alert. If ye see a myrnex, burn it.”

Jurom held his head a little higher. Normally, Ervig would have chuckled, but right now, he thanked the stars for a chance to rest and a hatchling who could breathe fire. He sat on the ground and rested his back against a bundle as he stared at the stretch of beach. No myrnex could come at him from behind. He glanced at the sky. The yellower of the two suns dipped closer to the horizon, with the red-orange sun not trailing far behind. Yellows and deep oranges smeared across the cloudless horizon as a light breeze rippled the water, stirring petals of color across the surface like burning embers. The sea air refreshed him. From the corner of his eye, a large shadowy object startled him from his reverie. He shot to his feet, thankful his knees no longer wobbled. His heart pounded, expecting to get a look at his first myrnex. Instead, a floating mountaintop hung in the air settling above the shoreline. Another followed behind it and another and another.

His jaw dropped as he stared at the impossible. "What is this?" he said to himself more than to his young dragon companion.

"It be thy new home until the temple be built," Nimbus answered from above.

He looked to the sky behind him and watched more hunks of mountain float toward him until they settled above the shoreline. His mouth hung open in amazement. Beside him, Jurom moved quickly. His tail whipped across the sandy ground and knocked Ervig's feet from beneath him. In a blink, fire shot from Jurom's jaws. Burnt flesh assaulted his senses as a large, long body fell forward, still smoldering. Ervig stared at the creature's large, square, flattened head and enormous sickle-like jaws armed with several sharp, hollow projections. The shape of the body reminded him of Kaibelle's spindle with yarn spun around the center. For the first time, he realized he gripped his dagger and held it, ready to defend himself. He'd drawn it and didn't even realize it. He studied the still smoldering carcass, and fear for his family's safety flooded him.

Nimbus landed near him. A rush of wind gusted from her wings, blowing the stench away. "Come, Young One."

He sheathed his dagger, climbed to her back, and held on to the goldenhorn, squeezing it like a lifeline. "Nimbus, I don't know about bringing the children here."

She took to the air without a word and circled one of the floating chunks of sandstone. From this height, even in the low light of the setting suns, he saw a pit in the soft sandy soil from which the myrnex had emerged. "That's a trap," he said matter-of-factly.

"Aye, it be impossible to escape unless ye can grow wings. The more prey struggles, the faster the sand drags them into their jaws."

Nimbus treaded air for a moment at the mouth of a mammoth cave in one of the floating mountains. The dragon flew inside and landed gently. "The myrnexes be the reason, these floating caves be thy new home, while the temple be built."

"But what then? You'll be leaving, and we'll be here with whatever those things are! Kaibelle's not going to like it. Dragon dung, Nimbus. I don't like this! We're putting the children in danger, and they aren't the ones who signed up for this! Why not use magic to wipe them out?"

"Calm thyself. Magic should never be used to take life. That be how the evil we fight started with the taking of life as part of a blood covenant. The temple be large. While ye and thy kind build it, we be helping gather materials and ridding the land of the myrnexes by fire. Thy family be living here, above the danger."

Ervig glanced out at the other floating mountains. Each was pocked with caves, and vegetation grew on the slopes. On the third floating mountaintop over, he saw shaggy sheep of good size. Nimbus was right. Everything they needed would be provided up here. "I can make bridges connecting them," he said as he thought out loud. "But how do they stay in the air? Is this safe? We didn't have such a thing…." He stopped himself. I need to stop comparing this to the world I knew. Every change they'd made was to stop the coming evil. How floating caves would help, he couldn't answer, but it was a way to keep his family safe from those myrnex monsters.

"Our magic be strong. These floating caves be set along the shore for thy kind, here and elsewhere, like restless mountains."

"How are we supposed to get up and down? We don't exactly have wings, and you certainly can't be planning to fly us back and forth."

"That be thy part. Ye speak of bridges. Somehow ye will make a bridge to reach the ground."

Ervig stood within the large cave, amazed that Nimbus had room to turn around and face the opening. They looked at the sea and over to the next floating mountain. The last of the red-orange sun melted into the horizon.

"We need to journey back," Nimbus said. "Be ye able?"

Ervig nodded reluctantly. "Let me add the bridges before we go. That way, I don't have to try to do it without the children seeing me use magic." He raised his hands and said, "Pontem iungere conjur unam alteri." A single rope appeared, then another and another. They wove into thick cables to form handrails. Soon, the floor of a suspension bridge spanned the sea below and connected the mountain tops like links in a chain. Wood and sticks turned it into a footpath. Ervig let his arms drop. "What am I allowed to speak of with Kaibelle? Can I tell her about the Midlands? Can I tell her I used magic to create these bridges?"

Nimbus' clicking laughter echoed in the large cavern. "Aye. She be aware. Beroan carried her there in a dream."

"In a dream?" Ervig shook his head. "I'm not sure that was bewildering enough. It can't really prepare a person for walking the Midlands."

"What ye speak be true. For most humans, it be a trap with no escape. It be death. But from thy line, a rare few with power to traverse the Midlands alone and see their way be born. Thy daughter be one."

Ervig shook his head. "I don't want to know more. It's too hard to have such secrets from Kaibelle. I'm ready to go back." He climbed to Nimbus' shoulders and readied himself to take flight with fear for his daughter gnawing at him.

"There be changes coming, Young One. Here in Five Marks, ye and thy mate shall talk of things secret and work together. Let me show ye."

A tingling sensation ran through Ervig's hand from the goldenhorn. Visions of the temple and how to build it flashed through his mind, along with secret elements of which he could never speak. The final pieces he and Kaibelle needed to put in place. Then their work, here, would be finished.

As the visions faded, Ervig felt afraid but excited. Things would be changing, but at least he and Kaibelle would no longer have to keep secrets from one another. While they still couldn't talk to others about being Dragonborn, he and Kaibelle were now allowed to discuss it with each other.

Nimbus and Ervig joined the others on the ground. The carcass of the myrnex was no longer there. Ervig decided not to ask. He was just happy that his family didn't have to see the monster when they arrived. For now, he elected not to mention the myrnexes to Kaibelle, or he may never get her on a dragon to fly here.

There on the shore, the dragons and Ervig once again made physical contact. This time he heard Nimbus say, "Transport in Dragonborn in vivis perdidisse Kylar in valle." He had never heard the ancient language until the Zaylan oracle. This time he understood it perfectly. "Transport to the Dragonborn living in Kylar's lost valley." The golden light wrapped around him and blinked him out of existence in his world. His feet hit the ground hard. Again, it caught him off guard, and he stumbled forward a step in the darkness to keep his balance. His stomach flip-flopped. A wave of nausea washed over him. He swallowed hard, ignored it, and moved forward. With practice, he could do this. It would never be his favorite mode of getting around, but he could handle it if needed. After all, he survived being trapped in a rat's body. Nothing could ever be worse than that!

He spotted the first circle of faded purple light beneath the shadowy slate ceiling. As they slipped through it, his upset stomach settled a little. This time he watched eagerly for each new ring. With each one, he felt better but still weak. Excitement built within him to know his family waited at the end of this experience. And to know he and Kaibelle would finally be able to share life on every level as they fulfilled one of the most significant tasks in their role in defeating the evil that started them on this journey. Building the temple.

CHAPTER TWENTY-TWO

As the suns set, Kaibelle worked to get her keyed-up children to settle down. Kylar followed her around while peppering her with questions. "What was that–that light? Where did they go? How did they disappear?"

"It's a special way dragons travel that's much faster."

"Faster? Can we do that instead of flying all day?"

"No, it's not safe for…." She swallowed the word Dragonborn. "Not safe for young ones and not for many adults. I've never traveled in that way, and neither has your father, but he took the risk so our belongings can already be waiting for us when we arrive." Kaibelle shoved Aurora into Kylar's arms as a distraction. "See if you can get your sister to sleep while I tend to your brothers."

She walked away as she sucked in a calming breath. *After all this time, I almost broke my oath!* Her other boys darted about with the younger hatchlings. *They are overexcited because of the way Ervig disappeared.* When Carn saw her coming, he stopped and slipped his dirty thumb into his mouth. "I don't wanna go to sleep yet," he complained around his thumb. "What happened to Da? Is that light going to get us?"

"Oh, he's fine and will be back before we know it. And while we wait, I thought maybe we could all get comfortable and enjoy a story." The boys perked up and huddled with the hatchlings on the ground, where they soaked up the warmth of the fire. "This is like Jur-Jurom!" Rikard said with a smile as he snuggled beside his mother. Even Kylar drew closer with his sister to hear the story. If this didn't work, she might have to resort to casting a simple spell to help them fall asleep.

"Once in a land of many cabins, people walked in the streets to go to a marketplace."

"What is a street?" Kylar asked.

"It's a path used again and again until it grows wider and wider and more and more people follow it." She took in a breath, let it out, and started again thankful for the distraction. It helped take her mind off Ervig. "The people traveled this street to go to a marketplace where they could buy whatever they needed. They could buy fruit, meat, bread, and even toys!"

Rikard looked up at her with wide eyes shining with the glow of the amber embers in the fire pit. "Toys?"

"What kind of toys?" Carn asked as he climbed onto his mother's lap and plugged his thumb into his mouth.

She hugged him and his brother close. "Whatever money could buy."

"Money? What is money?"

"In this land, money was something people used to get the things at the marketplace and to pay people who did work."

"What does it look like? This money? Can you eat it?" Kylar asked as he rocked from one foot to the other lulling Aurora to sleep.

Kaibelle laughed. "No, it is a precious metal made into small round-flat pieces called coins. Some coins are worth more than others. It depends on their size or what metal they are, but a single silver river coin buys enough food for a week. And these small coins are easy to carry in a purse or pocket."

Kylar's brow puckered with thought. "How do the people in this land get these coins? What kind of work do they do?"

"Much the same work we do. Like making pottery. Someone who needs an urn, a bowl, things like that can buy them. There are bread makers, candlestick makers, those who make furniture, cloth, and even clothing."

Kylar glanced down at Aurora and back at his mother. "I would like to live in such a place with roads, coins, and with the work shared among others."

Kaibelle nodded. "It would be nice to live in such a place, but there would be challenges as well."

Just as Kylar was about to ask what kind of challenges, a golden blaze of light lit up the small group, like the noon suns. They stared wide-eyed as warm air gusted and tussled their hair. The light blinked out. Nimbus, Beroan, and Jurom appeared beneath the full moon. Kaibelle's heart caught in her throat as she blinked to erase the ghost of the flash. *Where is Ervig?* To her relief, her husband's silhouette raised from Nimbus' back–near her shoulders. She sprinted over to greet him, but even in the low light, she could see he didn't look well. "What happened? Are you injured?"

He slid down Nimbus' scaled side, his tunic snagging briefly and softening his fall. He hit the ground, and his knees buckled made of softened wax. "I'm not injured. Just sick to my stomach. I feel like I've been on a ship tossed about on the high seas for days."

"Why? What happened to you?" Kaibelle crouched beside him feeling his forehead.

"Midlands." He swallowed hard; dirty grayish energy had overtaken his usual gold tinged with green. He was sick. "I'm never doing that again. I don't care how many days we must travel."

Beroan lumbered over to Kaibelle. *"The Midlands be disorienting to the untrained eye. It's effect befuddling. For humans, who be not Dragonborn, they never be right again."*

Kaibelle wondered, *How do they know this if we are the first Dragonborn?* Her mind worked it out like a puzzle. *Probably knowledge from living in the future*. For now, she helped Ervig to his feet. Her usually strong husband draped his arm around her neck and stumbled toward his gape-mouthed children staring at him in wonder. Kylar tried to hold Aurora close to his chest, his aura a pale yellow as if his father presented danger, but the bright flash had awakened Aurora, and she fussed and struggled against Kylar's grasp. Her aura showed no fear as she leaned to reach out to her father. "Da."

He smiled weakly. "Let me sit, daughter." He collapsed into the long grass. "Phew. I can't tell you how I feel. It's like I left part of myself, behind and I'm waiting for it to catch up."

Aurora wriggled free from Kylar's hold and slipped to the ground giggling as she darted toward her father. Kylar swiped to catch her but grabbed air. Aurora jumped toward her Da. Instead of reaching out, he lay there like a newborn fawn without the strength to stand. It all happened so fast, Kaibelle bent forward to snatch her daughter from the air, but Aurora just dropped and stood in front of Ervig. “Da.” She reached out; her chubby fingers gently touched Ervig’s shoulder. Kaibelle blinked as Aurora’s rainbow energy surged, surrounding Ervig and swallowing his sickly aura and returning it to the familiar gold fringed with green. He instantly sat up straight, grabbed his daughter, and held her at arm’s length staring at her with eyes wide with questions. Just as quickly, he drew her to his chest as she placed her arms around his neck. Their auras mingled for a moment, and things returned to normal.

“What are you all still doing awake?” he asked his sons. “We leave at suns rise, so you better get some sleep.” Kylar stood staring for a moment longer and turned to walk over to where Jurom lay, sat on the ground, and leaned against his dragon friend.

Aurora ran back to Kylar and climbed onto his lap. As he scooped her into his arms, he wondered about the bright light. About how his father and the dragons had appeared out of thin air. He fell asleep dreaming of flying to Five Marks and the new life that lay ahead with streets and many cabins and a marketplace where they bought toys with small pieces of metal called money.

CHAPTER TWENTY-THREE

The following morning Ervig packed up some of his potions, seeds, and dried herbs and placed them in the bag he planned to carry at his side. Hopefully, he could grow a garden of medicinals on one of the floating caves. He stared at the shelves of bottles to be left behind, thankful for the knowledge he'd gained. They loaded small bundles of food and blankets for when the air grew chilly above the clouds. For now, the two youngest hatchlings would ride on Nimbus' back because she was the largest and the stronger of the adults. Kylar mounted Jurom while Kaibelle harnessed Carn and Aurora to Beroan's goldenhorn and then joined them on the flat area between the dragon's muscular shoulders.

"It's too far to travel to Five Marks in one day. So we will stop late this afternoon," Ervig announced. "And tomorrow, we'll finish the journey." He took his place on Nimbus' back, where he joined the hatchlings, Erik, Rikard, and Tomas. He broke up a quarrel between Erik and Tomas as they squabbled over who would sit closest to the goldenhorn. "You can take turns." Tomas nodded and gave up the spot to Erik as they settled in.

Kaibelle marveled that Ervig and the dragons made a two-day journey twice in the amount of time it took for the fire in the fire pit to consume the wood the night before. Later, she would talk with Beroan about traveling the Midlands. For now, she just wanted to take in the view as she said goodbye to the only home her children had known–other than the volcano. Tears pooled in her eyes, but she wiped them away before anyone noticed.

The suns cast elongated shadows across the valley floor as they took to the air. Kaibelle watched their cabin disappear in the distance and shook off the sense of melancholy as she turned to her dragon, Beroan, for companionship.

* * * *

Ervig breathed in the crisp air and let it out slowly. He couldn't shake the sense of guilt nagging him since he returned from Five Marks… or what would be Five Marks. "*Why couldn't I bring myself to tell her about where we'll be living*," he asked Nimbus.

The dragon's laughter lightly clicked from deep in her throat. *"Have ye not told her the place we be going has no cover and the feral myrnex be plenty… and a danger to the younglings."*

"No. I haven't told her anything yet. I was so tired and sick. And she already regretted leaving the valley. I just couldn't give her more difficult news."

Ervig glanced at Kylar riding on Jurom. "*Living in the floating caves, temporarily, won't be any different than riding a dragon, I guess."* He glanced at his sons riding with him. *"It shall be well,"* he to bolster his confidence.

* * * *

As Beroan and Kaibelle talked, he brought up the myrnex and how Jurom had protected Ervig and even saved his life.

"Myrnex?"

"Aye, the feral ground-dwelling creatures–"

"Feral?" Panic filled Kaibelle as she absentmindedly put her hand on Aurora's back. *"You mean like animals that eat humans for food?"*

Silence.

"Beroan? You're taking us to a place where there are animals that eat humans?" she asked again.

"Young One, ye forget that this world be different from the one ye knew. Even from the one I knew, for that matter. It be wild and touched little by thy kind."

"You don't have to remind me. I have not forgotten." For a time, they flew in silence. Kaibelle worked to rein in her apprehension, but

when clicking laughter from deep within Beroan's throat touched her mind, it ignited hot anger. *"What is so funny?"*

"Ervig and Nimbus be talking of the floating caves."

The levity in his tone helped calm her. Logically, she knew she was probably overreacting because Ervig would never purposely put his family in danger. *"Floating caves? Why didn't Ervig tell me any of this?"* Just as she began to feel anger rise again, worry clouded her thinking. *Perhaps traveling through the Midlands damaged his mind after all.*

"They be thy home until ye build thy human roost," Nimbus said.

"Floating... caves?" Kaibelle repeated. *"Like floating on what? The air? The water?"*

"Aye, floating on air. We moved pieces of mountains and placed them above the sea for thy safekeeping."

"Safe? What are you not telling me?"

"There be no place for ye to take cover. Few trees. What trees there be have few branches. The flatlands be near the sea. No place to hide from myrnex and other wild animals."

Kaibelle rubbed her temples. *"I understand. You don't need to say anymore."* She rode in silence as she scanned the flattening landscape. A short time later, she spotted a ribbon of blue on the horizon in the distance. The sea. Then for the first time, she saw gray shadows in the sky.

"Are those the floating caves?"

"Aye. For tonight's roost, but this be not Five Marks."

Kaibelle pointed to the relocated mountaintops. "Carn, see those floating mountains? That's where we will sleep tonight in caves." Her three-year-old took the thumb from his mouth and stood, holding the goldenhorn securing him to the dragon with two hands. His eyes shined with excitement.

"I see. I see."

"Up in the air," she added with a smile she didn't feel. "*Better up in the air than on the ground to be mauled or eaten by wild carnivorous ground dwellers! Thank you for protecting us, Beroan.*"

The earth beneath them flattened, and the vegetation appeared rather scrubby and stunted. The dragons were true. No place to hide here, but she didn't see anything that looked like a predator either. As they crossed the Inkish River, the dragon's shadows drifted over broadleaf groundcover that grew thicker as they drew nearer to the sea. A small group of deer grazed on the shrubs but scattered as the dragons flew over. Kaibelle watched them gracefully gallop toward the river when suddenly the lead deer went down. It struggled for a moment as the rest of the deer scattered in different directions. The downed deer stopped its struggle. *"Is it dead? So quickly? I didn't even see anything."*

"The myrnexes inject venom with their jaws. The deer be paralyzed."

Dread cut through her. Details made it worse. It gave form to her fear. This dangerous creature was the reason for the floating caves. "Carn, sit down." For the first time in a long time, she worried for her children, alarmed for their safety. They would be settling out here in this wild, dangerous world. And once the temple was built, the dragons would retreat to the mountains. *And we'll be on our own.*

She let out a deep breath. *Why didn't Ervig tell me about this?* She stopped herself. Ervig had been so sick after visiting the Midlands. She'd never seen him so weak. So sick. Her eyes drifted over to him and found him looking at her with the same concern she felt.

CHAPTER TWENTY-FOUR

The floating caves loomed closer. Kaibelle marveled at the sight. "They are mountains! How are these things staying in the air?"

"It be dragon magic."

"How long can they stay up there like that?"

"They be up there until dragon magic brings them down."

"Brings them down," she muttered to herself. She thanked the stars that the dragons were her friends, but what would happen in this time–this future they were creating. Once the dragons moved back to the islands, how would life be?

As they drew nearer, the immense size of the floating caves stunned Kaibelle. They even dwarfed Beroan as his wings backstroked to slow his approach. Kaibelle leaned in and wrapped her children in her arms as her hands held fast to the goldenhorn. Beroan's cranial ridge missed the edge of the cave entrance by inches. For a brief moment, she thought about the smaller size of the Thornose dragons and how this would be easier for them. She often wondered why the Thornose weren't the ones who carried them here since the ancient dragon language belonged to them, the prophecies belonged to them, and they were guardians of the Labyrinth. It doesn't make sense. She pushed the thoughts to the back of her mind as they entered the cave. Not really a cave, she thought. It's a cavern. She turned to see the rest of her family on Nimbus' back and wondered how the larger of the two dragons would navigate the opening.

As they landed, Kaibelle lurched forward. Her stomach dropped, and fear of the floating cave dropping into the sea with the extra weight shot through her. She squeezed her eyes shut and clasped the goldenhorn tight as she encircled her children with her arms.

"These are the floating caves?" Carn asked.

She opened one eye and then the other and looked around. "Yes." She did her best to sound positive as she sat up straight and rubbed her arms. "It's cold in here."

"It be from high in the mountains. There be snow atop it when we first moved it."

Kaibelle dug out a sweater for each of the children. She slipped Aurora's arms into her sweater before untethering her and wrapped her in the sling across her back. How am I going to make sure my little free spirit doesn't fall into the sea below?

Carn leaned into his mother's leg with his teeth chattering. "This is like an i-ice c-c-cave." His lavender aura brightened.

She leaned forward and hugged him close to warm him. "My little daydreamer." It always amazed her how different her children were.

With Aurora wrapped across her back, she carried Carn in her arms and climbed to the floor of the expansive cavern. Once she dismounted, Beroan tipped his head back and shot flames overhead, heating the rock ceiling. "Come, Little One, climb higher and warm thyselves. Make room for Nimbus and the others."

She didn't argue but clambered up the slope nearer to the heat as the other dragons hovered outside. Her muscles burned under the weight of carrying two children up the angled incline. When she reached a flat outcropping, she sat to catch her breath and watched Jurom and Nimbus land. As her family dismounted, she called Ervig to come and collect Carn. Together, they found their way back to the floor of the cave. The family and hatchlings settled in the heated floating cave as Beroan and Nimbus took off to hunt. Soon they returned with a couple of deer, quickly disemboweled them, and cooked them for human consumption. Kaibelle's stomach rumbled at the delicious aroma as Ervig sliced off portions for each of the children with his dagger.

Kaibelle stepped up to get hers and elbowed her husband. "Floating caves? Animals that will eat us, and you don't say anything?"

"I didn't know what to say. I didn't want to frighten you."

The hatchlings swarmed the second uncooked carcass, and Nimbus flew out to get another deer for her and Beroan because the flight had left them depleted. As they ate, Ervig laid down rules for the children. “Don’t go near the cave opening because a gust of wind could come and snatch you.” Carn’s face showed he understood for the moment. But Ervig knew, if he started running after his sister or brothers, he’d forget. And Aurora needed constant monitoring.

Once they finished eating, the children and two younger hatchlings climbed and explored as they burned off some of their unspent energy except for Jurom and Aurora. The young dragon lay on the floor recovering from his first long flight. With a full belly, he quickly fell asleep as Aurora snuggled beside his head which was already the size of four men.

Kaibelle and Ervig sat side-by-side on a short outcropping a few feet off the floor, using it for a bench. Nimbus lay on her side with her head raised eye to eye with the humans. Kaibelle brought up the urn she’d made for Aurora. She’d given it much thought and still wondered about the symbols that had appeared on their own. “I made it for Aurora as a keepsake. When the symbols appeared, I didn’t know what to think. So what does it mean? What do we do with it now?”

Nimbus blinked, and Kaibelle could see the Mosaic eye lens at the center of her eyes deflect the low light. “The marks on the jar be prophetic and carry with them a message for the future. It be for thy daughter, for she shall be the priestess in the temple at Five Marks and the keeper of the jar. She be not only dragon-touched as thy child but Dragonborn of the Thornose through thee.”

“You mean she—what? Inherited being Dragonborn?” Kaibelle glanced at Ervig, whose eyes showed worry.

“Aye, and there be more. For she be the first Dragonborn through a Goldenhorn–mine Jurom.” She gazed at her sleeping son. “When the time be right, the jar’s magic will take it to the hands it needs to reach. For two orphans shall usher in a secret bond in marriage, and their offspring shall bring forth the deliverance of humankind. Until that time, thy Aurora shall be keeper of the jar of Five Marks and caretaker of the ancient Scroll of Prophecy.”

Kaibelle let out a long sigh and leaned against Ervig. "Such tellings make me happy and sad. Happy because we'll make a difference in the future and stop the evil that took my parents, but sad, for our Aurora. She had no choice about becoming a Dragonborn. She doesn't even know right from wrong!"

Beroan snorted. "She knows. Her abilities far outrank her tender age."

Kaibelle glanced at her daughter shrouded in the rainbow energy–the same aura that had melded with the young Jurom. The same force she'd witnessed with the healing of her husband following his time in the Midlands. Her young toddler did seem to understand things beyond what her age would allow.

The pupils of Nimbus' green eyes grew big and round. "Before we agreed to come to this time, we faced dreadful evil. Each of us agreed to come to this time in hopes of defeating that evil. And in doing so, to dispose of the Book Darkmore. Many summers be passed, but we must not forget why we be here. And we cannot forget that our offspring be part of the solution."

Ervig hugged Kaibelle against his shoulder. "She's right. I would love to have just stayed in the valley and lived out the rest of our lives in peace. But what future would that be for our children? Isolated and not knowing any other humans. And then what? Would the future change, or would our offspring face the same evil because they lived a life secluded from the world we are trying to protect?"

Kaibelle realized for the first time that all this pulled the dragons' offspring into this fight, too. She offered a half-hearted nod. "You're right." Nervous energy coursed through her as she wrestled with her emotions. She stood and brushed the dirt from the seat of her trousers. "Children, it's time to sleep. We will be leaving early again tomorrow."

Groans of disappointment echoed in the cavern. "Do we have to?" Rikard asked.

She laughed. "Yes. And when we get to Five Marks, you'll have more floating caves to explore."

They cheered the news as they climbed back to the floor of the cavern where Kaibelle laid out a couple of blankets. Kylar sat on one of the blankets and smiled at his mother. "The faster I fall asleep. The quicker morning will come. And the sooner we'll get to see our new home in the floating caves."

His brothers piled on top of him, which woke Aurora. She stood with a giggle and ran as fast as her feet would carry to jump into the mix. They laughed and tussled, but Kylar helped get everyone settled. Kaibelle bent to kiss each of them on the forehead and rub chins with them. As she kissed Kylar, he said, "Can I ask one thing?"

"Sure."

"Why is the place we're going named Five Marks?"

"Good question." Her mind raced to find a reasonable answer.

Ervig stepped up behind her and said, "It's because of my five sons." He wrapped his arms around Kaibelle from behind and smiled over her shoulder. "Each will leave their mark on this world."

Kylar smiled a toothy grin they didn't see often. In another eight years, he would be the age Ervig was when he joined the guard. When I fought the Red Knave…. When I became Dragonborn and agreed to come to this time to defeat this foe.

"Get some sleep," Kaibelle said in the sternest tone she could muster.

Together, she and Ervig walked back toward Nimbus and Beroan. If I hadn't come here, I wouldn't have met Ervig and would never have had these very children. She slipped her hand into Ervig's, leaned in, and whispered. "Good answer."

He smiled. "I knew that question was coming. It's the best I could come up with."

They sat with their dragon companions and talked into the night about their questions. "Sometimes, I feel like we are fumbling through the dark trying to find our way."

Beroan's clicking laughter drifted lightly. "We be doing exactly that many a time. Nimbus and I know prophecies, but they be Thornose prophecies. We know not always how they be fulfilled."

"So these orphans…. Do you know who they are?"

"Nay, we know not. But the magic of the jar knows. When the marriage takes place, the jar be on its way to them."

"And then what? What are they going to do with the urn?"

"It be their marriage gift, and it grants them the deed to the cabin in the valley."

"The cabin? You mean our cabin?"

"Aye."

The heat of anger colored Kaibelle's face. "Calm down," Ervig said as he rubbed her back. "Think about it. We came. We've had children. Within our family, we both have seen gifts–dragon-touched as our friends here call them. And Aurora…." He paused to gather his thoughts. "Our children are special and bring possibilities to this world that didn't exist in my time. Perhaps the next people will do the same."

Kaibelle studied her fingers in her lap and nodded in resignation. "You're right."

"And you and I are going to make a home in Five Marks. A real home."

All Kaibelle could think of was the ruins known as Five Marks in her own time, but she pushed the thought away. We are making a difference. A new future. "One more thing," she said. "I know that dragons travel through times through a Labyrinth."

"Aye, the Labyrinth of Times."

Ervig nodded. "Yes, I've done that and, if I never do it again, I'd be happy."

"You? You did that? And you traveled through time in the Midlands."

He nodded. "But that's different. In the Midlands, you move through–between time–it lets you travel quickly from one place to another without actually losing time."

"I understand that too, so what about the tears in time? Like the tears that brought us here? I ask because that is one of the five marks on the urn. What does that mean?"

Ervig looked at the dragons. “What does that mean?”

“Dragons, and humans who ride dragons through a tear as we did, be able to move from one time to another undetected by the dragons who guard access through the Labyrinth. Rents within the fabric of time form when the Labyrinth be accessed, illegitimately, by the power of the Book Darkmore. A dragon’s ability to see these tears be the first qualification for being chosen to travel to other times because these gashes in time pose a threat.

“Some tears move forward in time, some travel back. Until these tears in time opened in our skies, the only way to reach these other times be the Labyrinth. If these tears be visible from the other side, an enemy could slip through, and we be unaware. We cannot run from this problem, for if the spirit of the book be unchecked, the magic of the book could rule across all time and wipe out the dragon races and more. We decided it be best to take our stand here, in the past, to create a shift in the balance of power. For the prophecies say one be coming who will join with us. A human, like none other. She be the salvation of the dragon race–she be thy future kin. The Variel.”

The one mark on the urn they could not explain was the human female with the Thornose head. Between the four of them, they discussed their thoughts. Ervig talked about spells that changed people into animal forms.

Kaibelle wrinkled her nose. "Why would anyone do such a thing?"

Ervig almost let his experience as a rat slip but decided against it. The two of them had agreed not to discuss their lives, before the valley, for fear they would accidentally break their dragon’s oath. And now that they would be allowed to share their Dragonborn experience once they arrived at Five Marks, he wasn’t sure he could bring himself to tell her.

Kaibelle didn’t notice his hesitation as her thoughts drifted to Aurora and her rainbow aura. Could she be the one? This salvation of which the dragons talked? Her aura had changed in that exchange with Jurom, from a simple pink edged in orange, which showed her to be a sensitive, loving creature but confident and creative, to a rainbow aura that sent mixed meanings. But the head on the figure on the urn was a Thornose–not a Goldenhorn. She pushed the thoughts from her mind.

All this guessing could drive me to distraction, and if there's one thing I need to be at this time, it's focused.

"…the risk of time shifts," Nimbus' voice filtered into her thoughts, and suddenly Kaibelle realized she hadn't been paying attention. She would ask Ervig about what she had missed later. Right now, she needed sleep.

That night, the dragons lay in front of the cave opening as a safety measure, so a child couldn't accidentally topple out if they woke earlier than the rest. When Kaibelle opened her eyes, she found Aurora and Kylar leaning against Beroan, sound asleep.

"Good morning, Little One."

"Good morning Beroan. Where's Nimbus?"

"She be fetching breakfast."

CHAPTER TWENTY-FIVE

The band of dragons and humans took to the air with full stomachs and high expectations. They headed toward the brightening horizon as the suns peeked above the line where the sea met the sky. Low hanging layers of clouds blushed with peach pastels and transformed to a bright rose, while the opposite horizon dimmed to a lavender hue. Ervig held on to details like this as his anchor in such uncertain times. The suns always came up in the east and set in the west.

He held on to Kaibelle's love in the same way, but beyond those two things, he had no assurance of what to expect in this new setting–this, Five Marks. Knowing Aurora would grow to become the priestess in the temple they were about to build left him apprehensive. And what of the rest of his children? He hadn't seen them in the future vision Nimbus shared with him. With the vicious myrnex, would they even survive? And what of the other people Nimbus said would join them? Who would dare come together with them and build the village with such dangers? Then it dawned on him. *The temple ruins were all that remained of Five Marks. That could be because there never was a village, not in the sense I expected.*

"Nimbus, can it be the village of Five Marks lives in the floating caves?"

"We know not the future, for thy mate and younglings and mine mate and offspring bring change."

This leg of the trip didn't take as long as the day before. The floating caves at Five Marks displayed like dark specks in the sunny sky, about the time his stomach reminded him it was past time for their midday meal. The magic-Dragonborn part of him longed to take on falcon form and race ahead to ensure all was safe for his family. Luckily, the Thornose race had excellent far vision, and because of the Thornose magic bestowed upon him, he could see details sooner than the average person. For a moment, he thought of his trip through the Midlands and the faint rings of color. *If I were Dragonborn through the Goldenhorn, I wonder if I'd be able to see the bridges between time more clearly.*

As they drew closer, he waved his hand over his sleeping boys. He'd used magic to cause them to sleep to stop Erik's complaints about Kylar riding Jurom again and how it wasn't fair. The boys opened their eyes groggily. "Are we there yet?" Rikard asked as he wiped the sleep from his eyes and sat up.

"Almost." Ervig pointed ahead. "Can you see the floating caves?"

Rikard stood, holding the golden horn to help keep his balance. "I see them. I think they are even bigger than the ones we stayed in last night!" He started to jump up and down with excitement. Ervig grabbed his upper arm. "Rikard, be careful. Just because you are bound to Nimbus, don't risk falling to test the strength of the cord."

The boy stopped, stared wide-eyed at his father, and then at their shadow as it raced across the shoreline below. He glanced back at his Da, looked at his brother, who just shook his head, and collapsed to a sitting position without protest. Rikard tended to be an excitable sort but, with time, could be encouraged to think things through. Ervig's concern was for his eldest boy, Kylar. He was a good boy, helpful, and obedient, but if Ervig had to guess, his firstborn was, what Nimbus called, dragon-touched. His memory for detail was beyond usual. His mind recorded everything it saw and recalled it nonchalantly down to the minutest point. The map he drew of the way to Jur-Jurom was the most recent example.

Ervig's mind drifted from the map to the cabin where they left it. In his heart, he hoped that his family's time in Five Marks would be as fulfilling. So much had happened in the years since he'd come to this time. He glanced back at his wife riding Beroan with Aurora and Carn. The children were sleeping. Even though they never discussed the use of magic, in his heart, he knew she had used magic in the same way he did to keep the children safe.

He turned to face the floating caves. As they loomed closer, the size stunned him. *These are mountains, not just caves.* A light pine scent wafted on the breeze from dark-green pines growing on the slopes of the detached mountaintops. He breathed deeply as thoughts of his childhood home stirred. In some ways, this would be more like home than the valley. He chuckled to himself. As they passed the first mountaintop, the size still amazed him. *We will be able to grow food without living on the ground–until we must.*

As they passed the first mountaintop, he studied the ground looking for any sign of the myrnexes. His first order of business would be to clear the area of those dangerous beasts, but how? That he hadn't figured out since he couldn't use his magic to take a life. Any life. *Kai and the children will have to stay on these restless mountains until I decide what to do*. He'd discuss it with Nimbus, but this might require his ability to change into an animal that could take on this foe. But what? A dragon? *Could I use dragon fire, or would that be against the rules of magic?*

Inwardly, he laughed but caught himself. The image of the female form with the dragon head flashed into his mind. She could represent someone like himself, able to become a dragon or any animal they'd seen. The question that remained unanswered was who the woman was. In his heart, he feared it could be Aurora. He'd felt her healing energy after his Midlands' sickness. It was her touch that brought the five marks into the clay of the jar. "My little treasure," he said under his breath as tears stung his eyes.

Nimbus touched his mind. *"Be not sorrowful, Little One. Thy daughter be the priestess of the temple."*

Her words caught him off guard. Anger heated his cold cheeks. *"I wasn't talking to you, Nimbus."*

"Thy thoughts be so strong, like ye be shouting, and I can't help but overhear."

He didn't respond. She was right. This move hit him harder than leaving his own time. Then, he had been motivated not only to catch the Red Knave but to become a man again. Now, his emotions bubbled up to the point he felt like a dormant volcano ready to surprise everyone by spewing.

Nimbus broke in on his self-pity. *"This be the largest cave."* She circled it while Beroan glided through the opening, followed by Jurom and the other two young dragons. As Nimbus hovered at the entrance, a sense of safety washed over Ervig. A vision flashed within his mind. It showed him a glimpse of the future with this as a village in the air.

Nimbus carried him into the shadows of the cave as Kaibelle handed Aurora to Kylar before climbing from Beroan's shank. He untethered his sons, thankful to be able to stand. The boys ran around, happy to explore. The karst cave offered several small openings to explore. "Be careful!" Kaibelle called.

Kylar carried Aurora on his back. Her legs hooked through the crooks of his arms, and her arms clamped around his neck. "Not so tight," he said as he climbed a naturally forming ridge to an opening higher in the wall.

Ervig walked over to Kaibelle and hugged her. "We're here." A smile tugged at one side of his mouth. "Our new home." She could tell by the way his aura vacillated from pale yellow to bright yellow. *He is full of positive excitement and new ideas but struggling with the fear of losing control.* She felt much the same way.

"So we've become cave dwellers!" she said with a smile. "We have to figure out how to build shelves, our beds… I'm glad we brought what furniture we did." For a moment, she thought perhaps they could use magic to create replicas of things they left behind, but what would the children think?

Beroan walked up behind her and nudged her with his snout. *"This be why we be here–to help. We be able to gather what ye need to make thy new home."*

CHAPTER TWENTY-SIX

Nimbus carried Ervig to a clearing among the dense ground vegetation a good three or four thousand rods from the water. Thick rope-like vines made it tough to get around. He hacked them up to clear the patch of ground around him. As he worked, Beroan and his mate delivered materials. Ervig wondered where they were getting milled wood but chose not to ask. If they were slipping back to the future, he didn't want to know about it.

Ervig lined up the boards and rungs. Before using magic, he glanced up at the Restless Mountains with his enhanced vision to make sure his children weren't watching. *No sign of them.* Kaibelle was doing her part, keeping the children busy inside the home cave. He lined up the top corner of the ladder-like structure with the foundation leg and did the same with the other side. He counted the graduated rungs and, with a flip of the wrist, said, "Tabula ad navem." The rungs lined up and connected the boards with the top of the piece about as wide as two adults standing side by side. He fashioned all four sides with identical dimensions and trussed them side to side. It reminded him of when they had built the turret on the prison. *If I had to do this without magic or the help of the dragons, it would never happen.* For now, he wondered how he'd explain this to Kylar.

Nimbus grabbed the top of the tower. With two thrusts of her wings, she raised it into the air. Ervig sunk the bottom three rods of the legs into the ground, securing the foundation with his magic. He stood looking at the tower as he used his sleeve to blot sweat from his forehead. *Standing like that, it's nothing more than a four-sided ladder, that's what–*He shielded his eyes from the suns trying to measure it *…50 reeds tall?* "How is this going to be a temple big enough for us to live in?" he asked Nimbus.

"This be the core around which ye shall build the temple. Let me show thee."

Ervig walked over to Nimbus and placed his hand against the ridge of her brow, her smoky scent familiar and reassuring. The ladder-like tower stood before his mind's eye. Around it, a structure took form. Wide at the base and growing narrower with a flat platform at the very top. Rooms adjacent to the tower were all the same size, except for one side where a single massive hall took up four floors with smaller rooms at one end. On the outer edge of the structure, large rooms edged the first floor. Rooms grew smaller in size, with each floor working toward the top. On the outside of the building, staircases climbed the center of each side, linking floors with arched entries. *The inner-most rooms are only accessible through the central tower–the core.* When the vision ended, Ervig understood his mission to completion but still wished he could know the outcome. *How does any of this eliminate the quest to stop the Red Knave?*

He stood back and stared at the skeletal frame thinking of ways his children could help even as he used his dragon magic to make the work go faster.

A rustling in the foliage startled him. He caught a glimpse of a rabbit and relaxed. In the blink of an eye, the ground rumbled beneath his feet. Without thinking, he scrambled up the rungs of the tower. His heart slammed as he stared down at the rabbit as a myrnex depression sucked up vines and other brush around it. A depression of cascading pebbles turned into a growing hollow. The rabbit jumped free of the funneling slide and dashed into the underbrush. The ground belched the stench of rotting flesh as two long mandibles lined with long thorn-like teeth reached up to grab its prey that wasn't there. It reminded Ervig of the death and decay he had smelled in the dungeon as a rat. He raced up the tower another ten rods. *It wasn't after the rabbit. It wants me!* A wide-opened mouth with unhinged jaws broke through the surface. Its flat spindle-shaped body tried to rise to reach him, but its short insectoid legs weren't capable.

The rush of dragon's wings gusted around him, followed by the heat of dragon breath as flames shot past him and engulfed the monster. It screeched and tried to escape to its underground den without success. When the blaze stopped, a smoldering carcass lay within its trap.

Ervig clung to the rungs with a white-knuckle grip, his breath shallow and quick. *There is no way my children will be helping with any of this until we eliminate this threat.*

Nimbus tried to comfort Ervig. *"Be at peace, Little One."*

The dragon's words upset him. *"You're telling me to be at peace! After what just happened?"*

Nimbus reminded him that *"All things serve a purpose. Even the myrnexes."*

With his heart still pounding, Ervig questioned this. *"How am I supposed to be at peace knowing my children are in danger from these monsters?"*

"What do ye remember of the Five Marks of thy own time?"

"Nothing is left of it other than the temple. No one goes there. So why is this temple so important that I have to risk my family's safety?"

"Come, place thy hand upon mine goldenhorn."

Ervig climbed to the dragon's back and grabbed hold of the goldenhorn. Visions of the finished temple formed. *"Within these, the walls of the Temple at Five Marks, be many secrets."* They stood within the great hall. High windows large enough for a dragon to fly through flooded the hall with light. A large archway at the far end behind the dais flickered into existence. "*This be not visible without the aid of dragon magic. It holds a portal, like a hole in the floor, to another world where time be moving quickly for ye. Those who travel there be old before their time. It be here, for it be the portal through which one day the savior of the land arrives*."

Ervig wanted to ask questions, but the scene changed. He stood, within the core, clinging to one of many ladders lining the walls. Blue lines of light diagrammed booby traps within the core. *"These traps be designed to carry intruders into the Midlands."*

"Intruders?" Ervig's mouth felt dry.

"Be not concerned, Little One. The traps serve many purposes. Mostly they protect the shadowalkers."

The scene changed again. Ervig stood before an obelisk that glowed with energy. Other than that, he could see nothing but darkness. “Shadowalkers? What—what are shadowalkers?” He cast a nervous glance to his right and left, expecting to see shadowy figures stalking toward him.

“There be only two shadowalkers. They travel back and forward in time, bringing Dragonborn to their reward. Ye will recognize them when the time comes to understand.”

The visions ended, and Ervig blinked against the sunlight. *“This still doesn’t answer why I should be at peace knowing my children are in danger from these myrnexes?”*

“They be protection. Humans be not willing to live among them. The secrets of the temple be safe.”

Ervig still didn’t like it, but he understood it. He climbed the rope ladder back to the cave, equipped with a better understanding of his goal, and life in the floating caves became routine. The children thrived, and Kaibelle and Ervig grew closer now that they could share Dragonborn secrets.

CHAPTER TWENTY-SEVEN

Aurora fussed with the harness strap cutting into her shoulder. *It's time for Da to make a bigger harness.* She sat on an outcropping halfway up the eastern side of the floating mountain in which she and her family had lived until the temple's inner chambers were complete. Part of her missed sleeping in the caves. She stared down at the temple. While she enjoyed having a bedchamber of her own, she missed sleeping against Jurom. Longed for his smoky smell and the sound of his heart. When she wasn't sleeping, she felt claustrophobic. Her room was the smallest because she didn't share like Erik and Rikard or Tomas and Carn. And truthfully, Kylar's sleeping chamber situated across the core from hers was just as small as hers. *It's those booby traps. I know they are supposed to keep us safe, but what if I trigger one of them just going to visit Kylar in his room? And safe from what?* She always came back to that question. *Why can't I see the answer? Those traps hold me back more than this harness.* She hugged her knees to her chest. *I miss living up here where I can move about freely.*

The suns cast shadows across the left side of the temple as they warmed the northeastern slope where she sat. Now, as others joined them at Five Marks, she felt more alone than ever. She climbed up here to try and cheer herself. Memories flooded her young mind as she looked down at the temple. For its size, it had gone up quickly, but the finishing touches were still ongoing. Her favorite memory was when her Da guided the dragons as they carried the massive blocks of sandstone. Gradually the pyramid-shaped temple took form while Da helped his family learn to live within the Restless Mountains.

At least we only sleep in the temple. Up here was real life. Here they cooked and ate their meals, did laundry, cared for livestock, and gathered to sing and listen to the stories. Here, she was free to roam and explore. *But up here, I have to deal with the others.* It was hard for her mingling with the others who had found their way to Five

Marks even though they lived in caves of their own. Many of the older people didn't want the children near her because of Jurom. *I'd rather spend time with him anyway.*

But she couldn't help but think of the others. Some families had three generations living on one mountain. *I wonder what it would be like to have grandparents, aunts and uncles, and cousins. So many people.* In her own family, she was closest to Kylar, but his friendship with that newcomer was changing things. She pushed the thought away. It made her sad. She climbed higher as if she could escape thinking of that girl. *I can't bear to accept it. Sometimes I feel like I'm a square peg pounded to fit into a round hole. If I didn't have Jurom, I think I might go mad.*

Da and Mother often talked of their surprise that others were drawn here as news of the floating mountains spread to people who lived in the land even after they learned of the threat of the myrnexes. Most stayed because of the sea, the balmy weather and, even though they feared the dragons, they liked watching them.

Da fashioned harnesses made of strong goat hair cords for all the children living in the caves of Five Marks and required them to wear them any time they left the cave proper. Even her oldest brothers, who were now young men, were still required to wear long ropes made of leather which tethered them to metal rings pounded into the rim of every cave opening. Aurora marveled at all her Da and Mother knew and often asked questions, but her questions regularly led to more questions she decided to leave unasked. For instance, she had asked, "Where did the metal rings come from?"

"We had them when we lived in the valley," her brother Kylar had told her. But she saw, from his aura, that he didn't believe his own words. *He doesn't know about the magic. And I won't be the one to tell him.* She often wondered why the magic her parents wielded was a guarded secret–and why she could see it and others couldn't—a mystery she planned to solve. *Why do I know and see such things when no one else can? And why can't I see more when it comes to those booby traps?*

As she sat soaking in the warm sunlight, a cloud of sadness hung over her. Knowing secret matters about future things had an emotional impact on the seven-year-old. But when she didn't know them, and something happened that she didn't expect, it hit her even harder, like earlier when she had found her two youngest brothers in tears. It startled her not to know what was wrong. The two were inseparable and often whispered to one another as if they lived in a private world. Carn, who was just a year older than her, looked up at her as he wiped his nose on his sleeve and shook his head. Tomas let out a shuddered breath and said, "You know… about Kylar leaving. And Rikard."

Their words didn't surprise her. They often knew about events before they happened, much like her but not to the same extent. What troubled her was that she hadn't foreseen it in that way, and neither had they. The news hurt. As she tried to comfort them, she wondered if they knew their destiny to live in the Nalhdyn Mountains in Nalhdyn Hold. *As the youngest boys, they will be the last to leave.*

At this moment, she grieved the thought of losing Kylar. He wouldn't be with them much longer because of the young woman he met at the river while on a *foraging trip.* That's what Da called it anyway. She knew he was mapping the land for future settlement.

As much as she loved Kylar, he was responsible for bringing many others here. Like the young woman's family that he talked into coming to Five Marks. *Even with others joining our village here, it won't last.* In her mind's eyes, she saw it. And Carn and Tomas had confirmed it. She stared down at the temple. *Once it's finished, my family will leave. One at a time.* A tear rolled down her cheek, and she wiped it away. Eventually, all her family–all the newcomers–would be gone. Even Mother and Da. The temple below blurred through her tears. *And I'll be here alone.* She broke into full sobs. A sound from above caught her by surprise. She sat up and swiped her face with the edge of her tunic as she scanned the area overhead. A shaggy split-hoof sheep balanced on a boulder covered with flowering woodbine. The ram munched on the sprouts without giving a thought to her bout of misery.

The shaggy sheep lived on more than one of the floating mountaintops, and now many of the families kept small flocks in the upper chambers of their family dwellings along with goats for fresh milk, cheese, and wool. Up here, they also collected wild grain they called ulgar, which grew on the southern slopes. The ulgar beans could be ground into yellow flour or boiled to make a thick porridge. When they were fortunate enough to find cloudberries, the golden-yellow fruit offered a sweet but tart addition to breakfast or a tasty snack.

Aurora spent much of her time split between helping her mother forage, churning butter, or spinning wool. In her free time, her parents allowed her to ride Jurom, despite the protest of her three youngest brothers, especially Erik, who thought it unfair that she should have a dragon. *But, Jurom chose me.* Riding him was her favorite pastime. It taught her all kinds of new things. He'd even shown her the place the dragons selected to go to die in the future, just on the other side of the eastern mountains where the river ran into the sea at Pren Bay. It was when she flew west that she learned about Kylar and the young woman at the river. She saw him stroke her hair and lean in to kiss her and how their auras mingled in love. It startled her because her foresight had withheld it from her. She hadn't seen it until she came face to face with it. That day she turned Jurom around and went straight back to the cave.

Erik's raised voice broke into her thoughts from the cave below where Mother scrubbed the laundry in the tub of heated water with soft soap made from ash lye and animal fat. "You always favor her," Erik roared as if shouting for the world to hear.

* * * *

"It isn't me, or your Da, who favors your sister." Kaibelle measured her tone as she looked up from her scrub board to her hot-headed son. She reached with her wet fingers and brushed a strand of hair from her eyes. "Dragons decide for themselves who will ride them. Jurom and your sister grew up together. It's something that just happened."

"But you and Da ride–and Kylar, he sometimes rides Jurom. And I grew up with the dragons."

"Erik, stop fussing. Your Da and I won't be riding much longer. Others live among us now. The dragons will return to their home in the volcano once we finish the temple."

He stared at her with wide blue eyes. "Don't say that. I hate to think it. They can't leave us. How will we get food?"

"Now that much of the work on the temple is complete, your Da has plans to start training all of you boys to hunt, just like the other families living here do. He says you are rather good with the bow already."

Erik walked over to the entrance and stared down at the temple. The muscles in his jaw tightened.

* * * *

From the outside, the temple looked complete. Steps ran along the center of all four outer walls and mounted to a platform at the top. The exterior of the building was in place, but Erik and his brothers were still in the process of covering it in stucco made with sand, lime, crushed volcanic rock, and water mixed with bright red, yellow, green, and blue. His work was the red at the base. As second oldest and capable with a bow, his assignment was for the most sizeable and dangerous section closest to the myrnexes. His three younger brothers had the top tiers, with Carn having the smallest blue part near the top because he was the youngest of the boys.

Not fair. I have the most dangerous task. It couldn't be clearer that Da and Mother see me as the most expendable. And precious Kylar doesn't have to do any of the dangerous work. It irked him that Kylar didn't have to toil under the heat of the two suns. "Artistic talents," he muttered to himself. He cast a glance toward his mother, whose frown made it clear he best keep his troubles to himself.

Da had asked Kylar to use his artistic talents to decorate the interior walls with murals of life in the valley, life with dragons, even life at the dormant volcano, and living above ground in the floating caves. But he spent an awful lot of time in his private bedchamber joining glyphs and bits of the ancient dragon language. *Drawings. Stupid drawings!* Jealousy fueled Erik's hot temper as he clipped his harness to his lifeline and climbed down the rope ladder to get back to work. *Kylar always gets the easy tasks—inside where it's cool.* As he descended, his eyes scanned for any sight of his Da. *Probably inside, working on the booby traps with his favored son. If he's even here.*

Kylar was off-site more and more. Not in the temple and not in the floating caves of the Restless Mountains. *Probably, riding Jurom.*

* * * *

Later that evening, Ervig stepped from the ladder at the core into the small inner chamber where his oldest son chiseled glyphs into the sandstone as a decorative border around his most recent mural. He now stood almost a hand taller than Da and sported a full beard a shade darker brown than his red hair. “Kylar, your work is beautiful.”

“Thank you, Da. Did you see the relief on the ceiling in the great hall? I finished it today before I went surveying.”

Ervig stood quietly behind him. Kylar paused with his chisel and hammerstone in his hands with his back to Da. “Is there something more, Da?” He turned to look at his father. He studied his Da’s face. For the first time, he noticed small lines around his eyes. *He looks so weary.*

“How’s the map coming along?” Da asked.

“I still need to fly further along the river to the mountains in the west.” Guilt filled him. He needed to tell his Da about Juel. Her family had come to Five Marks because of him. He had invited her and her family to join them here because he intended to make her his wife.

“That’s fine. I know you’ll get it done.” Ervig rubbed the back of his neck and stared at the floor. “I know you understand that we are putting things into place, which we can’t discuss at this time.” He looked. “At least, not at this time.” He shrugged. “And, for a good reason.”

Kylar’s heartbeat quickened. Da never talked about such things; they just had a connection–an understanding. He nodded and looked back at the half-finished glyph. “I’ve always known that.” He glanced down at the chisel in his hand and back at his father’s reaction with a sideways glance.

A weak smile tugged at the corner of Da’s mouth. “You’re old enough… I have something I’d like you to do, need you to do, but it’s something you can’t tell anyone. Ever.”

Kylar dropped his hands to his side, still grasping his tools. He turned to look his father squarely in the eye. For the first time in his life, he felt free to speak about his knowledge. "I dreamed of this," he said. "It doesn't happen very often. I don't know things like Aurora—"

"You–you dreamed of this? What do you mean?"

"I know you've come to tell me there is a room, not very big. Well, big enough to hold a dragon. It's hidden here in the temple. Within it, there is a portal through which one day the savior of our land will arrive."

Ervig wiped his hand across his eyes and nodded. "That's about right. Do you know what message is to be added to the walls then? In that room?"

Kylar nodded. "I do."

Ervig walked over and hugged his son. "That's good. That's good." He stepped back, still holding his son's shoulders. "This isn't easy for any of us." He swallowed the emotion forming a lump in his throat. "Come with me. I'll show you the way."

CHAPTER TWENTY-EIGHT

Kylar carved high relief glyphs into the gypsum-stucco-faced sandstone walls of the hidden chamber. The time-consuming task filled him with a sense of sadness which clashed with his personal feelings of excitement. While he looked forward to starting a new life, knowing fragments of the future wasn't always an easy thing. The original glyphs he first chiseled when he began this project told the story of how they came here and of the building of Five Marks Temple. The artwork started as a border depicting the broadleaf vines, which covered much of the ground. Then he added a warning about the myrnexes to anyone who ever found refuge in this place.

His thoughts drifted to how he and his brothers named the plant 'ink ivy,' when the sticky liquid inside the leaves turned their fingers green which quickly turned black if they didn't wash it off. And if it was allowed to dry, it worked as a strong glue unless cooked. It was the first plant they learned they could eat after moving from the valley. It didn't take long to learn the more mature leaves tended to be fibrous and hard to chew. When picked young and tender, the leaves were delicious and could even be eaten raw or added to soups and stews. Saliva diluted the plant's juice eliminating the stickiness, but eating them raw left their lips looking like a dead man's if you didn't wash up immediately after eating them. He chuckled as he remembered he and his brothers pretending to be sick as a prank and startling their mother with their black lips. While she didn't think it funny at the time, today, she often told the story to others who had joined their village over the years.

A lot had changed since then. They all had once been so close, and now Erik treated him almost like a stranger–an angry stranger. And Carn and Tomas stared at him like they were waiting for something to happen. He blamed part of it on being so secluded from everyone. Before his Da had assigned him to decorate the secret chamber with messages for the future, the early stages of decorating the public temple chambers included artwork depicting the dragon family with which he'd grown up. It was fun reminiscing, but it left him feeling a bit melancholy. The dragons had moved on. Though Jurom still visited occasionally to take him on his surveying trips or his sister into the skies to who knew where. The thrill of his first flight was something he'd never forget. Not that he ever forgot anything.

Gradually, his pictographs here in the secret chamber between the great hall and the core had evolved to show the history he'd lived through in his lifetime, and the glyph borders spelled out specific historical details. As he turned back to the wall with his chisel and hammerstone, he wondered about the eyes that would see his work in the future. *What will they find here*?

He raised the hammerstone to strike the chisel, but before it rang out, the sound of soft footfalls startled him from his reverie. He spun around to see his young sister, Aurora, walk into the hidden chamber as if it were something she did daily. She stood staring at his handiwork as he fought to figure out what to say here within the room no one was supposed to know existed.

She turned to look at him with her mesmerizing green eyes flashing multiple colors for just a moment. He'd witnessed this before but rarely. "Tell me the story of when I was born." She smiled, showing off the gap left by her two top missing teeth.

What do I do now? he wondered. For a moment, he picked up the paintbrush he'd fashioned from finely frayed sticks bound together but changed his mind. He set it down and picked up the chalk rock he used to sketch his initial ideas before applying chisel, ink, or color. His eyes fell back on his sister. They were specially connected, and they both knew it. "I'm sure you could tell it to me by memory."

She giggled. "Tell me anyway. I miss you. We're always working!" He carried the chalkstone over to the south wall, which hadn't been layered with stucco yet. *She is right. We are working all the time.* He stood before the blank wall, unsure of what was supposed to go there. It would come to him, but for now, it would be the sketch of his sister's life. He could use a diversion.

As the words spilled from his lips, he sketched out basic chalk images as he talked. The rudimentary forms shaped the story. He'd done this in other rooms, but here in the secret chamber–it raised questions in his mind. For now, he went on with the story. He would cover the simple images with stucco later.

He told the story of her birth in the alcove, within the dormant volcano, life playing with the young dragons, making things from the white clay from the lake, and her mother making the jar for her as a baby.

Aurora walked over to the urn situated in a small niche and rested her hand on the shelf. "You know I'm going to be the priestess here in this temple." She glanced at him over her shoulder.

He paused and nodded but looked away. He didn't like thinking about her living alone in this temple, day after day, while she waited for the urn to pass into another's hands.

She walked over and placed her sun-kissed hand on his arm. "I know you'll be tying the knot with that girl who used to live down the river. What's her name? Juel?"

He nodded again. Aurora always knew things she shouldn't. He hadn't even told Mother or Da yet. *Much like me. But she knows the future rather than the past.* He knew bits of the things to come. Things revealed to him but here and there but nothing like Aurora. He'd given up trying to hide anything from her. "Yes, I do plan to make Juel my wife, and when we finish with the temple, she and I are going to move up the river where the farming will be more like how it was in the valley. You know I brought some seeds with me from the lost valley and, with the dragons' help, I planted fruit and nut trees downriver shortly after we arrived here. Now they bear fruit. So when I move there, you'll have to come to see us. And we'll be able to bring you things like apples. Do you remember apples?"

Her eyes flashed with amber energy. "I do remember. Golden apples, red apples, and green apples."

Whenever he saw that flash of ochre light, he wondered what it meant, but he never mentioned it. He feared people would think his sister strange or different. He'd had a hard enough time with being different himself. As more people joined their community, his memory was more a curse than a good thing. Enough so that he no longer let on that he remembered details–every detail. Instead, he kept most information to himself and learned to mimic the behavior of everyone else. He even pretended to forget a name or that he'd heard a story before.

"Now that Juel's family is here, too, we'll be back regularly to visit and trade, and you can always come to see me."

"I'm not sure how much I'll be able to do that."

"Why?"

"I'm an oracle, Kylar. Zaylan's oracle. Why I know that when I'm barely old enough to climb the ladder to the caves on my own, I don't understand." She shrugged and let out a sigh. "I do know that I am here to watch over the urn Mother made for me." She pointed to it and let her hand drop. "Don't ask me why. I just know I am. It's like it is part of who I am, like asking me why my eyes are green when no one else in the family has green eyes. I haven't seen anyone else with green eyes in all the people now living among the Restless Mountains."

Aurora stopped short of telling her brother about her visions of everyone leaving Five Marks. She knew it would break his heart to think of her alone here for ages. She didn't much like the idea herself.

He let his arm drop to his side, the chalk rock still in his hand, fingers white with chalk dust as he turned toward her. "I'm going to miss these times."

She smiled. "I know, but with your memory, you can remember all the times we've had and relive them over and over."

He laughed. "That I can." His face grew serious. She was the only one he ever talked to about his exceptional memory. "So what does it all mean, Aurora?"

She shrugged. "I don't know. I'm only seven summers old. Mother says when I'm 18 summers, I will understand." She paused. Her face grew serious. "That tells me that Mother and Da understand things they don't talk about in front of me. I know some things, but I don't understand."

"Can you tell me?" he asked. Guilt filled him with regret because he held his secrets, too. He'd given his word never to give away the whereabouts of the portal or even mention that it existed. He wanted to tell her, but he'd promised not, too. *Since she is here, she probably knows, but it doesn't give me the right to talk about it.* He'd seen the prophecies in the alcove at the lake and written of them in the scrolls, and yet he couldn't mention it to his sweet little sister, who would be stuck here without human contact for centuries.

"What I know is this building shall be my home for all my years." Even as she said it, she knew there would be an exception but not one she could mention. "This village will never be a village like that in Mother's stories." Tears pooled in her eyes and trickled down her cheeks. "Instead, this will be a province for good… the place where the spirit dwells that will fight the coming evil."

Her words chilled Kylar. He'd read those very words about the spirit and coming evil in the ancient language, back in the alcove, and now they came from the lips of his little sister. The sister he loved more than he could put into words.

She spun around like a dancer and stopped with her arms out to her sides. "I'm the guardian of the jar. The jar Mother made me when we lived with the dragons in the volcano." She pointed to the pictures sketched on the stone wall behind him. "… until it disappears to fulfill its purpose."

"Purpose?" Kylar's voice squeaked with emotion as if it hadn't quite finished changing. He cleared his throat and repeated in his new, lower voice. "Purpose?"

"The symbols." Aurora shrugged. "Each one of them will be fulfilled by the holder of the jar."

Kylar thought of the symbols–the tree, the volcano, the woman with the strange-looking dragon head, a bolt of lightning, and an eyeball with two irises–one looking east and another west. *Quite a puzzle*. Even with all his knowledge, none of them meant anything to him other than the volcano.

"Ky, did you ever think about Mother's stories?"

His focus turned back to his sister's sweet face. "Her stories? You mean the stories of places with pieces of metal called coins used to buy food and other things?"

"Yes." She crossed her arms and looked at him thoughtfully. "Have you ever thought that maybe those aren't stories just from her imagination?" She let out a long breath and rubbed her tongue over the gap left by her missing teeth.

"What are you thinking?"

"I don't know. It's just a feeling. I used to think it was my imagination joining with hers because it all seemed so real. But, now, I believe it is something that she lived. And Da knows how to do things, like the way he fights the myrnexes. His knowledge about how to craft a bow and make arrows, and how he taught the rest of you like one taught when he was my age. The way he handles his dagger–and have you ever seen such a weapon other than his. Just the way he moves when he is fighting. And, have you noticed how he stays aware of everything going on around him? While the rest of us are busy with whatever we are doing, he is paying attention."

Aurora's reflections hit Kylar hard. "You're right." That's all he could say because her ideas stirred so many questions he didn't know what else to say as details from the past flooded his mind. He set his chalk rock on the floor and brushed the dust from his hands. He wanted to get out in the fresh air to clear his mind. "I told Juel I'd help her with tilling the soil on the west side of their cave."

"Is she ready to live in a cabin downriver?"

He laughed. "Juel loves to hear about the trees that bear fruit, but when I talk to her about living on the ground, I can tell she is a bit unsure. It's like she can't imagine living in a place without the threat of the myrnexes."

"I can understand. I've lived here almost all my life. It's what I know. It's from your stories that I know it is not like this in all the world." But as she said it, in her mind's eye, she saw Juel and Kylar leaving with a bundle of belongings on a raft going up the river along with two of their brothers, Erik and Rikard, she assumed to help them set up his homestead. Sadness filled her as the vision faded. She knew they wouldn't return. By the time she was Kylar's age, they would all be gone. Even Tomas and Carn, though they'd be going to the mountains in the west.

Many would follow Kylar to live in a place without the myrnex — a place with food that grew on trees and hunting game was plentiful. *Why would anyone stay here?* While the thought troubled her, once all the people deserted Five Marks, Jurom would be free to visit whenever he wanted. He would be her companion. But this limited understanding of the future only skimmed the surface of what was to come. Jurom had said it was like a stone skipping across the lake in Jur-Jurom. She looked forward to the day she came of age and would know in full the answers to her questions.

CHAPTER TWENTY-NINE

With the temple completed, the constant battle with the myrnexes, and the untimely loss of life that sometimes resulted, humans gradually abandoned life in Five Marks for a new start upriver, away from life in the floating caves. Many joined Kylar and his bride, Erik, and Rikard. Erik moved even further downriver and found a spouse. Their settlements grew, and back in Five Marks, Carn came of age.

At the dinner table that night, Mother set the birthday loaf on the table with a bowl of cloudberries and sweet cream. "Hard to believe you're 18 summers," Aurora said. She worked to keep the sadness she felt from her voice.

"Next year, we'll be celebrating your coming of age." He flashed a smile. "So, what is the surprise?"

Aurora placed her hand on his head and mussed his hair. "I know you know, silly. You don't have to pretend with me." She cast a nervous glance at her parents, but they paid no attention. They knew their sons were going. She could tell.

Carn's face grew serious as he smoothed the sparse mustache on his upper lip. "So you're going to take me…." He pointed to Tomas. "…and Tomas to the western mountains?"

She nodded. "The Nalhdyn Mountains."

The two young men stared at each other wide-eyed. "Told you," they said in unison and laughed as Carn grabbed the birthday loaf and pulled off a chunk, and handed it to his brother. He crumbled the bread into a bowl and sprinkled it with berries and cream.

Aurora smiled, but it wavered as she crumbled loaf into her bowl. *How much will they be laughing when they see what awaits them there?* "We leave in the morning, so figure out what you want to bring with you."

Carn looked up from his bowl with a startled look. "Tomorrow?" He glanced at his parents. Mother's eyes held that sadness that said goodbye before her lips did.

Carn glanced at Tomas and then stared at his bowl as he emptied it.

Aurora ate hers slowly. She wanted to enjoy this moment. It would be the last time all of them would share in a meal.

That night, she spoke mind to mind to Jurom and made plans for him to come to pick them up the following morning. For this trek, Jurom planned to bring his son. "*My son Cezzor be old enough to make the trip. We shall see ye at suns rise, Young One.*"

The following morning, she woke rested. She lit a few starstones and placed them in a chest lantern that allowed her to climb down the ladder to Tomas and Carn's room in the perpetual darkness of the inner core. She'd collect her brothers and head up to the platform. If all went well, they'd have time to eat something before they took off.

As she slowly followed the ladder rungs down to the next floor, she heard their voices resound with excited chatter. "You're already awake and ready to go?" she said as she swung from the ladder into the room. Each picked up a bundle wrapped in a tarp and slung it over their shoulders. "We can tether these to the dragon's goldenhorn, right?"

She nodded. "We don't have much time. Fetch your things, and let's go." Without another word, she climbed back onto the ladder and started heading up the rungs. The soles of her feet didn't thump against the rungs, with hurried steps. They never did. She silently climbed upward with slow, cautious steps. After all these years, she still didn't like climbing the ladder, even though she was aware of the location of every boobytrap. She couldn't get past the fear of triggering one. Her brothers always teased her about it as they'd race to see who could reach the top first, hopping from one ladder track to another. But she saw the trace of magic attached to each trap. The fact that no one talked about magic was one more warning signal that the traps were perilous. And it was one more pointer toward her father's undisclosed abilities. She was like him in many ways, and she hungered to know more.

At the top of the ladder, she stepped onto the short platform set against the wall and cranked open the hatch. The sound of her brothers' footfalls echoed as they pounded the rungs with frantic staccato beats in their last temple race. They reached the top in a dead heat and out of breath as they stepped onto the short platform and rushed up the few stairs onto the flat roof of the temple. In the distance, the violet sky brightened to purple at the horizon.

"Jurom and his son are going to be here at suns rise."

"Wait for us," Da called from below. He and Mother climbed to join them on the roof, with each carrying a couple of small bundles.

Da held out his hand and helped Mother onto the roof. Both wore solemn faces as they faced their eager sons. "Good day, Mother. Good day, Da," Tomas said. But suddenly, the smile disappeared from his face. "We aren't returning!"

Aurora watched with sadness as her brothers realized that it was time for them to move forward to meet their destinies. "Will we see you again?" Carn asked.

Mother stepped forward. "You know the answer to that question better than we, for you, are the first of the sages." She handed each of them a bundle wrapped in animal skins. "I've made each of you a robe to mark your profession. Think of us when you wear them." She smiled, but it wavered as her bottom lip trembled as the second sun peeked over the horizon, burning a pink blush across the sky.

Carn wrapped his mother in his arms in a warm embrace. "We shall never forget you, Mother. We love you." Tears brimmed in his eyes as he turned to face Da. "And you Da. Thank you for everything, for preparing us for this day." His lavender aura darkened to violet edged in red, showing a side of him Aurora rarely saw. The practical, survival-oriented part of him tempered with an unshakable determination.

Tomas accepted the bundle and hugged his mother as Jurom and his son Cezzor landed.

Auras of her entire family flared with emotion. For once, she considered her gift to see into the future to be good fortune. She'd known about this for most of her life. It prepared her on a base level, but it still stirred sadness because she knew it would be her parents leaving her next. She walked over to Jurom and met Cezzor for the first time. *"What a sweet boy you are,"* she said as she rubbed his eye ridge. She busied herself tethering the smaller bundles to Cezzor's goldenhorn and then secured the larger bundles. "We'll all be riding Jurom," she announced to her brothers.

They hugged their parents one more time and climbed aboard Jurom, and tethered themselves to his goldenhorn. As they took off, no one spoke. They watched Five Marks disappear in the distance. The dragons' shadows sped along the banks of the river. They passed over the village of Red Grove, where Kylar and Rikard lived with their young families, and then the smaller settlement of Man's Bow, where Erik lived with his wife. Beyond that, the suns shone against the purple Nalhdyn Mountains as Jurom chatted with Aurora about the future. He filled her head with the information she needed to pass on to her brothers as they stepped into the role of sages. Once again, she wondered, *Why can't we talk among ourselves so we can see the entire picture?*

CHAPTER THIRTY

As they drew nearer to the mountains, Jurom said, "Talk to thine brothers about the threads of history and magical energy."

She took in a breath, but the words didn't come. *How do I broach the subject?* She glanced at each of them as they stared out at the mountains with wonder. "How are you feeling? About all this?"

Carn let out a sigh and looked at his older brother. "We knew it was coming, but it happened so fast. I didn't realize I'd never see Mother or Da again when I woke this morning." Tomas nodded his agreement as he bit his bottom lip to stop it from quivering. "Sometimes I feel like I know so much, but really, I know so little."

"What do you know of your… your responsibilities at Nalhdyn Hold?"

Tomas shrugged. "We see things, but we haven't understood them." He gestured to Carn. "Go ahead and tell her about the strings of light that swim through the air."

"We've both seen shelves and shelves of books, scrolls, and other items."

"Tell them that be the library of Tachnir and that there shall be a second in what shall be the temple at Nalhdyn Hold," Jurom said as Cezzor worked his wings double time to keep up.

"There shall be two libraries," Aurora said. "One within Mount Tachnir where sages like you two will study newly created scrolls of history while fresh… recording events before they happen to see if there is evidence of a breach in time."

"Ye speak true, Little One. And in the future, these scrolls shall be delivered to the temple, in Nalhdyn Hold, where the temple prophets shall also study the scrolls. Their gifts be different—they offer another dimension to the interpretation of threads—an understanding of the

future before it unfolds. Then they shall be stored in the Nalhdyn Hold library, which shall be a big part of the temple."

Aurora wondered about the recording of events before they happened, even as she spoke of it. "The temple prophets will store tomes written by the sages. Some will be oral history written down, some written from memory, but the sacred scrolls will be woven with threads of history and magical energy and not written by the human hands."

"Temple prophets? Not sages?" Carn asked. "So, another temple?"

Aurora nodded. "This one will focus on the abilities of magic and prophecy, and many will live there."

"Will we be free to talk of such things? I mean, Tomas and I have talked about our visions with each other, but we never felt free to speak of these things to anyone else."

"Yes." She smiled at her brothers' wide-eyed wonder. "Not only will you be free to speak of it, but you will even teach and guide others with such abilities. They shall read the scrolls and learn from them as they search them earnestly." Her smile faded. "You two have the gift of visions of things, yet future, and with the dragons' help, you will grow to use magic. Those who are like-gifted will find their way to you. I'm speaking of things far future. In the beginning, prophets in this new temple will cultivate the students' talents in magic or prophecy. But after a time, initiates will be forced to choose between magic *or* prophecy. Eventually, those in charge will declare all magic as evil due to the spirit of coming evil and will declare all magic forbidden."

"So this will be a place of teaching?" Carn asked.

"Yes, and those who grow to maturity in the skills of visions and magic and are gifted to read the threads–these will be responsible for searching emerging history for strands of evidence of possible portal activation from the past or present."

"Wait, what are you saying?"

"You shall be the first of the Sages of Tachnir. You will be entrusted with the knowledge and guardianship of the great Labyrinth of Times along with the Thornose dragons when they come to this world."

As they approached the mountaintop, Jurom interrupted to point out a protruding ledge to Aurora. *"This be where we enter, Mount Tachnir. From here, there be a network of tunnels which be in their visions."*

When they landed, Tomas was the first to climb down. Aurora marveled at how bright his green aura shone even in the afternoon sunlight. "Have to confess I'm happy to have my feet on solid ground." He looked up at the great maw before them. "I've seen this. Carn, look!"

Carn stepped up beside him and threw his arm across his brother's shoulder. "Me too, brother. Come, Rora, let me show you the strings of light." He started toward the mouth of a tunnel on the right. "This is strange. Tomas, is it like you've been here?"

Tomas nodded as he stepped into the shadows. "But in my visions, there were lights… blue lights that came on when I stepped into the opening here."

Aurora stood back for a moment. Just hearing Carn call her by her childhood nickname took her back to life at the lake in the volcano when he couldn't say her name. *I'll miss them.*

Jurom nuzzled her with his snout. "*It shall be well, Little One.*" He followed her into the cavern with his son at his side. *"We shall rest here while ye prepare the sages."*

"Yes! Blue lights!" Carn agreed. "I saw them too!"

Aurora rubbed her eyes. "I believe I am the one to offer you the lights." She pulled out a handful of starstones from her bag.

"No." Carn shook his head. "I'm talking about lights in the tunnels. All the tunnels. Not carried in your palm."

She nodded. "I know." She stretched out her hand. "Imbed et multiplicamini. Lumen semitis sapientes Tachnir." The starstones glowed blue and lifted from her hand. Each one divided into two, half of the pieces drifted higher, and both groups split again. Soon the air within the tunnel shone with light like that of a full moon on a cloudless night as stones embedded into the tunnel ceiling. Others shot further into the tunnel; sapphire blurs, multiplying, scattering, and embedding.

Carn stared at his sister with his jaw hanging open. “How did you do that?”

She laughed. “We all have our secrets. You have your visions, and I have these ensorcelled starstones. They are in place to light the way for the Sages of Tachnir, of which….” She pointed at each of her brothers. “…you are the first.”

“Amazing! But these are not the lights swimming through the air that I saw in my visions. These are different. How long will they give light?” Tomas started down the tunnel with his eyes fixed on the magical lighting.

Aurora thought about it for a second. “As long as there is a sage.”

“This is what I saw.” Tomas led the way as he and Carn chatted excitedly about various “rooms” they passed. As they reached an intersection, Carn pointed down the tunnel on his right. “That leads to where people will live… on the east side of the mountain.”

Tomas pointed to the left. “And that leads to living quarters on the west side. I saw people in my visions. Many people. When will others come here?”

“I don’t know all the answers,” Aurora admitted. “I do know that in the beginning, dragons will bring them. Once the temple is ready, sages will come from the school.”

“Here.” Carn gestured with his hand for them to follow. “This is the way.” They trailed behind him as he followed another split in the tunnel system. After walking a short distance, they paused outside a great cavern on the right. “This is the great hall where the sages will gather to eat, and the adjoining cavern will be the library.”

“Yes,” Tomas said. “But come. What we are looking for is at the end of this tunnel. There we will find the strings of light.” The corridor ended at a large, arched entry. They stepped through it into darkness.

“We need light.” Aurora fumbled for more starstones.

“No,” Tomas said. “Wait. I can see them.”

“Yes, I see them too!” Carn said. “I-I feel a draw….”

Aurora stood surrounded by darkness as she listened to her brothers move through the dark. She stared into the inky black and blinked. “I can’t see anything. Do you mind if I light some torches?”

“Torch?” Tomas asked as if distracted. “Yes, yes, that’s fine.”

“Create et lux facula ardebat. Est….” She pointed. “Est… est… est… est.” Four torches appeared in sconces high on the walls with each point of her index finger. A warm orange glow spread overhead. Shadows oscillated across the room as she walked over to her brothers. They stood looking at a large rock in the center of the room. As she drew closer, she realized they were peering into a jagged crevice.

Carn looked up at her. “This is the colliery.” He placed his palm gently against the stone as if it were a treasure. Inside, she saw colored threads of light swimming like minnows through space. “Here, we will read these energy threads of place and time shortly before they intersect with the real-time.”

She suddenly felt uneasy. The brothers she had carried here had already changed. *These magical threads have touched and changed them. These are the filaments of energy that will create the sacred scrolls of history yet to unfold.* That familiar out-of-body sense washed over her but, with it came deep sadness. *This colliery will allow the sages to monitor and control people’s thoughts.* She took a step back but said nothing. Her part was to bring her brothers here and leave the dragons to help them.

She walked back the way she’d come. The sounds of her brothers’ voices faded as she followed the star stone lights back to the cavern where Jurom and Cezzor lay resting. Jurom lifted his bulk as she walked into the cavern. Without a word, she walked over, and he bent his neck until his snout was level with her chest. They looked at each other eye to eye. She placed her hand on the bony ridge above his eyes and cried.

“This is too difficult. I don’t want to know the future anymore.”

“In the end, ye shall be happy, Little One. And thy unselfish love and sacrifice combined with that of the dragons will help others find happiness in the future free from the evil to come.”

CHAPTER THIRTY-ONE

Aurora said goodbye to Carn and Tomas with promises that she would see them again soon. That was hard, but it was harder still to leave her beloved Jurom and his son Cezzor to help establish the order of the Sages of Tachnir.

"Travel well, Little One," Jurom said.

She rubbed his eye ridge. "I wish you were coming with me." She lay her head against his strong jaw drinking in his smoky scent. "If it weren't for you, I wouldn't be able to travel the Midlands alone. It's only by the Goldenhorn's ability to see the rings that I can make the trip alone. And I got that from you."

At one time, she was proud to be the only human able to travel the Midlands unescorted by a dragon, but right now, it felt lonely as the flash of golden light swallowed her. Her trip home to Five Marks through the Midlands left her drained as her feet hit the roof of the temple. She spoke the spell to open the trapdoor from above. "Apertum est sermo." The cylinder of the windlass turned as the crank inside the temple worked beneath the trapdoor. Even as tired as she was, she had to smile at her Da's magic. Though, he didn't call it magic. "It is security," he whispered into her ear. "Say, 'Open by the word.'" Then, he laughed heartily.

Her younger self had asked what he was laughing about, and he could hardly get out the answer as he tried to catch his breath. "There is… no word." She was still smiling as she climbed into the cool shadows of the core, closed the hatch, and used her magic to light the starstones in one of the chest lanterns hanging at the top of the ladder. She headed into the core on wobbly legs.

Silence wrapped around her like a cloak in the dim light. She stepped into her room and stared out into the core. All the other rooms were dark and empty, except for lamplight flickering from the room on the top level, across from hers–her parents' room. Next to it, what had been Kylar's room sat dark. The lamplight renewed her smile. Mother didn't like to use starstones, so she and Da always used an oil lamp. Da always said, "Lamplight makes it easier to find things." She paused, wondering if she should announce that she had returned. No. They heard the windlass working to open the door. If they want to talk to me now, they will come to me. She didn't want to allow them the chance to tell her they were leaving. Not yet. Today had taken enough of an emotional toll. Saying goodbye to Carn and Tomas was the hardest goodbye yet, and she would still see them from time to time. That would not be so with Mother and Da. Tomorrow, she thought. Tomorrow is soon enough. She climbed into bed knowing that tomorrow when they said goodbye, she would face the solitary life she had anticipated all her life.

As she slipped beneath the blankets, she wondered about Jurom's prophecy that she would again see her parents when the time came for her to leave the temple for good. What does that mean? Before she could ponder it further, exhaustion claimed her.

She woke to the sound of her parents opening the hatch to the temple roof sending beams of early morning light down the core. As she slipped out of bed and dressed, the sound of soft footfalls descended on the ladder toward her room. Mother leaned into the opening. "Good morning, Aurora. I'm glad to see you're up. I'm off to make breakfast, and I wanted to be sure you were joining us."

She nodded. "I'll be there in a minute."

Mother disappeared as quickly as she appeared. "How does she do it?" she asked herself as she tied her hair into a braid. "All of her children gone except me, and she's off to make breakfast as if it is just another day."

She grabbed the bar at the opening to her room, swung out onto the ladder, and looked up. White clouds tinged with gray scuttled across the sunlit patch of blue sky above. When she reached the floating cave, a fire burned beneath the pot of bubbling ulgar beans with the wholesome aroma already wafting in the air. Long ago, she'd come to realize the only way Mother and Da accomplished such things so quickly was magic. But the closest they ever came to talking about magic was when Da taught her the password to open the hatch. Yet the colors of magic reflected in their auras, just like Carn and Tomas. Thoughts of bringing up the subject were always at the edge of her mind, but she never felt the timing right.

"Da picked some cloudberries," Mother said without looking up as Aurora walked into the cave.

For the first time, Aurora heard emotional tightness in her voice. She walked over and draped her arm across her mother's shoulders. Mother spun around and wrapped her in her arms, buried her face against her shoulder, and cried. From the corner of her eye, she saw Da stepped into view with the bowl of berries.

"What's wrong?"

Kaibelle looked up at him with red-rimmed eyes. "What's wrong?"

He set the bowl on the table. "Kai!" His tone carried an unspoken warning as he led her by the hand to take a seat. "Come, Aurora, sit with your mother. I'll serve breakfast."

Aurora did as he suggested and sat beside her mother. "It will be alright, Mother. I know you're leaving."

"My dear Aurora, you are always so strong." Kaibelle sniffled. "Are you sure you'll be alright?"

Aurora nodded, but inwardly she longed for them to stay at least until her eighteenth birthday.

Da carried over two steaming bowls of ulgar and sat without getting his breakfast. His love-centered green aura gave way to a flood of red closest to his head, telling her how hard this was for him. A matter of survival. "This day is extremely difficult," he said. "But we all have a purpose in history." They glanced at each other and admitted that they longed for their family to stay together. "But we understand you can't join us for now. Just like Kylar's purpose is in Red Grove, and Carn and Tomas belong in the Nalhdyn Mountains, your purpose is here, and ours is–elsewhere."

They all left their breakfast uneaten as they talked about new starts and how difficult it had been to move from the valley, but they avoided the real topic on their minds. Finally, Da stood. "It's time." He didn't need to say more. A sinking feeling hit Aurora, unlike anything she'd ever experienced. She moved by instinct, trying to hide her sadness. She felt hollow. As she rubbed chins with Mother, she could see her doing the same as she fought to keep her lip from trembling; her loving, tender pink aura overtaken by red.

Da took her into his muscular arms. In her mind, she screamed for him, to never let her go. He whispered, "We shall see you again." Then he held her at arm's length and looked at her with sad brown eyes. "We'd rather you don't come to see us off. This is already difficult enough for all of us." She leaned against Mother one last time, and the two of them wept, soaking the necks of their tunics with tears. Da rubbed chins with her and guided his wife to the ladder. They turned one last time and looked at her. "Until we see you next," Da said, and they disappeared down the rope ladder. Aurora stood motionless in the cave, silent tears streaming down her face, the ulgar still bubbling on amber embers. She walked over to the table and stared at the uneaten cloudberries. She picked one up and thought, "Da touched this." She scooped up the berries to carry to her room in the temple and realized she'd forgotten her satchel. She glanced around the cavern for something to carry them in and spotted her mother's bag on the bench where she'd been sitting. "Mother," she said in a whisper as she picked it up. She threw the berries on the table and hurried to the rope ladder, hoping to catch her Mother before she was gone.

Aurora clambered down the rope ladder to the top of the temple. From here, she could see miles of the open sea, the Nalhdyn mountains in the west, the river snaking toward her brothers in Red Grove, and, beyond that, mountains in the east. She didn't see even a hint of her parents. Mother's satchel dangled from her hand in the light breeze. How can they be out of sight so quickly? Within a few heartbeats, she saw a speck flying from the west. For a moment, her heart thrilled that they were coming back, but it wasn't her Mother or Da. It was her Jurom.

The dragon landed with such skill his wings stirred a brisk wind but didn't kick up a whirlwind, ready to blow her over. He lumbered toward her and touched his great snout to her forehead. All be well, Little One. When the time be for thee to leave the temple, ye shall join them.

PART III

CHAPTER THIRTY-TWO

Summers came and went. With the humans gone from Five Marks, the myrnexes multiplied but didn't breach the temple. The ink ivy climbed the once colorful exterior temple walls now faded with time; the structure now almost hidden beneath a blanket of broad leaves. Aurora thanked the stars that Jurom could carry her away to see the world outside of Five Marks because while she could travel the Midlands, she didn't like how it drained her.

Jurom had grown into a magnificent green dragon, the color of evergreens that grew on the snowcapped mountains, and she had developed into a proficient rider. At times, she visited her brothers. It was always good to see them, but their lives were so different now. The village where Kylar and Rikard settled became known as Red Grove, for the apple trees turned a bright red in the fall. Erik went further upriver and settled in what became Man's Bow because he brought Da's knowledge of the bow to the people who lived there.

Rikard married one of Juel's younger sisters, and Kylar and Juel's family grew to three boys and three girls. In the beginning, Jurom dropped Aurora off far enough away from the settlement that no one saw him. From there, she just walked up to their porch and was welcomed into their home. Once she knew where she was going, she often crossed through the Midlands instead of riding the dragon, for Jurom needed to spend more time with his mate, Tozet, and his clan.

Travel through the Midlands upset her stomach terribly, but she considered the cost worth it because it offered her freedom. With practice, she learned to travel from the top of the temple to the fences surrounding her brother's fields or the ledge on Mount Tachnir outside the network of tunnels, where her brothers, Tomas and Carn, taught a growing number of students. She did the same in reverse when it came time to leave. Her nieces and nephews often ran to greet her. Their brightly colored auras shone with true happiness to see her. But time took its toll. Kylar aged until he looked more like her Da the last time she saw him.

His children tied the knot and became parents too. Some were gifted and even went on to become Sages of Tachnir. When Kylar passed on, Aurora stopped visiting her brothers or their families other than Carn and Tomas. The pain of loss was so great. She stayed inside the temple more and more. Some days she ventured out to the porch and stood beside the large pillars, now veiled beneath ink ivy. Her memories drifted to how the dragons had helped her Da craft the pillars and put them into place. But this too stirred raw emotions, and after a time, she let go of that small pleasure. Instead, she spent time in the great hall where sunlight still spilled through the large arched windows built high in the walls near the ceiling. She basked in the memories as she studied the murals, pictographs, and tomes. She relived the moments in her mind. It made her feel like her family members were all still here–still alive.

Each morning she climbed the ladder to the floating cave and sat at the table where her family had shared their meals. From time to time, she visited other abandoned dwellings for something to do.

Finally, she allowed herself to visit the bedchambers of her brothers–but, not Mother and Da's room. After all, they had no murals, no scrolls. She preferred to remember things as they were–to allow herself the fantasy that Mother and Da could slip out onto the ladder at any moment and join her on the roof. Above all, they did promise she would see them again. This thought stirred unanswered questions. *With all the future I can see, why don't I see that?*

Decades turned to centuries. The Sages of Tachnir now served within the Temple of Tachnir, but her youngest brother, Carn, had passed on. It hit her and Tomas hard, but Tomas kept busy with a flurry of students and responsibilities. Finally, she gave up her visits to Tachnir and grew to accept her solitary life.

One morning, after a couple of hundred years, she stepped out onto the portico again and stood beneath the curtain of ink ivy. Even with the shade of the overgrowth, the suns seemed much brighter. She separated the veil of vines and peered up as she shielded her eyes. "The floating caves are gone!" Her mind raced as she pondered what that meant. *Gone are the shaggy sheep, fresh herbs, ulgar beans, and cloudberries.* A soft sigh brushed past her lips. While she would miss the fresh milk and cheese, fortunately, she had spindles full of goat hair and sheep's wool and dried ulgar beans and herbs stored up. Other than that, the only evidence that her family had come to Five Marks was the temple. *And me.*

With Jurom's visits less frequent, Aurora busied herself with reading scrolls left behind by Kylar in the secret chamber where she regularly checked on the urn. It consoled her to have his words–his gift–and the knowledge that one day the cup would pass on to another and she would be free to leave Five Marks. *Where will I go from here?*

One day Jurom landed on the rooftop platform of the temple and trumpeted his greeting, but Aurora didn't come up to meet him. He called to her. *"Little One? Where be ye?"* When she didn't answer, he grew concerned.

He clawed the hatch leading to the core of the temple. The screech of his talons upon the petrified wood and stone was enough to wake the dead. Finally, the razor tip of his toe caught in the crack where the heavy door abutted the stone. He hefted the door up and slammed it against the roof. He peered into the dimly lit corridor and trumpeted again. Aurora stepped to the doorway of one of the rooms situated near the top of the core. With her arm outstretched, she pointed into the room behind her with a scroll in her hand.

"What be ye doing? I feared some trouble befell thee."

"Jurom! Kylar talks of a hidden portal here in the temple. A portal to another land–protected from view by dragon magic. Do you know of this portal?"

A curl of smoke drifted from his nostril as he stared at her from above. *"Aye. I be a dragon. Of course, I know of it."*

She dropped her arms to her side and stood a little straighter. *"And you never said anything? Why was this hidden from me? I mean, I'm Dragonborn! I should know about this. Instead, you leave me to die from boredom here. It says I will set up a home in this other land. A home?"*

"Aye, but the Scroll of Prophecy speaks not of a home for thee."

Aurora's shoulders slumped but just for a moment. She straightened and started pacing. "Not for me? Why not?" She frowned. "Who would I be setting it up for then?"

"This be different than traveling through time within Voldatha. This portal leads to a new land. It be a whole new world. In that world, time be different. There, ye age quickly like one, not Dragonborn. There, dragons age quickly as well. This be why I have not mentioned it. Time in that world must be limited, for we must protect thy long life to fulfill thy purpose here."

The thought of aging appealed to her on a base level. Everyone she knew and loved had already lived their lives and passed on, except for Tomas. He and she still looked young. But he had a wife. "What good is a long life if you don't have someone to share it? Someone to love?"

Jurom stuffed the front half of his body into the core with the ladders pressing in on his bulk as he stretched and reached forward with his foreleg, using the smooth scales on the back of his claw to brush her face. *"For now, ye have me."*

She placed her hand on his claw and patted it. "Yes, but you have hatchlings and a mate of your own. Your family lives long–mine did not."

He lightly clicked, and she smiled. *"Ye know that in time ye will have the opportunity to live and love and even have younglings if ye wish."*

She nodded. "I know I shall meet a young man with coal-black hair and sun-kissed skin. I've seen him many times in my visions, but it's just such a long journey to get there." She studied her feet for a moment as she ran her toe through the light layer of dust filled with her footprints. With her chin against her chest, she asked, "Do you know where the portal is?" She looked up at her dragon friend.

"Aye?" he said as more of a question than a fact.

"Let's see it. I've lived in this temple almost all my life, and I've never seen it. Where is it hidden? Even if dragon magic conceals it, I should see it, right?" She started looking around with renewed earnest as she talked to herself. "I can't believe my brother could keep this a secret. We never kept secrets from each other...." Her words trailed off. She knew that wasn't true. Some things she knew and couldn't share with him or anyone.

"Thy parents helped to construct the portal. That be how they departed this world."

The news stunned her for just a moment, but it quickly brought clarity to many of her suspicions. "They *were* Dragonborn. I knew it. That's why they could leave me here. That's why they didn't age like Kylar. And like Erik and Rikard. They grew so old. And Carn, I thought he was Dragonborn, might have been, but he died after he came back from that journey. It is clear that Tomas is, but he will never speak of it. My Mother and Da–. I wondered for a long time about why they left the way they did. But I guess they couldn't have people asking why they looked as young as some of their children. So where are they?"

"Little One, ye know I cannot say. But I can tell ye that in time, ye shall see them."

Her bottom lip curled into a pout. "You know, sometimes you can be maddening, Jurom. It's just you and me!"

His eyes narrowed. *"A dragon's honor be always in place even when we be alone."*

She laughed and waved off the suggestion as if she hadn't meant it. "I know, I know. But I still want to see the portal. We can, at least, learn about it and make the plan for when I set up this—this home that's not for me. It will give us something fresh to do. Something to look forward to."

Jurom let out a long snort, filling the core with a light layer of smoke that drifted into the unoccupied bedchambers. *"First, ye must read the scrolls. Learn what Kylar wrote, for he be chosen as the messenger carrying the message in the language of the Thornose."*

Aurora rolled her eyes. "Alright then, go back to the roof."

Jurom pulled back to the rooftop letting the light of the suns into the core. As Aurora climbed the ladder in her slow, methodical pattern while carrying the scroll in one hand, he wondered if Kylar's writings told of the second hidden portal. Once topside, she sat with her legs crossed, with the scroll rolled in her lap. "Tell me about these Thornose dragons," she started. "Why didn't they come here? Why don't we ever talk about them if they are so important?"

"They shall be here. Travel through the Labyrinth allows movement through times. So mine parents and thine came from the future. There the Thornose gave them the plans to build this portal to a land called America. It be not like one of the portals within the Labyrinth. It be one of the reasons this temple be built."

"America," she repeated the strange-sounding name. "What's it like there?"

"I have only seen it from this side of the portal. Scenes change, different destinations and times within this other land."

Aurora smoothed the scroll across the flat stone in front of her. *"Really? Different destinations? How will we know when to step through?"*

"That be thy part, Little One. Thy parents knew when to step through."

She turned her attention to the scroll. "I guess you're right then. I best study these scrolls to see what I must know and do." She started reading and shook her head.

"What be troubling thee?" Jurom asked.

"I–I just can't believe Kylar could keep all this from me? We were close."

"Did ye keep things from him?"

Her eyes grew wide like green pools. "I had to. I couldn't corrupt the oath."

"And he had to keep his."

"You mean.... But Kylar couldn't be Dragonborn. He has already passed on. He aged."

"True, Little One. But he be dragon-touched, from his birth. He be gifted and understood things beyond normal reason. His memory be like a trap that never lets things go. He be able to fit together happenings and deduce things not known by any other human. But

part of his gift be the innate ability to know what not to talk about. Most dragon touched be not aware of anything more than their gift of magic or ability to prophecy. These do not take an oath. In the future of this world, these two gifts shall cause division among thy kind."

"So he knew but didn't know in a way that he understood what he knew?"

"Only because he be gifted so. Thy brother be a special human for certain."

"And there will be others gifted… dragon-touched."

"Aye. Thy brother Tomas be Dragonborn, but thy brother Carn be dragon-touched. But these be things of which we speak not. I only speak of them now because thy role requires that ye understand. When thy parents were Dragonborn, we knew not if their offspring would show Dragonborn traits. It all be a test. Kylar inherited Thornose dragon gifts. Inborn gifts. The same be true of thy brother, Carn. Tomas be Dragonborn, through thy parents, as were ye. It be Thornose magic. But, thy gifts be something far more.

Thy Thornose gifts be powerful. So strong that through thy bond with me when we be very young, thou became Dragonborn also through the Goldenhorn almost before ye could talk. Ye be double Dragonborn through both the Goldenhorn and Thornose. Thy gifts be much more potent than mine parents thought possible, and they be maturing. But those who be dragon-touched shall not know their gifts be dragon gifts. In the future, some shall embrace their gifts, but some of thy kind shall hate magic and make laws against it. It shall cause dragons to leave the land. This be one reason the Thornose be not here as yet."

Aurora drank in Jurom's words. She stood and placed her forehead to his forehead. "I wish there was a gift for not being lonely."

A wave of emotion flowed between them. *"I understand"* He closed his eyes for a moment and then looked at her. *"Perhaps going to the portal be helpful, but ye cannot enter until thy destination is clear. Our destination."*

"Our? You're coming with me." Her spirits lifted. "And will there be people there?"

His multifaceted blue-green eyes shined. *"I know little, but there also be times I cannot tell ye things that may influence thy actions... thy choices. However, I do know humans be there."*

His cryptic answer filled her with excitement. Something to figure out that she didn't already know. A portal that would take her to another world... but a portal that would steal away her youth if she lingered too long. *It would be worth it to feel alive. Truly alive.*

* * * *

Aurora studied every scroll she could find. After each one, she asked Jurom if she could see the portal. And each time, he asked, *"Have ye found anything new?"* And when she said, "No," he put her off. *"Not yet, Little One, but soon."*

It only made her more determined. *There is something I'm missing. Something I must know before I enter that portal. I'll search again; maybe I overlooked something. I'll start in Kylar's room.* She pulled out a handful of starstones and stopped. Da had always said his lamplight made it easier to find things. The thought brought a moment of clarity she'd never considered. *Maybe he meant more by that than I thought.* This time she'd use one of Da's lamps.

She climbed the ladder in the dark to the walkway that joined her room to her parents' chamber. Her breathing sounded loud to her ears. She inched through the darkness with her hands stretched out in front of her. When her fingers brushed the wall, she groped for the door to their room and stepped inside. "Lux in lucerna." A lamp on the small table beside the bed lit with a single flame dancing in the darkness with a buttery glow. She blinked at the sight. Her parents' bed sat there made up as if mother had just tidied the room. A second lamp on the shelf beside the door also came to life. She lifted it from its place, stirring dust particles into the halo of light. On the other side of the door hung Mother's apron, on a hook beside Da's satchel. "He left his satchel too?" It reminded her of running to catch her mother and wondering how they could have disappeared so quickly. Now she knew.

She lifted Da's bag from the peg, surprised at the weight. "What's in here?" She put the lamp on the floor and untied the satchel laces. As she raised the flap, the slight glow of magic shined within. "What is this?" She pulled out a long but slender wooden box. Blue light leaked from the crack where the lid and bottom of the box latched.

"Jurom," she called out with her mind. *"Are you near?"*

"I be with Cezzor and the Sages of Tachnir."

"I've found something."

"What be it?"

"A box. I haven't opened it yet. I–I can see an aura of magic leaking from it."

"I be coming. Open it not until I arrive."

* * * *

Aurora slipped the box back into the shoulder bag, hung the strap across her torso, and hurried as fast as caution allowed back to her chamber with the oil lamp lighting her way. As she stepped into the room, the buttery glow of the lamp made it feel like a different room. Aurora had spent hours in this room, every day, hoping to find the thing needed to move on with her life, and it wasn't even in this room.

Excitement, tempered with apprehension, filled her as she changed into her best trousers and her one tunic with no holes. She re-braided her hair, went to the wall, and grabbed the rounded hood with a black veil from where it hung on a peg. It had been her mother's—a gift for when she came of age. She fingered the strange feeling headpiece on her head. Memories flashed through her mind of her mother's stories. Intuitively she knew the headpiece was from another time and decided not to wear it. She tossed it on her bed, slipped Da's satchel over her head with the strap across her body, and clattered up the rungs of the ladder faster than ever. She didn't even worry about the boobytraps. This time she cranked open the hatch without thinking about where her Da found the gears. Sunlight filled the core. When she climbed out onto the temple roof, Jurom was already visible in the western sky.

She waved her arms wildly in the air as if the dragon would fly faster. When he landed, she ran up to him and grabbed the box from the shoulder bag. "What is it?" she asked, eager with anticipation as he folded his wings close to his body. "Is this it? The thing I need?"

Jurom eyed the box with one eye.

"This be it, Little One."

Her fingertips rested on the latch as she looked at the dragon with the unasked question hanging between them. *"Aye, the time be upon us. Open it."*

Aurora's heart slammed against her ribs as if she'd just run from here to the Nalhdyn Mountains. She lifted the lid with shaking fingers and stopped. A frown creased between her brows. "A stick? I've been waiting to find a stick?"

"It be the therus rod."

"Therus rod?" She stared at the smooth stick in her hand with new interest. "It looks polished. I've read about this, but I thought it would look more–I mean less ordinary."

"It be not ordinary. If ye have read the scrolls, ye know this."

"Of course." She felt the blush of embarrassment burn across her cheeks. *"Let's see. I know it shows the way — it opens the door — the door that remains for the one to come."*

A light clicking sounded from deep within Jurom's throat.

"Why are you laughing?"

"I be thinking how proud Kylar would be to hear ye."

A smile tugged at the corners of her mouth as she thought of Kylar. Jurom was right. "It's amazing he knew all this. Even more amazing that he wrote all this down from memory! I don't understand how he could remember all this just from working with the tiles. The real question is: did he know what it meant? For instance, what is the door? What is the way?"

"He knew not what it meant, Little One. That be thy part."

"Are you sure? I thought the rod was to be used by a young man." She held the rod tightly and stared at it as if she could order it to work by sheer will, but it didn't show her anything other than an aura of residual Thornose magic.

CHAPTER THIRTY-THREE

Igasho crouched close to the short green grass wearing a biaguchu hide on his back. He approached the herd mimicking their behavior. He had been among the men who burned the tall grass on this bluff so it would come back greener to attract the biaguchu. Now, the massive animals grazed a few feet away. The smell of smoke lingered close to the ground like this. His heart thrummed in his ears. The honor of "fastest runner" had fallen to him to take the decoy position during this hunt. It excited him to think others trusted him with such a big responsibility. But now, the danger had him on edge.

He pretended to graze while keeping a watch on the herd from the corner of his eye. His cousin, Pu'ennaakan, came to mind. Instead of being excited for him, he had muttered, "He's not the fastest runner. This scrawny-one, he is chosen because he is the son of the Taikwahni." Anytime Igasho was honored, Pu'ennaakan tried to steal away the esteem. *He already wears two feathers! Has dreamed of the bear but acts more like the coyote trickster.* At this moment, Igasho pushed it all aside. He would not let his cousin's words distract him.

He looked out to the edge of the cliff and found the jagged outline marking the crevice. *I'm in place.* He bellowed like a stressed calf. Massive horned heads raised, among the alter herd, as Igasho bawled again and sprinted toward the cliff. The huge biaguchu stampeded as one thundering mass behind him kicking up a thick cloud of dust. His heart pounded as they closed the gap between him and them. If a biaguchu found him out, they'd fling him into the air with their horns, and if that didn't kill him, landing under the stampeding hooves to be trampled would. *The entire tribe put their faith in me as the decoy. I will not fail.*

He reached the edge of the bright red sandstone cliff and slipped into the safety of the fissure. The stone thundered and shook around him. As he stared out from his hiding place, everything seemed to slow. The sun hid behind a cloud as the first biaguchu jumped to their death. He closed his eyes as the rest spilled off the cliff like a waterfall.

As the dust settled, he climbed from his hiding place. A handful of biaguchu stood behind him. They would go on to build another herd. He stood at the edge of the bluff and stared down at the men from his tribe. They gathered around the fallen biaguchu that would feed and clothe the entire tribe for many moons. The sun slipped from behind the clouds. He sang a prayer song of thanks so it could be carried on the sun's rays to Appah. He started to work his way down to join the men. From this vantage point, he could not see the path by which his people traveled down to the valley from their summer mountain home. He glanced westward toward the circular field that gradually sloped into the valley leading to the winter camp. Between here and there, red and yellow masses of rock scattered across the landscape. His focus landed on the one red sandstone pillar that always reminded him of a headless giant.

As he picked his way to the bottom of the cliff, he thought of Kimama. *I shall earn my first feather here today. If only I'd have my vision or dream, so my parents could talk to her parents about marriage.* He and Kimama had been friends since they were children. *She is like a sister.* He stared down at the men working among the biaguchu. There were many more men than women in his tribe. *If I don't marry her soon, she will be wife to another, and I will have to abduct a bride from the Akai Tükka'a tribe*. He tried to push it all to the back of his mind, but he knew that without a vision or dream that the tribal court recognized as supernatural, he would be going on a vision quest once they returned to their summer home in the mountains. *By then, Kimama could be married.*

The work of moving the biaguchu back to camp took days. The women set to work butchering and preparing meat. With so many animals, the men helped. Igasho took the opportunity to walk over to talk with Kimama as he worked beside her. He couldn't wait to tell her about the part he played in the hunt. But as he told her, she didn't even look at him. "Once I give my telling to the tribal court, I'll have a feather for my headpiece." He hoped she'd recognize what he meant.

"You were very brave." Her eyes stayed cast down on her work.

"Is something wrong?"

She nodded. "I didn't want to say anything, but it's your cousin Pu'ennaakan."

"What has he done now?"

She looked up with tears brimming in her dark eyes. "He has asked to marry me."

"What? Surely your parents said, 'no'!"

She nodded. "They refused, but he requested the *nakweekkante tsappisuta*."

Fear shot through him. Kimama's mother was the weaker of the two mothers. *She is sure to lose.*

"If only I had my vision or dream—met my Spirit Guide. I would ask for you to be my wife."

She nodded. "I know. Perhaps you could be my second husband."

He shook his head sadly. "Second to Pu'ennaakan? I know you would have the say-so, but he would never allow it. And even if he did...." He let his words die on his tongue.

She nodded. "I understand."

* * * *

Taikwahni Ubirajara stepped from his grass house with his son, Igasho. "This day is an honor." He puffed out his chest and stood tall.

"Yes, Father." Lingering sadness over Kimama stole his joy.

"Walk with me, son." The Taikwahni walked toward the outskirts of the camp, where he often walked and talked with Igasho. "Tell me of the wolf and the trickster."

Igasho balked. Everyone knew the story well from childhood. "Long ago, Wolf and many other animals walked and talked like man. Coyote could talk, too, but our people stayed away from him because he was a trickster. Always up to no good and out to double-cross you."

His father nodded. "And what of the Wolf, Esa?"

"Our people respected him."

"And so what did the Coyote do?"

"He tried to trick the Wolf who said that if someone were to die, he could bring them back to life by shooting an arrow under them. And so the Coyote came up with a plan. He told the Wolf that if he brought everyone back to life, the Land would soon have no room. He said that once-dead people should remain dead."

"And why did he come up with this plan?"

"He thought that if the Wolf took his advice, the people would hate him."

"And so what did Wolf do?"

"He only nodded. He knew Coyote was up to no good. And he had a plan of his own to teach Coyote a lesson."

"So he did not have to use harsh words or a loud voice. He did not have to fight Coyote. Instead, what did he do?"

"A few days later, Coyote ran toward Wolf. A rattlesnake had bitten his son. Coyote pleaded with Wolf to bring his son back to life by shooting an arrow under him, but Wolf reminded Coyote of his own words that people should remain dead. That was the day death came to the Land, and as a punishment for his mischievous ways, Coyote's son was the first to die."

"Well told," Ubirajara said. "You say the people respected Wolf. Do you think they respected Coyote?"

"No."

"Why not?"

"People could see he was a trickster. He could not be trusted."

Ubirajara stopped. Igasho stood before him, looking up into his tawny face. "Do you think you are the only one who sees Pu'ennaakan for what he is?"

Igasho paused. He never considered that others saw what he saw. "Kimama sees it, but other than her, I do not know. I do not talk about him to know what others are thinking."

"Do you think he is respected just because he wears two feathers and claims the bear as his spirit animal?"

As he thought about it, the answer was clear. Most people stayed away from him best they could. "I don't think they do."

"I can tell you this, Son. People do respect you. Today, you receive your first feather. Do not worry about your cousin or even Kimama. Remain close to the Great Spirit. Treat the land and all living beings with great respect. Work for the benefit of all Mankind and give assistance and kindness wherever needed. I see great things for your future."

They continued walking in silence as they headed to the tribunal. Igasho held on to his father's advice and accepted his feather with thankfulness. But as he lay upon his mat that night, he thought of Kimama. *What of her? How do I do nothing and still show her respect?* But in the morning, he awoke with no dream, no Spirit Guide.

Days later, the tug of war between his aunt and Kimama's mother took place. Each of the women held one of Kimama's arms, ready to start. People stood in a circle watching as her mother battled to pull her daughter over the line. People cheered as the struggle went back and forth. Igasho noted that most people cheered for Kimama's mother as he stood near the back of the spectators. Then it happened. Kimama's mother lost her footing. She stumbled forward, and her grasp on Kimama's arms faltered. His aunt yanked Kimama across the line. Pu'ennaakan raised his arms in a boastful gesture as if he had pulled her over the line, himself. For a brief moment, their eyes met. Pu'ennaakan smiled as he walked over and claimed his bride. Igasho did not walk away or run from the disappointment. He did his best not to react in any way, but inside, he wanted to run and pull Kimama from his cousin's grasp. Instead, he watched them walk away together. As he walked back to his family's hut, he struggled to focus on the future and his vision quest in the spring. *I can't wait to meet my guardian spirit and get the power and wisdom I need for this life. Father is wise like the Wolf. I trust his advice.*

CHAPTER THIRTY-FOUR

Igasho sat dressed in his loincloth beneath the stars ignoring his rumbling stomach as he prayed. The rock he sat upon, still heated from the sun, warmed his legs. His eyes began to grow heavy, so he lay back and stared at the night sky. The half-moon offered little light as his mind drifted to thoughts of roasted rabbit. "Don't think it," he warned himself. The rabbit represented fear, and he certainly didn't want that to be his spirit animal. He'd come out here to the highest cliffs in hopes of meeting up with a lizard. As a spirit animal, it was said to represent the dream world beyond time and space. It could see into the future and even teach him how to create a new reality based on his dreams. His thoughts drifted to his own reality. Pu'ennaakan and Kimama expected their first child, and his cousin teased him just as he did when they were children. *"My wife carries my first child, and look at you. Still no mate, Igasho."* His stomach growled and pulled him back to his quest. *Tomorrow morning I will face the sun in the east again and sing a prayer song to be carried on the sun's rays and delivered to Appah.*

In the morning, Igasho requested that he fulfill his quest and asked for a squaw to be his mate. Many of his friends already had two wives, while he still had none. Most of the women were taken from other tribes, but Igasho had hoped to know the woman he married. To talk to her and test her heart. A deep sigh escaped his lips as he resigned to the idea of taking a bride. *Once my quest is complete, I will visit another tribe to find a wife.*

* * * *

"Salva me videre." Aurora spoke to the rod for help to see, hoping it would obey. The feel of the rod in her hand grew warm as an aura of magic encompassed her. She cast a nervous glance toward Jurom only to see the aura around him as well. "I'm not sure what I'm to do next."

"Walk to the hatch," Jurom said.

She moved over to the opening and stared down into the core. *Is that where the portal might be? It is well protected.* Sunlight lit the top-most floors accommodating the family bedchambers. For a moment, she thought she saw a light blink like a faraway star. *What was that?* She couldn't remember ever going that deep into the core. She repeated, "Help me to see," in the ancient language. Instantly, blue lines of light diagrammed each booby trap she knew, along with others she didn't know of deeper into the core.

"I see," she said to Jurom. "I see every trap. Does that mean I'm to go down there? I thought I saw a light. Is that where the portal is?"

"Dragons be not able to fit within the core. The portal ye seek be in a room next to the hidden chamber where the cup be held. Climb aboard, and I shall take ye to the portal."

Aurora scaled his foreleg and found her place on the flat, leathery spot where she stood holding on to the goldenhorn with her left hand and the rod clasped in her right. Light from the rod pointed over the temple roof and angered down the side of the building. Jurom didn't ask the way but followed the light's trajectory across the vine-covered outer walls to the large arched windows of the great hall.

The dragon tucked his wings and slipped into the room through the center window like thread through a needle. He circled once and landed on the floor in the great chamber where Aurora used to gather with her family. The rush of air stirred dust motes into beams of light slicing into the room from overhead. She dismounted and held the rod in front of herself. It was about the length of her forearm and cast a line of light to the other end of the hall to where a high table set upon the dais. Behind it were three archways leading to private rooms. The light pointed to the large center archway big enough to accommodate Jurom.

"That's strange. Until this moment, I've always seen two doors." She walked tentatively toward the newly exposed doorway. "Mother told me that someday one room would be the kitchen and the other a pantry." As she neared the newly exposed door, she pointed the rod toward the outer wall and watched the archway disappear. She waved the rod back toward the wall behind the dais, and the archway reappeared. Aurora proceeded cautiously and paused at the door. Beyond it, a swirling pool of images stirred within the floor. As she stepped into the room, energy brushed her skin with a prickly sensation. "I expected to see blue energy of a portal like you've told me about Jurom. This is different. It's like a window in the floor."

"From this side, it be like a window."

She stared into another world. A world where a patch of night sky sparkled with stars. As Jurom stepped through the archway to stand at her side, Arora stepped forward. The light of the rod went dark. It felt as if the floor dropped out from under her. Her breath caught in her throat. *"It's like the Midlands?"* Her eyes adjusted to a dim blue glow cast from the portal on this side. *"No. This is different."* She stared at her feet. *Solid ground.* She hadn't really dropped. It was more like a stepdown. No dizziness. No nausea. As Jurom stepped into the space beside her, his familiar smoky scent filled the confined space. She reached out and placed her hand against his side. Behind her, the portal swirled like a wall of blue energy large enough to accommodate the dragon. *"It is different on this side. Where are we? In a cave?"*

"Aye, it be a cave."

She clasped the rod in her right hand and brushed the fingers of her left hand along the wall feeling her way as she walked away from the portal to peer out at the world from the mouth of the cave. She marveled at the stars in the sky as she stepped out into the crisp night air. *Different stars*. Jurom lumbered up beside her. She stashed the rod in Da's satchel and climbed upon her goldenhorn.

* * * *

Igasho let out a deep sigh and looked up at the stars wishing his Spirit Guide would come quickly. Day three of his vision quest had proved to be the most difficult, and he wasn't really looking forward to day four. Fasting left him weak and his throat parched. He longed for a cool drink from the crystal waters of the Wind River and wondered how long it would take until he could taste it against his tongue. He got up and paced along the stone ridge, thinking of how his uncle fasted for seven days. *He even cut off three of his toes as a sacrifice before his quest Spirit Guide appeared to him in the form of a turtle. Why can't I be like father? He experienced his supernatural vision without going on a vision quest. At the rate I'm going, I'll reach the age of wisdom before I—*

A crackling noise broke the silence. *It sounds like... like burning kindling?* He crouched and scanned the dark landscape. *No sign of fire. No amber glow.* Overhead a loud rushing wind startled him as it whipped his hair over his head. *The thunder of wings!* He clambered toward the rock face and pressed his back against the cool stone as he squinted into the dark sky. Something blotted out the stars. *Something huge!* Another rush of wind pelted his naked chest with grit. His heart slammed against his ribs as his mind raced. *What could it be*? The noise faded, and he followed it as fast as his feet could carry him in the dark. *This could be it! My supernatural experience!* He whistled for his horse, Molala.

The stocky Cayuse with her high withers and unusually long cannon bone trotted up the ridge; the sound of her broken gait clear in the stillness. "Come on, girl," he urged her to hurry. As she drew near, he grabbed a hand full of her mane, threw his leg over her back, and turned her around. "Go Molala." She picked up speed but still moved slower than he wanted through the dark. Up ahead, the sound of a crashing tree branch reverberated through the stand of whitebark pines.

Igasho tugged Molala's mane gently, and she slowed to a stop. He slipped from her back as silently as a snake and crept into the woods. A snort unlike he'd ever heard sounded almost like the call of a ram's horn. He used the trees for cover and stole toward the noise. Then he heard it. *A voice! A woman's voice speaking in a strange tongue.*

Ahead, unnatural blue light shined within the trees. He crept forward and peered beyond his hiding spot to see a young woman holding the caerulean light in the palm of her hand. *Some sort of magic rocks.* In the surreal glow, it looked as if her other hand rested on the wing of a lizard the size of at least four giant boulders too big to be moved by men. Fear stole his breath for a moment. *This is my vision!*

His fear melted away, and he stepped forward to meet his powerful Spirit Guide and the woman with hair of fire who could hold light in her hand. "Tsaangu yeyeika. ene'e. E aise hakate? Ne ene'e?" (Good evening. Who are you? My spirit being?)

The woman spun to face him, the blue glow of the stones in her hand cast an eerie glow across her face, her eyes wide with surprise. The giant reptile turned its head to face him.

"It's him," the woman said. "The man with the coal-black hair!"

He stepped closer. Her voice sounded friendly enough. He placed his hand on his chest. "Igasho."

She nodded, took her hand away from the lizard, and placed it on her chest. "Ah-rohr-ah." Just as quickly, her hand returned to rest on the muscular chest of the giant lizard, its neck thicker than the tree which he had hidden behind. "Jurom," she said as she patted the lizard. Igasho pointed to the lizard, "Jurom." Then he gestured to the woman. "Ah-rohr-ah."

She nodded and walked toward him.

"Igasho," she repeated his name and stopped in front of him. She dropped the glowing stones to the ground, touched her head with her palm, and then reached out with her other hand to touch his head.

"Can you understand me, now?"

He jumped back and grabbed for the stone knife at his side. "I-I heard you in my head." He held the knife at the ready, trying to figure out what exactly he would try to attack. *This-this is the answer to my vision quest. It must be.* He blinked as he tried to make sense of it.

She motioned slowly with her hands with her palms toward the ground, much like he would do if trying to approach a wild horse. "I just wanted us to be able to understand one another," she said. "Can you understand me now when I speak?"

"I understand," he said as he sheathed his weapon. "You are truly a powerful spirit being." He wondered at his destiny. No one had ever returned from a vision quest with a woman guardian. Before he could even begin to grasp the idea, the lizard trumpeted and shot a stream of fire into the air. The woman, Aurora, turned to look at the giant lizard, and the fire stopped. She placed her hand on the lizard's great snout as smoke curled from its nostrils.

Igasho edged forward with his arm extended and stopped with his hand inches from the lizard. He glanced at the woman who took his hand and placed it on the great snout. *Her touch is flesh!* "You are not a spirit then?"

* * * *

Aurora tried not to stare at the young man, Igasho, as he crouched across the fire from her, testing the rabbit roasting. His stomach rumbled. "I look forward to this," he admitted. "I've been fasting."

"Fasting? For how long?"

"Three days. In fact, when I skipped the evening meal, it was the start of my fourth day." He pulled the rabbit from the fire and tore off a rear leg, handing the steaming meat to her.

She accepted it, but it was too hot to hold and so laid it on the rock beside her and licked her fingers. "Why have you been fasting?"

"I am on my vision quest."

He went on to tell her of his quest as they ate. Aurora drank in his story as well as his looks. His coal-black hair draped over his naked shoulders and down his back. His dark skin glistened in the firelight as if oiled. His red aura revealed he was strong-willed but realistic and survival-oriented. All good qualities in a husband. Especially a husband destined to return with her to her own land. His dark eyes looked from her to the dragon behind her and back to her.

She glanced over her shoulder at Jurom, who sat like a statue with his eyes narrowed on Igasho. His wings weren't folded close to his body but stayed partially extended. It was easy to see he felt uneasy in his new surroundings. *Does my dragon's oath hold here in this world?* she asked.

"Yes, thy oath holds true wherever ye be."

"But I can tell him I come from a different world?"

"Aye."

She turned back to face the fire, still impressed that Igasho had gone out and actually hunted this rabbit, skinned it, and cooked it. Jurom had hunted her meat for hundreds of years, and his skill reminded her of her brothers and Da. "This is delicious," she said as she searched for a way to start a deeper conversation.

Jurom let out a snort. *"I be going to find mine own dinner, and it shan't be such puny prey."* Without another word, his wings stroked the air and lifted his bulk into the air. The wind fanned the campfire. Igasho stared wide-eyed, watching the dragon disappear into the night sky.

"Where is the firebird going?"

Inwardly, she smiled at the thought of Jurom being called a bird. "He is hunting."

Igasho's dark brown eyes grew even wider. "Are my people safe?"

She liked that he thought of others. "Yes. He does not eat people."

He used a stick to scrape the embers of the fire toward the center. "I'm in awe of you," he said matter-of-factly.

"Me? Why?"

"You are a powerful guide." At the heart of his aura, the red transformed to pink, showing his sensual side or—thoughts of a romantic relationship. *He must know why I am here.*

"I am more than your guide," she said as she wondered how her own aura must look at this point. "I am here to become your wife. It is why I have come." As the words tumbled from her lips, she'd never felt so vulnerable—so exposed. He pushed to his feet. The rash movement startled her. *Is he leaving?*

"On my vision quest, I hoped to find a powerful Spirit Guide able to protect me–and a wife." He started to pace. "I came here to fast and pray and to return to my people with answers. I hoped for a lizard to be my guide. I thought maybe at least a turtle."

"A turtle?" Aurora swallowed hard, trying to fight the smile tugging at the corners of her mouth. "Why a turtle?"

"A turtle gives the ability to cure the sick."

Her amusement turned to confusion. "In my world, a turtle is a reptile that has a shell… its head and legs can pull into the shell for protection. Is that how it is here?"

He nodded. "And here the turtle can see through the water and can help a healer see through the patient to see why they are sick or hurt."

"Ah, that makes sense." She took another bite of meat.

"My people, the Newe (*nuh-wuh*), live in cliff dwellings or in the warm valley depending on the time of year. What are your people called?"

"My people," she repeated, wondering how to explain things. "My parents came from a far country I never knew. They settled in a valley. There they became friends with the—the firebirds. My parents had a family of five boys and then me."

"Do they all have hair the color of fire?"

Her hand self-consciously moved to the braid draped across her shoulder. "No, not all of us. Some have light hair, others brown hair."

"Perhaps I shall call you Waianten."

"Waianten?"

"The names of my people grow with life. Waianten means fire. I know no other woman with hair of such color." He placed his hand on his bare chest. "And my name, Igasho, means wanderer."

"Interesting. My name, Aurora, means light in the sky. And I think Igasho is actually a good name, for as my husband, you will wander to a far-off land."

"So I would be chief among your tribe. Tell me more about this land you come from."

She stood up and brushed the seat of her trousers. "Better yet, I can take you there."

"Now?"

"Yes. It won't take long."

"It is far, but it will not take long?" He stood proud and tall but could not hide his puzzlement. "Shall I call my horse?"

"Not this time." She reached out her hand. "Come."

"Jurom!" she called with her mind. *"Come! I'm taking Igasho to the temple."*

Igasho stepped toward her and clasped her hand. His touch thrilled her. It had been so long since she made physical contact with another person. She walked back the way she came with Igasho in tow. When they reached the cave, Jurom circled overhead and landed quickly, peppering them with grit. Igasho protected his eyes with his forearm. Jurom lumbered into the cave complaining that he hadn't had a chance to eat. Aurora started to follow, but Igasho stood like an anchor staring into the darkness of the maw and still holding her hand. "How can this be the way?"

"Do not fear Jurom. He is my protector. He leads us to a gateway that takes us from your land to mine. It is a secret only known to me—a secret I now share with you." She reached into her satchel with her free hand and pulled out three starstones. Almost instantly, they glowed and lit the mouth of the cave. She rested her hand on the therus rod within the satchel and used it to activate the portal as she tugged Igasho forward. He willingly followed with cautious steps. Deeper into the cave, Jurom stood beside the swirling blue light of the portal on the farthest wall. "This is it," Aurora said. Jurom walked through the churning energy.

"A gateway of light." Igasho stared at the mysterious vision with the portal's light shining like blue stars in his dark eyes.

Aurora nodded and followed her dragon through the portal with Igasho in tow.

CHAPTER THIRTY-FIVE

The couple stepped into the great hall behind Jurom as late afternoon sun spilled through the arched windows through curtains of hanging ivy, which created dancing shadows across the stone floor. Behind them, the archway blinked out of view as Igasho stared into the diffused sunlight squinting. "It is day here in your land!"

Jurom stepped over the table on the dais like it wasn't there, while Igasho almost bumped into it as he stared at the vastness of the room. Aurora yanked his hand and pulled him like a child around it and, for the first time, saw him clearly in the light dressed in nothing but a loincloth.

"This is a strange land," he said.

"We are in the Temple of Five Marks. The land is beyond these walls."

Jurom flew to one of the great-arched windows near the ceiling, stirring a great wind within the hall before he slipped out of view and into the daylight. Aurora stopped. Jurom's quick departure without saying anything surprised her. *What do I do now?*

"We'll take the stairs," she said.

"Stairs?"

She pointed toward the flight of steps leading up to the door that would take them to the terraced outer walls of the temple. "That way."

Before they reached the door, Igasho paused before the mural on the southernmost wall.

"I have never seen such images."

"My brother Kylar's work," she said. "This is what life was like when my family first came here. She explained how they lived in mountaintops that floated in the air, how the "firebirds" helped with the cutting and moving of the big stones, and how they worked with her Da and brothers to construct the temple.

"What is that?" He pointed to a young man on a rope bridge with his bow trained on a myrnex on the ground.

"Myrnex. They are the reason no one lives here any longer. They are ground dwellers that eat people and animals. If they come up under you, it creates a funnel in the ground and takes you by surprise. The ground drops out from under your feet and swallows you." She made a circular downward motion with her finger. "If they even touch you with their razor-sharp teeth, venom paralyzes you, they drag you below, and you are gone."

His hand moved to the stone blade at his waist. "So you live here alone? In this huge structure? With those deadly meernex outside the walls?"

"I have Jurom," she said, "but all my people have moved down the river."

"Why did you not go with your tribe?"

"I must stay here for now. It's complicated. I have something I must accomplish before I can leave here. A responsibility I must fulfill." Frustration mounted as she tried to explain her life without breaking her innate Dragonborn vow. She sucked in a deep breath and let it out little by little, surprised at the emotions ready to erupt within her. "But I long to belong to a tribe—to have children." She glanced at him to see his reaction but quickly turned away as she felt a rush of color burn across her fair cheeks. *I don't even know if he is willing to be my husband. How could I say such a thing!* She focused on the heavy door at the top of the stairs and changed the subject. "We go out up there." She pointed and hurried up the stairs regretting that she had said such a thing to a man she didn't know. *But I did say it, and I can't take it back.*

Her heart quickened as she wondered what he thought—what he would do. She reached out to Jurom but felt detached. The disconnect scared her as Igasho's bare feet slapped against the stone slabs behind her. *Jurom!* she reached out again. A sense of panic filled her as she lifted the latch and tugged the door. It refused to open. "I-I can't open it," she admitted. "It hasn't been used in a long time." She glanced up at the row of windows. *Jurom, the door is stuck*!

Igasho stepped forward, lifted the latch, and pulled. The muscles in his shoulders worked, and the door swung open enough for them to squeeze out. He pulled aside the veil of ivy and stepped out into the sunshine. Aurora followed and, with her foot, scraped aside the blanket of ivy to expose the steps. "These lead up the side of the temple to the roof. We're going up there." She scanned the sky for any sign of Jurom, wondering where he had gone and why he wasn't answering her.

The two of them made short work of climbing the stairs. They passed arched entries to other levels draped in ivy until they reached the flat roof. They stood there catching their breath. Igasho's torso glistened in the sunlight as he pointed to Jurom standing on the rooftop. His eyes grew wide as he stared at not only Jurom but a second dragon. "There is my Guide and another. Is that your Spirit Guide?"

Aurora blinked in disbelief. "That? That is Tozet. Jurom's mate." She marched toward Jurom, who stood like a majestic statue staring at her. Aurora reached out in anger. *"Jurom, why didn't you answer me? Why is Tozet here?"*

* * * *

Jurom flew through the arched window tearing through the ivy. His leathery wings beat the air taking him higher above the temple. He felt like he needed to get away—away from the Newe man from America who had come here too soon. The man who now caused him to ignore Aurora's calls to him. "*Tozet!*" he called to his mate. "*I need ye here with me now.*"

"What be wrong, Jurom? Be thou injured?"

"No. It be worse than that. Hurry. Travel the Midlands. I need ye at mine side. The man to be Aurora's mate be here."

"It be too soon!"

"Aye, I know this. Come, perhaps ye can see a way to rectify this. I need thy help."

Again, Aurora called to him. It hurt him not to answer, but he did not know what to say to her. He could see how happy she felt, finally to have a mate. *How can I tell her it be too soon?* Before he could begin to ponder his question, a burst of light exploded at the corner of the flat temple roof. Tozet stepped from the golden halo of light brighter than the suns; her iridescent purple scales shimmered with a rainbow of colors. The light blinked out, and the rooftop returned to dappled sunlight as clouds scuttled across the sky.

The two dragons greeted each other as they rubbed their boney eye ridges. The throat pouch at the base of Tozet's neck bulged with life. Suddenly two hatchlings peeked from the white marsupium.

"Ye brought the hatchlings?"

"What would ye have me do with them? They be too young to fend for themselves." As they spoke, the two hatchlings squirmed free of the pouch, dropped to the ground, and flapped and stretched their wings before climbing aboard their mother's back to the flat area around her goldenhorn.

Aurora and the dark-haired Newe man stepped onto the rooftop from the northern stairs. The man's dark eyes grew wide as he looked from Jurom to Tozet? But Jurom was caught by Aurora's icy stare. *"Why didn't you answer me? Why is Tozet here?"*

"I know not what to say to thee, Aurora."

"Aurora? You never call me by my name. What have I done to offend you?"

Jurom looked behind her at the Newe man who had his back to them as he looked out toward the Inkish River.

"I see the river you spoke of," the man said, "but where are the floating mountain tops?" He glanced up to scan the cloudy sky. "But two suns!"

"They have moved on," Aurora said without taking her eyes off the two dragons. "I don't know where. Perhaps the-the firebirds put them back where they took them from." She turned her attention directly to Jurom *"Jurom? What have I done? Why won't you answer me? You're scaring me."*

"Ye have done what dragons feared all along. Ye be Dragonborn, double Dragonborn of the Thornose and the Goldenhorn. And now ye

have invited this man here from another world without the agreement of the dragons?"

"Wait. What are you talking about?" She gestured toward Igasho, who still had his back to her as he stared out at the vast land around them. *"He is the man I saw in my vision. You even said he was the man."*

Jurom turned and looked at her with his blue-green multi-faceted eyes narrowed and violet in color. *"He be the man. This be not the time. This be why I called Tozet from Jur-Jurom. For her gift of foresight may help us repair any damage caused by thy mistake."*

* * * *

Aurora's jaw dropped. She didn't know what to say! Jurom's answer stunned her but, even more, his coolness toward her hurt her feelings.

"If it was such a mistake to bring him here, then why didn't you stop me?"

"When should I have done so? Before or after ye said, "I'm taking Igasho to the temple?'"

She froze. *What have I done?*

"I'm sorry. I didn't realize." In her excitement, she'd impulsively done what she felt like doing without talking about it. She glanced at Igasho, who turned and looked at her with the unasked question of what to do next. The once simple question was, now, riddled with problems. *"What can I do now?"* she asked Jurom.

"Is something wrong?" Igasho asked as his eyes looked from Aurora to the dragon and then at the heather-colored dragon with young sleeping upon its back.

Aurora looked at Igasho and shrugged. "I guess we are early. You are to be my husband, but…." She glanced at Jurom. *"But not yet?"*

Igasho walked over, placed his palm against Jurom's side, and patted him as if he were a horse. "Perhaps my Spirit Guide will show us what to do next. After all, he is the one who led us here."

The bony ridge above Jurom's eyes raised about an inch as he stared hard at the man and released tendrils of smoke with a frustrated breath.

"Aurora, we must return him to his world." Jurom's large head swung to face her.

Aurora spluttered for a moment as she looked from Jurom to Igasho. She stretched her arms to her sides and let them drop. "Now that you've seen my world, maybe we should go back so I can meet your tribe."

Tozet let out a short snort followed by a light clicking.

"This be not humorous!" Jurom scolded.

"This child be always a challenge, Jurom. Why not take the two of them to see the land before they go back to his world? It will give them something to talk about over the next year before they come here to stay."

Jurom swung his face to meet his mate. *"What! Do ye mean for her to stay in his world until they come here? Do ye understand what that portends for her?"*

Aurora took Igasho's hand. "Come, your Spirit Guide is going to take us back to the, um, the gateway of light." When Jurom didn't offer his foreleg for her to climb, she ran up his broad tail, avoiding the stunted barbs that formed a protective ridge, and hurried to his goldenhorn. Igasho's bare feet followed as if he'd run the tail a hundred times with practiced ease.

Jurom pondered the problem pushing in on him. *Is this how we should handle this—this inappropriateness that goes against the plans laid down by the Thornose so long ago?*

* * * *

As Igasho's hand reached out to hold Jurom's goldenhorn, the connection startled the dragon. He could hear the man's thoughts! *He truly believes I be his Spirit Guide! Perhaps I can use this.*

Igasho! he reached out in a stern voice. *I be thy Spirit Guide.*

Igasho's dark eyes grew wide with wonder. "I hear you, Spirit Guide, and I listen."

Aurora's brows raised in mild surprise.

"Mine mate and I shall show ye the land where ye shall live with thy wife and tribe in the future, but the time be not yet."

The young man's bronze shoulders sagged just slightly. *Without her, who will believe me? But who am I to question my Spirit Guide? I will trust him.* He nodded. "I understand."

"Will I have Ah-rohr-ah to be my wife before I reach the age of wisdom?"

"She shall be thy wife when the suns go down this day, and tomorrow ye shall return to thy people until binangu daza–summer next."

Igasho placed his hand on top of Aurora's on the goldenhorn. "Tonight, you shall be my wife—my Waianten."

A blush burned across Aurora's face as she nodded. "Yes, I shall be your Waianten."

Tozet's voice broke into their private moment. *"Aurora, ye shall ride upon mine back to spy out the land."*

"But—Jurom?"

"Tozet be right. Go. Ride mine, mate."

After explaining the plan to Igasho, she dismounted and climbed aboard Tozet, where she nestled her legs between the two hatchlings. When her palm touched Tozet's goldenhorn, visions flashed through her mind. She saw herself in her bed-chamber with Igasho, traveling through the portal to his world, a crowd of dark-haired, brown-eyed people staring at her as she stood beside her husband, living in a house made of grass and a baby! She saw a baby in her future. And then? A second baby? *"How can this be?"* she asked.

The dragons flapped their vast wings and lifted off the temple roof. They followed the river to the west, but Aurora hardly noticed. *"How can I have two babies if we are only to be there for a year?"*

"Time be different in thy mate's world. Ye will age faster there, and so will thy children. And thy pregnancies shall pass by quickly."

"I'm so sorry," she admitted again to Tozet as she clasped the female's goldenhorn with two hands. *"I didn't mean to cause such trouble."*

"I know. But the trouble be trouble, and it be not just thine, for the time ye spend in thine mate's world will cut short thy life in this world. And one will have to take thy place as the priestess of the temple to close out thy responsibilities."

Aurora heaved a deep sigh as she glanced over at Igasho riding on Jurom's back. She could see Igasho's lips moving. He and Jurom were communicating, but she couldn't hear them! They traveled over Red Grove and Man's Bow and finally swept across the Nalhdyn Mountains and Tachnir before turning back toward Five Marks and the temple. But to her surprise, they flew beyond Five Marks following the Inkish River to the east where it met the sea. Here the soil was fertile and the sea full of life. It was here the dragons came to die in the mountains along the eastern shoreline. *"This be where ye and thy tribe shall live."*

Hope renewed in her heart. She had made a mistake, and it came with a cost, *but I can't change the past*. She thought about her parents and how they had traveled back in time to change the future. *If I'm not careful, I could ruin all they sacrificed so much to change*. She looked over at Igasho, and their eyes met. Her misgivings unraveled as a thread pulled on the tapestry of what might be. She drank in his broad smile. *His heart is bright*. Her fingertips brushed the smile on her lips, knowing she mirrored his happiness as they banked over the eastern mountains and headed back toward the temple where Igasho was to become her husband.

CHAPTER THIRTY-SIX

Aurora awoke in the dark to the whisper of steady breathing beside her. The sound exhilarated her. It had been so long since she had shared human companionship. Now her husband slept beside her. *Husband!* She threw back her bed fur and slipped from her bed. In the inky darkness, she spun around in a dance of joy before lighting a handful of starstones. She set the stones on the small table where she had spent hundreds of years alone studying. They cast the familiar blue glow across her bed and the man who had changed her name and promised her a new life. He opened his eyes and reached out his hand, inviting her back to their wedding bed.

"Come, Waianten."

She walked over and accepted his hand. His warm touch sent a thrill through her as her knees met the mattress. He pulled her to him and kissed her gently. She placed her hand on his bare chest and asked, *"What shall your new name be?"*

His smile faded. "It could be Waci-ttikih."

Her brows knit into a frown. "What does it mean?"

"It means to keep secret, or to hide something."

She let out a long breath. "Yes, that could be your name, but it's too hard to say. And if you have a secret, you don't tell everyone by your name. Don't you have something easier?"

"How about Angitsuku? It means flying-man. I still can't believe I flew on the back of the firebird."

"You can have that name when we come here to live. For now, let's call you the lying down man." She laughed a lighthearted laugh that drifted into the booby-trapped temple core. "How would you say that?"

"Happitsuku." He pulled her toward him and kissed her again.

Aurora sat cross-legged on the rooftop, eating the meat Jurom delivered and cooked, just the way she liked it. Igasho squatted across from her. He ate while he rambled about the firebirds and how they not only hunted but cooked the food. But Aurora hardly listened as she pondered the things Tozet had shown her the day before. Part of her was so excited about having children, but the dire prophecy about causing someone else to take her place in the temple bothered her. She didn't wish such a lonely existence on anyone. Plus, it meant that at least one of her offspring would be Dragonborn.

"Waianten? Waianten, did you hear me?"

Aurora snapped out of it. "I'm sorry! I was thinking about our future."

He placed his hand on her shoulder. "My people will love you. I can't wait to return from my vision quest with a wife. No one has ever done such a thing."

His excitement made her laugh until Jurom said, *"It be time to leave."*

* * * *

They stepped down through the secret portal carrying nothing but her father's bag, which held the therus rod, a few of her personal belongings, and a supply of starstones. Jurom followed them through the portal's pool of light and into the cave. As the portal blinked closed behind them, the light of the full moon spilled across the floor through the opening. They stepped to the mouth of the cave, where the crisp night air chilled them.

Igasho rubbed his arms for warmth. "I forgot that it is night in my land when day in your land." His brow furrowed. "But how is it already the daza-mea summer moon? I was only away for one day."

"Ye must tell him that time here be quick moving for thee. That if ye stay, ye will be an old woman before thy time."

"I will tell him when the time is right."

"Do not keep it from him, or it be trouble hiding around the corner for thee."

She placed her hand on his side. *"Please, Jurom. Let me take care of this."*

"Very well. I will check with thee in a couple of days." Jurom started to make the tight turn to swing back toward the portal.

"Wait, where are you going? Aren't you coming with us?"

"My place be not in this world, for here I, too, age quicker. It be not fair to mine mate nor mine hatchlings."

The thought of quickly growing old scared her. She didn't like it. "*How old will I be when I come home?"*

"For every turning of the four seasons here, thou shall age five times that."

She nodded. That wasn't as bad as she thought as long as she didn't overstay her time.

Igasho walked up to Jurom and placed his hand on the dragon's snout. *"Aren't you coming with us? My people will never believe me when I tell them of your size, or your breath of fire, or that I flew through the sky upon your back. That you are truly my spiritual guide."*

"I will return from time to time and reveal mineself to thy people. For now, thou must bring thy bride to thy people and tell them of thy vision quest. Tell them that Aurora be from a faraway land beyond the gateway of light. Gather and ready thy tribe. Those who believe shall be willing to follow thee through the gate of light at the next summer moon. Unbelievers and the fearful shall stay here. It be a journey for the stout-hearted."

Igasho stood a little taller and nodded. *"Then I shall see you soon, Spirit Guide?"*

"Ye shall see me soon, mine spirit child." Jurom turned around. His long tail scraped across the ground, stopping just short of knocking their legs out from under them. He swung his mammoth head back to face them and glanced at Aurora. *"Be ye good, Little One. I shall miss thee."* He stepped into the swirling blue light, and as

his tail cleared the threshold, it blinked out of existence, leaving Aurora and Igasho standing just outside the cave in the bright moonlight.

* * * *

Aurora suddenly felt very out of place. The only thing she knew of this land was that it was home to a man she already cared for deeply. "What do we do now?"

He smiled and stared at her without answering.

She smoothed her hair self-consciously. "What are you looking at?"

"Even in the light of the moon, I can see your hair is the color of fire. It brings to mind a poem. 'The white star at twilight is fair, and the sky clears at the day's end, but she is more fair to me, more dear to me, she is my heart's friend.'"

Aurora rested her head on his shoulder. "Thank you. So what do we do now, husband? Go to live with your tribe?"

"While I enjoyed the simple marriage custom of your land in sharing your bed, I think before I take you to the tribe, we should take a day to teach you the steps to the Sacred Fire Ceremony."

"Steps? How many steps?"

"Do not fret about it. It's a beautiful ceremony symbolic of two lives becoming one."

"We have a ceremony like that. We call it tying the knot. It includes dancing."

"Really? Then when we move to your land, maybe we can combine the two and start a new tradition. For tonight, do you want to sleep within the cave or beneath the stars?"

"I've slept in the dark for many years. I think I'd like to sleep under the stars in the moonlight."

"We shall sleep within the trees where the white pines sprinkle a cushion of soft needles." He glanced around.

"What are you looking for?"

"Molala, my horse."

Horse? She thought of her mother's stories which included animals called horses. *Perhaps they came from here.*

He placed his fingers to his lips and let out a shrill whistle. About a minute later, the broken gait of the horse joined the sounds of crickets. The stocky roan pony walked up the slope toward them, easily visible in the light of the summer moon. As she neared Igasho, she whinnied and trotted toward him. He greeted the horse much like Aurora greeted Jurom.

"Molala this is my wife, Waianten."

The horse took a step back when Aurora reached out to touch her. *"I won't hurt you,"* she thought to the animal. The animal didn't answer. It didn't even seem to hear her. She hadn't used her magic much in a long time. Perhaps, it didn't work here.

"Don't worry, she will accept you soon enough." Igasho patted the horse's flank. "Be a good horse, Molala." He stepped away from the animal and crouched. "I will start a fire warm us during the night."

As he kindled the fire, it stunned Aurora that he did it all with no magic. She took advantage of the moment and cast a quick spell, "*Aperire aures et audire ad bestias hoc mundo vocem meam."* If it worked, the beasts of this world would be able to communicate with her. To test it, she reached out to Molala. *"I won't hurt you. I love Igasho and want to be your friend."*

The mare shook her head, whinnied. *"How is it I understand you?"*

"It is a gift. I can hear and speak with you and other animals."

"But why? It is not natural?"

"Where I come from, it is very natural. I hope you will be my friend."

Molala nuzzled her hand, lifted her head, and gently blew air through her nostrils into Aurora's face. *"Now, when I am thirsty and want to stop for a drink, I will not have to wait for Igasho to figure it out."*

Aurora giggled.

Igasho looked up from fanning the flame. "What is funny?"

"Your little horse likes me. I find it pleasing."

In the light and warmth of the fire, the two talked. Since both ate breakfast before coming through the portal, neither were tired nor hungry. "Let me teach you about the Sacred Fire Ceremony."

"Very well, what do I do?"

"First, my people will build a fire circle with stones. They build the sides high." He motioned with his hand to indicate the height. "Then the shaman cuts seven types of wood from specific kinds of trees. Three separate fires burn within the circle. The largest fire at the center of the fire circle represents the Creator and the holy union of two people. Two smaller fires will signify us and our individual lives before the ceremony. The shaman sprinkles things like tobacco, sage, corn, and sweetgrass on the fires and us with songs. We will offer a prayer."

"A prayer? How will I know what to say?"

"You will be fine. We can pray silently. And after a short time, we will push the two small fires into the large fire in the center as everyone sings praises to the Creator as our two lives join as one.

"That sounds easy enough."

"Yes, it is. Very special. And then we dance."

"Dance? We do that too in tying of the knot." She thought back to her brother Kylar and how silly he looked as he danced before his bride.

"As we dance," Igasho said, "we will make our vows. I will start." He pulled Aurora to her feet and pointed a few feet away. "Go stand over there."

She took about four steps and turned to face him. "Here?"

"Yes, that's fine." He walked in the opposite direction and turned to face her. "Now imagine the large fire circle between us. We will each take seven steps sunwise around the sacred fire. With each step, we will make a vow."

"Out loud?"

"Of course. All family and friends form a circle to hear us." He flashed her a smile, but she worried about the language. Jurom had fixed it so they could understand each other, but what about the people of his tribe? *I might just have to come up with another enchantment.* "Who goes first?" she asked.

"I do. We do this until you make your final vow and we have circled the fire completely. Then friends and family join hands around the fire."

"Can you tell me these vows? What to say? So I can prepare?"

"There are many words to learn, so I will begin to teach you, but I have an idea that could help. Do you think my Spirit Guide, Jurom, would come to the ceremony?"

"Jurom? I-I don't know." Mentally she reached out to her lifetime companion to ask him, but just as quickly realized he wasn't there. It would take time. "Why do you ask?"

"I can see he talks to you as he talks to me. I know the words for the vows of the Sun Dance and can tell him the words, and then he can tell them to you. You will know what to say, and those of my family and friends will think nothing of it."

Aurora ran toward Igasho and threw her arms around his neck. "What a wonderful idea, my husband!" But just as suddenly, she let her arms drop. *Have I said too much? Did I break my oath? I must be careful.* She changed her tactic. *I can use the information he gives me.* "How do you hear him?"

"Mind to mind. It first happened when I touched the great horn when we flew. Jurom confirmed that he is my Spirit Guide."

That's what she needed. "But can you hear Jurom if you're not touching him?"

Igasho looked into the distance, his lips pouting in thought. "Every time I heard his voice, I was touching him."

"What would your tribe think about that? Having your Spirit Guide at the ceremony?"

"That is an interesting question. Those not on a vision quest may see Jurom as a creature to be conquered and even killed."

Aurora stared into the flames. “Maybe I should return to the temple and talk to Jurom to see if he has a solution.” She turned her gaze to Igasho, who let out a deliberate breath and nodded.

“You can go tomorrow, and I will wait here for you.”

“Are you sure?” It felt odd to her that he wanted her to stay, and after centuries of doing as she pleased, the way he gave his permission for her to go slightly annoyed her.

Igasho walked over to her and took her hand. “If you want, you can stay, and I will go talk to Jurom.”

He doesn’t realize how the portal works. “Why not go together?”

He shrugged. “As it is with the fire dance, everything my people do is in a circle because the Power of the World always works in circles, and everything tries to be round. The sky is round, and the earth is round like a ball. Birds make their nest in circles, and even the seasons form a great circle in their changing. And they always come back again to where they were. The life of a man is a circle from childhood to childhood. So it is in everything where power moves. You and I are creating a circle, and if one of us stays, it does not break that circle in my world.”

Her annoyance melted. Igasho wasn’t bossy or overbearing but following beliefs that would bring the best life for them.

“I’ll go,” she said. “And I’ll hurry.” She leaned into Igasho and hid her face against his bare chest. She drank of his scent and turned her head to listen to his heart. It eased her fears of the unknown. *I will get used to this new world. I know I'm destined to spend my future with this man.* She looked up at him. "When should I go?"

“As much as I don’t want you to leave, I think you should go now. Jurom may still be at the temple, and the sooner we talk with him, the sooner we will know if this plan can work, for he is my Spirit Guide.”

CHAPTER THIRTY-SEVEN

Igasho walked back to the cave with Aurora. In the half-light of the moon, he appeared wraith-like. "I'll hurry back." She kissed him on the cheek and disappeared into the cave as she drew the therus rod from her shoulder bag and opened the portal. Unseen energy brushed his skin as she walked through the swirling force and stepped up from the gateway within the floor on the other side. Daylight leaked into the large hall from the vine-covered windows high above her. The familiar stale smells of the temple hit her. Compared to the fresh air in America, out under the stars, here it hung heavy and stagnant.

"Little One!" Jurom sounded excited.

"Yes! I'm back. I need to talk with–." Before she finished her thought, the flap of wings drew her attention to the large center window the dragons used to come in and out of the room. Jurom's green-scaled underbelly looked darker as he extended his legs to land. Behind him, Tozet glided through the same window and landed beside her mate.

Aurora ran over to them, excited to share about her new home. Jurom leaned his head forward and let her rub his bony ridge. *"We be waiting for thee."*

"Waiting? How did you know I'd be coming back?"

"Tozet foretold ye be back."

She turned to stare at Tozet. *"How?"*

"I be able to see things future. Sometimes far future, other times near future."

Aurora patted Jurom's snout and wondered why she hadn't seen her return with her personal ability. She walked over to rub the ridges of a hatchling whose head popped free from his mother's neck pouch. She turned to look at Tozet. *"Do you know why I am here?"*

"Nay. But we know ye would not return so quickly if it be not important."

"That is true. Here is the situation...." She explained about the Fire Dance and how they hoped that Jurom might be able to help. *"Igasho is the one who thought of it,"* she finished.

Tozet swung her head toward Jurom as if to whisper something. Instead, she said, *"loqui?"*

Jurom didn't answer right away. *"It be a tool used yet future for humans to communicate with dragons."*

"That's it!" The news filled Aurora with hope. "*So what is it, and where do I find it?"*

"It be far off in the mountains north."

She walked over, sat on the stairs, propped her elbows on her knees, and cupped her chin in her hands. *"I told him I'd hurry."* Her eyes brightened. "Maybe we can take the Midlands!"

The two dragons looked at each other. Tozet said, *"Ye talk to her. She be thy Little One."*

"What! Why are you two acting so strangely?"

"Let us go to the roof and talk. Tozet ye go and gather the loqui."

Aurora climbed Jurom's foreleg and sat upon the familiar flat spot around the goldenhorn. But it felt different. *Things have changed.*

They cut through the ink vine draped across the high arched window and broke into the sunshine. Blue skies stretched overhead. With eyes closed and face tilted toward the suns, the familiar brought happiness. Almost instantly, they landed on the roof. Aurora expected to see Tozet, but the dragon was nowhere in sight.

For a moment, she lingered next to the goldenhorn. Who knew the next time she'd be able to ride. *"So why did you send Tozet instead of you and me going to collect the loqui?"*

"There be not time enough."

She laughed as she slid to the ground. *"You know that's not true. Traveling the Midlands eliminates the time element."*

"That be true, but ye cannot travel the Midlands."

"What are you talking about? I've traveled the Midlands since I was a child!"

He swung his massive head to look her in the eye. *"Ye cannot travel when with child."* His eyes were pinning with excitement.

"With—with child? Are you sure?"

"I be sure, and ye shall be sure soon enough."

Aurora placed her hand on her stomach. It felt no different, *but I feel different.* A flood of emotion washed over her, and tears flowed down her cheeks.

"Why be ye crying? I thought ye wanted younglings."

"I do. I do. It's just so much change all at one time. And I thought I would give birth to my children in Jur-Jurom."

Jurom snickered. She cherished the light clicking mirth. "*Ye be the only human born in Jur-Jurom, Little One. Ye be a one-and-only. And ye be right about change. I face not your absence well."*

"So, will you come to America and help us with the wedding?"

"I shall come, but I know not if the loqui shall work within the America world."

"What is it?"

Buttery golden light flashed, and Tozet stepped through the opening from the Midlands. She shook herself much like a wet dog, and Aurora laughed. "So I'm not the only one that feels like that when I step from the Midlands."

Two hatchlings spilled to the ground from her neck pouch, each carrying a pink crystal. They hurried toward Aurora. *"Can you hear me? Can you hear me?"* they asked in unison.

Aurora went down on one knee and welcomed the hatchlings. *"I hear you."* They dropped the crystals in front of her and scampered off, chasing one another as if her answer startled them. She lifted one of the pink crystals in the sunlight. *"This is loqui?"*

"That be it."

He went on to explain how it opened communication between humans and dragons. *"Thy Igasho can wear it and hear me… if it be the same in the world America as it be here."*

"Can you come with me then so we can test it?"

He glanced at the cloudless sky and then bowed his head before her. *"I will come, Little One. Let me say farewell to mine mate, and we shall be off."*

She watched the tender moment as the two dragons intertwined their necks and rubbed their bone ridges together. The two hatchlings ran up to Jurom's goldenhorn, but Tozet ordered them to come to her. As Aurora climbed aboard Jurom's back, she felt selfish for taking him away from his family. *"You will be back soon,"* she said as she patted his neck. But he took off without a word, and for the first time, a sense of the unknown flooded her. She hadn't realized it until now, but her gift of foresight was no longer working!

CHAPTER THIRTY-EIGHT

Daylight surprised Aurora as she and Jurom passed through the portal. "It is daytime?" She clambered to the ground. "I wonder where Igasho is." She rushed to the mouth of the cave and scanned right and left. "I thought he would be here. Let's go down this way." She pointed to the stand of whitebark pines where they had watched the stars through the branches.

"Waianten!" Igasho called from the base of the slope riding Molala. The horse whinnied with fear of the giant lizard and froze in place with her head held high. Igasho slipped from her back and hurried uphill, and embraced Aurora. "I have been worried about you."

"Worried? Why?"

"After two days, I started to think maybe you changed your mind. By day three, I thought perhaps something happened to you. I went to the gate of light, but it was dark—nothing but rock. On the fourth day, I started fasting and prayed as I faced the sun in the east in the morning and singing a prayer song to be carried on the sun's rays and delivered to Appah that you would return. And here you are today."

"You mean four days have passed?"

"Today is the fifth day. Why? How long did you think you were gone?"

"I didn't even sleep yet. I went, picked up something that might work for our plan, and I returned!"

Igasho shook his head. "Times are certainly different, but what is important is that you are here. Tell me, what did you bring?"

She pulled the loqui crystal from her shoulder bag and handed it to him.

He turned it over in his hand. Sunlight glinted off the pink crystal.

"Can ye hear mine voice?" Jurom asked.

Igasho glanced up at Aurora with wide eyes and nodded as he looked to Jurom. *"I do hear you! I do hear you, my Spirit Guide!"*

"It works," he said to Aurora. "I hear him clearly in my thoughts."

They caught up on all that had transpired in their time apart while Jurom went off to hunt. "I have something for you, too." Igasho walked over the rock wall, reached into a crevice, and pulled out a folded animal hide. "I have made this for you because your strange clothing will cause my people to be suspicious." He lifted a garment in front of himself and let it unfurl. He stretched out his arms measured it in front of her. "It might be a little too big."

His words brought a smile as she thought about the fact that she was with child. The garment looked to be made of deerskins, with the yolk painted gold and outlined with fur and decorated with a deer's tail on the front. "I've never seen anything like this," she admitted.

"Put it on. I want to see it on you."

Suddenly she felt awkward. "Turn around."

"Turn?" A scowl knit his brow. "For what purpose?"

"I don't want you to see me until I am wearing it."

He rolled his eyes but did as she asked and stared into the sky as he waited. When he turned around to see her, his eyes shined with pride. "You are a beautiful woman, Waianten. Here are the belt and bindings for your braids. My work is not as good as that of a woman's delicate work, but it will pass until you learn to make a belt, yourself."

"Braids? You mean more than one?"

He nodded. "Our women wear their hair in two braids."

After she braided her hair into the two-braid style bound with red cloth, he said, "Just one more thing, and you will be ready. But first, I have something to show you."

Excitement filled her. Everything was new and different. Igasho slowed and looked at her with dark eyes shining with mischief. "Now, it is your turn to close your eyes." A light laugh left her lips and carried on the breeze as she closed her eyes. They walked about twenty paces beyond the portal cave with him leading her by the hand. When he stopped, he said, "Open your eyes."

Before her, red rock paintings depicted a sun–the one sun of this world–a woman holding something in her hand with lines indicating light surrounding her. And there beside her, a rudimentary drawing of Jurom with his wings outstretched. Aurora stared. *Is this good or bad?* She wasn't sure. *Is it alright to record me being here in this way?*

"My people record their visions and history, much like your brother, Ky-lar, did. These symbols mark the history of my vision quest. He pointed to the sun. It represents me facing the sun in the east and singing a prayer song to be carried on the sun's rays and delivered to Appah for me to fulfill my quest and for a squaw to be my mate. Now, this is a most sacred place for it represents the intimate connection between me and my spirit world—my Spirit Guide—and the wife I prayed for."

Aurora reached out and touched the image representing her and looked at the trace of red on her fingertips. "What did you use to paint this?"

"It is found in the rock and crushed." He picked up a small ceramic bowl on the ground at the base of the rock. "I brought this with me to record my vision quest. My chronicle is not yet complete." He dipped his finger in the red pigment and ran it down the center part of her hair.

She grabbed his wrist. "What are you doing?"

"This is a decoration worn by the women of my people."

She released his hand. "Decoration?" She'd never heard of decorating one's self.

As he finished, the stir of wind overhead warned of Jurom's return. He carried a large animal like a deer but grander in size with antlers almost as high as she was tall. "What is that!"

"Wapiti," Igasho said. He looked at Jurom as he dropped the animal. "Do not burn the wapiti until we harvest all we can use. He rushed over and slit its throat and busied himself. It had been a long time since Aurora witnessed such a thing, for all the time she lived in the temple, the dragons hunted for her. "The last time I saw someone do this was my brother Kylar when I visited him…." She bent to help Igasho.

"Wait. Do you want to get blood and other fluids on your new clothing? The women of my tribe usually wear an apron to do such work." She nodded, and for now, changed back into her clothes from home. As they worked, Igasho taught about how they used the hide for clothing, shoes, and blankets.

"Shoes? You don't wear shoes."

"I am dressed for my vision quest. Normally, I wear moccasins—what you call shoes. We might even use it to make snowshoes. Do you know snow?"

"I know about it. But it is warm here."

"We are still under the summer moon. Right now, my people live in the cliff dwellings where it is cooler during the summer heat, but we will be moving on as the seasons change. While we live in the valley where it is warmer beneath the winter moon, we still hunt in the hills where the snow falls."

As the two of them worked together, he said, "Usually, the women are in charge of gathering materials and building the homes. All of this will be a good start for our home when we move from the cliffs."

The sun cast long shadows by the time they finished. Aurora's back ached, and she felt slightly weak. "I need food." She slowly dropped to the ground with her back against the rock bearing the painting of her arrival. "And I'm thirsty."

"We are not close to the water, for I came here to this place too fast. I neither ate food nor drank water."

* * * *

Aurora's pale pallor alarmed Jurom. *"She must eat, for she has worked hard all day after having no sleep, and she carries thy child."*

Igasho looked at his Spirit Guide with wide eyes and then to Aurora. "Waianten? You are carrying my child?"

She glared at Jurom for a moment, ready to scold him but nodded weakly. "At least that is what Jurom says. It is too soon for me to know." She cast a quick frown toward the dragon and then closed her eyes. She didn't have the energy to be angry. "I need to rest while you get water. Go."

Jurom stretched his wings. *"Come, mine child of the spirit. I will take thee to fetch the water."*

Igasho seized an empty waterskin from his campsite and fearlessly climbed the dragon's leg to the flat spot, and grabbed hold of his goldenhorn. "*Let us be off.*"

Jurom lifted into the sky as Igasho directed him to the river. Together they made a plan for introducing the firebird and his bride to his tribe.

CHAPTER THIRTY-NINE

After drinking and eating, they watched the sunset. Aurora fell asleep, and Igasho carried her to the cave. Once sure she hadn't awakened, he hurried out to Jurom.

"Are you ready?"

"Aye."

They took off into the night sky. "Tell me of thy people," Jurom said as they headed westward.

"Within our tribe, I live with family. My parents, grandparents, aunts and uncles, and their children. Most men my age already have a wife or two. Parents and grandparents share the ancestry and history of our people through stories told to their children. I first want you to drop me far enough from our village so they cannot see you. Then I will go and tell them the story of my vision quest. I am sure many will laugh when I tell them of the great firebird and that I have a wife with hair the color of fire. But when I call for you, I want you to come and breathe fire into the night sky. It will confirm you are real, and you will become one of the great stories of our tribe. I will tell them I will be back with my bride tomorrow for the fire dance, and then you will carry me away. Doing this will open the path for you to be present during the Fire Dance ceremony, and my family and friends will be ready to meet Waianten."

"Spirit Child, why speak ye of Aurora as Waianten?"

The two of them talked about names growing with the person. "I like this tradition," Jurom admitted. "Perhaps mine mate and I shall consider such a practice."

"We are getting close," Igasho announced. "I can see the village fires there on the south-facing slope."

"Mine eyes see. It be near the whitebark pine stands."

"Yes, find a place to land."

Jurom circled and landed on a smoothed stone mountain top above the village but out of sight. Igasho climbed down and rubbed his chaffed inner thighs. "I need to make sure I have hides on my legs in the future." He started down the slope and stopped. "Will you still be able to hear me even when I'm in the village?"

"As long as ye hold the loqui stone on thy person."

Igasho's hand moved to the pouch holding the precious stone. "I will call you when my people are ready." He worked his way down the smooth rocky slope, thankful for the intermittent moonlight. Indistinct voices and laughter wafted on the breeze. His heart beat faster. So much had changed since he set out on his vision quest. As he dropped to the ground, firelight flickered from the lodge where everyone gathered. He hurried over and stepped through the door. The tart scent of pine filled the room as many women worked food-grinding tools to extract nuts from pine cones.

His grandfather sat smoking a pipe among the men and was the first to spot Igasho standing at the door. He stood quickly and used the shoulder of the man beside him to steady himself. "Igasho returns!"

Heads turned, and many rushed over at once to question him. His mother pawed him as if checking that he wasn't hurt as his father cut through the crowd and reached his son. "Was your vision quest successful?"

"Yes, father."

His father stood proud and started to lead him toward the center of the lodge. "Tomorrow, we shall hear your story."

Igasho stopped. "Father, I must tell my story tonight."

His mother blinked and looked at her husband along with all the crowd. It was out of character for Igasho to speak in such a manner. His father nodded once. "Very well. Everyone come; Igasho shall tell the story of his vision quest."

Everyone crowded about in a circle sitting on horsehair mats. Some ran to collect missing family and friends who wouldn't want to miss his telling. When his cousin Pu'ennaakan walked in with his pregnant wife, Kimama, they locked eyes. Since Pu'ennaakan's marriage, Igasho did his best to avoid his cousin. But now, for the first time, Igasho felt bold enough to face him, for his disgrace no longer clung to him like a garment.

His family and friends gathered around. It felt strange. Usually, he hung toward the back of the gathering, but now he had completed his vision quest. He started his story slowly and gathered momentum. When he mentioned the sound of the wind and the dark form flying overhead, he had everyone's attention. Even as he told of riding Molala toward the danger, his heart drummed against his ribs, reliving the excitement. "I urged her on. 'Go Molala.' She picked up speed. Up ahead, I heard the crashing of a large tree branch in the stand of whitebark pines. I brought my horse to a stop and slipped from her back, and crept into the woods. A snort unlike I'd ever heard sounded like the call of a ram's horn. Then I heard the voice of a woman. Ahead of me, a blue light shone within the trees where I found a woman holding magic rocks in her hand making the light."

Chatter filled the room with everyone talking at once about his successful vision quest. A couple of dogs sleeping near the fire woke and wandered through the crowd to figure out the reason for the commotion. His mother and father were at the center of the uproar. Igasho raised his hand. He shouted over the tumult. "I have more. Please listen."

His father looked at his son with admiration and raised his hands. "Quiet. Let us hear the rest of the telling."

"The woman, Waianten, has hair the color of fire and was sent as an answer to my prayers. And I was an answer to hers." Now tears spilled down his mother's face while others questioned how anyone could have hair of such color. "And beside her stood my Spirit Guide who delivered her upon his back. For it was her flying overhead, on the back of a gigantic winged lizard, that had blocked the moon and stars from my sight."

"Are you trying to say your Spirit Guide is the thunderbird!" Pu'ennaakan shouted over the ruckus. His lips curled in an arrogant sneer.

"Jurom," Igasho called out with his mind. "Can you make a loud noise? Like a clap of thunder?"

"Surely, but why?"

"My people believe you are the thunderbird. That may make acceptance of you easier."

"Very well."

"Well?" Pu'ennaakan challenged. "Is that what you are saying?"

Igasho did his best not to smile. But inwardly, he was. "I am."

Again, the crowd broke into a frenzy. The dogs barked at the unseen foe. Concern washed across his father's face.

"This was my vision, and it is true. The Thunderbird will come when I finish this telling, and I will ride him into the sky. And tomorrow, I will arrive on his back with my bride, Waianten. She comes from a far land through a gate of light. I have visited this land, but that is a telling for another time."

The men pushed to their feet, challenging him to prove the thunderbird was his Spirit Guide. Igasho stood. It all seemed surreal as he moved outside under the stars. He turned. "Come, I will show you."

Pu'ennaakan stepped into the cool evening air with others following. "Where is this giant thunderbird you speak of, Igasho? Is he going to block out the moon and the stars again?" A couple of snickers peppered the crowd behind him.

"Come, Jurom. But fly overhead first, for they do not believe you exist. It will be better for them to see your shadow before they hear your thunder."

"Watch the sky and see for yourself," Igasho said.

Within minutes, a rush of wind sounded overhead. All eyes watched the sky as the blackness of a large form flew overhead. Before they could express their wonder, a loud clap of something like thunder tore through the air. The women ran back into the lodge with their children and fought for a place at one of the few windows or the door, while the men stood their ground to show their bravery as the village dogs barked wildly. "Quickly, bring wood for a fire so you can see the thunderbird for yourself," Igasho shouted.

The men who believed him quickly piled wood in the fire circle, but when they knelt to kindle it, Igasho said, "Do not worry yourself with that, for the thunderbird breathes fire." Even in the dark, he could see the men cast nervous glances at one another. "Do not fret. My Spirit Guide is not here to harm but to guide."

The whoosh of wings fanned the air above them. "Stand near the lodge," Igasho said. "Give him room."

The men scampered to stand near the outer wall of the lodge, resembling frightened rabbits as Jurom landed. His claws skidded against the stony soil as his feet sought to gain purchase. When he stopped, Igasho walked up to the dragon and placed his hand on his side. "This is my Spirit Guide, the thunderbird. Tomorrow you shall see him in the daylight but for now, let us light this fire so you can witness his existence," he shouted over the barking of the dogs.

"Jurom, light the fire."

Jurom's chest expanded, allowing threads of fiery light to escape between his scales. Light exploded across the settlement as flames burst from his powerful jaws. The wood ignited, and flames shot up from the fire circle. The surrounding area lit up like daylight as the dogs tucked tail and ran into the shadows.

"Perhaps if ye invite them to touch me, they be not so fearful of mine presence."

"Father, come. The thunderbird invites you forward."

His father stepped forward with his chest puffed out and chin held high. Jurom swung his head and looked at the man allowing smoke to curl from his nostrils. "Are you sure, son? He allows me to touch him?"

"I am sure. The thunderbird is with those who are with me."

His father reached out and touched the dragon's muscular neck.

"For now," Igasho said, "I must go to my bride. I need water, food, and warmer clothes. And leggings for the ride." His mother and aunt scurried to gather what he needed and rolled it in a blanket.

Igasho slipped the leggings on and fixed the blanket over his shoulder, tethered it in place, and slung the water skin across his opposite shoulder. “We have much to prepare, for she and I will dance the Fire Dance tomorrow when the sun sets.”

Jurom bent his foreleg, and Igasho climbed to the goldenhorn and grabbed hold. A couple of dogs tentatively entered the circle of light, sniffing the air. “I shall see you all about midday tomorrow.” With that, Jurom raised his wings and took off with a great thrust of air. Igasho glanced down to see his village people looking up at him as they never did before. “I know there must be a reason you have chosen me, Spirit Guide. I look ahead to our destiny.”

CHAPTER FORTY

Igasho found Aurora awake, dressed in the garment he'd given her, and sitting cross-legged warming herself at a small fire. The gilded glow painted a circle of light around her. "Did you wonder when I'd be back?" he asked.

She smiled and shook her head as she stood and brushed dirt from her behind. "No. Jurom told me you were on the way and to be ready to leave. Are we going now to meet your tribe? At night, in the dark?"

"No." He placed his arms around her. "Tonight, Waianten, we will spend the night in the Spirit Cave."

Her green eyes grew wide. "The Spirit Cave?"

A light clicking emanated from deep within Jurom's throat. *"Igasho believes it to be the home of the spirits, Little One. And since I be his Spirit Guide, it shall be mine home while we be in this land. Tonight, we shall sleep there."*

"We?" she asked as she climbed to his goldenhorn. *"Are you planning to stay then?"*

"I shall come and go, for Tozet does not wish to visit this land and grow old before her time."

Neither do I, she thought to herself as Igasho climbed behind her. She leaned against him, soaking in his warmth as they took to the star-studded sky. The cool mountain air made her eyes water as her mind wandered to the temple and the cup. She, too, would have to come and go because of that responsibility. But for now, as she wiped away the tears, she pushed the thought aside and relished this moment with the feel of a man's arms around her and holding Jurom's goldenhorn. *I'm no longer alone.*

They climbed higher and higher. The darkness erased the landscape below, making it impossible to know how high. "We are into the tallest mountains, Igasho. How do you get here without a– firebird?"

"I have never been. No one has. And my people now call Jurom the thunderbird."

Before she could ask, Jurom explained how he used magic to create a clap of thunder before showing himself to Igasho's people. She turned her attention back to this place called the spirit cave. "If you have never been to this spirit cave, then how do you know there are spirits?"

"At times, they can be seen, like smoke without a fire."

Aurora sat forward with her back straight and turned to look at Igasho. In the darkness, she could hardly make out his silhouette, but she could feel his breath on her cheek. "Why are we going there now then? In the dark?" Fear churned her stomach as she stared into the surrounding darkness wondering how people lived day to day facing the unknown in this fashion. Until now, she knew what to expect most of the time because she was aware of it before it happened. But her gift didn't work in this land. *What are these spirits?* "Are you sure it is safe to go there?"

Igasho leaned with his mouth next to her ear. "Jurom tells me it is safe. I believe him, do you?"

"Rest easy, Little One. There be no spirits living there."

Stress building across her shoulders and neck relaxed at Jurom's words, and curiosity set in. "What made you decide to do this, Igasho?"

"We will be able to say we slept within the spirit cave. My people will recognize me as a *taikwahni*."

A chief? It made sense, but the question remained, "*Jurom, how do you know where to go if you've never been there?"*

"Thy mate pointed out the cave when I carried him to see his tribe. And stop fretting, Little One. Remember, mine multi-faceted eyes can see in the dark."

Jurom's wings quit beating the air as they glided on the currents above the mountains. Aurora leaned into Igasho's embrace and stared at the stars.

Jurom's body shifted as his wings angled to land. She grasped the goldenhorn tighter. "It's so strange landing in the dark," she said more to herself than to Igasho. The stars disappeared as they entered cold inky blackness. The sound of Jurom's razor-sharp talons scraping against the cave floor scared her at first. Breaking, shattering noises were followed by clinking sounds scattered around them like a shower of broken pottery. As they came to a stop, she realized she was holding her breath. She sucked in a lungful of air and let out a deep sigh. "I can't see anything." For the first time, she realized her dragon-enhanced vision wasn't working either.

"Do you have some of your magic stones?" Igasho asked.

"Yes! The starstones." She fumbled with the tie on her shoulder bag, reached inside, and pulled out three starstones. She rubbed them together, and a blue glow shined from her palm, casting a cerulean hue across multicolored jewel-encrusted walls.

Igasho's mouth dropped open as he stared at the sight in total wonder. "I've never seen anything like this." He reached out and took her free hand. "You have changed my life Waianten. No one will believe we have seen such beauty."

"Will they believe you if we bring them some of these gems?"

A smile spread across his face. "That is what we shall do." Vaporous balloons formed in front of his lips as he spoke.

Jurom stretched his neck and shot a stream of fire against the ceiling providing instant warmth. Aurora wondered about using magic to start a fire for light, but she wasn't sure if she should. Instead, in the dim glow of the starstones, she grabbed the therus rod from the bag and cast a silent spell placing a torch, there, there, and there, and asked Jurom to light them. As he did, buttery light glinted off a rainbow of colored crystals and gems as she silently slid the rod back into the bag. They spent the next hour examining the cave and gathering small samples that fit into her shoulder bag. "Too bad Jurom's mate isn't here," Aurora said as she stashed a green crystal into the bag. “She has a large pouch on her neck and could carry larger crystals.”

“I shall be thankful to carry what we can and to be in this magical spirit cave with my wife and Spirit Guide. Waianten, I can’t begin to tell you how happy I am at this moment.”

The events of her long day started to overtake her as she nodded. “Igasho, I feel the same as you. But I am so exhausted I can hardly hold my eyes open.” She glanced around, trying to figure out where they should sleep.

Jurom lumbered toward them and curled against some of the rocks. *“Come, sleep on mine back.”* She climbed to the flat spot around Jurom’s golden spike while Igasho unpacked the items his mother and aunt had packed in the blanket. He carried the cover to Aurora and lay beside her.

They cuddled beneath the blanket, and the warmth of Igasho’s body lulled Aurora to sleep. Dreams carried her back to her childhood. She slept on her mother’s dragon, Beroan, as they left the valley. Kylar rode a younger, Jurom, beaming with a rare and genuine smile. She woke with lingering homesickness. *No!* It was more than homesickness. “I’m going to be sick!” she muttered as she slipped down Jurom’s foreleg as quickly as she could and headed to the mouth of the cave and vomited. Her head swam as she sat with her head between her legs, gulping for air.

Igasho walked up behind her and placed his hand on her shoulder. “You are ill?”

She nodded. “My stomach.”

“I will go gather *bohobi* to make you well.”

She didn’t argue but lay back on the cool rock ledge in the morning sunlight, trying to ignore the awful taste on her tongue. *Some wedding day!* She closed her eyes, listening to Igasho climb until she heard him no more. A few minutes later, the soft sound of footfalls sounded above her. She opened her eyes just in time to see Igasho jump onto the ledge with a handful of green leaves. She shot to a sitting position, and her head spun again. She collapsed back onto the coolness of the stone with a moan.

"Just lie there Waianten, I will make medicine to help you feel better."

He walked into the cave and paused. *"Jurom, I need a fire to heat water."*

"Place rocks in a pile, and I shall heat them."

Igasho poured water from the skin into a stone bowl his mother had packed and set it on the glowing rocks. He dropped a handful of the green bohobi leaves into the liquid and let it heat. He reached back into the bundle of items his family had packed, pulled out a few fistfuls of pine nuts, and placed them on the hot stones. He found a stick to stir them until they dried, ready to crack open. Before they dried enough, the water came to a boil. He picked up the bowl and quickly set it on the ground to cool enough to handle.

Aurora sat up slowly and watched her husband. "What are those?" She pointed to the nuts.

"Pine nuts. We gather them in the fall when the rabbitbrush turns yellow. They provide food throughout the year."

Aurora stood. Her stomach still felt queasy, but the worst seemed to have passed. She took slow steps toward the heated stones and sat cross-legged on the ground to warm herself. Igasho picked up the bowl and offered it to her to drink. "Sip this, and you will feel better."

She accepted the stone bowl and sipped the light gold liquid, worried she would throw up again. To her surprise, her nausea subsided. "It worked! I feel almost normal!"

Igasho stirred the nuts among the rocks and gradually picked them to the side with the stick. They cracked them open with stones and ate their fill. When they finished, he packed up his belongings in the blanket along with a larger piece of violet crystal and slung it onto his back. "Are you able to travel?"

Aurora nodded. "As ready as I'm going to be."

They climbed aboard Jurom, who swooped from the Spirit Cave and soared over the mountains. Aurora leaned against Igasho's chest. "I feel fine now. Thank you."

"That is good. I wouldn't want you to throw up at our wedding!"

His light laughter filled the air, and she relished the moment. *I'm getting married! Kylar was right–always right.* For a brief moment, she thought of her family–longed for them to share this precious moment. To meet, Igasho.

"There," Igasho pointed. "Our summer village."

Aurora glanced down at the collection of grass huts. *It's all so different.* She didn't know if the butterflies in her stomach were excitement or a warning that she would be sick again. "Medere languoribus," she whispered under her breath, but her stomach started to flip flop. She reached into her bag as Igasho stared at her with warm brown eyes. "Are you going to be sick again?"

She nodded as she felt past the crystals, pulled out the therus rod, and held it in her hand. A trickle of power flowed up her arm as she repeated the words. "Medere languoribus." The wave of nausea subsided, and she let out a deep sigh. "It has passed." Igasho narrowed his focus on her face but nodded once.

Jurom broke into their conversation. *"Be careful, Little One. The more ye use magic in this world, the faster age shall overtake ye."*

"Why, Jurom? Why will I age faster here?"

"*Magic be a gift from the Thornose, who be guardians of the Labyrinth of Times. And from the Goldenhorn who be the sentinels of the Midlands. Just as traveling the midlands drains energy from ye because ye be between time–being in America drains thy long life and mine for we be out of the realm of dragons. Living within the dragon realms converts ordinary dragon energy into magical power. But outside of the dragon realms, the power that extends long life must be used just to live life and even more so to perform magic. It causes rapid aging.*

She slipped the therus rod back into the bag with a resolve not to use it again until she reopened the portal to return home. *That will mean no magic!*

CHAPTER FORTY-ONE

"There." Igasho pointed. "You can see our village."

Aurora blinked against the tears caused by the cold air and saw her first glimpse of the village located on the south-facing, sunny slope of a mountain. Nestled near a whitebark pine stand where a river cut through the landscape and flowed toward a valley, it looked unlike the settlements along the Inkish River back home.

"What do you call the river?"

"Piaqogwaiq."

"Big Wind River," Jurom interpreted.

She stared in awe at a land so different but beautiful. As they drew nearer, a central lodge became the first discernable structure. A handful of cone-shaped grass huts stood scattered, but most people poured from holes in the hillside as they circled overhead. "Your people live in the mountain?" Memories of her brothers, Tomas and Carn, living in Tachnir flooded her mind. "Two of my brothers lived in a mountain. One still lives there. My brother, Tomas."

"Really? But you had to stay in the temple?"

She nodded. "All my other brothers moved downriver." Melancholy reared up to steal her joy, and fear of the unknown stole her breath as a crowd gathered below.

"Be ye ready, Little One?" Jurom asked.

It felt strange not to know what to expect next. *"I guess. Let's do it."*

As they circled lower, Igasho pointed again. "That man standing apart at the head of the others is my father, Taikwahni Ubirajara. His name means Lord of the Spear. And that woman in the front line, the one with one braid hanging over her left shoulder and the other behind her right shoulder—"

“Yes.”

“That is my mother, Hāwitche.”

Aurora took in a deep breath and let it out slowly. Her brothers and parents were gone, but she would represent them well. She sat straighter and steeled herself to meeting so many strangers at once and squeezed the goldenhorn tight as she readied for landing.

When they came to a stop, most of the people stayed back toward the large circular building Igasho called the lodge. His father walked forward to greet them as they climbed down to the ground. “Father, this is my wife, Waianten.”

Aurora stood there with the sun chasing away the chill of riding. *What am I to do?* The man had the violet aura of a magical visionary. *At least I can still see his colors. Should I hug him? Rub chins? Stand here, like a stump?*

Jurom said, *“Say ‘behne.’ It be their friendly greeting.”*

“Behne.” She smiled but wondered if it was appropriate to do so.

The man started to speak to her in words she didn’t understand. Behind him, Igasho’s mother led the way for others to come forward. The edges of her green love-centered aura were red, showing her to be strong-willed but realistic. *I don’t need my powers to know we will get along well.* As his mother reached out and handled one of Aurora’s braids, she spotted at least three women carrying babies on their back and another great with child. Suddenly a flutter within her lower abdomen surprised her. *It is too soon to feel my baby quicken! What does this mean?*

The chattering around her disoriented her. *“Jurom, help me. I can’t understand.”*

Just as quickly, the gibberish turned to words she understood. *“What did you do?”*

“I extended the power of the crystal Igasho carries to hear me. If ye be near him, ye shall hear the people speak in thy tongue.”

“Can I touch your hair,” one woman asked.

“Igasho, she is beautiful,” his mother said. “You are now a powerful man.”

Igasho took Aurora's arm and said, "You will all have time to talk with her later. For now, we must get ready for the ceremony."

His father pointed up toward the holes lining the cliffs, "Take her to our home."

Igasho led her by the hand up the slope. They walked past the lower levels of dwellings and stopped at the lodge at the top. As they stepped inside, it surprised Aurora to find a fire burning vented through a hole in the ceiling. "This is cozy," she said as the tension in her shoulders relaxed.

Igasho said, "We will live here with my family."

"All of us together? In here?"

"Yes, that is the way of my people."

"And Jurom will be living in the Spirit Cave?"

"Waianten, relax. You will be happy here."

"I know, but you need to make sure your family understands that I can't stay here. Not for long."

"Because of the faster aging?"

"Yes, but not just that. I think it may be affecting our baby, too."

His smile vanished. "Our baby. Why do you say that?"

"I felt it move! Just now, since we've been here. That doesn't happen until maybe 13 weeks–uh, a little longer than one moon."

He stepped away from her and paced back and forth. "How will I explain this? People will think the baby belongs to another father."

She walked over to him. "What matters is that you know it is your baby. And if I am right about this, we can expect the birth of our child within two moons."

"I will prepare my tribe."

"How? I don't even know how to prepare myself."

"I will include it in the telling of my vision quest, of being carried away to your land where I learned the only way you could be my wife would be to live there after a time because for you, here," he made a wide-sweeping gesture taking in the room, "time passes more quickly."

“And you think they will believe you?”

“When they see your stomach grow, quickly, I believe most will. Until then, cover yourself, so it is not evident. Once you reveal the truth, if they don't believe what you say, they will surely believe when the child is born. And after they believe, I will tell them that I am allowed to bring along those of my tribe who want to come to your land, and we can start to prepare for the journey. It is for the best we stay here until the melting moon. By that time, we shall have gathered plenty of pine nuts, seeds, roots, and grasses, and other food to bring with us until we learn to harvest and hunt the new tüpi.”

“New tüpi?”

He sat up and placed his arm around her shoulders. “Our new homeland.”

“Tupi.”

She nodded. “And you will explain about the time difference? I don’t want them to shun our child because they don’t believe it to be yours.”

“If you are right about the passage of time, you will go from looking like this to giving birth within two moons. Who will be able to argue with that?”

That reality stunned her, but she had no time to absorb it as voices warned that others were on the way to join them. She tugged on Igasho’s arm. “If we are separated, leave me with the crystal that allows you to hear Jurom because it lets me hear your people speak in my tongue, and they hear me in yours.”

He pulled the crystal from the pouch at his waist and handed it to her. She stashed it among the other gems in her bag as Taikwahni Ubirajara and his wife walked in. He marched over to his son and grabbed him by the biceps. “You have made me very proud. Appah has heard your prayers.”

Igasho stood a little taller as his mother fussed over him. “You can leave your bride with me. I will help her get ready, and you can help your father gather the wood needed.”

“You don’t have the wood?”

His father sternly said, "For the fire dance, seven types of wood will be specially cut from specific types of trees by whom?"

"The spiritual leader."

"That is right, and so you are going to help me."

It started to sink in. Igasho would be viewed as a leader now. "Me. You are allowing me to help!" He turned to Aurora. "I will see you at the ceremony. I know you are tired, so if you need to, take time to rest."

How kind he is to me. "I will see you at the ceremony."

His mother and aunts busied themselves getting Aurora ready for the wedding. One aunt who looked younger than Aurora carried a flat basket filled with purple flowers into the room. His mother said, "These symbolize faith, hope, and wisdom, and so you shall carry them with you as you take your vows."

"She is your sister?" Aurora asked, pointing to the younger woman.

"No, she is my daughter. Igasho's sister. The rest of these are my sisters."

The girl beamed with excitement. Her white teeth shone against her dark skin. "Do you truly come from a different land, as Igasho said? What is it like there? Do all the people there have pale skin and hair of fire?"

"Now, now, Aponi, we will have plenty of time to talk of such things. For now, let us all get ready for the celebration. My only son is getting married."

After a short time, Aurora relaxed and enjoyed the time with her new family. When they finished, she donned the dress Igasho had given her decorated with feathers and quills and wore a laurel of purple flowers in her hair. And she wasn't alone. After centuries of solitude, the clamor was music that reminded her of life back in the floating caves. As the sun hung low in the sky, they all started toward the door.

"Wait!" Aurora ran to the shoulder bag and pulled out the pink loqui crystal. She clasped it to her chest, thankful she hadn't forgotten.

"What is that?" Aponi asked.

"Among my people, the bride gives one gift before the ceremony. It is my gift to my husband."

The women gave one another a questioning look but accepted the idea quickly and headed out the door. She paused on the ledge and stared down at a large fire burning in the center of the circle where it cast light across the men milling about. In her heart, she thanked Igasho for preparing her for this. That circle represented the Creator and the holy union of two people. She followed the others down the path toward the fire. The scent of the flowers in her hair wafted around her. As they threaded their way toward the circle, the men worked at lighting the two smaller circles of fire. The southern fire caught, followed by the fire on the north. She stepped into the circle and walked directly over to Igasho as the people gathered around the perimeter holding hands. She stared at his painted face and wondered if the markings meant anything or were just decorative. "My gift to you, my husband." Firelight danced in his eyes as he accepted the crystal and slipped it into the pouch at his waist. A smile flickered across his lips as he took her hand and positioned her to stand by his side.

Taikwahni Ubirajara, as the holy man, sprinkled tobacco, sage, sweetgrass, and corn on the fires. It was time for Aurora and Igasho to offer their silent prayers. Among her prayers was one for her child, who would be born before its time. All those gathered sang praises to the Creator, for the two lives merging into one.

Igasho let go of Aurora's hand and took one step forward. "My beloved, our love has become firm by your walking as one with me. Together we will share the responsibilities of the lodge, food, and children. May the Creator bless us with noble children to share. May they live long."

Aurora's heart beat faster as he voiced much the same as she had in her silent prayer for her unborn child. *How long will it live? How much life will it lose because I chose to stay here for now?*

Jurom broke into her thoughts as he circled above the ceremony. *"As ye take thy step to join Igasho, this be what ye say."*

She repeated the vow. "This is my commitment to you, my husband. Together we will share the responsibility of the home, food, and children. I promise I shall discharge all my share of the responsibilities for the welfare of the family and the children."

Igasho's father sprinkled the fires with the fragrant herbs and grass again, sending amber sparks floating toward the clear night sky. As he did, Igasho said, "My beloved, now you have walked with me the second step. May the Creator bless you. I will love you and you alone as my wife. I will fill your heart with strength and courage: this is my commitment and my pledge to you. May Appah protect the lodge and children."

Tears of happiness stung Aurora's eyes. Her emotions soared and dropped, only to rise again. "My husband, at all times, I shall fill your heart with courage and strength. In your happiness, I shall rejoice. May Appah bless you and our lodge." She took a step to join Igasho and silently thanked Jurom for playing his part.

The last traces of sunlight diminished on the horizon, and firelight flickered across the faces of his tribe as he took another step around the fire. "My beloved, now since you have walked three steps with me, our wealth and prosperity will grow. May Appah bless us. May we educate our children, and may they live long."

More tears flowed down her cheeks. All these vows about their children caused her to realize she didn't know how to be a parent, but she did want them to live long. Jurom broke into her thoughts. *"Little One, all will be well."* She wiped her face with the back of her hand as she took her third step. "My husband, I love you with single-minded devotion. I will treat all other men as my brothers. My devotion to you is pure, and you are my joy." She stopped to swallow, to clear the emotional knot forming in her throat. "This is my commitment and pledge to you." She stepped forward and marveled at the way the firelight reflected on his face, highlighting the paint on his chiseled high cheekbones.

Igasho looked at her and said, "My beloved, it is a great blessing that you have now walked four steps with me. May the Creator bless you. You have brought favor and sacredness in my life." He took a step.

She repeated the ensuing vow as Jurom related it. "My husband, in all acts of uprightness, in material prosperity, in every form of enjoyment, and divine acts such as sacrifice, worship, and goodwill, I promise I will participate and always be with you."

Igasho took his fifth step of the seven. "My beloved, now you have walked five steps with me. May the Creator make us prosperous. May the Creator bless us."

She replied, "My husband, I will share both in your joys and sorrows. Your love will make me very happy." And in her heart, she meant it as she stepped to be beside him.

Firelight danced across all the family and friends still holding hands in a circle around them. Taikwahni Ubirajara sprinkled another handful of herbs on the fire filling the air with a fragrant scent. Igasho said, "My beloved, by walking six steps with me, you have filled my heart with happiness. May I fill your heart with great joy and peace, time and time again. May the Creator bless you."

Aurora followed with her sixth vow. *He does fill my heart with joy!* Once more, she repeated Jurom's words realizing it was Igasho who was relaying the vows to the dragon. It created a layer of specialness to this ceremony that no one but them would ever understand. "My husband, the Creator blesses you. May I fill your heart with great joy and peace. I promise I will always be with you." Even as she said it, she wondered how long she would be with him. How would time pass for him when they returned to the temple and their new life in the plains in the east? She pushed those concerns to the back of her mind and stepped. *Only one more step, and he is my husband in both worlds*.

Igasho took his last step. "My beloved, as you have walked the seven steps with me, our love and friendship have become inseparable and firm. We have experienced spiritual union in God. Now you have become, completely, mine. I offer my total self to you. May our marriage last forever." He reached out his hand toward her.

"My husband, by the law of the Creator, and the spirits of our honorable ancestors…." Thoughts of her family played in her mind: Da, Mother, Kylar, and all her brothers. "…I have become your wife. Whatever promises I gave you, I have spoken them with a pure heart. All the spirits are witnesses to this fact. I shall never deceive you, nor will I let you down. I shall love you forever." She took her final step and wrapped her hand around his.

CHAPTER FORTY-TWO

A whirlwind of activity filled the first couple of weeks of life among the tribe for Aurora. Igasho's family embraced her as their own, and his sister Aponi quickly became the sister she never had. As she rolled to her side on her sleeping mat, her unborn child kicked—not a flutter but a real kick against her ribs. It surprised and scared her as she rested her palm against her growing abdomen. Igasho stirred on the mat beside her. His brown eyes fluttered open. He smiled until his focus shifted to her hand, still resting on her rounded belly. His startled gaze flashed to her face and met her eyes with wide-eyed wonder. "Our child grows fast!"

"Yes, I don't know what I should do? Each day I awaken and don't know what to expect. What will your tribe think when I can't hide it? Should I go back to the temple until the baby comes?"

He reached out and placed his hand on hers upon her abdomen. "No. It is time to let them know. I must perform a telling of our story, including the fact that we are going to have a child very soon."

"But what will you say? What will they think? I don't want them to think the baby isn't yours."

He propped up on one elbow and rubbed his hand across her stomach. "I am going to tell them our child will be called *Nahma mea*."

She smiled. "Two Moons. I like it." She sat up, grabbed her dress, and slipped into it as she hid her concerns.

That evening as everyone gathered in the main lodge. Igasho walked to the center near the fire and called for the attention of those gathered. He pulled one of the logs from the pile of firewood and set it on end, and used it as a seat. Aponi sat beside Aurora cross-legged on a mat near the back wall.

Aurora's heart beat faster. *Jurom, are you near in case I need to leave?*

"I be within the spirit cave. I know mine spirit child be telling his people about the times and thy child. Be ye sure to tell him we must return to the temple to check on the urn once a moon."

"I will. Just be ready if I need to leave in haste."

Aponi looked at her wide-eyed, and Aurora suddenly realized she had not been paying attention to Igasho's telling! "And while in her land, I became her husband according to her customs. It was that night her name changed from Aurora to Waianten." As he spoke, his voice held a rhythmic quality as he gestured with his hands offering a graceful, visual aspect to his storytelling. "But amid our happiness, we faced one problem. Time in her land passes differently for her than it does here. Here, it moves very quickly, and if she stays here, she will age swiftly. And so she has agreed to stay here in our land for *symmy tommoppyh* (one year), but then we will return to her land. We invite anyone who wants to join us to come. As I have considered this, as her husband and father of the child she carries, we will leave sooner–at the time of the thawing moon. By then, we will have gathered food for the coming year and can carry that with us."

A buzz of conversation filled the room like a poked hornets' nest. Igasho's mother, Hāwitche, sat with her mouth hanging open while his cousin, Pu'ennaakan, stood with his arms crossed and chin held high. "You expect us all to go to this other land?"

Igasho stood. "No, I don't. But I am going, and Waianten has invited all of us. The invitation is only for those who want to come."

"Why so soon?" his father asked.

"Waianten, come up here."

She stood, but she wanted to turn and run. *What is Igasho doing?* She threaded her way through those sitting on the floor. When she reached Igasho, she just wanted him to hold her in his arms and to whisk her away back home.

"I remind you that this woman is the answer to my prayers, and my Spirit Guide carried her to me. She now carries my child, and in just two weeks, she is over the time of sickness and feels the child move."

Many of the women gasped or covered their mouths in astonishment. "How can this be?" Igasho's mother asked.

"I do not understand it," Igasho admitted, but in this short time since she has been with me, I have watched her stomach grow. Before we knew she was with child, she warned me time would pass differently for her if she came here to live. Our child is within her, and so it too is aging faster. Mother, come place your hand here, and perhaps you will feel your first grandchild move."

Hāwitche stood and glanced from one of her sisters to another. They patted her on the back, congratulating and encouraging her. Aponi rushed to her feet and walked toward Aurora along with her mother. Hāwitche tentatively placed her palm on Aurora's stomach. "Oh yes, she has a little belly." Suddenly a sense of warmth and reassurance flooded Aurora, and Hāwitche's eyes grew big as the child kicked. She squealed with delight as Aponi placed her hand on Aurora's stomach. Delight danced in her dark eyes, even though the baby didn't kick a second time.

"I think perhaps the baby is taking a nap," Aponi said. "All this excitement has tired it out!"

Many women laughed, along with the children and a few men. But a handful of those gathered cast nervous glances at those around them and looked to Pu'ennaakan. They didn't say anything, but it was clear to Aurora that they did not trust her. Especially Igasho's cousin, Pu'ennaakan. The muddy green hue of his aura had warned her early on of his jealous nature, but murky-red and lemon-yellow colors radiating closest to his body warned of raging anger brewing. He feared losing respect. She would talk with her Igasho about it later when they were alone.

For now, she laughed with the aunts, new mother, and sister hovering around her, and she basked in the joy she hadn't felt for so long. Part of her wished she could stay and live this life in this place, but she didn't allow the thought to linger. She reached out to Jurom and let him know, *"All is well."*

As she lay on her sleeping mat that night, she thought about Jurom. A memory tickled her mind deep within. She somehow knew her dragon companion even before she was born, and she wondered about her unborn child. Would it be dragon-touched like Kylar? Or Dragonborn like her? She fell into a restless sleep and dreamed of her childhood life at Jur-jurom playing with her brothers. When she woke, she felt tired. Her hand slipped to her abdomen and found it had grown larger again overnight. Soon she would not be able to hide her stomach beneath her loose-fitting dress. By her calculations, by her fourth week, she would look very much pregnant.

She got dressed and walked into the main chamber of their living quarters to find Aponi helping her mother roast and shell pine nuts. She walked over and squatted beside them with one of the sticks used for the job.

“Mother and I were talking about going to Tupi. Can you tell us what it is like there?”

Aurora nodded. "It's a vast land and varied. It is mountainous in the east and west. A smaller range in the south, but wasteland surrounds those mountains. Nothing lives there. A large river, the Inkish River, runs through the land with many tributaries. Some valleys grow tall grass that will be perfect for making baskets. The plains where we will live have such grass, and the land reaches the coast where blue waters extend for as far as you can see. The weather there is not often cold but tends to be warmer.”

“Is the weather warmer all the time?” Hāwitche asked as she separated three more nuts, which had cracked.

“Most of the time, as far as I know. I haven’t lived there.”

Hāwitche glanced up from her work with a furrowed brow. “You do not live there, but that is where we are going?”

“I have a… a responsibility. Once fulfilled, I will get to move to Tupi and live out my life in the land.”

Hāwitche smiled. “Soon, you will complete this responsibility?”

“Yes, soon.” Inwardly, Aurora didn’t know when her responsibility as Oracle would be over. All she knew was that she would have a husband and family and would be free to live with them in the east once the urn disappeared. It was one unknown piece of the puzzle. *But why don't I know?* she wondered. *When we move to, Voldatha, I can live in Tupi, travel through the Midlands, and almost no one will miss me as I check on the urn–unless I'm with child. Jurom or Tozet would have to help me then.* She wondered if her idea would be acceptable to the dragons.

Hāwitche asked, "And these plains of long grass. Are they filled with wapiti, biaguchu, and horses?"

Aurora didn't know what to say. Her land had none of those animals on which the tribe depended. *We don't even have the dogs they use.* "As I said, I have not lived in that part of the land. I will ask the Thunderbird what is there."

She reached out to Jurom. *"Jurom, can we move some of the animals from here to our land?"* A lengthy gap of silence lasted long enough that she started to wonder if Jurom heard her.

"For the larger animals, if I shrink them for travel, I be able to carry several at one time through the portal."

"That would be perfect, Jurom. If we move them soon, they will have time to adjust to their new home before the people arrive."

As expected, she grew markedly more pregnant-looking each day. At five weeks, she told Igasho that she would rather stay inside until the baby came. "Everyone looks at me like a spectacle."

"I understand, but you must see it from their point of view. Never has such a thing happened before."

"Oh believe, me! I understand that!" She let out a long sigh. "Before I can stay inside, I must go back to the temple and check on the urn."

Sadness and concern filled his eyes, and she placed her hand on his forearm. "Remember, I told you that I had a responsibility to fulfill."

He nodded reluctantly, and they made plans for the next day.

The following day, Igasho carried Aurora outside the village on his horse to a stand of whitebark pines where Jurom landed. Aurora climbed aboard. "I will return tomorrow," she said. "I'm going to look for some items for the baby while I am there." He nodded, but his emerald green aura, now tinged with dark blue, told her he feared the future.

"I will be fine," she reassured him. "Meet me back here tomorrow." She kissed his cheek and boarded the dragon. As she flew away, she looked down at her husband until he disappeared from her sight. Then she enjoyed the cool mountain air and a sense of freedom away from all the prying eyes watching to see how big she had grown.

When they reached the site of the cave, Jurom landed, and she disembarked. She stretched her back and rested her hand on her stomach. *"How much my life has changed!"*

"And mine as well, Little One."

She let out a deep breath and patted the dragon's side. "I'm sorry. I forget that I am not the only one going through such changes. Come, let us go home."

She took the therus rod from the bag and opened the portal of swirling energy. Jurom stepped through first. Aurora followed. The stale smells of the old temple wrapped her in familiarity. "I never thought I'd be happy to be back here, but I am. I'm going to check on the urn. Then can you take me to the rooftop?"

"Aye, mine Tozet shall be arriving there soon."

Aurora walked through the great hall into the "pantry" room and slipped through the door hidden by the shelves into the secret chamber where she had spent so many hours since her parents' departure. "Lux locus." Light filled the room like daylight. She walked over to the urn. It sat like a shrine within the niche in the wall on the wooden box containing the ancient Scroll of Prophecy. She picked it up and blew dust from the lid. Her fingers traced the symbols. Even after all this time, she wondered about the story they foretold and why she couldn't foresee beyond the urn disappearing. "I long for the day I see you disappear." She set the ancient jar back on the box and wondered where it would go. "And why will it return?" The Zaylan prophecy played through her mind. '*When the urn returns to the temple, one of thine line shall understand the sacrifice that must occur. A sacrifice never made before and never to be made again.*' She rubbed the last of the dust from the lid and let go of what she didn't know. "I can only do my part."

Aurora stepped into the Great Hall and climbed to Jurom's goldenhorn. His mighty wings lifted them into the air and out through the large arched window. As they landed, she saw Tozet in the distance. "I'm going down to my parents' chamber," she said. "And I plan to sleep in my bed for tonight."

Jurom trumpeted to his mate in greeting as she approached, and Aurora hurried toward the trapdoor and used her magic to open it. She carefully picked her way down the ladder. Growing with child certainly changed how her body fit on the ladder. A little over a month ago, she wouldn't have given a thought to traversing the ladder with such care. She inched toward her parents' room and called for a floating lucium sphere to provide light instead of lighting one of the chest lanterns. The orb appeared in an instant. *It feels good to be home*, she thought, as she stepped into her parents' chamber.

She took her time going through the chest that held Mother's belongings, searching for the wrap she used to carry her children. She found it, along with a few baby clothes she decided to bring back to the village. She thought of taking a change of clothes for herself but decided against it. She didn't need anything to set her apart as different right now. Her hair and skin color already did that, not to mention her quickly progressing pregnancy.

That night she lay in the comfort of her room and read the scrolls. While it felt good to be home, she missed Igasho. She lay her hand on the mattress beside her. *This bed is where I first became his wife.* She fell asleep thinking of him and wondering if he missed her as she missed him.

The following morning the baby woke her early. She placed her hand on her stomach. "Are you trying to tell me you are ready to go back to be with your Da?"

She dressed and climbed the ladder to the rooftop. "*Jurom, are you near?*"

"Yes, Little One. I be near. Are ye ready to depart?"

"Yes."

Within minutes, the rush of dragons' wings filled the air. Jurom and Tozet crested the side of the temple and landed on the roof.

"You slept in the temple?" Aurora asked. And for the first time, she realized how little she communicated with Jurom these days. Before Igasho came into her life, the two of them were always in touch.

"Yes, we slept in the temple. I needed to regain mine energy."

Guilt wrapped around her like a cloak. *"Living in the America land steals your energy, doesn't it?"*

"No, it does not steal mine energy but, it be not refreshed."

She rested her hand on her stomach. *"I wonder what it is doing to my child?"*

"Thy child be fine for now, but he shall mature quickly in that land."

"How do you know he is fine? Wait! He? You know I will have a son?"

A light clicking filled the air. It erased the tension building in Aurora's shoulders. *"I miss this,"* she said. *"The sound of your laugh, the feeling that I belong."* She shrugged. "*There in the village, I am out of my time. I love it, but I'm not in harmony. I feel more like a spectacle on exhibition. In my home, it is fine, but when I step outside...."* She shook her head, struggling to find the right words.

"That be right. Ye be not in harmony, for ye be not in synch. Nor should ye be, for it be not thy time. Ye know what needs be done."

"I do?"

The dragon's blue-green eyes transformed to light violet as he focused on her. She let out a quick gasp. *"I do! Why didn't I see this? It's like I've gone blind to my foresight!"*

Tozet stepped forward. *"Ye see again?"*

Aurora nodded.

"What do ye see?" Jurom asked.

"I see I will live in the land America until the winter thaw. And then I will return with my two children, husband, and some of the tribe." She rested her hand on her stomach as if she could protect the baby from losing his early childhood. *And what of the second child which I carry in a sling upon my return?*

A tear trickled down her cheek. She wiped it away angrily. *"And why do I still not see the day the urn disappears from the temple? The day I am released to live my life as others do? When will that happen? Is it so wrong to long for life, as others live?"*

"Ye know what ye must know."

His words felt unkind–uncaring. Anger shot through her. *"And what about you? What do you know, Jurom?"*

His aura changed to a muddy gray, and it scared her. "Jurom? Are you sick?"

"Little One, I be not the focus, but mine life be not much longer. The less time I spend on the other side of the portal, the more time I shall have here."

She rushed over to him, wrapped her arms around his snout, and hugged him. *"Then stay here. I will be back here to check on the urn and will see you then. You will be here when I come back here, right?"*

She looked from Jurom to Tozet. "Right?"

"We know not the answer for living out of mine time has changed... things."

She nodded. *"I changed things. I am so sorry, but I didn't know about living outside of the dragon realms or what would happen."*

Smoke curled from Tozet's nostril, and Aurora let it go. Saying goodbye to Jurom tore her up inside, but she knew it must be so. This time, when she stepped through the portal, she felt an odd sensation–a separation as the portal closed. For the first time in her life, Jurom let go of his connection. *I am making him sick because I'm living beyond the dragon realm. But I saw Igasho in the visions–and Jurom didn't tell me until it was good late.* She couldn't second guess herself.

Instead, she clung to the thought that Igasho was waiting for her, *and soon I will be a mother. And I will have a second child before I leave this America-world.*

She tucked the therus rod into her bag along with the folded sling that would soon carry her child. *My son.* She stepped into the sunshine and stopped. *How am I going to get back to the village?*

She reached out with her powers to see if she could communicate with Igasho's horse, Molala. She felt the mare's mind, but it wasn't open in the same way as talking with animals back home. She tried to call her, but the animal didn't answer. *What am I going to do?* Birds hidden among the trees chattered to one another like small children calling questions. They offered no answers because she couldn't understand them. Her moccasins padded down the ridge where she first met Igasho hoping to find him there. She paused to look at his stone drawings of her holding the starstones and Jurom with his wings outstretched. Her fingers brushed the image of the dragon. "I've longed for change most of my life. Now that it has arrived, I find I'm longing to hold on to what I've always known."

When she reached the stand of white pines, she wondered if it was possible to travel the Midlands here. *It's too much of an unknown. If there isn't a Midlands, I could find myself trapped in rock or something. Or even if there is, I may not see the way. What am I thinking? Jurom said no Midlands travel when with child.* The thought of what could have happened if she tried sent a shudder through her.

If I walk back to the village, I could get lost. The baby kicked against her ribs. "And you could be born before I ever reach the village." For now, she would stay here until she had a plan. She gathered kindling and added it to the remnants of the firepit she and Igasho had used when they slept here, but she didn't want to go searching for wood to keep a fire burning. Instead, she'd use magic to start a fire that burned without fuel. She pulled out the therus rod to manage the magic. Holding it in her hand inspired her. *I know how to reach Igasho!*

Igasho kept his eyes trained on the skies watching for Jurom and Waianten. Concerns bubbled within him because Waianten had said she would return the following day but had not. He tried not to worry, but he couldn't help it. His eyes turned skyward one more time, and he spotted a message in the clouds. *Igasho, come to me where we first met*. "Look at the sky," he said to his father.

"My son, never point at or talk about a cloud. You'll scare the rain away."

Igasho averted his eyes from the sky and nodded his agreement. *Father cannot see the message!* It stunned him that Appah wrote a communication for him in the clouds from his wife. It gave way to a different worry. *Perhaps the baby is coming, and she cannot ride! Maybe, she is injured*. He didn't speak of it but walked to the outskirts of the village and whistled for Molala.

Within minutes he mounted his horse and urged her forward. As he rode, he marveled that two moons earlier, he had traveled this way for his vision quest. His Spirit Guide and spirit-blessed wife had changed his life, and now he was expecting his first child any day. As he thought about it, his apprehension eased. He trusted Appah would not bring him to this point in his spiritual journey only to take away his wife or child. He sent up prayers as his horse's hooves pounded out his unspoken urgency.

Igasho followed the upward trail, heading toward the small plateau and the portal cave. He slowed his horse and threaded into the white pines to let her cool down. The bed of pine needles muted Molala's footfalls as the light scent of a campfire wafted on the air. As he reached the stony ledge, he called out, "Waianten!"

"Igasho!" Aurora wailed, followed by a soft moan. "Hurry!"

He slipped from the horse's back and ran on foot. "Waianten?"

"The baby, Igasho. The baby is coming."

He broke through the tree line and into the campsite. Waianten lay on her side near the fire. He rushed to her side and picked her up.

She wrapped her arms around his neck. "What are you doing?"

"I'm moving you into the cave. It will be the birthing hut."

She didn't argue but lay her head against his chest.

"Are you in much pain?"

“Some. But it is expected.” She let out a thin laugh and winced.

He carried her into the cave and set her down. “I wish my mother and aunts were here to help.”

She reached up and brushed his cheek. “You are here.”

Within the hour, the baby arrived. “It is a son,” Igasho said with pride as he handed the child to his wife. “We shall call him Two Moons.”

She looked down into the baby’s red face and quieted his cry. “I would like to call him Kylar Two Moons after my brother.”

“Ky-lar.” Igasho nodded. “It is a strong name. Ky-lar Two Moons.”

Love for the child filled her, his aura shined emerald green, but when his tiny hand wrapped around her finger, rainbow beams sprang from his clasp. Warm power wrapped around her. In a blink, the negative effect of this world and the drain on her energy disappeared. *He is a healer.*

Igasho moved to the mouth of the cave and scanned the area. “Where is Jurom?”

“He isn’t feeling well. Living here is difficult for him.” She stood. “Would you mind if we introduce him to the baby before we travel back to the village?”

“Are you feeling up to it? Perhaps you should rest.”

She laughed as she held the child in one arm and opened her bag with the other, and pulled out the sling she had brought from her parent’s room. “I feel fine.” She swaddled the baby against her body and smiled. “He looks like you.” She walked over and kissed Igasho. “I’m so thankful he has dark hair.”

Igasho didn’t know what to think. The women of his tribe were happy to stay in the birthing hut for a few days after giving birth. The men often joked that they were glad to have time off from their chores, but Waianten acted as if she’d never given birth.

She stood ready to open the portal with the baby swaddled in the sling across the front of her body. As the blue light swirled into existence, Aurora stuck her head through enough to call to Jurom. *"Jurom, are you here?"*

"I be here, Little One. Tozet and I sleep upon the temple roof."

It left her surprised but happy to hear he was still at the temple. *"Come meet my son."* She pulled her head back to the America-side of the portal and reached out her hand to Igasho. "Come. Let us introduce Kylar Two Moons to Jurom and his future home." The new family walked into the ancient Temple of Five Marks as Jurom landed in the great hall, and Tozet glided through the large arched window near the ceiling. Jurom stepped forward. His head and snout seemed unusually large as he sniffed the tiny lump created by the child in the sling. Igasho rushed forward with his hand on the stone blade at his side.

Jurom paused. *"Do not be fearful, Spirit Child, for I will not harm thy child but rejoice to see him before I go the way of mine ancestors."*

His words struck fear in Aurora as she stared at the muddy gray edges of the dragon's aura. "Jurom?" She reached out and touched his snout. "You are very sick!"

Tozet stepped to his side. *"So kind of thee to finally notice. Using magic to carry all those animals from there to here be a terrible toll. Thy reckless behavior has carried him to the door of death."*

"My behavior?"

"He is dying?" Igasho stared wide-eyed. His arms hung at his side. "Why? What does his mate mean it is because of you?"

Aurora's mouth felt dry. She had forgotten that Igasho could hear their conversation when he carried the loqui stone. Her hand cradled Kylar Two Moons within the sling; grief quickly tinged her joy. "It is because I walked through the portal earlier than planned, and so it caused him to stay on the other side… your land… longer." Her words trailed off into tears.

"It be well enough," Jurom said. *"Cry not at this time of happiness. Let me see thy child whom we have awaited so long."*

Her breath shuddered into a muted moan as she forced a smile. She pulled the child from his hiding place within the folds of the sling and raised him with two hands toward the dragon. His green snout drew near as if sniffing the child who stretched and kicked his legs. The soft clicking rising from deep within Jurom's throat brought Tozet closer.

"What be humorous?"

"I recall when Aurora be born. This child looks nothing like her. He be black-haired and ruddier, but he be like his mother in that his power be quite strong."

"Power?" Igasho echoed. His shoulders relaxed, and a smile tugged at his lips. "He looks like me, Waianten, but is powerful like you. His future will be that of a taikwahni."

The child stretched his arms and legs. When he started to fuss, Jurom leaned in to touch him with his snout. The child wriggled, and his hand brushed the dragon's powerful muzzle. A rainbow of color burst around them. The dragon's head swung to the side as if hit by a giant fist. Aurora reflexively clutched the baby to her breast as if protecting him from danger.

"What is wrong?" Igasho asked. His lips pressed into a straight line as his eyes darted from Jurom to Aurora.

The familiar struggle returned and wrapped around Aurora like a musty, old blanket. She wanted to talk about it but wasn't allowed to tell him what she saw. She glanced at Jurom. His aura had returned to the green of health with no hint of the sickly muddy gray she had witnessed moments before. Instead of answering Igasho, she asked a question. "What happened?"

Tozet trumpeted. *"Mine mate be healed. Thy Kylar Two Moons be a healer!"*

"What?" Igasho looked from Tozet to the child in his wife's arms. "The baby—my son is a healer? He is only hours old."

Aurora nodded. "It must be so. Jurom is well. That means he will be able to visit us more while we live on the other side of the portal and prepare your—our people to come here to Tupi."

"Kylar Two Moons shall be a leader among his people, and from his line shall come one who walks alongside the Variel." Tozet's multifaceted eyes transformed from amber to a deep lavender as she

focused on the child. *"I be honored to be part of thine life, and I be regretful for the way I treated thee in the past."*

Aurora laughed lightly and walked over to the female dragon. "Kylar Two Moons, meet your Grandmother Guardian."

Tozet bowed her head and lightly stroked the child with her snout. *"I be happy to become thy Grandmother Guardian."*

With his renewed strength and health, Jurom agreed to go along with Igasho and Aurora through the portal to carry them back to the village. Tozet rubbed her bony brow ridge against her mate's and said, *"Mine mate, if befitting, I be willing to join thee and carry Zaylan's Oracle and Kylar Two Moons, and to meet the others who shall be coming here to live."*

Everyone agreed to the plan, but as they traveled over the mountains toward the village, Aurora wondered at her blindness. For she hadn't perceived Jurom was so ill, and she hadn't foreseen that they would all be traveling to the village riding upon the dragons. For a moment, Aurora questioned her health. Then the baby stirred against her bosom, and she let her concerns go. Perhaps her inability to see had something to do with her pregnancy or even motherhood. If that was the case, it was a price she would willingly pay.

As they circled over the village, Jurom let them know, he and Igasho would land first, which pleased Igasho. *"Give me time to tell my family about the arrival of the baby."*

Aurora smiled not only because Jurom perceived the human ways of this culture but because Tozet did not try to argue or complain. As they circled above the village, Aurora nursed her son. As he suckled, she wondered at the rainbow of power shining from him and what it would mean for his future. Maybe that's why I've gone blind. As a mother, it might be better not to know. She thought of her parents and wondered what they understood about her future when she was young. *I wonder if my mother lost any of her abilities when she became a parent.*

She marveled at her son, and then he opened his eyes and focused on her with eyes of green. For a moment, it filled her with fear. *What does this mean?* His eyes had been dark, but they had changed color, and he could already focus.

Tozet began her descent, and Aurora tried to let go of her worries. A crowd gathered around Jurom and Igasho, but as Tozet came in for a landing, Aurora marveled at how every face was upturned and waiting for her and the baby.

The people kept their distance from Tozet, except for Igasho's parents, who hurried to meet their *daughter* and the mother of their first grandchild. She climbed to the ground and peeled back the sling. "Say *behne* to Kylar Two Moons."

They finally made it to the cave-dwelling amid a whirlwind of activity. Aurora and Igasho stood outside on the ledge and wished the dragons farewell before they turned and walked inside. They sat in the main chamber, where Hāwitche happily held the baby and cooed her delight at how much he looked like his father.

That night, Igasho and Aurora whispered about everything that had happened. They talked some about how much the child had changed since he was born, but Igasho left questions unasked because he had more important things to discuss.

"Pu'ennaakan's wife had her child yesterday… a girl. And I've already heard my parents talking of arranging the marriage of Pu'ennaakan's daughter and our son."

Aurora sat up. "My people have a different custom. We are allowed to choose a mate. Is such a decision up to the parents or the grandparents or the children?"

Igasho rolled his eyes. "It will be our choice." She lay back and cuddled against his chest, and the two of them fell asleep with the baby swaddled in a cradleboard her mother-in-law had crafted. It was dark when Kylar cried for his night feeding. As she lifted him, he felt heavier. When she put him to her breast, she felt a palpable difference in his size and the strength of his suckle. *He is developing quickly—aging rapidly like me.* When he finished eating, she lay him beside her as if she could somehow hold on to him as he was, but in the morning, when she opened her eyes, Kylar lay on his stomach and lifted his head to look at her. He kicked his feet with excitement and cooed and smiled. Igasho opened his eyes at the sound and stared at his son as if he were dreaming.

Now, the rapidly-growing Kylar Two Moons became a spectacle to all, but he also served as a confirmation that the story of Igasho's vision quest remained true. About the time Kylar began to wean, Aurora grew ill. At first, she wondered if age was overtaking her more quickly than she thought, but Hāwitche hit her with a new reality. "You are with child again."

Kylar was walking, running, talking, and often by his father's side learning. He helped his father gather bohobi to make the tea that made her feel much better.

With a second child on the way, Igasho spoke with his people about moving to Tupi during the thawing moon. By then, Kylar would be like one who had lived five summers, and if the new baby aged in the same fashion, it would already be walking about and learning to talk. He wanted to get to Tupi, where Aurora said time would slow to normal for them because he could see Waianten youth fading, and he wanted to enjoy his children a day at a time.

"Those who want to make the journey will have to plan to bring food stores, for the land of Tupi is different. We will have to learn new hunting, but I can tell you there will be plenty of fish because there is a lot of water. However, I didn't see a single pinenut tree there, so I planted seeds when I was there from the back of the Thunderbird, but it will take time for those trees to grow and produce."

Tupi became the constant topic of discussion. Some feared that they would age quickly in the new land "like Igasho's child." About half the tribe decided they would make the journey, while the other half wanted to stay in the land of their fathers. It created a sense of excitement mingled with sadness.

Their second child came within two moons like his brother. "We shall call him Nakaah," Igasho said. "It means 'last born,' for he will be our last born in the land of my forefathers." Everyone said this boy looked more like his grandfather, with the deep brown eyes of his father.

Nakaah developed rapidly, like his brother, but his lavender aura made Aurora think he would be better named *Nabusai*, daydreamer. But, it wasn't something she could talk about, so she treasured the name in her heart. *Perhaps, he will be Nabusai as he grows and earns a new name.*

The two boys were very different but got along well. Kylar Two Moons and Nakaah had a special relationship, but Aurora feared the other children might shun them because they were different. To her relief, the opposite was true. The other children looked up to Kylar, who had already matured to the size of children three summers old. Everyone wanted to be his friend. Nakaah was just over two moons old and already looked to be nine moons in age and starting to take steps without holding on to something. The other children often played with him to see how much bigger he'd grown and what new things he could do.

While the other children were eager to be friends with her children, the other women often treated Aurora as if being with her would bring them good fortune. They frequently asked her to be with them during childbirth, and she learned to make relationships for the first time in her life. Bonds grew closer, and more and more of the tribe made plans to travel to Tupi to start a new life with her and Igasho at the time of the thawing moon. Pu'ennaakan was one clear exception. It was no secret he wouldn't be among those who planned to leave. This pained Aurora, for she and Pu'ennaakan's wife, Kimama, had become close friends. She glanced over at Kimama whacking the pine nuts from the upper branches of a tree with her daughter sleeping on her back. The two of them often worked together.

Kylar Two Moons eagerly gathered pine nuts from the ground among the trees and tossed them into the basket. As summer drew to a close, the mountain air grew colder, and the tribe prepared to travel into the valley soon. Kimama often talked of life in the valley and how she preferred it to life on the cliffs. The one thing she didn't talk about was her husband and why he didn't plan to come to Tupi, but what bothered Aurora most was the unhappiness she saw in Hāwitche's dark brown eyes.

Aurora pointed deep into the trees where other children helped gather. "Kylar, collect the nuts over there until I've knocked the pine nuts from this tree." He ran deeper into the dappled sunlight as she whacked the long stick against the tree branches. Nuts thumped the ground like hailstones. Nakaah fussed, to be freed from the sling tethering him across her back. Kimama walked over and cooed to the fussy boy, speaking in the rhythmic language Aurora had learned to love. Nakaah kicked his feet and giggled.

"In some ways, you are fortunate that your children mature so quickly," Kimama said. "Soon, Nakaah will be running with the other children while my daughter is learning to sit up on her own."

Aurora turned to look into the woman's sad brown eyes. "In some ways, yes, I'm fortunate. I already have two children, and they are rapidly maturing." She shrugged. "I'd rather they could grow at a regular pace. I feel like I'm missing the opportunity to enjoy them as babies. At least when we go to Tupi, they will grow normally, and perhaps I will have other children and enjoy them as babies."

Kimama glanced up at the tree as tears pooled in her eyes.

Aurora reached out and gently touched her forearm. "What is it?"

She looked at Aurora and swallowed. "I am torn. I feel I must warn you, but if I do, I betray my husband."

A sinking feeling washed over Aurora. Her lack of prophetic ability in this world hit her squarely. "Warn me? If my family is in danger, please tell me."

"It is Pu'ennaakan. He thinks you bring evil spirits among our tribe in the form of your children and that you have deceived Igasho." Tears spilled down her cheeks. "He plans on killing you and your sons." She broke into full sobs and buried her face in her hands. "If he learns I have told you, I fear he will kill me too."

Aurora dropped to her knees and sat back on her heels. For a moment, she didn't move as she absorbed what her friend was saying. "Kill… us?" Frantic with fear, she searched for her son among the children helping to gather pine nuts. "Kylar Two Moons," she called as she pushed to her feet. "Kylar!"

Kylar ran from the shadows into the sunlight. His dark shoulder-length hair bounced with each step as he held out his tunic filled with pine nuts like an apron. A few sprang free and hit the ground with each step. "Look, Mère, I have gathered many!" He dumped his haul into the basket as Aurora reached out and gathered him into her arms.

"Thank you, Kimama." She placed Kylar's feet on the ground. "I owe you my life and the life of my children."

Kimama nodded and looked away to focus on the uppermost tree branches.

Aurora understood. *She can't say another word about it without bringing herself harm*. She picked up the large basket of pine nuts and grabbed Kylar's hand. "I'm going to take these back to our lodge." She hurried back to the lodge without another word. Her mind raced. *I need to leave with the children.*

"Jurom? Jurom, can you hear me?"

"Yes, Little One."

"Hurry, come to me at the edge of the stand of white pines. If possible, bring Igasho with you!"

CHAPTER FORTY-THREE

Aurora's fearful words about Kimama's warning alarmed Igasho. He ushered his children and wife onto Jurom's back. "Take us to the gateway of light."

Jurom's leathery wings carried them upwards and over the mountains toward the portal cave. "What are we going to do?" Aurora asked.

"You will take the children to Tupi now. I will return to the village and let the people know now is the time to leave. Perhaps it will throw Pu'ennaakan and his followers off."

"Perhaps! Perhaps! Igasho! He could kill you. Come back with me to Tupi, where I have powers that don't work here. Remember how I told you I came here because I had seen you? There, in Tupi, I will be able to see who we can trust. Please, husband, come with us for at least a day."

"I will come with you, but I will not stay. Once you and our sons are safe, I must go to my people and warn them of this *isa'awih*. For if his lies and tricks go unchallenged, he will deceive hearts to believe you are the *isanai.*"

She dismounted at the mouth of the cave with mixed emotions. If she had her way, she'd walk through this portal with her family, never to return to America. As they stepped through the gateway into the stale temple air, Aurora marveled at the way Kylar's aura brightened. Within a moment, she understood. It wasn't that his aura brightened but her ability to see it had strengthened.

Igasho turned to return to his homeland, but Aurora grabbed his arm. "At least see us to the rooftop. Then, you can return with Jurom, so he can help protect you, and he can alert me to when you want to come through the gateway of light. And while you're gone, I will work to set up a detour that will lead all your people straight into the land of Tupi rather than into the Temple at Five Marks." Even as she said it, she hoped Tozet could help her. She'd read about a mirror-portal among all of Kylar's scrolls, and while she knew such a thing was possible, she didn't know how to create it.

Igasho climbed back onto Jurom with Kylar Two Moons. Aurora ran up at his heels with the baby strapped to her back. They slipped through the arched window into the evening twilight burning orange like dying embers above the Tachnir mountains in the west. The first sun had disappeared, and the second dipped close to the horizon. They landed on the roof, and Igasho looked at her with a sadness she couldn't interpret. A vision of a struggle flashed through her mind. Two dark-haired men, *Pu'ennaakan and Igasho!* She wrapped her arms around Igasho with a desperate need to cling to him. "I don't want you to go."

"I know. But I must. Our people will wonder where we are, and the longer I am gone, the longer Pu'ennaakan has to stir up lies and false accusations." She dismounted with her children and watched Jurom carry her husband into the air before plummeting down the side of the temple and slipping through the arched window.

Kylar held out his hand and touched her hip. "Don't feel sad, Mère." Energy flowed from him in a way she had never experienced. It renewed her depleted strength.

"Thank you Kylar, Mère feels much better."

"Where are we?" He looked around with eyes wide like two emerald pools.

Before she answered, she reached out to Tozet, *"Come. I need your help."* With the dragon on her way, Aurora knelt to look her son in the eyes. "This is where Tupi is… where we are going to live." She pointed toward the east. "It is beyond those mountains where the river runs into the sea."

"What is the sea?"

"It is a lake so big that it seems to be without end."

"When will we go there?"

"Soon. Soon. For now, I want you to rest before the trip."

Kylar fussed but obeyed as he snuggled with his younger brother, Nakaah, on the bricks still warm from the suns. Nakaah was more interested in sticking his finger into Kylar Two Moon's nostrils than falling asleep. The older boy reached out and brushed his hand across his brother's face. The younger boy's brown eyes grew heavy-lidded and closed, lulled to sleep.

Aurora stared at her son with amazement. *Life on the other side of the portal hampered his powers. Will it stunt his abilities?* As Kylar's eyes closed, Aurora spotted Tozet flying toward the temple. *"Try to land as quietly as possible. The children are sleeping."*

Tozet hovered and gradually dropped onto the flat temple roof. *"Where be Igasho and Jurom?"*

"They have returned to bring Igasho's people."

"It be sooner than planned."

"It is." Aurora nodded. *"Someone planned to kill the children and me, so Igasho decided to bring us here, and now he has gone to bring those planning to live here. And since things happened so fast, I was wondering if you know of a way to create a mirror-portal."*

"A mirror-portal?"

Aurora nodded as she started to pace. *"I read about such a portal in the scrolls my brother left behind. At the time, I wondered why such a thing would be necessary. But if it could work, it is a perfect option for what I would like to do. If possible, I'd like to create a portal on top of the secret portal to carry the people directly to Topi. I don't want to reveal the temple to them. We don't know if there might be people among them who think I am an evil spirit. People who believe I should be destroyed, along with my children. Even if something were to happen to me, I must protect the temple from that possibility."*

"Aye." Light tendrils of smoke curled from the dragon's snout as she thought. *"We be able to create a mirror-portal."*

"That's what I hoped."

"We shall create it atop the true portal, so as they step through one, they will continue through the second without realizing it."

Aurora ran over to Tozet and lay her head against the white pouch on her throat. *"Thank you, thank you! That is what we need. So how do we create this mirror-portal."*

"Ye need the therus rod."

Aurora pulled it from her shoulder bag. "I have it." Just then, Nakaah started to fuss, and Kylar Two Moons sat up and pulled him onto his lap. "What am I going to do with the children?" Aurora wondered out loud. Her thoughts flashed to her husband's mother and aunts and how much they helped with the boys. She looked at her boys, and it came to her. *Tozet!* Tozet lightly clicked her approval.

Kylar Two Moons eagerly climbed into Tozet's neck pouch, but Nakaah wasn't so sure and clung to his mother. Instead of fighting with him, she wrapped him in the sling across her back and climbed aboard the dragon's back.

As they stood before the portal, Aurora felt blind as to what to do next.

"I must warn thee. It be dangerous magic. For the mirror-portal must match the shape, size and the kinetic energy of the portal exactly."

"What if it doesn't?"

"If it be flawed in fit, energy leaks into the Midlands. Those who cross the threshold risk being pulled into the Midlands and lost forever."

"Wait! What?"

"It must mirror the shape and size of the portal. The two must fit as one."

"Have you done this before? Create a mirror-portal?"

"Nay, I have not." She hesitated.

"What are you not telling me?"

"I know not if it works. It be Jurom's father Beroan who worked this magic in time past."

"And you don't know if it worked? How can you not know?"

"It be when he left this realm... this time."

The news stunned her. She'd always wondered what happened to the dragons she'd grown up around. *"Were my parents with him?"*

"Ye know I cannot tell thee."

That's all she needed to hear. Her parents, Beroan, and Nimbus had all disappeared at the same time. She'd wondered about it but let it go. Her parents had prepared her to let it go, but now she wondered where they had gone–if they might still be alive somewhere even after all this time. *Da said I would see them again.*

For now, she let it go again. She had to worry about Igasho and the tribe coming here. *"Okay, what do we do?"*

"This magic takes two, for it be too powerful a tool to wield alone." She went on to explain what they must do. As they stood at the edge of the portal, Tozet would mentally speak the spell in the ancient dragon language passed on by the Thornose, and Aurora was to say it.

Tozet began. *"Laici hoc prodigium"*

Aurora stared into the swirling energy, "Over this portal lay."

"Plaga est plaga, zone pro zona."

"Stroke for stroke, zone for zone."

"Alter pelle."

"A second skin."

"In speculo. Ostium secundum."

"A mirror image. A secondary gate."

Suddenly, a frosty-looking layer crept from the farthest edges toward the center of the glowing portal. The skin formed and then disappeared.

"What happened? Where did it go?"

"It be there. Ye cannot perceive it."

"Can you? Are you sure it is there?"

"Say, 'Mirror detect.'"

"Mirror detect." The filmy frostlike layer appeared, and she let out a sigh of relief. *"And now when they step through, they won't be here in the temple but will arrive in the area we are calling Tupi?"*

"That be correct."

"But where? How will we know where?"

"Ye must go activate it with the therus rod from the other side."

"So how did Beroan do…." *My mother or father had to help. They all disappeared at the same time–went to live somewhere together. But how if they left the therus rod?* Without a doubt, she knew her father was the one who risked the first passage through their mirror-portal, and now, in a sense, she would follow in his footsteps. A lump formed in her throat. *"If something goes wrong…. I'm going to leave Nakaah here with Kylar in your pouch."*

Tozet didn't question the decision. *"I shall carry and care for them until ye return."*

Aurora placed her children within the neck pouch, pinning their arms at their sides. Nakaah took it in stride because he was still used to the cradleboard, but Kylar Two Moons squirmed. She kissed his forehead and told him to, "Be good for Tozet; Mère will be back soon." She rested her hand on the dragon's bony eye ridge. "I will bring our mates home."

She spun around and stepped into the portal before she changed her mind. The energy of the portal felt different. The prickly sensation she'd grown used to itched like creeping nettle rash. She wasn't sure if it was her imagination or if she could feel the filmlike mirror skin. For now, it didn't matter as she stood within the familiar cave where Kylar had been born. Good memories flooded her mind as she pondered all that had happened since then. She mentally reached out to Jurom, and he answered.

"Yes, we be coming, but it shall take three days if all goes well, for the people have loaded their belongings on what Igasho calls a travois. They be pulled along by puny four-legged creatures."

"Dogs."

"Yes, dogs. While many of the people walk upon their two legs."

Aurora knew what he meant. It was how they had moved from the cliff dwellings into the valley. The dogs dragged the sleds loaded with their things, and it was slow going. *"I understand,"* she said. *"The portal is set up to arrive in Tupi."*

The pause told her he knew that she knew or at least suspected what had happened to her parents. It hurt slightly that he never mentioned it, but she understood. It was the same for her with Igasho. And it was the same for her parents, but she didn't understand why. But with this newfound knowledge, she wondered if she might learn something more if she read Kylar's scrolls or studied his artwork again. *In my pompous pride, have I overlooked things because I could see into the future and thought it more important than the past?*

"I shall bring thy mate to thee." Jurom's voice pulled her from her self introspection.

"I promised the same to Tozet, but I didn't think about it being days. I need to open the gate with the rod, and I must go back to feed Nakaah. I know time passes more quickly here, so how shall I count the passage of time as I wait on the other side?"

"It shall be little more than half a day, so get a good night's rest, feed thy younglings, and we shall see thee tomorrow."

"Very well, I will meet you in the cave to open the portal."

CHAPTER FORTY-FOUR

Aurora stepped through the activated portal feeling encouraged. To her surprise, instead of stepping into the dimly lit temple, she stood in the evening twilight on a triangular tract of land at the mouth of the Inkish River, where it split into several channels. The second sun still hung low in the sky, and a herd of wapiti grazed on the other side of the river. "This is perfect," she said to herself. She had ridden with the tribe down the Wind River on rafts in America when they moved to the valley, and now this river would carry them to what they all referred to as Tupi–the new land. *The thing that is not perfect is that I'm here, and my children are at the temple.*

"Tozet, I'm back."

"Shall I bring thy younglings to thee?"

"No, I will travel the Midlands and meet you on the roof of the temple soon. We will spend the night there."

She opened access to the Midlands. The golden swirl of light shined like a bonfire sending petals of buttery color scattering across the water's surface in the twilight. Brightness wrapped around her like a whirlwind and exploded in a brilliant flash, initiating a wave of dizziness. The Midland's fog settled over her mind as she disconnected from real-time. Her head throbbed as she forced herself to focus. She closed her eyes for a moment, and the nausea stirring in her stomach subsided. One foot in front of the other, she reminded herself. In the back of her mind, she dreaded the fact that she'd be making this trip regularly to check on the urn until time released her from the responsibility.

Aurora opened her eyes within the swirling distortion of the bubble protecting her as she passed through the dusk between time. She spotted the translucent purple ring floating ahead of her and pushed against the invisible resistance slowing her movement. As she stepped through the gossamer ring, her nausea subsided totally and the struggle to move forward eased beneath the steely ceiling hanging above her.

The green ring came into view ahead of her. She'd forgotten how the ground in the Midlands felt beneath her feet. It wasn't wet or dry. It wasn't hardpan, and it wasn't grass. Not cold or hot. It was there, but it wasn't. She wouldn't be able to return this way with the children, for Jurom warned her that those not Dragonborn lost their minds in the Midlands if they survived. As she stepped through the green ring, she thought about what Tozet said about the mirror portal. "If it be flawed, in fit, energy leaks into the Midlands. Those who cross be at risk–can be pulled into the Midlands and lost forever." With so many people flowing through the portal at once, what are the chances that something can go wrong? If dragged into the Midlands, they will be blind to the rings–lost forever. She pushed the thought from her mind. She needed to stay focused.

Excitement filled her as she neared the gossamer ring, the color of the midnight sky which held within it the violet ring. She visualized the temple rooftop as she stepped through the circle into muted dark swirling colors. Beyond it, she saw the last bridge. The dark green loop of subdued light was easy to spot for those who knew what they were looking for and the vision to see it. She pushed against the resistance dragging her feet. As a mother and wife, she had more reason than ever to return to real-time. She stepped through to the other side. Energy wrapped around her and jerked her upward. Just as her stomach dropped, her feet slammed into the ground. She tripped one step forward and caught herself as she pulled in a deep breath of fresh air.

"Mère, you back already?" Kylar Two Moons' rainbow aura burned bright as he squirmed to free his arms from the dragon's neck pouch and reached toward his mother. She collected him in her arms. "Yes, I'm back, and tomorrow your father, grandparents, aunts, and all the others will be here too." His face brightened with genuine happiness. She hugged him, thankful for Kimama's warning. If she hadn't said something, her precious boys could be dead.

She shrugged away the ugly images the memory brought to her mind, collected Nakaah from the dragon's pouch, secured him in the sling on her back, and fastened Kylar in front of her body. "Where are we going?" he asked.

"I'm going to show you where Mère used to live."

Tozet agreed to sleep on the rooftop. "I be ready to carry the younglings to the east in the morning while ye open the portal so thine mate and his people can cross."

"And your mate, too." Aurora smiled.

Kylar didn't stop chattering about climbing down the ladder, about the furniture, the lamp offering light, and the bed with a mattress as he explored her old bedchamber. She pulled out a few items from her childhood, but he stared spellbound by the paintings and sketches hung on the wall. As she fed Nakaah, she explained that the artwork was from her brother Kylar. "You are named after him."

He sat beside his mother on the bed. "Tell me about this, brother. Where is he now?"

She told him the story of Kylar and his "very excellent" memory, his love for art, and how he wrote everything down. Kylar Two Moons enjoyed hearing about floating caves and life with so many brothers. But when she said, "He took a wife and moved down the river to start his tribe," he let out a long yawn. She went on to describe the village of Red Grove. First, Nakaah fell asleep, and soon Kylar's eyes grew heavy. After he drifted to sleep, she lay her two sons, side by side, on the bed and made her way to the secret room to check on the urn.

She stared at the urn under the blue light of a lucium sphere hovering over her shoulder. "How much longer will you be my responsibility?" Her fingers brushed the ceramic urn as she thought back to her first memories in the dormant volcano of Jur-Jurom. In a flash, visions danced through her head. Images of Igasho's people crossing through the portal. A struggle between Igasho and Pu'ennaakan. She yanked her trembling hand free from the urn. Hot tears stung her eyes. I need to warn Igasho! She ran from the room and called to Tozet as she climbed the ladder. "We need to talk." The dragon met her on the temple rooftop, and the two of them made a plan.

After feeding her children in the morning, Aurora tucked her sons into Tozet's neck pouch. “Keep your brother, Nakaah, safe,” she said to Kylar.

“I will. I will.” He turned to his little brother. “We are going to fly like Mère, and her brother Kylar, did when they came to Tupi.”

She brushed the dark hair from his forehead and kissed his soft skin. “That’s right. Just like me. I will meet you there.”

Tozet took off carrying the children to the river where the mirror-portal would deposit the people to settle in the region to the east.

CHAPTER FORTY-FIVE

Aurora stepped through the portal into the cave where Kylar Two Moons had been born less than a year before Sunlight outlined the mouth of the cave. Diffused light dappled the uneven stone walls near the outlet. She walked into the sunlight and reached out with her mind to Jurom.

"I am here," she announced.

"The people be to the other side of the white pines where Igasho first met us."

"Jurom! Is Pu'ennaakan with the people?"

"He be not, but his wife, Kimama, and youngling be among them. Why ask ye?"

"I had a vision. In it, I saw Pu'ennaakan struggling with Igasho as he stepped through the portal."

"I shall watch over thy mate. We be almost to the path leading to his vision quest rock drawing."

"I will meet you at the cave." She took out the therus rod, activated the portal, and hurried out into the sunshine. Crisp mountain air reminded her of why they had moved to the valley as she rubbed her arms to chase away the goosebumps. The sound of voices and dogs barking in the distance took her mind off the cold. Soon, the people, her people, would be here. They would come home with her. *I'll never live alone again.*

The first group of people to show up included young men, a travois piled with belongings hidden beneath hides, dragged by one of the younger dogs, and with them, Igasho's father and a couple of horses. "Taikwahni Ubirajara! Come this way." She motioned toward the cave as her eyes scanned the line of people behind him looking for her husband. "Where is Igasho?"

“He sent us ahead. I am to lead the people into the new land and be there to greet them. He shall follow.”

She nodded, but she didn’t like it. Her mind reached out to Jurom. *“Am I to lead the people into the new land or let them enter without me?”*

“Ye shall lead them. I shall watch after thy mate. We shall see ye in Tupi where I shall join mine mate, never to return to this land.” She glanced overhead and shielded her eyes against the harsh light of this world’s one sun as it dropped closer to the horizon. The dragon’s reassuring shadowy silhouette circled high above the trees.

“I will see you there.” As she led the people to the cave, she explained to them about the gateway of light, but she couldn’t shake the memory of the vision. “It is much like the setting of the sun in the west. The following day it rises in the east and brings a new day. You shall step through the gateway here and rise in Tupi to a new life.”

The Taikwahni stood before the portal calming, the dog who ferociously barked at the swirling energy. He spoke to the people who crowded into the cave. “I will step through this gateway of light before you and as your Taikwahni will be there to greet you on the other side.” He stuck out his hand, touched the energy, and pulled it back. “Just step through it?”

Aurora nodded. “Yes, and as my Taikwahni, I shall follow you. Each one here will tell the next to step through just as you did.”

Before he did anything else, he took a rope from the sled and tied it around the dog’s neck. “Come,” he said to the dog as he stepped into the light. The dog sat like a stubborn mule, unwilling to move. “Come,” Taikwahni Ubirajara’s dark eyes shined with pride as the dog obeyed. The chief stepped into the portal pulling the rope, dog, and sled behind him. The dog whined, but once through the portal, left the others staring at each other quietly.

“That’s a good idea,” Aurora said. “We will make a chain. That way those, who are brave, can encourage those who are fearful and weak to follow you.” The young men laughed, but with their shifting gazes, she could see they were nervous. Who could blame them? The chain of people strung outside the cave and down the hill as the message spread. Some held hands or arms, while others just rested a hand on a shoulder or one of the sleds or horses.

Aurora stepped through the portal with apprehension gnawing at her. The Taikwahni greeted her with a big fatherly hug and spoke of the beauty of the land. He directed people to sit along the river to wait for the others. “Then we shall travel together.”

Everyone relaxed until Tozet flew low overhead and landed just east of the people. They shot to their feet and talked excitedly. Buzz filled the air like a poked hornet's nest with everyone talking at once. Aurora ran to Tozet to collect her children, and the people grew noisier until Kylar Two Moons ran over to his grandfather beside the portal and the stream of people arriving.

* * * *

Every muscle in Igasho’s body tensed with anticipation. Since Jurom shared news of Waianten’s vision, he’d hung back from Kimama and her daughter. If Pu'ennaakan showed up, he would likely drag them back to join the part of the tribe that chose to stay in the valley. Pu'ennaakan said he wasn't coming, and Kimama left him in favor of life in Tupi. *She has shamed him.* Even so, Igasho did not blame her. He had experienced his cousin's anger first hand and feared for Kimama.

When they stepped from the tree line, he relaxed some. The rockface to the right cut the risk of a surprise attack. When they reached the rock bearing the images of his successful vision quest, he pointed to the drawing of Waianten and Jurom. Kimama smiled. “I am happy the spirits brought her to you, for in her I have a trustworthy friend.”

The people in front of him touched one another hand to shoulder, hand to arm, or holding hands to form a human chain. One of his mother’s sisters took Kimama’s hand and said, “Waianten says to stay connected as we walk through the gateway of light.”

Once they entered the cave, Igasho relaxed. *It seems her vision has not come true.* Kimama carried her daughter on her back as she stepped through the portal with his aunt. One more sled and Igasho would follow and rejoin his wife in Tupi. The dog followed the women through, and Igasho pushed the sled from behind. Suddenly, out of nowhere, an arm grabbed his neck and pressed against his windpipe, trying to cut off his air. Igasho knew better than to lean back, or Pu'ennaakan would bring him to the ground. He pressed his chin to his collarbone and squatted forward, thrusting his elbows back to strike his assailant. He caught Pu'ennaakan off guard, shoved his arm back, and hit him in the groin, but Pu'ennaakan didn't lose his grip. Igasho leaned forward and pulled Pu'ennaakan to the ground. The sled disappeared through the portal, leaving the two men struggling on the cold floor of the cave. Pu'ennaakan scuffled to his feet with the gateway behind him, cutting off Igasho's access. He picked up a nearby rock poised to bash Igasho in the head. Igasho kicked him in the stomach sending him back a couple of steps toward the gateway of light with his arms flailing. He lost his balance, and his back slammed the edge of the portal where it met the wall. Purple light sparked and started to leak from the edge tainting the blue energy and swirling like a small storm cloud that held Pu'ennaakan fast.

As much as he fought, he couldn't break free. "What is happening!" he screamed, his eyes wide with panic. "Igasho! Help me!" He clutched at Igasho but couldn't reach him.

Igasho clambered to his feet, grabbed Pu'ennaakan hand, and tried to pull him free, but Pu'ennaakan's body distorted as if being stretched like wet clay. His dark brown eyes grew bulbous in his elongated head.

"You have ruined my life, you *tizipe*!"

Igasho didn't know what else to do but get help. So he stepped through the portal and grabbed Pu'ennaakan's arm on the way through. His father stood waiting for him on the other side. "Here he is," Taikwahni announced.

"Help, father!" Igasho called, "Something has happened to Pu'ennaakan!"

His father grabbed Pu'ennaakan's shoulder and pulled. With the two of them working together, they yanked him through to the other side. He fell to the ground unconscious. Little Kylar stared at the man for a moment and dropped to his knees. Aurora ran to join her husband and stared at Pu'ennaakan on the ground.

"What happened!"

"Just what you said would happen," Igasho said as his chest heaved. He didn't want to say more in front of the others. He didn't want to say more in front of the others. Aurora leaned into him, drinking deeply of his scent, her heart overjoyed that Pu'ennaakan did not injure him. She bent to pick up Kylar but stopped. His green aura shined brightly, and his hands rested on each of Pu'ennaakan's temples. Rainbow energy surrounded the top of the man's head. After a moment, Kylar Two Moons stood and took his mother's hand. "He will be well." A deep sigh escaped Pu'ennaakan's lips.

Kimama timidly made her way to the front of the crowd with her daughter on her back. When she saw her husband, her eyes filled with tears. "Is he… dead?"

"No," Aurora said as she walked over and placed her hand on her shoulder. "He is going to be alright."

She reached out to the dragons. "*Tozet? Jurom? What happened?*"

"The human breached the mirror skin," Tozet answered. *"He be fortunate that he be not pulled into the Midlands, but there be no guarantee that he shall be normal, for the pull of Midland energy scrambles one's thinking for the rest of their life."*

Astonished gasps followed by a light moan behind her spun her around. Pu'ennaakan sat with his hand on his head. "What? What happened?"

Igasho stepped forward. "The sled cocked out of your hand as we were coming through and threw you to the ground. You hit your head."

"I… I hit my head?"

"Yes."

Igasho's father ordered everyone to set up temporary shelters for the night. "We will stay here for the next two nights and move out the following morning."

Kimama stood with her daughter on her back, not knowing what to do. She had defied Pu'ennaakan, and now he had followed her. She feared for her life.

He reached up toward her. "Kimama."

She stepped forward, casting nervous glances in every direction. "Yes, husband." She knelt beside him. He looked at her with eyes full of wonder. "My beautiful wife. I am sorry I almost let you leave me forever."

She blinked and looked away. "I am happy you decided to join us, my husband. For now, my family is complete again."

He grabbed her, and she flinched, but he drew her to his chest and held her as one precious.

Aurora picked up Kylar and held him. She whispered. "What did you do to Pu'ennaakan?"

"I made him well, Mère. He is *anta-piccyhhad.*"

Aurora looked into her son's eyes. "A man of much anger," she repeated. He nodded. She stared into the innocence of those green eyes. Everyone knew Pu'ennaakan had a hot temper, and now he sat with his arm around his wife and daughter.

Igasho's mother walked over to them, carrying Nakaah. "I think Tupi is a good land." She glanced at Pu'ennaakan and Kimama and back at Aurora. Nakaah just took his first steps!

CHAPTER FORTY-SIX

The tribe rested at the fork in the river for two days so the animals and young could recuperate from their journey. A knot of women gathered at the river's edge to wash clothes, talking about the warm weather. Aurora sat with Kylar Two Moons' head in her lap, stroking his dark hair. He looked at her with dull green eyes and felt feverish to the touch. She didn't know what to do. She'd never been sick. She reached out with her mind.

"Jurom, Kylar is sick. I don't know what to do."

"Heal him."

"Me? How?"

"It be a part of thy Dragonborn powers ye received in Jur-Jurom. Ye first used them to heal thy Da when he first traveled the Midlands."

The memory of that moment lingered in the back of her mind. "I was a toddler… is this the same gift Kylar has displayed?"

"No. they be different. Thy gift be of the Goldenhorn clan, his be of the Thornose."

The scene at the lake in the dormant volcano made sense now. When Aurora remembered it, it felt more like a dream. Over the years, she realized she was born gifted with Thornose magic, but Jurom had also gifted her with Goldenhorn powers as a young hatchling. Zaylan foretold it. She looked down at her son. But how do I use this healing power? Before it just happened. What do I do?

Kylar's breathing grew shallow, his lips tinged with a blue hue.

She scooped him into her arms. "Kylar, please hold on. Mère is here." Suddenly all her fear disappeared. Her mind cleared, and she tapped into what she realized now was dragon energy. It flowed through her arms and wrapped around her son as Jurom's shadow circled overhead. Kylar's eyes fluttered and popped opened, staring wide-eyed at nothing. He sucked in a deep breath and coughed, expelling a cloud of squirming gray ethereal thread-like worms that dissipated on the breeze.

Aurora swallowed hard, her mind frantically trying to figure out what just happened. Jurom landed nearby and lumbered toward her. “What…?” She rocked back and forth with Kylar in her arms, tears painting wet tracks down her cheeks. “What was that?”

“That be the evil thoughts thy child has absorbed from others around him to prevent them from doing wickedness.”

“Evil thoughts? I thought he was a healer.”

“It be Thornose ability. Thornose can purge evil thoughts, but thy son can only partially purge them. What ye witnessed be evil released only to return from whence it came. In Kylar’s case, it be best not to absorb such thoughts, for they be like poison to him.”

Aurora hugged Kylar close. “You need to stop taking evil thoughts from people, my son.”

“But Mère, if I do not, Pu’ennaakan shall kill you… and father too.” Tears pooled in his eyes as Igasho walked up from the river.

"I've been searching for you," Igasho said as he squatted beside his wife. "I have set up a temporary lodge, and Mother says it is time for Nakaah to eat." His gaze fell to Kylar. He looked at Aurora and finally at Jurom. “What is wrong?”

Aurora’s mind raced. Pu’ennaakan cannot continue with us, but what can I say? She stood and held Kylar on one hip. “Come, show us the lodge. Your mother is right. Nakaah is hungry.”

Jurom spoke first to Aurora, “Be safe, Little One. And, Igasho, I must talk with thee.”

“Very well, I will return in a moment, Jurom,” Igasho said as he took Kylar into his arms.

Aurora cast a questioning glance over her shoulder toward the dragon. “What are you going to do?”

“I must tell him to cut Pu’ennaakan from the tribe.”

Aurora walked away, wondering how things would turn out. In her heart, she wished the man had been pulled into the Midlands instead of into her world. Why did he have to come! What of Kimama and the baby?

When Igasho returned to Jurom, the dragon warned him of Pu'ennaakan's intentions to harm his family. "He not only thinks thy wife be an evil spirit, but that thy children be what he calls little demons. And he has talked thus to others in thy tribe."

Igasho crossed his arms before his chest and scanned the makeshift settlement at the river's fork. A few dogs milled around, marking their new territory. He regretted saving Pu'ennaakan. "Day and night cannot dwell together." He thought of his family. "I know what to do."

He headed out to look for his father to ask for his help.

CHAPTER FORTY-SEVEN

Igasho spotted his father standing on the river bank, poised with his spear in his hand, watching for fish. He walked past a group of women harvesting rushes to craft baskets, happy to see them adjusting to Tupi so quickly. "Father," he paused with the Taikwahni on his left. He searched for the right words as his father turned to face him. The sound of the rushing water soothed his nerves but didn't ease his burden.

"What troubles you, my son?"

"Walk with me." He stepped away from the river, cutting a path through the tall grass.

The Taikwahni didn't argue but followed his son with his spear grasped in his right hand. Igasho turned to face him when they were far enough away to prevent someone from overhearing. "It is Pu'ennaakan. The spirits have warned me that he has murder in his heart. He intends to kill my family and me."

Anger flashed in the Taikwahni's eyes as he thumped the end of his spear against the fertile soil, his brow knitting into an angry scowl. "We should not have allowed him to walk through the gate."

"It's too late for that." Igasho let out a sigh. "But I have a plan, and I wanted to see what you thought." Igasho shared his plan, and as they walked back toward the river, they went separate ways. Igasho walked off to find Aurora and the children. He spotted Kylar Two Moons running in the tall grass smashing a circle path in his wake. Aurora stood with Nakaah propped on her hip. Her eyes met Igasho's as he cut a straight line to join her. "Father," Kylar cried out with glee and ran toward him. Igasho scooped him up and carried him toward his mother.

Aurora studied his face. "I've set up our lodge for the night."

"Let us go there and sit in the shade. The warmth of two suns will take time to get used to."

They stepped through the opening and sat in the coolness. Kylar leaned against his father while Nakaah nursed. Igasho wished Kylar would fall asleep because the boy was too smart to hear what he had to say. He couldn't risk the child repeating something not meant for his ears. To his relief, Kylar fell asleep quickly. He rested his large hand on the boy's head, and for a moment, marveled that he had a son this "old."

Aurora reached out and touched his forearm. "What are we going to do?" She cupped Nakaah to her breast a little tighter.

"Don't worry, Waianten. I have talked to my father. I've given him my plan, and he has agreed to help me. At this moment, he walks upon the people along with my mother's family, individually listening to what people are saying. But spreading a message."

"A message?"

"Yes, a message. But I would say more like gossip. Did you know the land we are going to is too dry, won't have enough food to support us? But that the land to the north is better? There's a lake there and plenty of fish."

"The land where we are going has plenty of room and food. The dragons have already carried biaguchu and wapiti from America and seeded multiple herds."

He reached out and placed a finger on her lips. "I know."

* * * *

Such behavior didn't make sense to her, but she had to admit she still had much to learn from these people.

As the first sun drew near the horizon, the people gathered. Igasho stood in the crowd with Aurora as his father stood on a rock before the gathering. "The great spirit smiles upon us in this new land of two suns. Tomorrow, we shall travel beyond the mountains to a valley that reaches the sea. There shall be food—"

Pu’ennaakan broke in. “Enough food? I’ve heard there isn’t enough food to sustain all the tribe.”

“Igasho has seen the land. He has said it is a rich land,” the Taikwahni announced.

“A rich land? A land without enough water? There is better land to the north. A land with a large lake with many fish.”

Murmurs spread throughout the crowd. Igasho’s heart beat faster. *Will he take the bait?*

“A better land,” the Taikwahni thumped the base of his staff against the rock. “A better land? Perhaps, we should separate the people into two tribes. One can go to the rich land promised to us, and the other can go to the better land.”

Voices erupted, everyone talked at the same time. Igasho closed his eyes and listened. When he opened his eyes, Pu'ennaakan stood directly next to the rock, looking up at his father, and turned to the people motioning with his hands for quiet. “What the Taikwahni suggests is a good plan. I...." He struck his chest with the palm of his hand. "...am willing to go north? How many are willing to take the northern route?"?” About a third of the people offered to go.

The Taikwahni looked at those willing to follow Pu’ennaakan. “And who shall be your Taikwahni?”

“I beg you to consider me to lead,” Pu’ennaakan said loud enough for all to hear.

Taikwahni Ubirajara’s eyes darted to his son for just a moment and then looked down at Pu’ennaakan. “Because of your prowess and leadership, you shall be the Taikwahni of the northern tribe, and as Taikwahni Pu’ennaakan, you will name your council.”

“And Igasho, my son, shall be Taikwahni of the eastern tribe.”

Aurora leaned in to speak softly into her husband’s ear. “How did you know he would accept?”

“The weakness of the enemy makes our strength. I know his pride.”

That night, the tribe celebrated as one. The following morning, they would follow two different paths at the fork in the river.

At dawn, the people said their goodbyes and climbed aboard packed sleds used as rafts to float people, belongings, and dogs along the river. Aurora's sled swiftly drifted, along with the current. Nakaah slept in the sling on her back while Kylar sat upon a bundle. Igasho and some of the other men rode horses along the bank. Pu'ennaakan and those hostile toward her family took the northern fork of the Inkish River. When they were no more than a speck, a sense of relief flooded her knowing that Jurom flew the skies to keep an eye on them.

It took three days to reach the river delta beyond the eastern mountains. The smell of the sea filled the air. In her heart, she knew she was home. She cradled Nakaah asleep in the sling across her chest as Kylar Two Moons prattled on and on and pointed at birds, animals, trees, and his father and the others riding along the river. For the first time in her life, she belonged. Her relationship with the dragons and her responsibility to the urn was her only real tie to her old life, and she could feel that time drawing to a close.

As they set up lodges and the village took shape, people talked about Tupi as the land with two suns. A smile played across her lips as she remembered how odd it felt to live in a world with a single sun. She settled into her new life. Their diet now relied more on salmon fishing, deer, and small game, as well as roots gathered by the women while the wapiti and biaguchu carried from America were left to multiply. Once a week, Aurora slipped into the Midlands, traveled to the temple, and checked on the urn. Only then did she visit with Jurom and Tozet face to face.

"The urn shall soon travel to its new destination," Tozet said.

Jurom closed his eyes. "Yes, and the time of dragons and humans living side by side shall come to an end for a time."

Aurora let out a sigh. "I've seen it, too." She reached up and rubbed the underside of Jurom's jaw. "But I've seen a time in the future when dragons and humans come together again. Goldenhorns and another kind of dragon, like on the urn. It is the Thornose, is it not?"

"Aye, it be so," Jurom said. *"Tozet has witnessed the same."*

"I'm going to go check on the urn," she said. "I'll be back in a moment. I want to watch the suns rise with you like we used to do."

A light clicking from Jurom's throat eased the seriousness of their conversation as Aurora raised the hatch and climbed down the ladder into the temple lit with lucium spheres. She thought of visiting her old bed-chamber but decided against it. She wanted to get back to her lodge bedchamber her children woke.

She made her way through the core to the secret chamber. The spheres, floating behind her, cast a blush of blue across the urn. Seeing it always ignited a rush of memories. The lake in the volcano, her parents, her brothers, knowing she was different–Dragonborn. Suddenly a rainbow of color filled the air around the urn. Aurora gasped as a new vision filled her mind with an audible voice. A voice from long ago—Zaylan's voice. *"When the urn returns to the temple, one from thy line shall understand the sacrifice needed. A sacrifice never made before and never to be made again."* With that, the urn dissolved before her eyes and disappeared. She stood frozen like a statue staring at the spot where the urn set for centuries. "It's–it's gone." The freedom she had longed for, for centuries, left her relieved but sad. And the cryptic message left her with questions. *One from my line? One of my descendants has to make a sacrifice no one has made before?*

Her heart slammed against her ribs as she rushed up the rungs of the ladder. The first hint of suns rise brightened the eastern sky. The dragons sat on their haunches side by side as her feet thudded against the roof toward them with tears streaming down her cheeks. "It's gone," she said over and over. "It's gone."

"Aye," Tozet said. *"Thy responsibility to the urn be complete in the temple. Only one more thing ye must do."*

Aurora wiped her tears with the back of her hand. "What? I have to do something more?"

Jurom chuckled. *"Be not concerned, Little One. Ye be free from the temple, but ye must teach Kylar Two Moons about the temple and the prophecy."*

"The prophecy? About the sacrifice?"

"Aye."

New fear quickly tinged the joy of freedom–fear for her children. The sacrifice required was going to be more than she had ever had to do. *Will it be Kylar who has to sacrifice?*

She sat with the dragons in silence as they watched the suns rise. As much as she would miss this, she looked forward to living life with the tribe and raising her children. Maybe one day, she would bring them here again. She didn't know. For the first time in her life, she didn't know, exactly, what was next for her life.

Instead of traveling the Midlands, Jurom offered to take her home. It would be the last time. As the tribe came into view, he said, *"Little One, life shall be good but be aware, ye shall see thy husband grow old and die. When he joins his ancestors in eternity, ye shall return to the secret portal in the temple. I have removed the mirror skin. It shall carry thee to where ye must go to live out thy life. Carry with thee the Scroll of Prophecy and the therus rod."*

He circled to land, and Aurora sputtered as she tried to voice all her questions. *"Ye know what ye must know."* When he landed, Igasho walked toward him in the morning twilight. Aurora climbed down and hurried to his side. The two of them talked briefly with Jurom and watched him fly away. When they walked back to their lodge, Kylar Two Moons stood in the doorway. "Don't be sad Mere. In the far-away future, you shall see Jurom again."

The way he said it sent a chill through her. It wasn't just what he said, but how he said it. He knew this as if it had already happened. She understood because she'd lived it. She knelt before her son and scooped him into her arms. Jurom's words from the day in the cave replayed in her mind. *"Kylar Two Moons shall be a leader among his people, and from his line shall come one who walks alongside the Variel."* She squeezed him tight and didn't want to let go. Finally, he squirmed free and ran off toward his grandmother's hut.

* * * *

Time passed. While Aurora lived a happy life, her eyes often scanned the sky looking for a glimpse of the dragons, but they were gone. She and Igasho had two daughters and one more son born into the family. Their children grew up and married. They buried Igasho's parents and sisters in Tupi, and 50 summers after they had become husband and wife, Aurora buried Igasho. Their children and grandchildren gathered to honor him, and when the ceremony closed and all returned to their homes, Kylar Two Moons invited his mother to come to live with his family. She stroked his cheek and said, "You know what I am about to do."

He looked away and nodded. "I don't want it, but I do know it is what you must do."

"Always know that I love you, son, and be sure to remind your brothers and sisters of that fact." They embraced, and she held him a little longer and watched him walk away. He glanced over his shoulder one time. Tears shimmered in his green eyes as he gave her one last wave, turned, and walked toward the setting suns.

"I never want to have to live through this again," she muttered under her breath.

"Come, Little One. Meet me at the temple."

"Jurom!"

She packed the Scroll of Prophecy along with small mementos, which held a special place in her heart into the well-worn satchel that once belonged to her Da. She traveled the Midlands with heavy sadness in her heart. Not only was Igasho gone, but she would never see her children or grandchildren again. When she reached the temple, she found Jurom waiting for her. She ran to him and lay her head against his immense foreleg. His familiar smoky scent comforted her. In some ways, it felt like no time had passed, but her heart told her differently. "Should I leave the Scroll of Prophecy here?"

"Nay, take it with thee."

"When is it no longer my responsibility?"

"When the shadowalker comes to find thee, it shall no longer be thy responsibility."

"Shadowalker? That's not something I've heard before. Who is that?"

"Ye will know when the time comes." She let it go. *"I'm tired of trying to figure things out before they happen. I'm going to trust you, Jurom. I always have."*

He glanced down at her with emotions transforming his eyes to violet. She lay her head against his side, listening to the beating of his heart as they watched the suns set. As the second sun dipped beyond the horizon, they walked together to the secret portal. She didn't watch the shifting scenes but drank in the sight of her dragon. "I don't want to go."

"Trust me."

She let out a long breath and threw her shoulders back. One last glance at Jurom told her this would be the last time she saw her friend. *Too much loss*. But she did trust him. "I love you, Jurom."

The dragon blinked his violet eyes. *"Ye know that when the Thornose die, they leave a Donum... a gift."*

She nodded. "Yes, I know."

"If I could leave a Donum in that way, mine gift would be the ability to remove evil from the world."

She reached up and ran her fingers across his boney ridge, and then kissed her fingertips and placed the kiss on his snout. *"That's what we are all trying to do."* With that, she straightened her shoulders and stepped into the portal that had brought her home decades before. As her feet hit the ground on the other side, she stared into total darkness. She pulled out a handful of starstones casting light across a narrow room. Questions flooded her mind. Before she had time to think, voices from beyond the door at the far end of the room lured her cautiously forward. She opened the door enough to peek beyond. An older man with a balding head fringed with shoulder-length gray hair and a woman with stooped shoulders and white in her hair sat at a small table. Aurora cleared her throat and stepped into the room lit with sunshine streaming through two windows. The man looked over at her, and she recognized his eyes.

"Da?"

The woman looked up. "Aurora!"

"Mother!"

Her mother stood up so quickly her chair tipped and clattered on the floor. "You're finally here." They ran toward each other and hugged. Da embraced the two of them as the three stood in a cluster. Aurora's mind tried to catch up.

"How is this possible," Aurora asked as the three sat at the table and talked. "I can't believe we're sitting here together. After all this time…."

"You knew you'd see us again, right? We came here through a tear in time about ten years ago in this time."

Aurora nodded. "Are we in America? The last time I walked through that portal, it led to a cave. The cave where my son Kylar was born."

Her mother covered her mouth. "Kylar? You have a son? And you named him Kylar after your brother!"

"I have three sons and two daughters. And I have grandchildren." They talked about her family, the loss of Igasho, and saying goodbye to Jurom.

Da let out a long breath. "Hearing these names brings back such memories. We haven't seen a dragon for more than a decade… since we came here. This is where we will grow old and follow our ancestors into eternity."

"Is this America?" Aurora asked again.

They nodded. "When we arrived here, this was a cave such as you described. That's why the room you entered is shaped the way it is. Those walls are within the cave. It is a room crafted by magic, and if you look at it now, what do you see?"

She turned and blinked at a wall without a door. The room had vanished. "Our purpose here was to build a home, for this will be a sanctuary in the future to hide the child who will save our world from the spirit of the Book of Darkmore."

"And me?" Aurora asked. "What am I to do here?"

"You brought the Scroll of Prophecy?"

She nodded.

Her Da smiled. “You will be the caretaker of this home until you welcome another who walks through the portal to become the gatekeeper. Then you too will be gathered to your ancestors in Nomuria.”

About the Author

Originally from the Chicago area, author Donna Sundblad now makes her home in the foothills of NW Georgia with her husband, cat and birds. As a child she entertained friends and family with tales from her overactive imagination. By the time she was a young teen, she started to put pen to paper and her love for writing blossomed.

Donna treasures time spent with family, is an avid reader, loves animals and enjoys the outdoors. She retired from editing and ghostwriting in 2019 to focus on her own works. Dragonborn is her fourth published fantasy novel and book one in a series of four. Stay up to date on the Dragonborn world through Facebook at Dragonborn@donnasunblad.

While writing fantasy is her first love as a writer, she also offers an imaginative approach to writing in her book *Pumping Your Muse.* Other published works include inspirational short stories found in a variety of collections including *Life Savors* and *Cup of Comfort.*

Made in the USA
Middletown, DE
07 December 2022

17393892R00195